SPICE AND THE DEVIL'S CAVE

"The group in Abel Zakuto's workshop hitched chairs closer to the table spread with a huge map."

SPICE AND THE DEVIL'S CAVE

AGNES DANFORTH HEWES

ILLUSTRATED BY
LYND WARD

DOVER PUBLICATIONS, INC.
MINEOLA, NEW YORK

Bibliographical Note

This Dover edition, first published by Dover Publications, Inc., in 2014, is an unabridged republication of the work originally published by Alfred A. Knopf, New York, in 1930.

Library of Congress Cataloging-in-Publication Data

Hewes, Agnes Danforth.
    Spice and the Devil's Cave / Agnes Danforth Hewes ; illustrated by Lynd Ward.
        p. cm.
    "This Dover edition...is an unabridged republication of the work originally published by Alfred A. Knopf, New York, in 1930"—Copyright page.
    Newbery Honor, 1931.
    Summary: In 1490s Portugal, Abel Zakuto, a Jewish banker with a keen interest in mapmaking and sea navigation, encourages explorers Magellan, da Gama, and Diaz to find the elusive sea route around the "Devil's Cave"—the Cape of Good Hope—to India, which would enable Portugal to dominate the spice trade.
    ISBN-13: 978-0-486-49287-2 (pbk.)
    ISBN-10: 0-486-49287-7
    [1. Explorers—Fiction. 2. Magellan, Ferdinand, d. 1521—Fiction. 3. Gama, Vasco da, 1469–1524—Fiction. 4. Jews—Portugal—Fiction. 5. Portugal—History—Period of discoveries, 1385–1580—Fiction.] I. Ward, Lynd, 1905–1985, illustrator. II. Title.

PZ7.H448Sp 2014
[Fic]—dc23

2013028952

Manufactured in the United States by Courier Corporation
49287701   2014
www.doverpublications.com

To the memory of
ARTHUR STURGES HILDEBRAND
BECAUSE OF HIS BEAUTIFUL
MAGELLAN

CONTENTS

Contents

SPICE AND THE DEVIL'S CAVE

CHAPTER I

Out of the Night

THE GROUP in Abel Zakuto's workshop hitched chairs closer to the table spread with a huge map, eyes intent on Captain Diaz' brown forefinger, as it traced along the bulge of Africa's west coast.

∞ I ∞

∽∽∽ *Spice and the Devil's Cave* ∽∽∽

" Cape Verde, Guinea – all that's an old story to Portugal now; and this . . . and this . . . as anyone can see by our stone pillars all along the way. Then " – the brown forefinger that had slid rapidly southward stopped short – " then, the big Cape. . . . And the last of our pillars! " he added under his breath.

The circle of eager eyes lifted to the tanned face with something very like reverence, for not one around the table but knew that, if Bartholomew Diaz had had his way, the stone pillars would never have stopped at the Cape.

Into the mind of young Ferdinand Magellan, hunched up over the table, flashed a memory of the first time he had heard of Bartholomew Diaz. Up to the family home, in high, lonely Sabrosa,[1] had come the story of this man who had marked the farthest bound in the search for the sea route to India, which he had named the Cape of Storms. Ferdinand quickened to the picture that the story had called up to his childish fancy: the man gazing from his fragile, tossing ship at the awesome rock, while the great Cape, waiting through the ages, bared its storm-swept head to hail this first white face.

He suddenly leaned over the map and closely inspected it. Then he looked up at Abel Zakuto. " What does this name mean? "

Abel glanced where he pointed. " Why, that's really the big Cape. But Fra Mauro[2] showed it as an island which he called *Diab* – probably from the legends of the Arab sailors that the surrounding sea was the Devil's Cave.

---

[1] Magellan's birthplace, in Portugal's most northern province, Traz-os-Montes.

[2] A Venetian cartographer of the fifteenth century.

∽∽∽ 2 ∽∽∽

You know King John liked to call it The Cape of Good Hope."

" I like Devil's Cave! " exclaimed Ferdinand. " Sounds exciting."

Diaz gave him an amused look. " You'd think 'twas exciting," he told him. " Greatest commotion of wind and water there ever I saw – like ten thousand devils set loose – just as the Arabs believed."

He sat back in his chair, his smile gone. He appeared to have forgotten the map as he stared absently before him.

Across the table a man eyed him as if pondering something he wished to say. A black-bearded stocky figure he was, not much past thirty, with a long-nosed, forceful face – Vasco da Gama, a gentleman of King Manoel's court. His father had once been Comptroller of the royal household, and had been intended, in John's reign, to head an expedition to explore a sea route to India. Vasco, himself, had seen service at sea and had soldiered in Spain and Africa. Lately, with all Europe agog over the Way to the Spices, he'd begun to brush up on navigation, and occasionally came to look at Abel Zakuto's maps.

" Have you any doubt, Captain," he at last ventured, " that the coast east of the Cape makes up to India as Mauro showed it? "

" No, I haven't," Diaz replied bluntly. " But what use is that if I can't say I *know* it does? No, Gama, all I know is only what I've seen, and that's the coast this side of the Cape – barring some score leagues beyond."

Young Magellan made an impatient gesture. " Covilham had no doubts about the coast east of the Cape," he said, pointedly.

His tone made the older men smile. This youngster just missed being a nuisance with his ever ready willingness to challenge one's statements, only that he was always so sure of his facts, and so amazingly well informed! Covilham! – What other lad in Lisbon would have known enough to ask this question? For Pedro de Covilham had started out on his great errand to verify by land what Bartholomew Diaz was sent to verify by sea, when this boy was hardly more than waist high – at least half a dozen years before he had come down from Traz-os-Montes to the palace at Lisbon for his page's training.

"Covilham said it was clear sailing," Ferdinand persisted, "east of the Cape, now didn't he?"

From under his grizzled brows Bartholomew Diaz studied him with amused pride. After his own heart, this lad, with the great, sombre eyes that seemed to see beyond ordinary vision. That readiness to question, that rebellion against the passive acceptance of the mass – ah, *that* was the stuff of which pioneers were made! His own kinsmen, for instance: suppose they had believed all that nonsense about there being nothing beyond Cape Bojador but a chaos of boiling seas. But now, no one would soon forget that John Diaz was the very first of his race to take the dare of the great promontory and double its forbidding coasts; that Diniz Diaz was first to reach Cape Verde, and Vicente Diaz first at the Cape Verde islands; that he, Bartholomew, had sailed farther than any of them – though he did say it, who shouldn't! And young Magellan, you could depend on it, would go as far some day; perhaps farther.

"But Covilham didn't come home to tell what he'd found, as Captain Diaz did," Gama observed. "All we have to go by is that he sent word back from Cairo to Lisbon that he'd got down the east coast of Africa as far as Sofala, and that if our ships would just keep on from Guinea they'd find a clear passage to India and the spices. But, if he didn't get beyond Sofala, how could he be sure of that?"

"Well, even so –" Ferdinand's arm shot out to the map, thumb on the Cape, and little finger on Sofala – "all that's left to prove is the gap between *this,* where you left off, Master Diaz," tapping with his thumb, "and *this,*" tapping with his finger, "where Covilham left off." Triumphantly he looked around the table to score his point, as he flattened his palm to indicate the reach from thumb to finger tip.

"Yes, anyone can see that's ' all,' " Gama drily retorted. "The point is, how much of an ' all ' is it? If the coast runs north from the Cape to Sofala, well and good; but if, somewhere in between, it should happen to make out to the east, and then down into the frozen south . . . "

Ferdinand heaved a long sigh. "I'd be willing to stake everything I had to settle it!"

Captain Diaz shrugged. "So would any of us, if there were only one's self to consider." Wouldn't he, he meditated, have "settled" this tantalizing gap, ten years ago and more, only for having to turn back for that doubting, homesick crew of his?

"The one thing to do, King Manoel won't do – go and find out!" Abel Zakuto quietly stated.

Everyone always listened to what Abel had to say. He always struck at the core of a situation; led you back to the main argument when you inclined toward side issues.

"He's too busy trying to manoeuvre his head into the

Spanish crown to bother with finding a passage to India!" Ferdinand said, sarcastically.

"He'd have no trouble getting crews," Diaz grumbled. "Everybody'd want to go! All he has to do is to finish the ships that King John began for an eastern expedition and would have sent out – under your father, Gama – if death hadn't blocked him."

There was no one in the room who had forgotten that it was Diaz, himself, who had designed those ships and watched over their beginnings; but only he knew the bitterness of seeing those idle hulls and their half-finished rigging left to rot – for all Manoel seemed to care – in the dockyards.

"It always seemed to me," Abel took him up, "that John got just what he deserved. Here, years ago, John Cabot came all the way from Venice to beg an outfit to discover a passage to India; the same thing happened again, in the case of Columbus, and John turned both of them away – deliberately lost two great chances for Portugal. Life doesn't go on holding the door open, you know. There comes a time when it slams it shut in your face!"

"But wouldn't you think," Diaz demanded, "with Spain so keen over Columbus's two cruises that they're outfitting him for a third voyage, and news that the English Henry is getting John Cabot ready to find a sea passage, that Manoel would be afraid they'd find the way to the Indies first?"

The evening always finished that way: eager speculation, comment, mounting hopes, finally ending against the dead wall of Manoel's callousness to the big issue of the time.

Bartholomew Diaz pushed his chair back from the table, got up, said good night and went out. Gama soon followed, and only Ferdinand and Abel remained. In fact, it was the usual sequel of these meetings, that the boy would stay on to talk of the all-engrossing topic.

Abel studied him now, as Bartholomew Diaz had, earlier in the evening. But where Diaz had noted evidence of personal traits, Abel read evidence of the national character. The sturdy build, the air of ruthless determination coupled with a certain arrogance toward danger, all reflected, Abel said to himself, generations that had been trained on Portugal's littoral to the combat of the sea, or hardened in struggles with the Moors.

At this point in Abel's meditations, his wife, Ruth, came in with a dish of figs preserved in grape treacle from a famous recipe that she claimed came from Palestine. Ferdinand sprang up and greeted her with an affectionate little gesture. He'd been a favourite with Ruth ever since she had seen him as a toddling youngster, when she was visiting friends at Sabrosa, and he knew those figs had been brought in especially for him.

" Help yourself, child, they'll sweeten your dreams after all that dry talk," she told him. " How you can spend so much time over those stupid old maps I can't see. Stuffy in here as a dungeon, too, with all you men hived up together! "

She pushed the map to one side of the table, set the dish at Ferdinand's hand, bustled across the room, and flung open the door into the garden-court.

Ruth was short and stout, with a way of trotting about as she talked, while she punctuated her remarks with little sidewise nods that reminded one of a bird cocking its head from side to side. Everything about her was intensely practical. When other women's skirts swept the ground, Ruth's neatly cleared, and homespun for every day but the Sabbath was, to her mind, wasteful and frivolous. She prided herself on a fresh muslin cap each morning as much as she did on her clean house and the trim flower beds. Her mind was as practical as her capable hands: anything, for instance, outside of established fact she treated as cobwebs or weeds, and neither Abel nor his friends were under any illusions as to her opinion of the discussions in his workshop.

"You'd stay here in this close air till you choked!" she scolded, as she sat down; then, "Aren't you going to sample my preserves?" she impatiently demanded, while she pulled at the girdle of her tight-fitting waist.

Abel reached over and helped himself to the confection, meditatively gazing into the darkness beyond the open door. Ferdinand, seething to continue the theme of the evening, watched the older man for a sign to begin.

"Well, Ferdinand, let's have it!" Abel finally said, his eyes twinkling.

"Yes, sir!" The boy's hand smote the table with a blow that made Ruth jump, and his sombre eyes blazed. "I can't get over it, Master Abel – the shame of it! Here's the merchantmen of Venice and Genoa bringing back the goods of the Orient, and trading with everybody all up and down both sides of the Mediterranean, their flags flying as complacent as you please, here in Lisbon harbour, as if they owned the place, while our ships sometimes – only sometimes, mind you – get left-over cargoes that no one else is keen about. Think of it – Portugal taking the leavings of Venice, by heaven! Why shouldn't *we* be bringing back the cargoes from the Orient? I don't mean by way of the Mediterranean, either!"

"I know, I know," Abel nodded. "You mean direct from the Orient, around by the Devil's Cave."

"Heavens, yes! Of course that's what I mean," Ferdinand snapped out. "*Then* where'd Venice and Genoa be? And Spain and England?"

"I declare," laughed Ruth, "I believe you'd like a chance to spite Spain and England!"

"Don't you think for a minute that they don't feel the same way about us!" the boy retorted. "Aren't they both doing their best to crowd us out of the race for India? And we could have been there before Spain ever thought of sending out Columbus, if we'd only followed Captain Diaz' lead! But now, Spain claims that Columbus has reached the Orient; by way of the west, to be sure, but still reached it."

"There is no doubt Columbus has found something," Abel said thoughtfully, "but whether it's the Orient, or even any part of the Orient – Look here, Ferdinand," he broke in on himself, "you know, and I know, that those half-naked savages and those rude gewgaws that Columbus brought back don't tally with the great cities and the costly trade that men who've been in the Orient tell about – men like Marco Polo and his compatriots Conti, and Cabot, and even our own Covilham."

"Well," Ferdinand offered, "to do Columbus justice, all he claims is that what he's found is the undeveloped outskirts of Cipangu [1] or Cathay. [2] But if we could settle what we've all but proved," he pursued, in a low, vehement voice, "if we could reach India by way of the Cape, then, Portugal – Lisbon –" He broke off, his face working.

"Lisbon would be," Abel finished for him, "the port

[1] Japan.   [2] China.

of entry to Europe of the Orient's trade. Lisbon would be –
what Venice now is! "

" But if we lose," the boy choked out, " if we lose, we'll
have to stand by, while Spain, or London gets the trade.
And yet, Manoel can't see it! The biggest chance the world
has ever offered – and he letting it slip through his fingers! "

" Just listen to the child! " cried Ruth. " Breaking his
heart over something he doesn't even know exists! "

" Don't say that! " Ferdinand said, sharply. " I'd – I'd
– stake my soul that the Way of the Spices lies as plain as a
road from us to India, just as Covilham says." He turned
almost pleadingly to Abel. " *You* believe that, Master Abel,
don't you? "

As Abel started to speak, the two others saw his lips,
even in the very act of forming an answer, freeze into stark
amazement, his eyes focused on some object behind them.

With one impulse they whirled about to see, poised in
the doorway, as if in arrested flight, a bare-legged, ragged
figure. Out of the pallid face stared great, dark eyes dilated
by a madness of fear that wiped out every other expression.

For an astounded moment Ferdinand waited for the
apparition to vanish – as it had come – like a wraith. No!
. . . That was *flesh*, human, alive, that quivered under the
torn breeches, and that was blood on the thin hands – one
could even see where it had stained the tattered coat. Just a
poor, frightened lad, of perhaps his own age!

A chair scraped the floor – Ruth ran past him to the
door, and drew the pitiful figure inside. All at once he heard
her cry out, saw her draw back. He started forward – as suddenly halted. Had he seen – or imagined – two braids of long,
dark hair tucked under the ragged coat?

"It's a girl, Abel – a *girl!* " Ruth was stammering.

At the sound of her voice the terror-stricken eyes glanced back into the court; then, like a wild creature seeking cover, the girl seized Ruth's hands and dragged her into the room beyond the workshop.

"Someone is hunting her! " Abel cried. "The door, Ferdinand – quick! "

Ferdinand was out of the room, across the court, and already turning the key in the outside gate, when Abel, coming up, a little out of breath, reached out and tried the heavy door. Too amazed to talk, they stood, looking at each other.

"You'd think," Ferdinand said under his breath, "that we'd have heard her come in, or that someone would have seen her climbing the hill up here."

"Suppose you'd gone away when the others did, and I'd locked the gate after you," Abel meditated aloud, "where might this poor creature have wandered? "

"I'm glad I stayed," Ferdinand said, soberly, falling into step with Abel who had begun to pace slowly up and down the court.

Without speaking, they walked its length and back. Unconsciously they muffled their steps on the stone flags, as though they listened for some clue from the night.

To Abel, the very garden about them was an expression of what was in their minds. The gray old fig tree, the laden damsons that his own hands had trained along the wall, even the beds of dew-sweet flowers seemed to listen, to wait. . . .

"Where in the world did that child come from? " he mused aloud.

"She might have been brought in on a slave ship,"

Ferdinand threw out at random. "But slaves are black as ebony," he quickly amended, "and this girl has skin – well – like ivory, with sunlight striking across it."

He was a little embarrassed at this lapse from his usual literal speech, but Abel seemed not to notice it.

"Exactly," he rejoined, "like yellowed ivory, or like those lilies of mine in moonlight. However, that idea of yours is something to follow up. We can very soon find out at the docks whether any slave ship has put in here."

From the court they could see Ruth's shadow moving about in the lighted room where the girl had fled. At last, the light went out, and Ruth appeared at the workshop door.

"She's quieted down a little," she whispered, as Abel and Ferdinand stepped into the room.

"What does she say?" Abel eagerly demanded. "Did she tell you –"

"'Tell' me!" Ruth echoed with fine contempt. "I don't believe she can speak a word of our language. I tried to talk with her, but all she did was to huddle in a corner, and stare at me with those big, terrified eyes. She acts almost as if her brain was turned. But when I gave her some warm milk, she drank it like a kitten, and she let me bind up her poor hands."

"Did you see how they'd bled over her coat?" Ferdinand broke in.

"It's clear enough that she's had a terrific fight to escape," Abel thoughtfully observed.

Ferdinand got up to go. "I'll look around the docks tomorrow, and see what craft are in," he said. "Perhaps I might pick up a clue about her."

Ruth started up with an alarmed face. "But mind you

don't do or say anything that'll rouse suspicion! Those she was running from must be lying in wait for her, right here in town, and if they should find her, it's my belief the child would die of fright."

"Don't be afraid, Ruth," Abel assured her, curiously touched by this new tenderness. "Not a soul outside of us three shall know she's here."

"I'll keep my mouth shut," Ferdinand declared, "and my ears and eyes open. No one shall drag a word out of me! "

"Right! " Abel took him up. "So it's just between ourselves to discover where she comes from."

"Compared with which even finding the Way of the Spices might be simple! " Ferdinand laughed, as he took himself off.

CHAPTER 2

Nicolo Conti

F R O M the rail of the Venetian merchantman, the *Venezia*,
Nicolo Conti watched her crew send the last of the
Lisbon consignment of sugar hurtling to the long quay. The
Venezia had come in late the day before, and by the time she

∽ 14 ∽

had made her way past Portuguese fishing boats and English vessels, Spanish galleons and Dutch, and found a berth
between the craft tied up to the sea-wall, there had not been
time to finish unloading. The crew now was hurrying, for
they were already overdue, and it was nip and tuck to catch
the flood tide over the bar.

Someone behind him spoke his name, and Nicolo turned
to see a rugged figure coming toward him. " Got your lug-
gage together, Conti? We're about ready to go."

" It went ashore first thing this morning, Captain. All
I've to do is to get myself ashore."

" Unless," said the *Venezia's* captain, looking hard at
Nicolo, " unless – you change your mind, and go back with
me. I'll give you the best accommodations on board! "

Nicolo laughed good-naturedly. " I'm not going to
change my mind, sir! "

But the captain was not to be put off: " Venice was good
enough for all your people," he insisted. " That's where they
built their fortune and there's where you should stay and
increase it, instead of risking it on the wild talk these Portuguese have started over this chap Bartholomew Diaz – "
He broke off as the mate came for orders; then, " Don't go
yet," he told Nicolo, as he went off with the officer. " I'll be
back to say good-bye."

With rising excitement Nicolo glanced at the quay.
There was his box. Presently he would be with it, ready for
this Lisbon venture from which his old friend had so tried to
dissuade him. Then, he must look up lodgings; lucky that he
could speak Portuguese.

A boy's head and shoulders, leaning out over the edge
of the quay, suddenly crossed his vision – what in the world

was that chap about? Nicolo watched him peer down at the *Venezia's* bow. Trying to read her name, was he?

The bent figure straightened up, and he saw a young fellow, rather younger than himself, well set up and stocky, with the most remarkable eyes – eyes that made you stop and look, for they seemed like fires under his thick black brows. He was sorry when the boy moved away to scrutinize the vessel next the *Venezia*, and wondered idly why he was interested in the names of ships.

A shout from the crew! – The unloading was finished. A hatch cover slammed down. There was a cry to stand by and slip the hawsers. Next thing they would be drawing in the gang plank – he must go. He glanced at the captain hurrying forward.

"Well, Conti, so it's really good-bye? Sure you won't change your mind? "

Nicolo laughed and grasped his hand. "Not till I've given Portugal a fair trial, anyhow."

The captain shrugged. "Personally, I like to be at the hub of the wheel. This settling yourself on the edge of the world – "

"*Edge!* " Nicolo broke in. " I'll remind you of that word when the trade is roaring around us and *this* is the hub! "

" A fine, loyal Venetian you are! " retorted the other as he gave him a friendly shove.

"Good luck, sir! And look out that you don't have another brush with pirates! "

The man's eyes glittered. "Pirates better watch *me!* They can't afford to lose any more pilots to Christians! "

"We were in great luck to get that chap to take the place of our own pilot – he certainly knew his business."

"As good a pilot as I ever saw," the captain heartily endorsed. "I tried to get him to stay with me, but he'd had enough of the sea for a while."

Nicolo sprang up the gangplank and from the quay called out his last word: "Let me know when you're in again —I'll be right here!"

On the impulse he decided to wait for the *Venezia* to clear, and, after he had arranged for the storage of his box, he loitered about until he could see her tall mainmast with the familiar Lion of St. Mark beyond the harbour shipping. He watched the flag out of sight, and had turned to find the main thoroughfare, when a sound of angry voices made him look back.

Around the *Venezia's* discharged cargo he saw several prosperous looking men engaged in a vehement discussion. They had evidently halted the stevedores, for only part of the load had been removed. Nicolo watched, as they made gestures toward it and consulted indignantly among themselves. Gradually, he approached them. His Portuguese was not too good, but he gathered that there was something wrong with the freight that the *Venezia* had left.

"There it is—see for yourselves," one of the group was protesting. "Empty as a sucked egg! And I'm out the price of a barrel of sugar."

Nicolo edged up and looked over the speaker's shoulder. With real dismay he saw that the barrel was empty.

"You could get a consideration, if you hadn't signed the bill of lading," someone suggested.

"But I *have* signed it. And talk of consideration—why, a Venetian'd rather sell his soul than part with a ducat!"

"The captain of the *Venezia* wouldn't!" Nicolo spoke

up from behind him. "How do you know your own men aren't responsible for that empty barrel?"

The other wheeled around and stared at him. "Because I was standing by when my men discovered the shortage," he retorted. "And what's the *Venezia's* captain to you, young fellow, that you're so free to put your nose into other people's business?"

There was a murmur of approval from his companions. A heated reply was on Nicolo's lips – when all at once the humour of the situation struck him, and he laughed. Here he'd come to establish himself in a strange city, and the first thing he did was to get into a full-fledged quarrel.

"It happens that he's a good deal to me," he said good-naturedly. "I've known him all my life, and the last thing he'd do would be to cheat anyone out of anything. Now, here " – he took out his wallet – "what do you figure that sugar is worth?"

"Oh, I didn't mean anything like that," the man awkwardly protested. "I can stand the loss, but it's – it's the principle of the thing!"

"Just so," Nicolo agreed, biting his lips to keep a grave face, "the 'principle,' for the captain's a great stickler for principle – like yourself, sir! Now," opening his wallet, "what do we owe you?"

The man named a sum, which Nicolo handed over. "No hard feelings, I hope," he said, a little sheepishly, as he took the money. "If there's anything I can do for you at any time –"

"I'll take you up on that," laughed Nicolo. "Can you tell me where I can get a bite?"

"I can that! If you aren't particular about style –"

" Not in the least – I'm hungry! "

" Well, then – " the man turned Nicolo around, and pointed down a narrow outlet from the quay – " that'll take you to the main thoroughfare. Follow along to a big square, and, to your right, in an alley way, you'll see a little tavern, The Green Window, kept by an old fellow they call Pedro. It's not much to look at, but you can get the best mutton and vegetable stew in there that's made."

Once clear of the noisy quay, Nicolo stopped to look about him. Portugal . . . Lisbon . . . after all these months of doubt, of inward debate, of final decision, here they were, bright reality. His eyes, accustomed to the levels of Venice, mounted, with a sense of adventure, hillsides up which quaint, high-roofed houses seemed to climb on each other's shoulders. Enchantments of colour caught, and held, his exploring eyes: sunlit walls broken by sociable little balconies and outside stairways; bursts of blossoming shrubs, a glowing patch of tiny, steep garden. Everywhere, Nicolo noted, was colour, virile, vivid, of an almost primitive quality, as if the crude essence of it had been laid on without care of shade or tone. The sky itself blazed, from zenith to horizon, a deep even blue. Where, he wondered, was the palace? Perhaps it was the solid gloomy structure that crowned that hill or, more likely, that larger building with dome and pillars half-way down the hillside.

Mentally he contrasted the disciplined beauty of Venice – mellow sumptuousness, noiseless waterways – with the gay helter skelter of this hill city and the clatter of its cobble-stone pavements. Life moved faster here, and more simply. That boy, for instance, milking his goats from door to door! . . . This woman urging you to buy from the tray of glistening

fish she balanced on her head, and those men telling you
how fresh were the vegetables in the baskets slung across
their shoulders.

In the square that the merchant had mentioned, Nicolo
noticed the shops of linen drapers and silk mercers – not so
different from the displays of the Merceria, only that a Venetian instantly missed the enormous variety which the Oriental trade gave to the shops of Venice.

He found The Green Window without trouble, an amus-
ing little place with one huge, green-cased window set into
its diminutive, peaked front. Several men, unmistakably
sailors, were eating and talking at a table. Nicolo sat down
near them, and was promptly served with a bowl of the
famous stew. The innkeeper was a quaint little man with
kind eyes, and scrupulously anxious to please. Nicolo at once
took a fancy to him, and ended by ordering a second portion
of the stew.

Half-way through his meal, he absently noticed that
someone came in and dropped into a seat at the far end of
the room, but immediately he forgot the incident in the talk
of the sailors. They were now topping off with good red wine,
and were in high spirits. Nicolo made out that they belonged
to crews which were to sail that very day.

" You'll be bringing back sugar and lumber, I suppose? " one of them asked.

" Yes, all the yew and cypress we can load without sinking her."

" They say there's no better hard wood than this Madeira timber," someone commented, "but, for big money,
give me a good shipful of black men and a ballast of gold
ore! "

So that was where they were going, Nicolo said to himself – Madeira, one of the important Portuguese colonies. As for the reference to " black men " –

" From your talk of blacks and gold," cut in another, " I reckon you're bound for Guinea."

Ah, the much talked of Guinea Coast – another of Portugal's discoveries.

" That's what! " was the hearty rejoinder, " And a bonus if we get back on schedule time! "

" That for your bonus " – a snap of the fingers – " when they get the water route to India going in good shape! Watch me enlist on the first trip! "

More talk followed, of places that to Nicolo had been half myths: Cape Verde, the Azores, the Canaries.

They went out, laughing and scuffling, and Nicolo, his fancy on fire, watched them roister down the street. As he got up to pay for his meal, he glanced at the one remaining customer in the room, the one who had come in so quietly. – The boy with the eyes!

Arms folded on his chest, head dropped a little forward, the great eyes seemed to burn far into some future world. Glowing fires, thought Nicolo; the most extraordinary eyes ever lodged in a human head; uncanny, only for the sheer beauty of them.

The boy looked up, surprising his scrutiny. " Interesting, weren't they? " he said, nodding toward the departed sailors. " I saw you listening to them."

" You Portuguese have a right to be very proud of your navigators," Nicolo said warmly, responding to this friendly ignoring of formalities.

The boy seemed to seize at the last words. " Have

you done any voyaging – seen any sea service? " he demanded.

"Only in the Mediterranean – but enough to get my sea legs," laughed Nicolo. "I take it you've been to sea, or expect to go? "

"As soon as I can! "

Nicolo caught the note of impatience in the brief reply. "Perhaps your people won't let you go? " he suggested.

"No – not till I've finished my tour of duty at the palace." He flushed as though embarrassed at revealing so much to a stranger. "You see, I'm a page," he explained with a little grimace, " and I've a half dozen more years of service."

Their eyes met, understandingly, and Nicolo laughed. There was something refreshing, lovable, in this frankness. "So in the meantime you get the sea at second hand from The Green Window! "

The boy nodded. "Every chance I see, I slip out of my uniform and into some old hunting clothes they sent me from home, and come down here. It's good to be quit of those stiff things that saw your neck in two, and keep you laced up so tight you can't breathe! " He ran his fingers around the open throat of his loose leather jacket and squirmed luxuriously.

"A homesick, country lad," Nicolo silently mused, as much touched as he was amused by the ingenuous gesture. But well born, you could tell, from that forthright way of his. No heritage of the yoke in him! Aloud, "Old clothes *are* a comfort," he agreed. "What do you have to do at the palace? "

"Oh, play errand boy, serve the King at table, stand by

when he rides or drives out, wait on the ladies for this, that, and the other."

" Not too exciting, eh? I don't believe I envy you! "

"It's deadly," the other pursued, " the routine that a page has to go through, like a dog at its tricks. I never could see the sense of pulling on the King's hose for him! And – " he lowered his voice, " why the devil shouldn't a woman pick up her own handkerchief when she drops it? "

" Sh – careful! " Nicolo laughed under his breath. " Women have a way of getting back at rebels like you! By the way," he ventured, " didn't I see you on the dock this morning? " Almost, he had added " What were you looking for? "

" I was certainly down there," the boy returned, " and I saw *you* – twice! You made a friend for life out of that sugar dealer! "

" To tell the truth, I was thinking of my own interests as much as his! It was hardly good business to make an enemy the moment I'd set foot here, where I expect to stay."

The great eyes lighted up. " You really mean to live here? Good! I thought I heard you say something like that, when you and the captain were talking. I – I – " the colour rose to his cheeks – " listened to you! "

" Oh, so you understand Italian? " Nicolo laughed, inwardly amused with the ingenuous admission.

" After a fashion; you know, we pick up a smatter of everything in the palace. But you have me beaten, the way you speak our language. Didn't I hear you mention pirates? " he continued. " What happened? "

" Not very much – to us! The pirates and a Venetian vessel had been having it back and forth, when we overhauled them. After that we were two to one, of course, and the pirates broke and ran. That was all."

"There was something else that you said: that Lisbon was going to get all the trade. What makes you think that?"

"What I've heard about Diaz. I believe he's on the right track to India."

Something leaped in the boy's eyes, and his hand shot out to Nicolo's. "Diaz is the greatest man in the world! I know him . . . if you'd like to meet him."

"Would I! – That's a chance in a lifetime."

"Then I'll arrange it. Now," with a little grimace, "I must be going back to the palace."

Nicolo rose and walked with him to the door.

"Where is the palace?" he inquired. "Up there on top of the hill?"

"That? Oh, that's the Castle of St. George – old citadel that dates back to the time of the Moors. Here – " Magellan drew Nicolo from the doorway – "step out where you can see. Might as well begin to get your bearings! Now, that big bulk of a building with the dome and arches, half-way between us and the Castle, is the Sé Patriarchal.[1] That's where St. Vincent's tomb is – Lisbon's patron saint, you know. Some say it used to be a Moorish mosque."

"I noticed it first thing and wondered if it weren't the palace."

"Why, the palace is in the other direction!" exclaimed Magellan. "It's down by the harbour, you know – faces square on the Tagus. You must have seen it this morning."

"I'm afraid I was too busy with the empty sugar barrel!" laughed Nicolo.

[1] Old Lisbon's Cathedral.

The other grinned sympathetically. " Don't know that
I blame you! But the next time you're down at the water
front, take notice of a great three-sided building with an enormous square in the middle that opens on the river. That's
Manoel's palace."

"Where you pull on the royal stockings, and pick up
handkerchiefs that the ladies drop! " bantered Nicolo.

The boy made a face. Then, a little bashfully, he asked,
" Perhaps I'll see you here soon again? "

" If there's a chance to see *you,*" Nicolo said heartily.
" And what do you say we exchange names? "

" Oh, I know yours, already! I heard your captain say
it; Nicolo Conti, isn't it? And mine's Magellan – Ferdinand
Magellan."

From the door of The Green Window Nicolo looked
after him with a warm little stir at his heart. Those brilliant,
brooding eyes . . . that lovable frankness, even if indiscreet
. . . the sensitive colour, and, again, those altogether extraordinary eyes!

He stepped into the alley way and stood, for a moment,
stretching himself in the warm sun and exultantly breathing
in the tang of the clear air. He had made no mistake in leaving Venice for Portugal. Here the future was in the shaping,
with a chance to share in the process; in the result, too. For
the moment, Life seemed a joyous effervescent that foamed
gloriously over the edge as he drank. He was glad to be here.
Glad!

He started to walk on, when an idea occurred to him.
He turned, amusedly contemplated the big green window in
the tiny front; then he re-entered the inn.

Pedro was giving a final scouring to the long board top

of a table. He had taken it off its trestles, the better to clean it, and, now, as Nicolo watched, he lifted it back.

"You forgot something, perhaps?" he asked, as he suddenly perceived Nicolo.

"I was just wondering if – well – I don't suppose you'd consider a lodger, would you, Pedro?"

"I've never taken lodgers, Senhor. I have nothing but a small room overhead." The tone was deprecatory but Nicolo could see that the kind eyes were pleased.

"Let me see it," he said. "All I want is a place to sleep in. I'm sure of good food here at any rate."

Eventually it was agreed that he should move in at once. The room was small, but it was clean and sunny and had a tolerable bed.

"I'll have my box brought here," Nicolo concluded, "shall I, Pedro?"

Pedro nodded. "If you're satisfied." Then, "Are you staying in Lisbon for long?" he inquired.

"For always, I hope!" Nicolo told him, good humouredly.

"So! Then you have friends here?"

"Only one, so far – the young fellow I was talking to, downstairs. But presently I expect there'll be more. There's a banker here that I mean to look up, a Master Abel Zakuto. You don't happen to know him, do you?"

"Of course! Who, in Lisbon, doesn't? A kind of a sailor-fellow on land, he is; always pottering with navigation instruments, and hobnobbing with anyone who's either been to sea or is going."

"Oh, that isn't the Zakuto whom I've heard about at

home," Nicolo broke in. "My man is a banker, a Jewish banker."

Pedro nodded. "He's that, too, a Jewish banker; same person. Yes, I can show you where he lives."

Directed by a graphic finger, Nicolo's eyes finally made out, high on the hillside, a certain house at the head of a long stairway. Along the front a row of windows were bright gold in the afternoon sun. It struck Nicolo's fancy – perched up there with an air of satisfaction at having out-climbed all those other climbing houses! He would go there some day soon and make acquaintance with this banker that he'd heard of in Venice – Abel Zakuto.

CHAPTER 3

Abel Zakuto's Workshop

A BEL quietly let himself through his gate, and crossed the court to the workshop. A little breathless from the last few stairs, he sat down and reviewed this morning's work.

It had been just another fruitless search for some clue to the Girl. He could think of nothing more to do, and he had to own himself completely baffled. Presently Ruth would come in to inquire if he had any news. He could hear her moving about in the further end of the house. Whatever she was doing, he knew she was near the Girl, for from the first she had watched over her with a fierce tenderness that amazed, while it touched, Abel. Later, perhaps, Ferdinand would drop in, with some light on the mystery.

Meanwhile – the whole of a golden afternoon with his tools and his instruments, and the blossoming court lovingly watching him through the open door!

He looked about the room like a boy who has successfully manoeuvred an afternoon for play – triumphant, but a little guilty; for, after his morning's search, he had deliberately come home instead of going to business. A feeling of happy seclusion and security stole over him. It was like a fortress, this room of his, high above streets and noise, and the wide outlook from its windows gave him a sense of command. Beneath him lay Lisbon's hills, and, in the blue bowl of a harbour that the widening Tagus had made at their feet, he could even distinguish the flags of the crowded shipping. He could, too, look directly down on Manoel's palace; on the massive wings and the huge colonnaded quadrangle open on the south to the river front.

He never gazed through his windows without recalling his friends' comments and Ruth's protests at his choice of large panes of clear glass in face of the fashion for mullions. He had let them talk. But he had gone on fitting those panes into casements that ran the width of the workshop – for one of Abel Zakuto's necessities was a view.

They'd laughed a little, too, when he'd made such a huge lamp to hang over the table. But when he'd got it done – a sturdy column of wrought iron and glass – they'd all admitted that it made studying the maps at night as easy as by day. "A regular lighthouse" someone had laughingly dubbed it – and the name had stuck.

But he must get to work; before he knew it, midday would be afternoon. There was so much to do . . . the astrolabe . . . the compass box. He opened a cupboard, and stood looking at two plates of copper within. Gently he took one up – almost as if it were alive – turned it in his hands. No, not that today; too much else to be done. Besides, before he could cut the copper into the proper discs, he must first put on paper the design that he had pretty well in mind. Already he could see in its completeness the new instrument that he had in mind: a metal astrolabe like those the Arabs had used for centuries, but as yet unknown to western navigation. This was Abel's newest and most precious secret, and that was why his fingers trembled a little, as he put the plate back into the cupboard.

He'd better go on with the compass box, he decided, since it was begun; but the piece of mahogany on which he'd started was so hard that first he must sharpen his saw.

As he began filing, he had a mental picture of Ruth – Ruth as she would presently stand, in the doorway, fix him with her bright, black eyes, and say – he knew well enough what she would say: "The time you waste in this workshop of yours, Abel! . . . Think of the money you could be making!"

Ruth had a heart of gold, he reflected, but when it came to imagination, one had to be patient with her. Besides, to

do her justice, she wasn't alone in her opinion; for he knew
it was said, here in Lisbon, that Abel Zakuto's astuteness
could have made him rich even in this city whose Jews were
known over Europe for their sagacity.

"Rich!" Abel snorted contemptuously. "Money!"
What money could buy the wealth of this room? Poor enough
it might look to some with its bare table and plain chairs.
But think of the men who'd sat around that table! . . .

Diego Cam, with his first glowing tales of how he'd
seen the Congo's vast flood rush far into the sea, of how
he'd set up at its mouth the stone pillar of Portugal; Christopher Columbus and John Cabot, who'd come here, sad and
disheartened by King John's indifference, but who'd gone
away fired with the courage that they'd found here in the
workshop; and Pero d'Alemquer, chief pilot of the Diaz expedition to the Cape; and Martin Behaim, the German.
Conceited Martin was, Abel reflected, but such charts as
he had made, with such German thoroughness! Would these
men have gathered in his workshop, if he'd been only a
money maker? Would Bartholomew Diaz come here night
after night, if he, Abel Zakuto, had been merely a rich man?

He laid down the sharpened saw, and stood up to reach
a partly worked piece of mahogany. He lingered to survey
a row of shelves on which were ranged delicate tools and
packets of metal and blocks of fine-grained wood. There was
one shelf that ran entirely to compasses. Mentally Abel contrasted them with the unwieldy "Genoese Needle"[1] – and
gave a sigh of content. . . . Not but what he could improve
on his present workmanship – and would! "Getting money,"

[1] A magnetized piece of iron floating on a raft of cork or reeds in a
bowl of water.

he mused, " when one could be making instruments to help find new worlds! "

His eyes roved to a niche in the wall, and lovingly dwelt there – his precious, even if tiny, library! What wealth would tempt from him those parchment treatises on astronomy and geometry, or that volume of Marco Polo's *Travels* transcribed from the very copy once owned by the Great Navigator,[1] and bound by Abel's own hands in boards half-covered with sheepskin.

He sat down at his carpenter's bench and made fast the mahogany block. This was to be a compass larger than those on the shelf, and in his mind it had already been dedicated to a certain enterprise – another of his secrets. By and by, he ran on to himself, when he had finished it and the astrolabe, then, *then* – he was going to make maps. . . . Maps!

He sawed on, till the severed block fell to the floor. Then he laid down his work, slid open the table drawer and began to lean over his copies of maps, inscribed with such signatures as Giovanni Leardo, Fra Mauro, Cadamosto. One of these days, he promised himself, he, too, would make maps – not, as these other chaps made them, as they fancied or hoped the earth was – but as it really was; but for that, of course, he would have to wait till Diaz put the final link in the sea route to India, and could give him facts.

He closed the drawer and went on with his sawing. Then – as he had foreseen – Ruth stood in the doorway.

" Abel – "

When Ruth began that way, and then paused, it was a sign that her mind must be unloaded.

" Yes, Ruth? "

---

[1] Prince Henry of Portugal called The Great Navigator.

Abel Zakuto's Workshop

She came into the workshop, and sat down, without so much as a glance at the litter of sawdust to which she usually objected. "Abel – I'm worried about that child. Why doesn't she talk?"

Abel took up a chisel and ran his thumb over its edge. Vaguely he was wondering at Ruth's silence about the sawdust. He stole a look at her. Her face was anxious, softer than he remembered.

"Shouldn't you think she'd talk," she continued, "and tell us what frightened her?"

"No, I shouldn't. Just think of the terror that was in her poor face; that still is. The child is simply beyond speech."

"Beyond speech, Abel? You don't mean – "

"Oh, nothing but what'll right itself," he hastily assured her. "By and by, when she feels at home with us – " He was absorbed, as he applied the chisel to an uneven edge.

Ruth watched him in silence. "I wonder," he heard her say, as if she were talking to herself, "I wonder what her voice will sound like." And not waiting for him to comment, she left the room.

What *would* the Girl's voice sound like? Abel pondered. If Ruth hadn't suggested it, he would never have thought of such a thing, but now he began to feel a growing curiosity to hear it. Perhaps if he approached her, spoke to her very gently . . . But so far she had persistently clung to Ruth, and had shrunk from him.

As he worked, his mind alternated between ways to persuade her to speak, and the mystery that so completely wrapped her. There was a last possibility that Ferdinand might have got hold of some clue.

But when Ferdinand finally appeared, late that afternoon, Abel saw at a glance that he had been no more successful than himself.

"That girl must have got here on wings," the boy declared, "for I was down at the docks first thing the morning after, and there wasn't a sign of anything like a slave cargo. I made sure of that: I got the name of every craft that had tied up here, where she hailed from, what stops she'd made, and what she was carrying. After that I inquired at the inns to find out who'd come in to town in the last day or two."

Abel nodded. "Just what I did."

"I saw something odd while I was hunting a clue down on the quay," Ferdinand continued. "Some merchant had just found a shortage in a consignment that a Venetian galleon had brought, and he was cursing Venice and Venetians for cheats and thieves, when, from behind him, up comes a young fellow with blood in his eye; says he's a Venetian and wants to know what the man means." Ferdinand stopped to laugh at the recollection. "In another minute I expected to see fists fly, when, all of a sudden, I noticed the young chap smile to himself, and pull out his wallet. 'I'll stand your loss, sir,' says he, and then there was some more about his being a friend of the captain who was responsible for the cargo. Well, you should have seen the merchant back water: money was nothing to him – it was just the 'principle' of the thing!"

"Nevertheless, he took the money?" Abel drily insinuated.

"Oh, of course! And then he couldn't do enough for the Venetian chap, told him where to find an inn, and so on."

"That young man has brains," Abel admiringly observed.

Ferdinand nodded. "At first glance you'd think him a

bit of a dandy, from his pointed shoes and the gold button
on his cap and the fur collar of his cloak, but when you saw
the swell of his chest under his doublet, and the buttons of his
hose all strained out at the calf . . . And he's plucky, too. I
met him afterward – in The Green Window, you know – and
he told me he had left Venice because he believed Portugal
was going to have it all her way with trade."

"Oh, so?" Abel exclaimed, with fresh interest. "That's
the kind of citizens we need. Bring him here some time, Ferdinand. Did you get his name?"

"Nicolo Conti. Of course he's anxious to meet Master
Diaz."

"Conti . . . Conti . . ." Abel mused aloud. " I wonder
if he's any connection of the Venetian traveller of that
name."

They returned to the search for the Girl, and Ferdinand
admitted he was at a standstill.

"If she would only talk!" said Abel.

The boy laughed. "One of these days she will – being
a woman!"

"But suppose she doesn't know our language?"

Ruth came into the room in time to catch Abel's last
words. "If she wanted to tell us about herself, she'd find a
way even if it was only by signs. My guess is that she's hiding from someone who's so crazed her with fear that she
doesn't dare tell anything to anyone."

"There's no doubt that she was trying to hide, and
meant to disguise herself," Ferdinand agreed. "I took her
for a boy, myself, until I saw her long hair."

Ruth nodded reminiscently. "Those eyes of hers are
just the same as they were that first night – they stare and

stare into space as if they were looking at ghosts. But the rest
of her is different, I can tell you, in the new dress I've made
her! You know, Ferdinand "–she became confidential–" I
hunted the shops over till I found the right stuff, all shim-
mery and gauzy, like . . . like moonlight on a misty night
. . . or like those lilies, out there at dusk."

Abel shot an astonished glance at her. Was Ruth, the
practical, turning poet? Was there, after all, a love of beauty,
hidden deep within her, that had welled at last to this sweet
outlet?

"Anyway," Ruth pursued, "she's as lovely a sight as
you'll ever see! "

Ferdinand's face lighted with sudden mischief. "Let
me see her, Aunt Ruth – I'll get her to talk! " He sprang up
and pretended to make a dash for the next room.

"You young jackanapes! " She caught his sleeve and
pulled him back. "You'd frighten her so, she'd never open
her lips! "

"Then I'll be going." He pretended to sulk, while he
winked at Abel behind Ruth's back.

"She'll talk," Abel comfortably observed, "when she
feels at home with us – feels that she's safe." But to himself
he wondered what would have happened if they had taken
the lad at his word and had let him see the Girl!

Ferdinand lingered in the door for a last word. "Your
cousin, Master Abraham Zakuto, said he and Gama would
be up here tonight."

"Good! " Abel was genuinely pleased. "I haven't seen
Abraham in some time. How is he? "

"Oh, Manoel and he are thick as thieves – Manoel's always consulting him."

"I'm glad Gama's coming–if for nothing more than to lend Abraham an arm up the stairs. On any account, though, I'm glad–I think a great deal of Vasco."

"I'd like him more," Ferdinand rejoined, "if he were keener on exploration–seeing as his father was to have commanded an expedition to India, if he hadn't died. Another thing: Gama's as stubborn as a mule–never gives you an inch in an argument."

Abel laughed indulgently. "Why should he, if the argument's worth anything? No–I like him for standing his ground."

"Well–have it your way," the boy retorted. "But when I'm his age," he shot back from the gate, "you won't see me content to dawdle around Manoel. Not while there's seas to sail and lands to be found!"

From the door of the workshop Abel's eyes affectionately followed him. "What should we do, Ruth, without that lad running in and out all the time?"

She came and stood beside him. "The saucy rascal!" she laughed. "Talking about the King and his court with no more respect than if they were common human beings!"

Abel chuckled. "Perhaps you'd do no better if you lived with Manoel day in and day out as Ferdinand does!"

She gave him a searching look: "I sometimes think, Abel, you haven't much of an opinion of Manoel."

"He seems to be treating Abraham as well as we could wish," he replied, evasively.

"You hit it just right," she declared, "when you thought of getting Abraham in as court astronomer."

"I doubt if I could have manoeuvred it without the

help of Manoel's physician. It's lucky he and I are old friends, for Manoel will do anything he advises."

"Poor old Abraham!" Ruth sighed. "Thank God he's sure of peace and safety here as long as he lives." A look of suffering crossed her face, and Abel knew she was thinking of those days of horror when they had seen thousands of Jews, driven from Spain and fleeing into Lisbon, starved, crazed creatures ravaged by disease. It had been months before Ruth could nurse Abraham back to even a semblance of himself.

"There's something unforgivable in persecuting an intellect like Abraham's, let alone his body," Abel sombrely mused.

"I can't bear to think of what our people have gone through," Ruth burst out. "It was wicked—wicked! Oh, Abel—" she turned troubled eyes to him—"what if King Manoel should drive us out of Portugal?"

"He won't, my dear, he won't."

She murmured something about supper, and left the room. Slowly Abel's eyes roved between workshop and court. Suppose that which had happened to his people in Spain should suddenly happen here, and he should be torn from this house, where he had brought Ruth a bride; from this court that together they had planted and set out.

He felt his heart contract; then, what a fool he was to borrow trouble, he sharply told himself, for hadn't Manoel always been friendly with his Jewish subjects? Hadn't he sought their advice and openly laid the country's commercial prosperity to the Jewish financiers? No, Manoel wasn't the man wantonly to drain his kingdom of the very sources of that prosperity. Spain had done exactly that, when she had driven out her Jews and Moors; but then, Ferdinand and Isabella were religion-mad, and Manoel wasn't, at least, that.

Rage surged through Abel at the thought of the paupered exiles, which Spain had made of her most useful subjects. Paupered, they who had made Spain rich! Homeless, who had made it famous for its learning and its scholars! It was hard to think calmly of them as wanderers, as cold and hungry, these people who had been so open-handed to encourage their country's progress. No one had had to urge them, he recalled, to give – and generously – to Columbus' first expedition. His face hardened as he remembered how the second expedition – after their expulsion – had been financed: from confiscated Jewish estates!

He became aware of a growing coolness in the air. The sun had set, and dusk was falling, while he had let his thoughts run away with him! He turned from the doorway, and began to put away his work. Shavings and sawdust were no matter, but a tool out of place – never!

It was dark enough now to light the great lamp, but Abel decided to wait till after supper. He liked to sit, quietly, by himself, in the half light, his chair tilted against the wall.

He found himself thinking of that strange night that the Girl had come. He was gazing out into the court, as he was now, he recalled, when, like a phantom, she had flashed on the square of darkness framed in the doorway.

It had always pleased his fancy that it was the workshop where she had first appeared – where the talk was always of the undiscovered and of the unknown. In a curious, mystical sense she seemed to fit the spirit of this room. She, who was as baffling as anything that had ever been discussed around the big table and over the maps! If only, Abel whimsically mused, some chart might be found to reveal her mystery! By heaven – as that idea suggested another – *that* might work!

His tilted chair came down on all fours. He would send a message to Ferdinand by Abraham or Gama.

Yes, *that* might work!

CHAPTER 4

The Two Abels

B Y keeping in sight its row of windows, Nicolo found the hillside house that Pedro had pointed out. Though the person who answered his knock acknowledged himself to be Abel Zakuto, Nicolo looked doubtfully at him. This spare,

youngish-looking man with sawdust clinging to his breeches
and to the turned-back sleeves of his plain round jacket, was
like no banker Nicolo had ever known; nor was the whimsical smile lurking in the boyish eyes that were so oddly
at variance with the high forehead. This was no banker, said
Nicolo to himself – never in the world; more like a skilled
artisan, or possibly a scholar, he looked, with that black
silk skull cap.

"I've often heard, sir, at home, in Venice, of Abel
Zakuto, the Lisbon financier," Nicolo began, "but here I
was given to understand that it was not banks you were
interested in, but navigation – exploration – something of the
kind. Are there two Abel Zakutos? And have I come to the
wrong one?"

"There *are* two Abel Zakutos," laughed Abel, "but
they both live" – he tapped his forehead – "under the same
roof. One of them is a banker – you're right about him. The
other is a conscienceless fellow who steals most of the banker's time to do things that don't bring in money! But come
in!" He pulled down his sleeves, seized Nicolo's arm and
guided him toward the workshop. "You say you're from
Venice? I wonder if you aren't the Nicolo Conti of whom
Ferdinand was telling me?"

"Ferdinand Magellan, you mean? You know him?"

"Oh, for years; he's always running in and out."

Nicolo took the chair that Abel pushed toward him,
while he glanced about. Tools . . . compasses . . . gay little ship models . . . a work bench littered with fine shavings. Yes, it fitted Pedro's comments about Abel: "A kind
of a sailor-fellow on land; always pottering with navigation
instruments."

"I understand from Ferdinand," Abel bantered, "that your first taste of Lisbon wasn't too pleasant! "

"Oh – that little matter of the sugar barrel? Well, it did seem foolish of that merchant to get heated about a few pounds of sugar, when we'd successfully brought him some thousands of pounds."

"Did you make any stops on your way?" Abel asked.

"No; that is –" Nicolo smiled at the recollection of the pirates – "no official ones! "

Looking at Abel, he saw his eyes change, and knew instinctively that some new thought had suddenly entered his mind. When Abel spoke again Nicolo was conscious that his question disguised the real motive:

"Did you see any slave trade along the way? "

Nicolo shook his head.

Abel seemed to ponder. "No craft with a slave cargo? " he carefully asked.

Something in his expression and attitude made Nicolo think, vaguely, of young Magellan – Magellan as he had leaned out over the sea-wall, and peered at the names of the anchored ships.

"Were you expecting such a cargo," Nicolo inquired, "or some particular craft? "

"No, oh no," Abel hastily disclaimed, and – Nicolo fancied – almost guiltily. "I noticed," he said, shifting the subject, "that you've the same name as the famous Venetian traveller – or rather, one of your famous travellers, for you have many."

"We've a bent for out-of-the-way places," Nicolo agreed, "though I didn't expect to find anyone as familiar with us and our doings as you are, sir."

Abel laughed. " Lay that to the scamp I was telling you about, the chap who keeps the banker from getting rich! One forgets about such stupidities as making money when one hears of exploits such as Conti's or reads chronicles like these." He reached for a book from a tiny library and handed it to Nicolo.

" Marco Polo! " Nicolo exclaimed at the title. " He's the master traveller of us all, isn't he! "

" And isn't it curious that, without any intention on his part, these *Travels* which he set down for people's entertainment should start – two hundred years later, mind you – the greatest sensation the world's ever known! "

" How do you mean, sir, ' greatest sensation ' ? "

" Why, it was Polo's account of the traffic of the East that started Christopher Columbus to thinking about a a water short-cut to it; he told me so himself, sitting in this room. And now all Europe is hot on the scent of a passage to India."

" We hear at home that Cabot has stirred up the English to send him on an expedition to find it. Do you know of him – John Cabot? "

" Know of him? " Abel ejaculated. " We've talked for hours in this very spot! "

Pedro's description of Zakuto as " hobnobbing with anyone who'd been to sea or was going," drifted across Nicolo's recollection.

" Yes," Abel continued, " Cabot's caught the passage-to-India fever. He saw enough of the Oriental trade on that trip of his down the Red Sea to convince him that it was worth trying for. About Conti's travels I know very little, but I've heard it rumoured that his special object was to get information about the source of spices, they being the richest item in the whole Oriental trade. Did he succeed, do you know? "

" Matter of fact, I hadn't meant to bring that subject up just yet, sir! But as long as you've put it to me – yes, I know a good deal about it, for I've read Conti's letters in which he tells how he discovered from where the different spices come. You see, sir, Nicolo Conti was my grandfather, and his letters are in the family."

" So! " Abel ejaculated. " So! " He drew his chair close to Nicolo's. " This is real news! Tell me all you care to."

" Well, sir, up to Conti's time, our merchants and explorers, even Marco Polo himself, had confused the ports where spices were shipped with the place where they grew. Whenever they asked an incoming caravan from where its spice cargo came, they were referred to the caravan's last starting point, and again, at that point, to one farther east; and so on. No one seemed to know where the spices grew and no one could find out, but it was always some place east of wherever the inquiry was made! "

" Looks to me," Abel interrupted, " as if all that evasion were intentional."

" Oh, Conti says it is, and charges the Arab merchants with it! So he made up his mind to keep on going east as long as there was an east. He finally reached Java and Sumatra, which was farther than any European had gone. And there he ran the scent down! "

Like an excited boy, Abel edged forward in his chair.

" He found out all about pepper and cinnamon," Nicolo continued, " and that cloves came from the island of Banda, and nutmegs from neighbouring islands to the eastward of India." He waited a moment, then, "Master Zakuto," he said, deliberately, "it was this information, together with my belief that Diaz has all but found the sea route to these islands, that brought me to Lisbon."

Abel's head went up proudly. "So you believe in Bartholomew Diaz?"

"If I didn't I wouldn't be here. I've come to Lisbon to follow up my convictions; and to you, in particular, Master Zakuto, because I've heard business men at home say they'd rather have your advice than each others'."

Abel made no reply at once; then, he said, carefully, "You would like financial counsel, or perhaps you wish to make a banking connection?"

The boyish eyes, Nicolo noted, had become quite astoundingly keen; unsuspected lines appeared around the mouth; chin and jaw, thrust ever so little forward, fitted the great forehead's testimony to a profound sagacity. This was Zakuto, the financier!

When Nicolo spoke he seemed to ignore Abel's question. "When Portugal reaches the Indies by sea she's going to take trade supremacy from Venice," he stated with a finality that brought an exclamation from the other.

"Strange, that, from a Venetian!"

"But it's true. My love for Venice can't change the lay of land and water!"

For several moments Abel studied Nicolo; then, he asked, "What do they say in Venice about this talk of a sea route to India?"

"You see, Venice has had the monopoly of Oriental commerce so long that she can't believe anyone can take it away from her. So, most of them at home laugh at the reports of the Diaz expedition, and a few take it seriously. I'm one of those few. Then, why live my life out in a city that shuts its eyes to what I'm convinced is bound to be? "

" So you're thinking of going into trade here? "

" As I figure, Master Abel – " again Nicolo waived the other's question – " when you get the Oriental trade to your side of the world, you'll need ships, more ships than you now have."

" Aha! " Swift comprehension broke over Abel's face. " So that's what you came to talk! Ship-building, eh? "

" That was my real business with you, sir – till we got started on Conti's letters, spice, and the rest of it! "

" Good! " Abel hitched his chair nearer to Nicolo. " You know, Conti, all they can think of, here in Lisbon, is getting their hands on that Eastern trade – but you never hear a word of how they expect to distribute it, after they have it. Of course they'll have to have more ships! Just as they'll have to arrange for more foreign credit. And the Jewish financiers have foreseen that. Why – " confidentially he lowered his voice – " my firm is already negotiating for branch houses abroad, even as far east as the Levant. But to come back to ship-building . . ."

They plunged into details of locations and sites and leases. Abel knew the right men for each connection.

" But above all, my boy," he warned, " lay in a stock of patience. Don't expect Manoel to send an expedition to India next week! "

" What! Isn't he interested? "

" When he can spare time from home politics! "

"But how does he dare risk delay, with rivalry so keen about reaching the Orient? Why, we've heard at home that His Holiness even had to make an imaginary 'Line' somewhere out in the ocean to keep Spain and Portugal from quarrelling over each other's discoveries."

Abel's eyes twinkled. "That 'Line' makes a fine talking point! But it doesn't prevent Spain's galleons from skulking around to see what we're doing on our side of it, down by the Guinea coast, any more than it prevents them from lifting one of our cargoes, now and then. Not that we neglect a good chance on their side of the Line, either! Oh, we're a fine, civilized lot, Conti! But you were asking about Manoel –"

"He's indifferent, you say, to reaching India? Doesn't he believe in Diaz?"

"Oh, in a way; but I suppose Diaz is an old story to him by now."

"You mean, that Manoel will have to be waked up before he'll send an expedition?"

"Something like that, yes."

Absently Nicolo drummed on the table. He hadn't counted on this sort of a situation – waiting for a royal imagination to be tickled.

From under his great forehead Abel watched him: "Push right on with your plans," he said, at last. "Diaz hasn't yet given up hope of completing what he began! As for myself –" He drew Nicolo to the windows. "See here a minute, my boy."

Below them, in the late sunlight, the roofs of the city stood up sharp and bright, with the streets, already in shadow, like black gashes between.

∾∾ *The Two Abels* ∾∾

" I never look down on this city, Conti," – Abel's
voice took on a new, deep note – " without saying to myself: 'Not Lisbon, the capital of Portugal, but Lisbon,
the emporium of Europe!' . . . I'm sure of it, Conti,
sure! "

There was a rush of colour to Nicolo's face, and his eyes
looked unseeingly before him; for, in fancy, he was gazing
on the Inland Sea that had nursed him, that had mothered
the childhood of man. Ah, sea of measureless blues and
crests of gold! Supreme through the marching centuries, it
was now to yield its supremacy. Those to whom it had been
highway and warpath would look henceforth to other waters;
already, in fact, were so looking, so seeking, faring forth with
the zest of the child who has outgrown the hand to which it
clung.

He was roused by Abel's suddenly hurrying to his carpenter's bench. From it he picked up an object which he
blew clear of litter, and then, almost reverently, held in his
palm for Nicolo's inspection: the frame of a compass. Just
that, and only that, it appeared to his layman's eye till Abel
enthusiastically pointed out the fine grain of the best Madeira mahogany. A long search it had been for this particular piece; sample after sample tested and discarded.
But at last, this! And when it was rubbed down, polished!
A swift vision of gleaming surfaces smote Nicolo's eye of
fancy. And then he must see just how Abel would set the
pivot on which the needle would rest.

"Makes the 'Genoese Needle' look pretty lame! " Nicolo admiringly commented.

All at once his arm was seized, Abel's face was thrust
close to his. This, Nicolo perceived, was the Zakuto of the

boyish eyes, and of the lovably incongruous features: the pilferer of Banker Zakuto's time!

"Conti . . . Conti . . ." he was stammering like an eager child – " do you know for what I'm making this compass? . . . For the first crew that sails out of Lisbon for India! "

CHAPTER 5

The Locked Door

ABEL ZAKUTO came thoughtfully up the long, stone stairway. Inwardly, he was a good deal perturbed. This thing that was to happen – for which, in fact, he had deliberately set the stage – must be so managed as to appear not

managed. It must be, he said to himself, like the unfolding of
a flower – as delicate as all that.

Perhaps it was this particular thought that made him,
when he crossed the court, stop to gather a cluster of late-
blooming roses. With them in his hand he went into the
room where Ruth sat sewing with the Girl.

"Ruth, see! Aren't they fine blooms?" He held them
up for her to smell, and then pressed them to the Girl's
cheek. Under his off-hand manner his keen, kind eyes noted
the rise of colour in the still face, and the flutter of the listless
eyelids.

"Come along into the court, Ruth!" He tossed the
sewing from her hands and caught her round the waist,
while his other arm swept the Girl up. If he saw Ruth's
startled eyes, or felt the Girl's slender body stiffen and hang
back, he paid no heed as, laughing and talking, he steered
for the court.

As they stepped outside, he was aware that the Girl
started violently, and, behind him, he heard Ruth's low
"What are you thinking of – taking her out so suddenly?"

"Fresh air and sunlight never hurt anyone," he comfortably returned, while he guided them toward the lilies
that had always reminded him of the Girl.

He picked one and put it into her hands, while he meditated aloud: "The narcissus bed must be thinned before
long, and these gilly flowers. There'll be enough for a new
plantation; or would a border be prettier, Ruth?"

His arm always around the Girl, he strolled on, stopping every few steps, to inspect a vine or a shrub; to notice
that the mint bed was a bit dry; to rub a bit of sage between

thumb and finger and hold it to his nostrils. Over her head he could see Ruth doubtfully eyeing him.

They had made tour of the court, and had halted under the old fig tree, when Abel heard a deep, tremulous sigh, and felt the Girl's arm drop from his. Quickly he glanced at her. As if she had forgotten his presence and Ruth's, she was gazing up into the sun-flecked shade while she stretched her arms like a drowsy child.

Almost holding his breath, Abel watched the pale cheeks warm with faint colour; then, as her eyes came back to him, he saw that they held something besides fear. She stood there, very still, between him and Ruth, and then, slowly, as if groping her way, she reached out to a jessamine vine, and picked a spray of its white stars. A look of triumph shot from Abel to Ruth as they covertly watched her smell the flowers, and Ruth found a chance to murmur in his ear, "I'd never have believed it!"

From time to time Abel furtively eyed the gate. At last, feet sounded on the stairs; the door swung back, and Ferdinand stepped inside. Abel saw him look hastily about the court, then draw back as he perceived the Girl.

Abel stole a glance at her. Thank heaven, she was not frightened! Soft, wondering eyes fixed on the figure at the gate, lips parted, head lifted as if listening, waiting – what was it that she looked like? Some young creature of the wild – ah, a fawn!

"I thought Master Abraham said –" Ferdinand broke off, then made another start: "Did you mean me to come now," he stammered, "or – or –"

"You're always welcome," said Abel serenely, "day

or night." He waved a hand at the flower beds. "Garden looks well, doesn't it?"

From behind the Girl, he caught Ruth suspiciously eyeing him. "Abel Zakuto," he heard her whisper, "I believe you sent for the boy on purpose!"

Without appearing to hear her, he strolled over to a fruit tree and made a pretext of examining it. From under his eyelids he observed Ferdinand slowly advance. He was trying hard, Abel noted with a chuckle, to appear at ease, and so was Ruth. – If she only knew how near the truth she'd come with her dark suspicions!

The Girl, he exulted, seemed less concerned than either. Stealthily he watched her. Never once did she take her gaze from Ferdinand, and, as he came nearer, she bent toward him, and held up the jessamine spray for him to smell – the ingenuous gesture of a child with a playmate! If Abel's blood quickened a little, he gave no sign, while he continued to potter about his tree, but he observed that Ferdinand had accepted the bloom, and was affably smelling it. He was making, on the whole, a fair show of manners – the young cub!

A new sound suddenly fell on his ears. Ferdinand's startled face, Ruth's eyes bulging with amazement, flashed before him. His gaze followed theirs – to the Girl. That sound . . . why, great heaven, it was coming from her! *It was her voice.* A voice, he noted, even in that first, incredible moment, that had the sweet vibrancy of metal struck on metal.

"Ruth," she was saying in that silver voice. "Ruth!" Then, "A-bel," she slowly pronounced, with a caressing little accent that brought a lump to Abel's throat. Her eyes now eagerly fixed on Ferdinand – eyes, Abel noted, that, for at least this moment, had almost forgotten their fright.

For a perplexed moment the boy's gaze questioned hers. All at once he seemed to understand what she wished, and, "*Ferdinand,*" he said, distinctly.

She repeated the syllables, pausing between them like a child trying a new lesson.

"That's right! " he nodded, laughing and excited. " I told you she'd talk some day! " he slyly threw at Abel.

"Now – *her* name! " Abel whispered.

Ferdinand came a step nearer her. " I'm Ferdinand " – he pointed to himself. "And you " – he made a quick gesture – " what's your name? "

Instantly they saw her face cloud, as she drew away from him.

"What's wrong? " he demanded in surprise.

"Abel – you try," whispered Ruth.

Ferdinand stepped aside, and Abel came close to the Girl. In the sunny stillness he could hear her quickened breathing.

"See, my child," he said, "*this* is Abel, *that* is Ruth, and *that* is Ferdinand." He touched her arm as if he were wheedling a child. "Who are you? . . . What is your name? "

She only looked blankly back at him. Could she, he wondered, be feigning? He drew her down on a near-by bench. "What is your name? " he coaxed.

"She doesn't understand a word you say! " Ruth's voice was as crestfallen as her face.

"But she understands what he means," Ferdinand declared.

Abel said nothing, but, secretly, he agreed.

"She's like a locked door without a key," sighed Ruth.

"There's always a key, my dear," Abel thoughtfully replied, while he studied the gently inscrutable face beside him – "if one can only find it."

"Well –" Ferdinand burst out laughing, "we have a key, sir! All we have to do is to teach her what she's begun to teach herself – our language. Then there'll be no trouble about unlocking the door! "

"Humph," Ruth sniffed, "if you think you can get her to open her lips one minute before she's ready . . . She's just what I said she was, a locked door."

Ferdinand's eyes glinted. "I'll guarantee she'll unlock, if *I* teach her," he teased.

Abel glanced down at the Girl. Out of the babel of words, of gestures, of varying expressions on the faces around her, what did she gather? Did some inkling of their import reach her? Again the image of a fawn flashed irresistibly before him – that attitude of pitiful vigilance, those wistful eyes that smiled at you, yet seemed never quite to forget a pursuing terror. He put out his arm and drew her to him. Never had she seemed to him so exquisitely piteous.

"I'll be here tomorrow," Ferdinand called back from the gate, "for the first lesson! "

"Abel," said Ruth, that evening, when they were alone, "did you send for Ferdinand on purpose? "

"Send for him? " Abel inquired innocently. "Why, he's been coming here for years, hasn't he? "

"You know perfectly well what I mean, Abel! "

"Come to think of it, I believe I did do something or other about it."

The Locked Door

"I knew it!" Ruth with her bright, black eyes and her head cocked to one side, reminded him of an exasperated blackbird.

"Well, what harm came of it? Seeing a young person – someone of her own age – did for our poor child what you and I couldn't have done in a hundred years. It started things going in that benumbed brain of hers."

"It certainly started something."

"What do you mean?" Abel demanded uneasily.

"Oh, nothing," was all Ruth could be got to say then, but, as he was dropping off to sleep, she volunteered, out of an apparently clear sky, "I don't believe Ferdinand will have to be sent for to come here again!"

And she was right. It had to be a full day at the palace that kept him from giving the Girl a lesson.

Ruth and Abel began by teaching her familiar, everyday words. Ferdinand went about it differently. As he talked to her, he would illustrate words by action; then, with infinite patience, he would make her re-tell what he had said, while Ruth and Abel sat by, sometimes laughing and always wondering at his ingenuity. And, gradually, almost without realizing what she was doing, the Girl began to piece words together.

One day, from a window where they could see the two in the court, Abel and Ruth heard him telling the Girl about his home away beyond the mountains; about the great forests, and the wolves he had trapped, and the boar he had hunted. Kindling to his own description, he said, a little regretfully, "I'd probably have stayed up there, if my father hadn't made me come down here to the King's court."

They saw her look strangely at him, and then, in her halting way, she asked, "Are you sorry, Ferdinand, to be here?"

"Ruth! Ruth –" Abel clutched her arm in his excitement – "do you see what that young rascal has done? Got her so interested that she forgot herself!"

They held their breath, while they listened to Ferdinand follow up the cue so unwittingly given him.

"Of course sometimes I'm homesick," he was saying. "Everybody is." Then, quite naturally, "Aren't you?"

They saw her eyes widen with fear. For a moment he appeared to wait for her answer. "Don't you wish sometimes you could go home?" he urged.

This time the two at the window saw the delicate face quiver.

"Abel, stop him!" Ruth whispered in a panic.

"Yes – he's going too fast." He strolled into the court and made a pretext of asking Ferdinand when he'd seen Nicolo Conti. Presently, the Girl went into the house.

"You pushed her too hard, lad!" Abel remonstrated in a low voice.

"She knew as well as not what I wanted, but she's downright obstinate!"

"Not obstinate, Ferdinand, but *afraid*. I was watching her while you were talking, and I know."

When Ruth joined them, she reminded them of her own prediction. "Remember what I told you – not to count too much on her telling you anything even when she knew how!"

As the days went by, Abel and Ruth found themselves less and less curious about her.

"I don't know that I care where she came from," Ruth would often say, "as long as she *stays!*"

"That's the point, after all, isn't it? What did we ever do without her?"

"I'm glad she's so lovely to look at, aren't you, Abel? If she were homely, now—"

"Your big heart would take her in just the same, Ruth! But I'm glad, yes."

Once, after one of these conversations, Ruth drily remarked, "Ferdinand doesn't act as if it were any great hardship to teach her."

Abel turned in his chair, and looked at her. "How could he? A hardship to teach that sweet child!"

"I sometimes think, Abel," she laughed, "that you've fixed your mind on such far things, you can't see what's under your nose."

Strange, Abel mused, after Ruth left the room, to go along for years and never know what you had been missing. The court, now, how empty it was unless the Girl were somewhere about, learning from him how to prune the grape-vine, or helping Ruth weed and water. Even the workshop, where he had been so content to be alone, seemed to take on a warmer life when she was watching him carpenter.

She asked him, one day, what he was making.

"Something," he told her, as he tested the accuracy of the compass frame, "to help sailors find their way on the sea."

He glanced up to find her half-fearfully watching him. What had he said, he puzzled, to bring such a look? And afraid lest he should blunder into worse, he said nothing, and went on with his work. But in his own mind he turned the thing over. Sailors and compasses and the sea – what could they mean to her?

"Poor lamb!" Ruth said, when he told her and Ferdinand of the incident. "To think of all she's carrying in her mind and doesn't dare tell us."

"She lives in two worlds," Abel rejoined, "our own and the one she came from!"

"At least I'd like to know her name," declared Ferdinand, "even if she didn't tell us anything more."

The corners of Abel's mouth twitched. "There's nothing to prevent our giving her one. What would you suggest?"

Ferdinand carefully considered. "I can't think of a name that would suit her," he came out, at last. "It would have to be something –" he hesitated, flushing a little – "something lovelier than any name we have, and –"

"Go on!" urged Abel, closely watching him.

"And different from our language anyhow!"

"That's it – different!" Abel's fist on the table confirmed his agreement. "I tell you, Ferdinand, she doesn't belong to our race. I've made up my mind to that. How about it, Ruth?"

"I believe you're right, Abel."

"The colour of her skin's not like any I ever saw," Ferdinand suggested. "It's not dark enough for a Moor."

"Nor blonde enough for northern Europe," Abel added, with an image in his mind of a dusky, golden lily.

"We aren't any farther along with her," Ferdinand fumed, "than when we started."

"Perhaps we never will be!" teased Ruth.

"There's a first time for everything, Aunt Ruth. You wait!"

CHAPTER 6

Sofala – The Devil's Cave

FROM where Ruth sat sewing, in the room next to the workshop, she could see and hear Abel and Ferdinand. They had a map spread out on the table, and their voices drifted past her in a jumble of strange names.

In the pauses of their talk she stopped sewing to watch the Girl as she moved about the court in the soft brilliance of late afternoon. Her eyes drank in, with a fulness of satisfaction, the grace of the figure that now was silhouetted in sunlight or tenderly outlined by leafy shade. That sharply delicate contrast of dark hair and ivory skin against a sweep of vivid bloom! Was there ever anything so lovely?

This child, Ruth often said to herself, was like some flower of golden grace, half hidden in shadow. And, again, when there was a sliver of moon behind a wisp of cloud, Ruth was as likely to say that she was like it, too. More and more, fear was leaving the soft eyes; some day, Ruth silently exulted, it would be wholly gone.

The hum of voices in the workshop rose again.

"It's the same old knot," Ferdinand was saying, "that we've still to cut: that reach between the Devil's Cave and Sofala."

As he spoke the last words, Ruth saw the slender figure start, and stiffen into tense, listening stillness, her face stark and white. Her impulse was to run out – but already the Girl was stealing toward the workshop. A glance at Abel and Ferdinand, with their backs to the door, told Ruth they were quite unaware of the presence behind them.

Noiselessly the Girl sank on the threshold, face turned to the court, hands clenched on her knees. Ruth could see the straining knuckles and the rigid shoulders. What had made this ghastly change? Was it something the Girl had overheard Abel or Ferdinand say?

In vain Ruth tried to recall the conversation, and at last she went into the workroom and dropped into a seat where she could watch.

"What are you two talking about?" she asked as casually as she could.

"Oh, nothing new," Ferdinand answered, without looking up. "I was saying that it was the same old knot that remained to be cut."

As he spoke, Ruth saw the head in the doorway turn ever so little. Just as she had suspected! Something connected with the map – and again she cudgelled her memory. Presently, with a yawn, Abel moved back from the table to where he could look at the sunset. She tried to draw him out, but he was no more inclined to talk than Ferdinand. After another pause, the Girl on the doorstep rose and Ruth heard her go to her room.

In an agony of suspense she debated with herself: should she follow? Should she tell Abel what had happened? Yet, after all, what was there to tell? No, she would delay a little, at least till Ferdinand went.

When supper was ready, she cautiously approached the Girl. She found her flung on the bed, her face turned to the wall. No, she wasn't ill – nor hungry. She wanted just to be quiet. Her voice was so natural, that Ruth's anxiety almost vanished. She went back to Abel, telling herself that her imagination had run away with her. She was glad she had had the sense to say nothing to him. But that night she found herself dropping off to sleep still puzzling over the curious change that had come over the Girl.

Suddenly, she woke, with an instant consciousness that Abel, too, was awake.

"Ruth," she heard him breathe, "someone's in the workshop."

A stealthy sound came to her ears. She recognized it

at once: the drawer of the big table sliding on its grooves. The drawer where the maps were kept!

" There! " Abel was sitting bolt upright. " Don't you hear? "

He seized his cloak, and stepped into the court. In another moment she was stealing after him to the workshop. Yet, even before they reached it, Ruth knew who would be there.

Through its open door a faint ray of light streamed into the dark court. Cautiously they avoided it, and then, from the shadow of a vine, they looked into the room, and saw – as the first sound of the sliding drawer had told Ruth she would see – the Girl.

Crazed fear in every line of her face, of her trembling body, she stood at the table staring down at something on it: a map! As if she searched for something on its surface, they saw her lean over it, and then reel back with a stifled moan.

Ruth grasped Abel's arm. " Shall I go to her? She's suffering so! "

He held her back. " Wait a moment."

The Girl was now forcing herself to the table, as if to some ordeal. Shuddering, she bent over the map, and this time they saw a trembling finger creep to a definite spot. Slowly it began to trace along the surface. On and on it moved – faltered – stopped short. Suddenly her hands went to her eyes, as though to shut out some horror, and her shoulders were shaking with soundless sobs.

" Oh, Abel, what can be the matter? " Ruth breathed in his ear.

Then, in utter bewilderment they were staring at each

other, while there smote on their ears a whispered wail:
" *Sofala – Sofala –* "

In terrified suspense Ruth watched the slender figure
within sway back and forth as if abandoned to despair,
when, again, came that stifled voice: " Sofala – The Devil's
Cave – "

"What, in heaven's name, does she mean? " Abel's
startled face was close to Ruth's. " Is the child gone mad? "

The Girl was standing quite still now, gazing before
her with wide, blank eyes. Suddenly and unexpectedly, she
reached out and snuffed the candle. The next moment Ruth
felt her brush past into the court. Breathlessly they watched
her pause, and scan the starlit sky, and then – steal toward
the gate.

In a flash Ruth had pushed Abel through the door of
the workshop. "Quick – go back to bed! " she whispered,
while from the threshold she called, " Trying to get some
air, child? Too warm to sleep, is it? "

She saw the distant figure start – turn back. In a minute her arm was around the trembling form. She was saying, gently, that she couldn't sleep, either, that a turn around
the court would make them drowsy.

From her manner no one would ever have suspected
that Ruth wasn't in the habit of taking strolls at midnight.
She rambled on about nothings; lingered, so they could
both smell the dewy jessamine blossoms. Sometimes, in
a dazed way, there were low murmured replies. At last
Ruth declared she was sleepy, and that she'd spend the
rest of the night on a couch near the door for the cooler
air.

On the pretext of laying back the heavier coverings,

she delayed in the Girl's room, and when she came out, she left the door ajar.

It was just before dawn, when she had made sure of the Girl's sound sleep, that she slipped back to Abel. He was dressed, and softly pacing back and forth, his head sunk on his breast – his habit when he was thinking out some problem.

She came close to him, feeling like a guilty child. "Abel – I – I saw her listening yesterday, when you and Ferdinand were studying over that map! I saw her face change – "

"You did? " Abel asked, in a startled voice. Anyone else would have added, "Why didn't you say something about it? " But Abel only said, very gently, "It was wonderful, my dear, just wonderful, the way you managed her in the court. I don't believe she suspected! "

A hurt look came into her eyes. "She was running away from us – though we've never done anything but love her."

"It wasn't from us," he comforted, "but from the same fear that drove her when she came to us."

"And I'd begun to think she'd forgotten! "

"That poor child must never know what we saw tonight."

"No; and another thing, we mustn't leave her to herself. I'd better go now and see if she's awake."

"Ruth," – Abel came close to her, and she saw that his eyes had an awestruck look – "did you notice that she said those words, *Sofala, Devil's Cave*, as if – as if, Ruth, they were familiar to her? "

CHAPTER 7

The Caged Bird

NICOLO's mood, as he watched his shipwrights at
work, late one afternoon, matched the sunless day.
Strips of sombre sky between the partly placed ribs of his
caravel gave her an aspect of desolation that made him

shiver. Would he have done better, he wondered, to have taken the advice of the *Venezia's* captain, and gone back to Venice? Suppose Manoel should remain indifferent to the Way of the Spices, and Spain or England should find it!

He recalled that Abel Zakuto had admitted, in so many words, that something was needed to awake Manoel to the situation. As if, Nicolo gloomily mused, anything more splendidly convincing than what Diaz had done were needed! If that couldn't spur the King into action, what could?

At this point in his reflections, he saw the men put up their tools and prepare to leave. He nodded to one of them whom he remembered hiring a few weeks ago, a short, wiry chap with a deeply tanned face and small, black eyes that looked like burnt gimlet holes in brown parchment. A rolling gait and an air of cat-like agility made one immediately visualize him as thoroughly at home at all heights and angles. Nicolo had hired him because the fellow had looked so in need, and because there was a haunting familiarity about him.

"Is she going ahead to suit you, sir?" he inquired, as he stopped at Nicolo's side to survey the caravel.

"I'm satisfied," Nicolo told him, "though I'm not as used to the Portuguese type of craft as I am to the Venetian."

At once the other looked interested. "You've been to sea, have you, sir?"

"I know the Mediterranean pretty well," Nicolo admitted. He scrutinized the tanned face. . . . Where had he seen it before? "You've had considerable experience at sea, I take it."

"All over!" grinned the other. "Up and down the Red Sea, and across to India, and over by Malacca."

"So! Some sight-seeing! How do you come to be in a dockyard at this end of the world?"

"Oh – everybody likes a change," the man evasively returned. "What trade are you reckoning on, sir?"

"Madeira lumber and sugar and wine till I can do better. Spices, eventually, I hope – if Portugal ever finds the sea route to them."

"Humph!" There was frank defiance in the grunt.

"Why, there's more in spice than in anything else," Nicolo remonstrated.

"You're right there is! You'd be surprised if you only knew how much of a 'more' it is!"

Nicolo studied the sailor with curiosity. Almost he appeared to bear a grudge against spice. "How do you come to know so much about it, then?" he demanded.

"Oh – worked for years on ships that carried it. What between hauling on board and heaving over rail I reckon I've handled more pounds of the stuff than you're days old!"

"You haven't by any chance been where the spices grow?" Nicolo ventured.

"Over Ceylon way, you mean? And Penang, and Banda?"

"Banda!" Nicolo seized on the name so familiar to him through the cherished Conti letters, "How'd you get over there?"

The brown parchment face wrinkled into a grin. "I took to the sea from pretty near the time I was born – and I suppose I just kept on!"

$\sim$ *The Caged Bird* $\sim$

Nicolo laughed. "And where were you born?"

"Down river – at Belem.[1] My father was a bar pilot and he taught me his calling. I cut my teeth, you might say, on the Cachopos![2]

Nicolo eyed him with fresh interest. "Belem and the Orient are some distance apart!" he suggested.

The other nodded. "After my father was lost at sea, and my mother died, I quit the land for good. I got to know every port in the Mediterranean. One day, in Alexandria, I saw a caravan starting out for the Red Sea, and I took a notion to go along. Everybody said there was plenty of work down that way, and they were right, too. The harbour at Aden's just chock-a-block with craft coming and going!"

Nicolo felt his pulses leap – the very East seemed to drip off this fellow's tongue! "Where does all that traffic come from?"

"Everywhere; mostly from India, Cathay, the mess of islands betwixt and beyond; in Arab bottoms of course. They do all the carrying, and I'll tell you they keep the ocean churning!"

Nicolo impetuously started on more questions, but suddenly checked himself: this first hand experience belonged to the workshop! "Would you be willing to talk to some of my friends about these places where you've seen the spices growing?"

The man silently eyed him, and Nicolo again sensed his hostility toward this subject over which Europe was seething.

---

[1] Belem. At the mouth of the Tagus River. The site of the chapel built by Henry the Navigator.

[2] Shoals formed by the bar at the mouth of the Tagus.

"Where are your friends?" he at last demanded.

"Up the hill a way – I'll take you there myself," Nicolo eagerly volunteered.

"Oh, I might go, some evening," the other agreed, as he turned away. "Perhaps I can tell you a thing or two about this spice business," he added over his shoulder, "seeing you're so keen on it."

Bursting with his news, Nicolo strode up the hill. Already he could see Abel's shining eyes when he should hear it: someone who had handled spices and seen them growing to tell about them first hand! They must arrange, too, for Gama and Diaz and the others to be there. It would be tremendous, epoch-making – and Nicolo quickened his step.

He found Ruth in the court, splitting figs from a heaped basket, and spreading them to dry in the sun. Abel was out, she said, but he would be back any moment.

Nicolo went into the workshop, took the Marco Polo *Travels* from its shelf, and sat down to see what he could make of the translation. At last, as no Abel appeared, he decided to delay no longer. He laid down the book and had started toward the door, when a stealthy sound arrested him, a sound which he knew instantly was not meant to be heard.

He glanced at Ruth busily dipping in and out of the figs. She, certainly, had not made that sound. There! . . . There it was, again.

On impulse he tiptoed into the next room, and looked into the room beyond. Back to him, by an open window, stood a girl, holding a bird-cage. Its tiny door, he noticed, was swung back, and the bird inside was fluttering uneasily. She lifted the cage to the window, and gently shook it. Nicolo watched her in amazement. Did she want to get rid of the little creature? Again she shook the cage, and, this time, out flashed the bird – not through the window, but into the room.

The girl wheeled around, and for a moment Nicolo had a swift vision of dark, velvety eyes in a face that was delicately, duskily golden. She seemed not even to see him. Her eyes were on the bird that was now darting about, and Nicolo perceived that they were very frightened. She had changed her mind, he guessed instantly – wanted her pet back!

He sprang forward, closed the door behind him, and then the window. Carefully he watched his chance, and when the downy little body dashed itself against a wall, his waiting hands closed gently around it. He held it so, until he felt the frantic wings and the fierce, tiny heart gradually quiet under his fingers – aware all the time that close to him a girl's breath came and went unevenly, that great, dark eyes wide with terror besought his.

He slipped the bird inside the cage and fastened the little door. Then, very gently, he turned to the girl, waited for her to speak, for he had the impression that something behind those terrified, beautiful eyes was waiting to be said. He could see the trembling of her clenched hands, and the pulsing of the soft, bare neck, and it came, curiously, to him that somehow she was the struggling bird that his hands had held and shielded; and suddenly he wanted, above everything he had ever wanted, to so hold and so shield her; to tell her that never again was she to be afraid – not of anything!

"You won't tell? " she whispered at last. "I was so frightened after I'd done it! He's Mother Ruth's pet – "

"Of course I won't tell! Not for worlds." He had all he could do to keep back a rush of tender assurances. "But why . . . why . . . did you? " He nodded toward the cage.

"Because–because–" her hands clutched at her throat–" I was once like that bird–shut up in a cage. And I couldn't–couldn't–get out! "

"In–a–cage? *You?* "

Something seemed to burst within him. This tender body behind bars! . . . This soft, throbbing neck! His nails bit into his palms to keep back that furious, inward tumult. He saw a half-fearful expression come over her face –ah, he mustn't frighten her, not even by his own feeling about her.

"Don't be afraid," he begged her, "not of anything– ever again! " Was it his fancy that she seemed to waver toward him? He came close to her: *"Who are you? "*

She caught her breath. Nicolo noted the quick colour that swept upward from the delicate neck. He waited for her answer, his eyes entreating hers. . . . A sound outside . . . Steps . . . Ruth crossing the court to come into the house, perhaps into this very room!

They sprang apart–somehow Nicolo reached the workshop, dropped into a chair, and snatched up the *Travels* he had dropped.

He heard Ruth enter the room he had left, listened until her casual tone assured him that she suspected nothing. He stepped into the court, and closed the door behind him with a little bang.

Exactly as he had intended, the sound brought Ruth hurrying to him. " You're not going, already? "

"I'll come again soon," he smiled back at her. "I have some splendid news for Master Abel!"

"He'll be sorry he missed you. Yes, come soon."

"Come soon" indeed! How was he ever going to keep away? Nicolo asked himself as he went down the long flight. "*I was . . . shut up in a cage.*" Great heavens! What did she mean? Why had Abel – or Ferdinand – never mentioned her? Something hotly-sweet surged through him: to hold her – even as his hands had held the bird – safe in the very hollow of his life!

CHAPTER 8

Scander

THE next evening found Nicolo and the sailor at the workshop. Nicolo had seen Abel down town that morning and had told him about his new acquaintance, and Abel had agreed to get word to the others to come that night.

~ 76 ~

All day Nicolo thought of that coming visit. Would he
see the precious secret that he had discovered, yesterday?
Did Abel and Ruth mean to keep her hidden? . . . What
did it all mean?

When he finally entered the court with the sailor, and
saw Abel waiting for them in the workshop, he realized
he'd forgotten to ask the man's name.

"Call me Scander," said he. "I got that name from
hanging around so long in Scanderia – Arabic for Alexandria. I had a Portygee name once," he explained, "but
'twould be like the coat I wore when I was a lad – wouldn't
fit now! "

"You've actually sailed in Arab vessels – been in the
Indies? " Abel eagerly began. He broke off to hail Diaz and
Abraham, who just then came in, with Gama a little behind
them. "Spice at first hand, gentlemen! "

"Hold fast there, Master Abel! " cried the sailor,
"I'm not giving a show performance! I came here only to
please Master Conti – said he had some friends who'd like
to hear what I know of the spice trade."

"Exactly what we want," someone replied. "Can't get
enough of that."

Young Magellan arrived in time to catch the last words.
"Can't get enough of what? " he demanded.

"Of spice! " laughed Abel.

"He's seen cloves and nutmegs growing," Nicolo
added. "Fancy that! "

"Lord! " Scander stared, open mouthed, at Ferdinand.
"Where'd you get those eyes? " Then, as the boy flushed,
"So you've gone crazy over spice, too? " he asked.
"Maybe " – a moody note in his voice – "maybe, I can tell

you a thing or two about the stuff that'll calm you down! "

They all drew up to the table and Nicolo noticed that Ruth had conceded enough to the current excitement to bring her chair to the doorway that opened into the next room. The door beyond, which, yesterday, had stood ajar, was now, he saw, fast shut. Was the Girl behind it? . . . Or where? Why this mystery and secrecy about her?

Old Abraham's voice broke in on him. "Did you say you'd seen the spices growing? " he was eagerly asking Scander.

The sailor nodded. "Seen 'em and traded in 'em, both."

"In India, I take it? " Gama inquired.

"Well, sometimes. But oftener, the Arab captain I shipped with regular, got his spice first hand from the growers: cinnamon from Ceylon, and pepper where it's plenty, 'round Penang, and cloves and nutmegs from Amboyna and the Bandas."

No one spoke. The very air was charged with profound suspense. Abel and Nicolo exchanged elated glances and Nicolo said, in a low tone, "That checks my Conti letters! "

Ferdinand's eyes, fixed on Scander, seemed more than ever like smouldering fires. "Is the spice trade the big thing in that part of the world, as it is with us? " he asked.

"Yes and no, lad. It's this way: all east of Aden it's about the same, gold, pearls, ivory, silk." He reeled the list off as casually as one would say flour, eggs, milk. "But *at* Aden there's a change and spice jumps into the lead."

"Why there? "

"Well, you see it's near enough to the Mediterranean to feel the European premium on spices."

"Then why couldn't a European," Nicolo quickly took him up, "who understood both ends of the business, make a good thing of it in Aden?"

"Humph! I was just waiting for someone to say that." Again that hostile note.

At once everyone was on the defensive: "Why not?" "What's the matter with that?"

"What's there against my Aden scheme?" Nicolo insisted.

"A European wouldn't be what you'd call exactly welcome at Aden. That's what there is against it!" Scander said shortly. He looked deliberately around the table. "You gentlemen thinking of going into spice?"

"Not so much for personal profit," Abel replied slowly, "as for the nation; for Portugal."

"Know anything about the other end of the spice trade, the *Arab* end? Well, before you break into it, I can tell you a thing or two that might save you some trouble."

In the words there was foreboding that riveted every eye on the tanned face.

"It was one time, some years back, when we'd just made Aden from Calicut," he abruptly began, "that we got wind of some gossip that had come up the African coast, about a Franj ship – their word for European – that had been seen away to the south."

There was a stir around the table. Everyone's eyes sought Diaz, and those near him saw his hands clench. But Scander, intent on his story, went on:

"It didn't sound sensible to me, but when we started

south to Melinde, for ivory, up popped the story again; kept on popping, too. Seemed as if every place we went, we heard about this Franj ship."

"Didn't they know you were a European?" Gama asked.

"Funny part of that was that I'd been there so long and got into their ways so, that I didn't think of it myself – at least, not at first."

"Where did you say that place *Melinde* was?" Abel interrupted, and jotted hasty notes as the sailor directed.

"The next time we were at Aden," Scander pursued, "talk about the Franj was running high, and in particular about – about – " he nervously wet his lips – "a Franj spice dealer there."

For a moment he seemed to have forgotten his audience, and his eyes, staring over their heads, had a curious, dazed expression. Someone moved uneasily, and at once he recovered himself.

"Odd, how talking about it brings it all back," he said, apologetically. "They were telling it around that this Franj had the finest spice concern on the coast, and the story went that he'd married an Arab girl to keep in with the native merchants – who are all Arabs, you understand. I'd seen the place, sorting sheds and warehouse, and his own house, too, a big palace of a place. Well, instead of putting to sea, the way we usually did, we hung around. I noticed several merchants come on board, and they appeared to be having some sort of conference with Captain. *He* had something on his mind, too. The way I noticed it first, he was so in earnest over his prayers; seemed almost like he was having a real talk with Allah!"

"How would you have happened to hear him at his prayers?" Abel inquired.

"That's so!" Scander exclaimed. "I've been among the Arabs so long, I forget you don't know their customs. You see, sir, every good Mohammedan prays three times a day: drops on his knees wherever he is, faces toward Mecca, and starts right in, loud and free. No whispering in dark corners or behind curtains the way you do here – nothing like that.

"Well, I began to suspect something was afoot, and sure enough, one morning, Captain told me that all up and down the African Coast and the Red Sea, across to Malabar and Cochin and Calicut, word had been passed to stand together against the Franj, to do no business with them, and to make way with them when it came handy."

"I'd like to take my chances with a good stout caravel and a Portuguese crew!" Gama quietly commented.

"All the time he was talking," the sailor went on, "I could feel something coming. Finally, he said Aden was going to start in by cleaning out the Franj merchant, and – 'Will you help?' says he, looking me in the eye. It went through my head like lightning that he was trying me, which side was I on, for I knew he'd not forgotten I was a Franj. 'What you going to do, Captain?' said I, playing for time. He didn't mince words: 'Burn,' said he, 'burn and – kill. Are you with us?'"

"'When?' said I, still playing for time, and thinking that, if I couldn't warn this Franji, I'd at least find a way to get out rather than take up against one of my own kind, as you might say. But he was too sharp for me. 'At once, when evening calls the Faithful to prayer. Are you with

us?' he asks again. But not a word did he say of *my* Franj
blood! 'Certain, Captain,' I said, 'I'll go with you.' I
reckoned that was the only way to save my skin. Later, I
figured, I'd find some way to get back to the Mediterranean."

"Why folks want to kill each other," Ruth exploded
from the doorway, "for stuff that makes your tongue smart
and your eyes water, is more than I can see!"

"Maybe you could, ma'am," grinned Scander, "if
you could sell it for half its weight in gold, as the Arab
traders do!"

"But the call to prayer?" Nicolo reminded him.

"Yes . . . yes." Again there was that nervous wetting
of the lips. "Well, just as soon as we heard it, Captain gave
the word, and we all started for the Franj outfit. Some carried long, two-handed native swords, and some had knives.
The warehouse was right on the water front, and I figured
that as soon as we got there I'd make a break for the house
and warn the Franj merchant.

"But no sooner had we reached the place, than Captain herded us around to the big sorting shed. Through the
cracks we could see the pepper and cloves and cinnamon
piled up, and the sweaty, half-naked natives with their
brown arms and hands gliding in and out as they sorted.
It was half-dark in there and hot – hot as hell's cockpit. And
all the time we could see those shiny, brown bodies and
their black eyes that sort of slipped around in their heads –
instead of their heads turning, as yours and mine would,
you understand!"

Scander paused, then, visibly bracing himself, he
plunged on. "Next thing I knew, Captain flung open the

door. 'At them! ' he yelled. 'Every one of them – in the name of Allah! ' "

Ruth cried out in the horrified stillness, and " You mean – in cold blood? " stammered Ferdinand.

" Did you . . . too? " someone gasped.

" How'd you suppose I know what I did in that hell's shambles? " he burst out. " Only thing I can remember is watching swords and knives, all red and dripping to their hilts, slipping in and out among those shiny, brown bodies just as *their* hands had been slipping in and out of the spices! "

A shudder ran through his listeners, but, apparently unmoved, Scander went on as if he were reciting by rote. " They killed, and they killed, and they killed," he deliberately pronounced. " Then I felt my head swim. I tried to get to the door – slipped – went down – " His voice broke, and he put his hand hastily over his mouth. " It was all warm and slimy down there – blood and spice mixed up together – "

" Go on," Abel hastily interposed. " Get to the rest of it."

" I promised myself," the sailor said slowly, " I'd never go over this, but seeing you all so keen on this spice business – these young chaps in particular – I thought you ought to hear the other side." He clutched his throat and swallowed hard. " That smell of warm blood and spice makes my stomach heave yet! "

" How about the spice merchant? Ever see him? " Nicolo inquired.

Scander ran his tongue around his lips before he answered. " I'll come to him in a minute. By the time we'd got through with the sorting shed, we could hear a terrible commotion all over the place and we could see the warehouse afire. 'Here's my chance to warn the Franji' thinks I, and I made a rush for the house, when – down jumps Captain from a wall behind me! 'Come on,' says he, 'you're the man I want,' and he drove me in front of him with that red, dripping blade of his at my back. I knew, then, he suspected what I had in mind.

"The moment we reached the house, we saw that others had been there before us. The place looked like the tail end of a typhoon; everything upside down, cupboards open, clothes scattered around. 'Where is *he?*' Captain kept asking. 'Where's the Franji?' We looked around for a while, and then, as we went into the court, we saw something on the stairs that led to the roof – something all huddled together. 'Go on up,' Captain orders me, 'till we make sure,' and he made me stand by whilst he jabbed at it with his foot – curse him. 'Twas a man with his arms around a woman, and a sword right through the two of them – the spice merchant and his wife. You could tell from his features that he was a Franji. She was an Arab; a real queen, poor creature, with long, black braids and big, dark eyes and slender hands.

"Well – that's about all," he ended, sombrely. "I stayed right by Captain, took his orders, and went back to the ship with him, quiet as a lamb. But I'd had enough. A night or two after, when we were to leave Aden first thing in the morning, I slipped over the side, got ashore, and shipped with a big slave vessel bound for Egypt."

There was a brevity in this winding up of the story that struck everyone with a feeling of something omitted.

Diaz drew a long breath. "You never heard any more of the Franj ship, I suppose?"

"Never a word, sir."

"Did your captain try to follow you?" asked Nicolo.

"If he did, I never got wind of it. From the minute I quit him I was right on my way, and I never stopped till I saw Alexandria and knew I was in western waters. I wanted to get as far as I could from spice! And here I've stuck my nose right into the cursed stuff again. I hate the sight and the smell of it," Scander spat out. "Smells like blood to me!"

"Why, man," said Abel, "there's always been quarrels and bloodshed over trade. What you saw the Arabs do to that European merchant is no more than the Europeans will do to each other in trade rivalry."

"Of course," Diaz agreed. "If anyone has doubts about what Spain, or England, or the Dutch would do to us, suppose we found the Way of the Spices first, I haven't!"

"How about what we'd do, if they happened to be first?" Ferdinand slyly retorted.

In the laughter that followed this sally, Diaz reached out and tweaked the boy's ear. "You young jackanapes!" he said, with a gruffness that deceived no one.

"Well, gentlemen" – the sailor shrugged – "war's what you'll get, any of you who're going in for spice, and don't make any mistake about that. And for every hatchful, take my word, you'll pay in blood. Way of the Spices! Way of Blood is more like it!"

"But look here," Gama insisted, "what if we beat the Arabs at their own game?"

"How are you going to, with them running the whole trade, and the carrying, too?"

"Well," Gama coolly maintained, "these Arab pirates aren't invincible!"

"'Pirates!'" Scander shot back. "They're no pirates, and don't you forget that for a minute. In their own eyes they're defenders of their faith, and it's the Franj that are infidels and thieves sneaking in where they don't belong and 've no right to go!"

"I suppose it was religion made them kill that Frankish merchant!" Nicolo said, sarcastically.

"Well, yes" – Scander laughed a little – "religion and business, together. It's religion with them to keep foreigners out, no matter how they do it. You have to live with them to see how 'tis," he continued. "Now, you'll go to your churches and mumble before images or whisper your sins to a priest, and then you'll come out into the streets and do business, and forget all about prayers and the saints till the next time. Not but what that's all right," he hastily interposed. "I make out to say an *Ave* once 'n a while, myself. But with the Arabs, religion's the whole thing all the time. Take that captain of mine now; he said his prayers three times a day, and so did his crews."

"What did you do – turn Mohammedan?" someone inquired.

"For the time being, yes."

"Show us how they say their prayers!" Ferdinand proposed.

The sailor gave him a glum look. "I'm not so particular about reminding myself of all that, but if 'twould amuse you – "

He dropped on his knees, arms crossed on his breast. Even Ruth left her seat, and eagerly peered over Abel's shoulder.

"They begin by calling out, twice, *God is great* – this way." His upturned face seemed to search an imaginary sky, and, with a savage fervor, "Allahu Akbar!" he cried, delivering each syllable with a sonorous precision. He bowed profoundly, forehead to ground, and as he swayed back, "Allahu Akbar!" he called again. "Allahu –"

A shriek from some distant part of the house froze the unfinished words on his lips. Everyone started up. Ferdinand jumped to his feet. Abel and Ruth exchanged frightened glances. They heard a door flung open . . . a rush of soft footsteps through the next room. Then – into the workshop burst the Girl – the Girl, as she had leaped from bed, black hair streaming loose, slender body rigid, eyes, as on that first night, oblivious of all but a madness of fear.

CHAPTER 9

Sugar

I N a flash Scander was forgotten. With one impulse Abel
and Ruth sprang to the Girl. Ferdinand still stood, transfixed. The others looked at each other in blank bewilderment. No one saw Nicolo start up, and then immediately

sit down; yet anyone who had watched him closely would have seen that his face was working with strong emotion.

But no one was heeding Nicolo. No one had eyes for anything save the astounding scene before them, more astounding than even the Girl's appearance.

Motionless, rigid, she was staring at Scander. He, still on his knees, hands grotesquely arrested in the gesture of prayer, eyes dilated past expression, was staring back. But in their faces was recognition, terrified, yet unmistakable, recognition.

For moments that deathlike silence lasted. Then, gradually, as if moved by common impulse, those two speechless figures drew near each other. Still kneeling, the sailor crept, inch by inch, toward the Girl, as, imperceptibly, she moved toward him. In horrified fascination the others watched that slow, ghastly approach, as if spectres, meeting in some dim unknown, should so peer into each other's faces.

The man's lips were moving, but no words came. They saw his throat twitch, heard him make what to them were unintelligible sounds. Then, slowly, with eyes locked on the Girl, he drew himself up by inches. And now, staring into his face, the Girl answered in those same strange sounds.

Slowly he looked around. "I – I – didn't tell all – all of the – Aden story. She –" he jerked his head toward the Girl – "she was on the steps, too – huddled up alongside of those – "

Ruth was first to understand. "Child! Child! Were they your father and mother? "

The Girl shuddered as if something had struck her. Abel

snatched up the cloak hanging on his chair and threw it around her. The gesture seemed to make her suddenly aware of the presence of others besides Scander. They saw her eyes drop and the colour rush to her neck and face. Gently Abel pressed her into a seat, and then he turned and looked deliberately around the table.

"Bartholomew – all of you – for this child's sake we – Ruth, Ferdinand, myself – have kept her a secret. Where she came from, who she is, her name, her language, no one of us has known."

"She came one night, months ago, after you'd all gone," Ruth breathlessly added. "She just stepped in here out of the dark. That's all we know – and that now she's ours." She moved nearer the Girl, with a protecting little caress.

"What?" cried Scander. "Stepped in here, did you say, ma'am?" He turned to the Girl and began to speak rapidly in the language of their first meeting, when Abel gently stopped him.

"She understands Portuguese, now, you know – and we all want to hear your story!"

"Well, then," Scander took him up, "how in heaven's name, did she get here, when I've been thinking she was dead – or worse?"

From where she sat between Abel and Ruth, the Girl looked amazedly up at him, and above the folds of the dark cloak her face was like shadowed ivory.

"That's what I thought about you," she whispered, "that when you rolled into the sea –"

"Just a minute, mates!" Scander wheeled around. "You've heard two ends of a story with the middle chopped

out. You see, there was a big night's work between where
I left off – with the spice merchant and his wife dead on
the stairs – and took up again with me on my way to Egypt.
As I was telling you, this child was lying alongside of them,
and we thought she was dead, too, till we turned her over.
I never could figure how she escaped alive. What did save
you? " he asked the Girl.

In a voice that was barely audible, she said, "We had
started up the stairs to the roof when – when – men rushed
into the court. For a minute they didn't see us, and my
father pushed me into a closet under the stairs. Then there
were shouts and running. I heard my mother scream out
to my father that she wouldn't leave him. And then –
then – " she paused, struggling with herself – "there was no
more noise. It was – all – quiet. I crept out – and I found – "
Her face dropped to her knees. "I didn't want to hide any
more," she sobbed out. "I wanted to be seen! I lay down
beside them – to wait – "

Abel threw back his head, as if in need of air. Nicolo's
hands, clenched on the table, were white at the knuckles.
Ferdinand kept his eyes on the ground. Diaz pulled at his
beard, and Abraham and Gama turned away. Over the
Girl's bowed shoulders Ruth openly wept.

"I'll never forget," Scander solemnly declared, "how
she looked when we found her. Just like what she said –
'waiting'! I thought of course Captain would make an
end of her, and, quick as a flash, I whipped out my knife
to get him first. You could have knocked me over when
he said, quiet-like, 'She'll bring a good price.' And to
make a long story short, we took her down to the slave
market."

"You mean," Nicolo fiercely demanded, "that you stood by, and saw her – *sold?*"

At his voice the Girl raised her eyes, and looked directly at him. Instantly she dropped them, but Nicolo had caught the signal: yesterday's meeting was to be still a secret!

"Yes," the sailor admitted, "in a way I did. My eyes saw her sold, but inside of me I knew, while they were haggling over her price and counting coin, that – that, somehow, I was going to do something about it. All the time Captain and I were going back to the ship I couldn't see anything but her: the only white thing among those naked, black cattle with their big, white teeth and lips " – he held thumb and finger apart – "that thick! . . . I couldn't get her out of mind! 'What'll come of saving her, suppose I could?' says I to myself. 'Nothing,' says myself back, 'but a sword up to the hilt somewhere in me. Go on, and forget her.' What'd I do with her, suppose I could buy her? thinks I. Anyway, I didn't have the price – and I walked on with Captain. All the while something inside me was snickering: 'Haven't the price?' I could hear it jeer. 'What's the matter with the price your captain just took for her?'"

He paused to survey the mystified faces about him. "I didn't see at first, either," he laughed softly, "same as you. But all of a sudden it came to me." Again he paused, and his hand tightened on the knife-hilt above his girdle, "What to do came to me at midnight when – everyone was asleep."

The Girl was leaning toward him. "You did – *that* – for me?" she asked, under her breath.

"Yes, thinking I'd buy you right back with what I'd

taken from – him. But when I got down to the slave market, they told me you'd been shipped out just after you'd been bought."

"Yes – that very night," she shuddered.

"It goes against you folks to hear talk of buying and selling her." Apologetically he met Nicolo's and Ferdinand's angry eyes. "But how else could I save her?"

"You're all right, man!" Diaz told him. "Go on with your story."

"I traced her," Scander resumed, "by her fair skin, to Alexandria, but there I lost her, till one day, in the big slave square, I noticed a ring of traders bidding – and there she was! I was just in time to see a big, handsome chap – a Moor he was – in a seaman's dress, leading her away. 'What'd he give for her?' I asked around, and the figure they named swamped me.

"What was I to do? I followed along behind them, turning my brains inside out for the answer. Finally, we got down to the water-front and I could see there was a heavy sea running. The tall chap walked her right along to a beached skiff, with a man in it, who grinned when his eyes lighted on her – and then my mind was made up: I was going where she went!"

There was a restless stir through the room, and men's eyes avoided meeting.

"Just as the Moor lifted her into the boat, she looked off at the water, and her face changed – as if lightning had flashed in the dark. Remember what happened, then?" he asked the Girl.

She drew a long, tremulous breath. "I meant to jump into the water," she said, in a low voice.

"The Moor saw what was up, too," Scander continued, "and in a minute he'd put her into the stern, and was holding her arms. I could have praised Allah, for then I knew the other chap couldn't make it alone, through that sea. 'Need another hand, Chief?' says I, with my heart in my throat, and before he even nodded, I shoved off the boat and scrambled in. The two men looked at me queer-like, and then sidewise at each other. 'Where to?' I asked, and they pointed out a fair-sized vessel that wasn't flying any colours, and I had a mind to ask why, but I thought better of it.

"I can handle a sail if I do say it, and I did my prettiest that day, so I wasn't surprised when they asked if I minded rough weather. 'The sea and I are like sweethearts' said I, and they grinned and wanted to know if I'd ever had a pilot's job. 'Twas my specialty, I told them!

"All the time this girl, here, never made a move; just sat there, head down; but I noticed *he* never quit watching her, never took his hands off her, either.

"When we came alongside I saw the ship's name was the *Sultana*. I made fast, and asked what to do with the skiff. 'Could you take us out?' said the tall chap, jerking his head toward the big craft. 'Sure job?' I asks, and he nodded, and then the two of them laughed. By this time the rail above us was thick with faces grinning down on us." Scander paused, with a significant look. "Five minutes after the girl was lifted aboard, I was there, too, skiff all shipshape and lashed down.

"The crew looked me over pretty sharp—as rough a gang as I ever saw. I edged forward as near as I dared to where she was standing between the tall fellow and another, who was older, and shorter by a head, but square-built and powerful. Moorish, too, he was. For all anyone could tell she might have been a corpse, with her face like ashes, and eyes blind-like. I listened a bit, and I made out they were talking a mixture of Franji and Arabic.

" 'With a jewel like this,' the tall chap was saying, 'we can make what terms we want, anywhere.' What did he mean? – and I edged nearer. 'The Sultan himself wouldn't be contemptuous of such a prize,' the older man answered, 'and we might even get a post in the royal navy out of it, Abdul, my boy! Shall we make the run to Constantinople, and bargain?' Abdul – the tall chap – looked up, surprised-like, and the other one threw back his head and laughed and laughed; and I didn't know why, but I wanted to kick him. Then Abdul says, easy and smiling – like one that's been caught off his guard but doesn't mean to be caught again – 'First, though, Captain, you recollect we've an appointment at Tripoli with the *San Marco*, bound out of Venice.' "

The Girl glanced up, and a look of understanding flashed between them.

"What? " Nicolo was asking, in a puzzled tone. " The *San Marco*, from Venice, did you say? "

Scander surveyed him in surprise. "Yes, why? "

"Nothing. Go on," with a careless gesture that contradicted a peculiar expression that had come into his eyes.

" Then, in a minute," Scander resumed, "I knew what kind of an outfit I'd shipped with, and why they'd all laughed when I'd come aboard so innocent: only one kind of crews has 'appointments' with merchant ships, and that's pirate crews!

"Well, a gale was blowing up, but I took the helm, and we began the run for Tripoli, all the way through head winds and heavy seas. We were so close to shore, you couldn't tell which yelled louder, the storm or the reefs. Sometimes, what with a black sky hissing above us, and the water like foaming jaws that couldn't wait to lap us down, I used to wonder if we'd make it."

"I used to pray Allah that we wouldn't!" the Girl said under her breath.

The sailor's face softened. "I expect so . . . I expect so," he murmured, while Ruth silently drew her nearer.

"You see," he told the room in a low aside, "Arab women of rank are brought up not to go out unless they're veiled. This girl had probably never been in the streets at all. And there she was, set down, all of a sudden, in the roughest gang I ever saw – not to mention what she'd suffered in the slave markets. I could tell from her face the hell she was going through, and sometimes I 'most wished she'd die. So, all those shrieking hours, that my hands were around the tiller head, there wasn't a minute that they weren't ready for the business end of – this!" Scander tapped the knife handle in his belt. "I'd pretty well made up my mind that seeing her dead was better than – than – Anyhow, I kept my knife ready.

"Well, it cleared, and when we reached Tripoli, the expected merchantman hadn't arrived. Right away, the captain and this chap, Abdul – first mate he was – held council, and I hung around to listen. They were considering offering the girl to the Bey of Tripoli. It was the captain who made the proposition. Slaiman, they called him.

"They talked all around the subject, and finally Abdul

says, 'Let's wait till we get to Tunis. We might get better terms there.' But at the next port "– Scander's eyes narrowed – " it was the same thing over. The same thing over," he repeated. " And then I knew what was up: each man was blocking the other to get the girl for himself. From that minute, I lived with just two things in my mind: to get her away from that hell-ship, and to keep my knife sharp.

" I used to manage to be in the same place, just at sunset, fiddling with the rigging or something or other, but 'twas always at the same time, in the same spot, right opposite her cage, and – "

Puzzled voices stopped him: " Cage? " " How do you mean – cage? "

For an instant the Girl's downcast eyes were raised, and between her and Nicolo shot a swift glance.

" She'd have thrown herself overboard. It didn't take half an eye to see that. So, first thing, they'd built her a cage of spare timbers they had in the hold, and they kept her in it day times. Well, one sunset, I caught her looking at me; next evening, same thing. Then I knew she understood that – that – "

" That I needn't be afraid! " The Girl's eyes, shy and tender, were raised to his.

He, in turn, for a moment, looked at her, and under his deep tan they saw him slowly redden. Then his head went up, and he plunged on.

" Well, finally, something happened. One day the lookout called a merchantman bearing to the west. Everybody was excited, and crowded forward. The captain ordered all sail made and the grappling irons got ready. I knew that my chance to save – or to kill – her was coming. I pressed up to her and whispered – speaking Arabic, of course – that when I opened her cage, to follow me."

The Girl's hands clasped and unclasped on her lap. "You said something else, too," she reminded him, in a low voice: "that nothing should harm me."

"Did I?" he asked, brusquely. "Well, by this time 'twas agreed that this was the ship they'd missed at Tripoli, and on her way to Malaga."

At mention of Malaga, Nicolo folded his arms across his chest, and leaned forward, as if to lose no word.

"We crowded sail and ranged alongside. Our long boats were lowered and manned, and then, from port and starboard at the same time, the crews closed in – and there she was, caught between our jaws! I hung back, thinking that in the scuffle I'd get the girl away, when, all of a sudden, there was Abdul, talking low and fast in my ear:

"'What'll you take, pilot,' says he, 'to keep everyone – friend or foe – out of the cage?' Of course, I knew he meant Slaiman. Before I could speak, he put a sword in my hands. 'A double share of the spoils, pilot,' says he, 'but if anything happens to her, I'll spit you through like a roasting capon!' It flashed through my mind that he'd guessed my thoughts, but, with his sword and my own knife, I was ready to take chances.

"By that time, men from the long boats were hanging to the *San Marco's* forechains, knives between teeth, waiting for orders to board. Then, both crews were fighting like cats, and the passengers were hiding in corners, and scrambling into the rigging. A shot or two plopped down on our deck, and I heard a blade sing past, but it was mostly slashing right and left with cutlasses. I managed to keep my eye on both the mate and the captain. Here was my chance, plain enough, to clear out with the girl. But where to? If the *San Marco'*d had a ghost of a show, I could have got aboard her, but she was having the worst of it, and I saw that, presently, we'd be towing her back to some pirate nest. The *Sultana's* men had pinned some of the crew clear through to the rail with pikes. They'd bound one poor devil to the mast and knocked his teeth out – so's he couldn't untie knots, I figured."

"Heavens, man," Gama exploded, with a grimace, "leave a little paint out of your picture! "

"'Twas a mess, sure enough," the other impartially conceded. "But just like that," striking his palms together, "something happened. In the thick of the fight, and before anyone saw her coming, right down on us bore a big merchantman, the *Venezia!* "

In the absorbed interest of the room, no one noticed that Nicolo's eyes flashed, and his fingers tightened on his folded arms.

"'Twas a surprise all around." Scander's burnt gimlet holes twinkled. "The *Venezia* swept up, grappled the *Sultana*, and on to our deck burst her whole crew. When I saw those grappling irons, I knew my chance had come. I ran below, snatched a pair of breeches, and climbed back with them to the girl. It took about two shoves to pry loose the cage bars, and then, with my coat over her head, and my arm around her, we were ducking through a shrieking hell to the rail where the fighting had slowed up." He paused to draw a long breath. "Saint Vincent, but 'twas a hell! "

"I was figuring," he went on, "that we'd both jump

overboard and then find some way of boarding the *Venezia*. All of a sudden, something made me look back, and there – "

"It was so horrible! " the Girl shuddered out. "That long knife, up to its very hilt . . . "

Scander assented. "We were just in time to see Abdul bury his knife in Slaiman's back. I didn't wait for more. We sprang for the rail, and were all but clear of it, when there was a yell from behind: 'You'd take her from me would you, you –' and there he was on top of me – Abdul. I can feel his boots in my face now, as he wrenched her away, and sent me into the water."

She leaned suddenly toward him, her eyes large with profound excitement. "I thought he killed you! " she cried. "What happened then? "

"Great heaven! What difference does it make what happened to me? " he choked out. "What happened to *you* is what I've asked myself ever since I felt that devil wrench you from me."

"But he didn't! It was I who tore loose from you! " she exclaimed.

In the stillness the sailor's lips moved without sound. "He – he – didn't – didn't get you? "

"I never saw him again! You see I – But first, what happened, when you fell overboard? "

"Well, you see the *San Marco's* mainmast had been cut down and the mains'l was trailing, and when I came up, I was under it. I worked around to the *Venezia*, and finally climbed up her forechains – and took my passage to Lisbon! " he ended, with a grin.

At these words, Nicolo's face cleared. Now he remembered!

Sugar

"Incidentally," said he, raising his voice a little, "you did a first class job after the regular helmsman was disabled in the fight!"

The sailor stared stupidly at the laughing eyes, while the others looked on, dumbfounded.

Suddenly, Ferdinand started up. "The *Venezia!*" he shouted. "Why, Nicolo, that was the ship you came on!"

"Of course! And Scander brought her in over the bar as smooth as silk, though the captain had expected to take on a pilot."

A quick little cry broke from the Girl. "You were on the big ship, both of you? . . . So was I!"

Out of the bedlam that followed, Nicolo recalled only one thing: the Girl's question had included both him and Scander — but she had looked only at him.

"But from the *Sultana* to the *Venezia?*" Ferdinand asked her. "How did you manage that?"

"All I knew was that I must get away from the *Sultana!* I ran through the fighting and the noise, and I got across to the *Venezia*. I'd pushed my hair under the coat, and no one seemed to notice me. At first I hid behind some rope. Then I noticed a ladder leading below, and when it was dark, I crept out and slid down it. I could feel boxes and cases, and I could hear the water so plainly that I knew I was in the bottom of the ship. I don't know how long I stayed there."

"It was several days before we docked at Lisbon," Nicolo quietly said.

Ruth's hands flew up in consternation. "And you had nothing to eat, child?" she cried. "No wonder warm milk tasted good to you, that first night! Do you remember?"

"I shall never forget it," the Girl said, fervently. "There were some barrels of water, and I used to steal out and drink, when no one was about. But what was I going to do when the cargo was moved? That was all I could think of. What if – those – men – on the *Sultana* should find me again?"

"Didn't you know?" Scander broke in. "The *Venezia's* men scuttled the *Sultana!* She went down like a pup with a stone 'round its neck!"

There was a long sigh of relief from the Girl; then, "And Abdul –"

Scander's tone was dubious. "Wish I could say as much for him and his crew, but –"

"You don't mean they were too quick for you?" Ferdinand exclaimed.

"Wait till you see those pirates in action, young fellow," countered Scander. "They take the edge off a streak of lightning. Isn't that so?" he demanded of Nicolo. "Besides, there was a plenty to do, without chasing them, what with nursing the *San Marco* along to Malaga, and a storm coming up, and all. Well," picking up the Girl's story, "when the ship docked?"

There was a quick gleam behind the dark eyelashes. "I was part of the cargo – *then!*" she announced. "I was a barrel of sugar!"

"Sugar!" Nicolo repeated. "Sugar!" He looked hard at Ferdinand.

Ferdinand was staring back. "By Saint Vincent – that 'short' barrel!" He whirled on Abel. "Do you remember, Master Abel, Aunt Ruth, my telling you of the row on the quay about the shipment of sugar?"

"The time you were trying to find a clue to this child?"
exclaimed Abel.

"Yes! When the merchant who'd bought the sugar was
threatening trouble for the *Venezia's* captain, and Nicolo
paid—" He checked himself awkwardly at a sign from Nicolo, but not before the Girl had caught at the word.

"Paid?" she repeated, while the colour mounted to her
forehead.

"How did you make room for yourself in the barrel?"
Nicolo hastily interposed.

She made no answer at once, but her puzzled eyes
searched his. "I scattered the sugar here and there," she
said at last, "where it wouldn't be noticed. The hardest
thing was to knock the top in. I was so afraid I'd be heard."

"You managed that, child—with those hands?" cried
Abel. He unclasped them from where they lay clasped on her
knees, and measured their slenderness on his own broad
palm.

She smiled faintly. "It wasn't easy," she admitted, "but
I found a piece of iron. Besides, that was nothing to what I
had to think of: how to get ashore, without being seen."

"There!" Ferdinand exploded. "That's what I've been
waiting for!"

"At first," she went on, "I thought I could be taken
off in the barrel, with the rest of the cargo. I thought I could
somehow pull the head in, after I was inside, but—"

"You poor waif," Diaz interrupted her, "didn't the risk
of that occur to you? Freight piled on top of you, for instance?"

She regarded him for a long moment. "Nothing seemed
a risk after Aden, or the *Sultana!*"

An impatient movement from Ferdinand roused her.
" But when the *Venezia* began to unload? " he reminded her.

" As soon as I felt the ship stop, I knew they would unload, and I got into the barrel. I tried and tried to put the
head in, but I couldn't!'"

" Of course you couldn't," Abel murmured, pityingly,
" Nor anyone else – from the inside."

" Then I heard them begin to move things in the hold,
and I knew that unloading had begun. I was frightened, oh,
frightened! " The delicate ivory face contracted with the
terror of the memory. " I saw that all I could do was to hide
as far back as possible in the hold. And I kept hoping that
before they got to me, something would happen. By and by
the noise died away, and everything was quiet, and I was
sure it must be night."

" Yes! " Nicolo exclaimed. " That was it. We had to
stop at dark."

Even in the hushed suspense of the room, the Girl's
voice was a whisper. " I waited. Then, I felt my way forward and, all at once, I looked up – and there were the
stars! "

" Yes," Nicolo said, again. " They'd left the hatches
open."

" I climbed over the cargo," the low voice went on, " to
a rope that was hanging from above, and, finally, I pulled
myself up by it to the deck."

There was a low exclamation from Ferdinand, and his
sombre eyes, fixed on the Girl, were very soft. " That was
why your palms . . . that first night . . ."

" Ah," Ruth murmured, " do you remember how bruised
and bleeding they were? "

~~~ *Sugar* ~~~

The Girl contemplated her hands. "I didn't notice, then, how I'd torn them," she said, reminiscently. "I was too afraid someone would see me. But I remember, when I got up on deck, I crouched down behind something, and wiped them on my coat. For a long time I waited there, and listened. It was very quiet, and no one seemed to be about, so I crept along behind a row of barrels, and, at the last one, I saw a plank between the ship and the dock. I went across, but after that I can't remember – my head was so dizzy. But at last, I found myself climbing stairs, climbing, climbing. . . . And then – I saw a light!" She caught her breath sharply. "There was never anything quite so beautiful as that light – and Master Abel's face!" Her voice broke pitifully. "I wanted to stay here, always, until – until I heard you and Ferdinand say those dreadful names."

"What names?" Ferdinand began in a puzzled way, while a quick glance shot between Ruth and Abel.

Very gently, Ruth put her arm around the Girl. "My child, can't you trust us enough now to tell us everything?"

"I did trust you," she faltered, "but when I heard them talking of those places on that map – I was afraid. Afraid! I didn't dare to stay here, for if my father had never gone down to – to the Devil's Cave and Sofala –"

"What?" cried Diaz. "*Sofala* – of which Covilham sent us word?"

The Girl turned amazed eyes on him. "Covilham? Pedro de Covilham? Why, he was my father's friend!"

CHAPTER 10

Nejmi

IN the stunned silence the faces around the table stared at
the Girl, and then at each other. Their ears had heard her;
but their minds still groped for her meaning.

At last: " Covilham was your father's friend? "

Diaz' gruff voice was so shaken that, involuntarily, the others glanced at him. He, himself, was oblivious of anyone except the Girl – but on her his whole rugged self was focused.

" Yes, my father's friend." She waited, looking from him to the others. " Why? " she asked, timidly. " What of that? "

" Nothing – nothing," he murmured, " or perhaps – everything! "

He rose from the table and went to her, and, as if in reverent acknowledgment that this moment was his own, the others drew aside for him.

" Child, will you tell me about – about him? All that you can remember? "

The very room held its breath for her first, quiet words:

" He came to our house in Aden, I don't remember how long ago, but when I was a little thing, and he and my father talked a great deal together in a strange language. I couldn't understand what they said, for my father always spoke Arabic with us. You see, my mother was an Arab.

" After Covilham went away, my father kept saying to my mother, ' If he finds what he expects, I shall build warehouses down there.' By and by, he got a letter. He rushed to us with it. He was more excited than I'd ever seen him. ' Covilham has been to Sofala, and he says what he hoped is true,' he told my mother. ' Think of the business that it will bring me! ' "

A strange sound from Diaz interrupted her. His breath was coming fast, and the pupils of his eyes were dilated.

She studied him a moment. " That was the way my father looked, when he got that letter – his eyes on fire, like yours."

A little impatiently he motioned her to go on.

" One day I heard him say, ' I must go and see for my-self.' And he did go, in a ship. It was a long time before he got home, and my mother was frightened about him. When he came back, he was grave and quiet. He said he would need a great deal of money because he was going to build a ware-house at " – her voice suddenly sank – " at Sofala."

At the familiar name, Ferdinand impetuously leaned forward, as if to speak.

" Let her tell her story! " Diaz sternly ordered him, without taking his eyes from the Girl.

" My mother kept begging him to stay in Aden, and at last he said, ' In a short time everything is going to be changed. The Franj are going to take trade away from Aden.' ' What makes you think they will come? ' she asked him. I remember that he didn't answer for some time, and at last he said, very low, ' They have already come! Their ship was seen some time ago by the natives.' "

" There! What'd I tell you? " the sailor broke in.

" Then he said that a native pilot had sailed with him from Sofala to a place, near the Devil's Cave, where there were two white stones with Franj writing."

" Name of heaven! " Diaz sprang to his feet, seized her arm. " ' Sailed,' did you say? " he cried. " Are you sure he told you, ' *sailed* ' from Sofala to the Devil's Cave? "

Half fearfully she stared at him. " That was what he said."

He sank back, breathing like a man at the end of a race. Slowly the hand which had been on the Girl's arm went to his forehead in a sailor's salute, and they heard him murmur " Thy dream . . . Great Navigator! "

He glanced up, as if for the first time he remembered the others, and his gaze rested on each face in turn. " This child," he solemnly said, " has answered the question that all Europe is asking."

" She is the Way of the Spices! " cried Abel.

" And Covilham was right! Covilham was right! " shouted Ferdinand. In his excitement he had leaped on his chair, and was wildly swinging his arms. " The old fellow knew what he was about – just as I always said he did! "

The men burst into a furor of talk, of questions, of speculation. They had hoped and dreamed so long that, now reality had come, they hardly dared believe it.

The Girl surveyed the commotion with puzzled eyes. " Why do you care so much? That little bit between Sofala and the Devil's Cave – what of it? "

In the complete hush that followed this astounding innocence, Ruth raised a triumphant voice: " There! That's what I've been asking for the last ten years, and you all thought I was stupid! "

There was an uproar of laughter, and everyone was volunteering explanations to the Girl, when Abel put them all aside.

" There's only one way to make her understand," and, diving into the table-drawer, he brought out a map.

But no sooner did she see what he was about, than she shrank away from him, her eyes full of dread. As it happened, no one noticed her but Abel and Nicolo. Nicolo was already starting toward her with that overwhelming impulse of protection which her fright roused in him, when he heard Abel murmur, " My poor child, forgive me! I didn't think."

"Wait, Zakuto!" Diaz reached out for the map that Abel was hurrying back to the drawer, spread it on the table, and for several moments studied it. Finally, his finger rested on a certain spot. "Those 'white stones,' of which this child says her father told, are – or were – here."

"I saw them go aboard when you set out from Lisbon, sir!" Gama broke in.

"So did I!" rejoined Abel. "Don't you recollect, Bartholomew, our watching the men cut the King's name and yours on them?"

Diaz' eyes glistened. "The last thing, just before we put about for home," he said, in a moved voice, "d'Alemquer and I, and one or two others, set those two pillars up as near as we could to the big Cape – the Devil's Cave, as you call it."

"It's pretty clear," Scander thoughtfully said, to the Girl, "that someone knew what your father had in mind when he went down to those parts. Wasn't it just after he'd got back to Aden that – that – "

Her brows drew together as at a stab of pain. "Yes," she murmured, "just after. So, when I heard Master Abel and Ferdinand talking about those places I thought – I was afraid to think!" She suddenly turned to Abel. "Where is Master Covilham now?"

"No one knows," he mournfully told her. "In the same message that he sent us from Cairo, about the sea route to India, he said he was bound for Ethiopia for further information of the Orient. That is our last news of him."

"And that," Gama gravely added, "was a long time ago."

"You don't know, child, from where your father came," Ruth ventured softly, "nor his name?"

The Girl shook her head. "No; and I never heard him called anything but 'Effendi.'"

"Like you'd say 'sir,'" Scander explained. "And that reminds me," as a sudden thought struck him, "I've always wondered what your name was."

Ferdinand jumped to his feet. "The time I've spent trying to find out without her suspecting me!" His eyes, luminous with mischief, challenged her, and Nicolo, observing that intimate glance, was devoured with envy.

"As if I didn't know, every time!" she shyly retorted.

"Well," Scander insisted, "what is it?"

But it was to Abel that the Girl turned entreating eyes. "How could I tell you before? I was afraid you would guess from it my language, my country – all. And my only safety was to wipe out every clue. But now – " she made a pleading little gesture – "now, that there's no more need to be afraid, it's – Nejmi!"

"Nejmi!" the sailor repeated. "Star! That's what it means in Arabic," he announced to the room, with an air of large satisfaction. "Star!"

"As lovely a name as I ever heard!" Gama's usual reserve melted into boyish enthusiasm.

"I'll agree to that!" Abel caught him up. "And the best of it is, it suits its owner. Isn't that so, Ferdinand?"

The boy's eyes danced. "Couldn't have chosen a better, myself, sir!"

"It's easy to say, too," Ruth comfortably contributed, with her arm around the Girl. "Not like some of those

Spice and the Devil's Cave

outlandish, foreign words that tie your tongue in a knot."
Softly she tried it over: "Nejmi – Nejmi."

"And who shall say," Abraham asked, looking from face to face, "that it's not a portent from the heavens that we shall find the Way of the Spices? For it's the *stars* that steer the mariner's course!"

"I'm thinking, Master Abel," Nicolo spoke up, "that what we've been hoping for has happened: the thing that will start Manoel up!"

"Right! I fancy he won't dally much, after he's heard what Nejmi and Scander have told us. Who's to take it to him? You, Bartholomew?"

"Wait a bit, sir!" Gama's voice was perturbed. "Was it your idea that someone of us should repeat to the King what we have heard tonight?"

"Why not?" Abel challenged. "Have you any doubt about the truth of it?"

"Do you remember, sir," Gama asked, in his turn, "that Master Abraham said, just now, the name *Nejmi* might be a favourable portent for the Way? Now, if he could put this matter to Manoel as coming from the heavens, instead of from . . ."

"You're right!" Diaz declared. "I see your point, Vasco."

"So do I," Abel ironically rejoined, "and I'm not afraid to put it into plain speech, either! You're trying to say, Gama, without being disrespectful to the King, that he might be jealous of Nejmi's and Scander's part in this business; that he'd get more glory out of sending an expedition to find the Way if he joined hands with heaven rather than with mere humans!"

"Any way you like, sir – " Gama was laughing and a little embarrassed – "but the thing is to carry our point; and everybody knows Manoel pins his faith to what's read in the stars!"

"Master Abraham is the man for us," Diaz agreed, "and the less said about what's gone on here, tonight, the better."

"You can tell Manoel," Abel said, happily, "that the last word in navigation instruments will be ready for the Captain-Major of the expedition!"

Involuntarily, everyone's eyes sought Diaz, for it was quite understood to whom Abel was speaking over Manoel's shoulders.

"We must put down the names of those places you mentioned," Abel told Scander, and he eagerly bent over the map. He began to sketch in the new landmarks while the sailor named directions and laid off distances with a stubbed thumb.

"There's Aden, of course, and Malacca, considerable away to the east'ard – "

"An island?" Abel's pencil hovered in mid-air.

"A big port, thick with traffic as carrion with flies," Scander inelegantly replied. "Then there's the Banda Islands, of course, where the cloves grow; and Macassar away over at the tail end of things."

Ferdinand eyed him with envy. "I suppose you'll get the job of master pilot to the new expedition."

"Me?" Scander's fist banged on the table. "Nothing in God's earth'd make me take that blasted trip. I've had enough of spice!"

Under cover of the talk that followed, Nicolo watched

for a chance to speak to Nejmi. He had seen her shrink back
when Abel had brought out the map. Now she was standing,
alone, at the windows. As often as he dared, he stole a glance
at the delicate face, flowerlike above Abel's black cloak. This
was his time he decided, but before he could reach her, he
saw Ferdinand step ahead of him. As he hesitated, wondering how to join them, Ferdinand beckoned to him.

"Come here! We've a question for you."

Nicolo noticed, as he approached them, that the Girl
was grave and perturbed, and in her eyes was a hint of the
old fear. Ferdinand's were dancing.

"Nejmi wants to know who paid for that sugar," he
grinned. "You don't happen to know, do you?"

Before Nicolo could muster a reply, Gama approached,
and took Ferdinand by the arm. "Come along, youngster,"
he said, good-naturedly, "or you'll get a reprimand for late
hours."

"And for deviltry in general!" Nicolo murmured, in
an aside, as Ferdinand passed him.

"Do you know?" the Girl insisted, as they were left
together.

"It was I." He tried to make his voice casual. "The
captain is a friend of mine," he hastily added as he saw the
colour flame in her face, "and he wasn't on hand to speak for
himself."

She looked at him with distressed eyes. "That makes
twice that I'm in your debt! If you hadn't caught the bird
the other day –"

A thousand things rushed to his lips. "Let it stand that
way," he said, trying to laugh off the incident. "I'll promise
to claim payment when I need it!" Then, lest he should say

too much, he turned the subject: "I saw you go away, when Master Abel brought that map out."

"I hate it!" she told him in a low, vehement tone. "I wish I need never see it, never hear those names again. Are you –" she paused as her frightened eyes searched his – "are you like the rest of them?" She motioned toward the heads bent over the table. "Do you want, more than anything else, to find the Way of the Spices?"

For a moment he hesitated. How should he answer her?

He looked meaningly at her. "Not more than *any*thing else!" he said, very low.

*   *   *

N I G H T   W A S graying into dawn when Nicolo went silently down the long stairway behind Diaz and old Abraham. Out of these incredible hours he carried an indelible image of the fright in Nejmi's eyes. Already he called her so to himself. Around her fear his mind revolved. To banish it, forever drive it away, ah, what would he not give?

He hugged to him the thought that, all unwittingly, they had made port together; together become citizens in a strange land. Dear fate that had singled him out to make good that empty barrel! He could have found it in his heart to envy Scander – Scander, who had veritably snatched her from death, stood between her and worse than death. A wave of gratitude rushed over him. That chap should have the best he could give!

Had she, he rambled on to himself, noticed that he had been the only one to say nothing about her name? How could he, with the whole room talking about it? Something had taken him by the throat, paralyzed his tongue. But some day all those dear, suffocating things should be told to her.

Nejmi! He said it over to himself, and across his fancy smote the vision of a star of palest gold set in a tender, evening sky.

CHAPTER 11

Debacle

A L L day, at his office, Abel answered questions and gave
advice to those who dropped in to talk over a rumour
which was said to come from the palace; for his intimacy with Abraham Zakuto and Bartholomew Diaz was

known to give authority to his information about court matters.

How much truth, he was asked, was there in the report that an expedition to India was on foot? Were John's ships to be finished, or new ones built? What about prospects for contracts to outfit such an expedition with supplies, clothing, arms? Would his bank loan to a small firm that was competing for such orders?

Just as he had finally contrived an excuse to slip away, a new-comer seized his arm.

"A minute, Zakuto! What's behind all this gossip? They're telling it around that Manoel's started things going on the strength of some nonsense he's got from the stars. Know anything about that?"

"What do you care," Abel evaded, "from where his authority came, so long as he's acting on it?"

"Have you faith in a sea route to India?" the other pressed him. "Fact is, my firm would buy up land for warehouses, if there were good prospects for the Oriental trade."

"Man," Abel assured him, "the sea route to India is just as sure as the ground under your feet!"

He went off inwardly amused. If they all, Manoel himself included, could know what was really behind this tremendous business: a girl and a sailor!

At every corner he heard men eagerly discussing the new excitement. Little boys, importantly beating their drums, bumped into him. What was that they were shouting? – "Enlistments in the Expedition of the Spices!"

So they, too, had caught the fever! From every tavern door, between drunken snatches, there floated out to him the name of Diaz. Yes, thought Abel, Diaz was the unani-

mous favourite for the new command. No question about it.
What a splendid piece of fortune for Portugal that she had
the right man for the great crisis which was upon her. For
once, at least, the times and the man fitted!

Bartholomew, he mused, would soon be up to tell him
the latest developments; perhaps even today; and, with that
in mind, he hurried along.

"Master Abel!" he heard someone call, and looked
around to find Gama out of breath behind him.

"Vasco! Where'd you come from?"

"I've been trying to catch up with you, sir. I had to see
you at once."

Abel looked closely at him. "Why, man, what is it?
You look ill."

"I am, sir! I'm sick at heart, and you might as well
know why, first as last: the King has named me to head the
Expedition."

Like a man stunned, Abel stared at him.

"I knew you'd feel that way about it," Gama murmured. "I could hardly speak when he told me what he
wanted me to do."

"Wasn't there even mention of Bartholomew?" Abel
managed to get out.

"Not a word. 'I want you to go, Vasco,' Manoel told
me – just like that. I protested that my brother Paulo would
make a better leader than I, but the King wouldn't hear of
that, though he promised me Paulo should command one of
the ships."

"But Bartholomew's experience, what he's actually
dared and accomplished, does all that count for nothing?"

"There's every reason in the world why he should have

this appointment, and not a single one why I should," Gama said deprecatingly. He suddenly threw back his head and looked Abel gravely in the eye. " But now that the King has named me, I have sworn before God that I will see this thing through."

" Does Bartholomew know? "

" I begged permission of His Majesty to tell him, myself. It was the hardest thing I ever did! "

" Gama, you're a man! " Abel's hand shot out to him. " That was hard to do. But I'll warrant that Bartholomew, too, took it like a man! "

Tears stood in Gama's eyes. " Nothing ever so wrung my heart, sir. He would have no apologies, no explanations; just held me together with those eyes of his. And when I asked him if he'd take charge of the whole thing – a good many, you know, sir, under such circumstances would have refused altogether – he stood like a soldier at attention, and merely said, ' When shall I begin? ' "

" Magnificent! " Abel cried. " I'm going to find him and tell him so as soon as I can! Where is he, do you know? "

" I believe, sir, he meant to see you at your house, perhaps is there, now."

There was a subtle note in Gama's voice that made Abel look sharply at him. Was the man withholding something?

A minute later, he forgot the incident, but as soon as he caught sight of Diaz' face, at the workshop door, that hint of foreboding in Gama's tone vaguely recurred to him.

They stood a moment without speaking, hands on each other's shoulders.

" I've just come from Gama," Abel at last said.

Understandingly Diaz nodded. " Then you know that I'm to superintend preparations for the Expedition? "

" That's one way of putting it," Abel sorrowfully answered. "Ah, Bartholomew – Bartholomew! Who'd have dreamed that things could have taken such a turn? Everyone talking of you, and no one even thinking of Gama! "

" I've had my chance, man," Diaz calmly told him. " Why shouldn't he have his? "

" But surely you're to go with the Expedition? "

"I doubt it. The King was hinting, yesterday, that I was needed at the fort at Mina.[1] But," he broke off, "that isn't what I've come to speak about."

Again reminded of Gama's tone of foreboding, Abel glanced apprehensively at him.

" You must brace yourself, Abel! " Diaz said, very low, and he squared his own shoulders. " You knew, didn't you, that the marriage contract between Manoel and the Infanta of Spain would be signed within the week? "

" I supposed as much. Well? " Abel's voice was as puzzled as his face.

" The Infanta of *Spain,* Abel! "

At the marked emphasis on that dreaded name, Abel's face changed, and over it crept a slow fear.

Diaz turned away his head. " The price of that contract," he faltered, " is. the exile of your people from Portugal."

For a moment Abel wavered, put out his hands as if to steady himself. " You mean we must – go? "

" Would that I could have borne this blow for you! " Diaz cried out in an anguished voice. " I couldn't bear to

---

[1] A Portuguese military post on the Guinea coast.

have it first reach you through the public announcement, so, with the King's sanction I came to you myself."

Abel sat down heavily, and motioned to close the doors. "Ruth mustn't hear this just yet – nor Nejmi. This edict – is to be pronounced – when? "

"In a few days, after the signing of the royal contract."

"Does Abraham know? "

"Oh, yes; Manoel told him first of all, and afterward Gama and I were called in. Abraham was too prostrated to come to you, so – "

Abel's hand groped toward the other's. "I'm grateful to you, Bartholomew. It's something to know there's one I can look to in this world that's fallen around me."

"All your friends feel as I do, Abel! There's nothing we wouldn't have foregone to prevent this. Nothing! And I doubt if there's a soul in Lisbon or in Portugal who wouldn't abolish this cursed edict. Manoel, himself, never would have consented to it, if the Spanish sovereigns hadn't made it the condition to his marriage. But of course it's no secret that the great thing with him is a Spanish alliance."

"Why couldn't I have foreseen this, after what they did to us in Spain? " Abel groaned. "But I was so sure of Manoel – oh, God, so sure! "

"To do him justice, I don't believe he had an inkling of what they were going to demand of him as the Infanta's price. He seemed really sorrowful when he talked with us about it; said, repeatedly, that Portugal owed her financial prosperity to her Jews."

"And it's nothing to what we've planned: new branch houses and agencies abroad, and Lisbon the commercial center of Europe. . . . But what's the use of talking about it now? " Abel turned his head away and Diaz heard his stifled voice: " We must leave it all – all! "

" It's taken the heart out of everything for me. This Expedition that we'd all revolved around for so long is ashes in my mouth."

" Yet Lisbon will go on just the same," Abel bitterly predicted. " The Expedition will sail, and who will ever remember the part the Jews have had in it? Who gives a thought as to how Columbus' expeditions were financed? "

" It's cold comfort," said Diaz, " but the King himself was speaking to Gama and me of what your people have done for exploration. He even reminded us that it was Rabbi Joseph who brought back Covilham's great message from Cairo."

" Yes! " Abel passionately broke in. " He's taken all we could give of brains and wealth, just as Spain did of the Moors and of us; and now, because we don't worship as he does, he casts us out like chaff! " His face dropped between his hands, and Diaz, himself rent with grief, heard a sound of anguish: " My garden . . . this workshop . . . Ruth and I exiles! And my poor Abraham . . . "

After some moments he raised his head. " How did the King take Abraham's advice about the Way of the Spices? "

" Just like a boy! Couldn't wait to start preparations. He promised Abraham his reward should be a Court residence for life."

" What will his word ever mean more than that – now? " Contemptuously Abel snapped his fingers. He looked steadily at Diaz as if he were forcing himself to some dreaded issue. " When – must we go? "

" In ten months," was the almost inaudible reply.

Neither spoke until Diaz rose, and then Abel faltered out, "With all you have on your mind, Bartholomew, it was good of you –"

"Abel – Abel – don't! " And as if unable to trust himself, Diaz rushed from the workshop and out of the gate.

It was characteristic of Abel that, without delay, and briefly, he told Ruth the news that Diaz had brought. She listened to him with a blank look in her bright, inquisitive eyes.

" But Abel," she gasped, " you said – you said – we were too useful to Manoel to have him treat us as they did our people in Spain."

" I thought we were! I thought we were, my poor, poor Ruth. But it seems he needs Spain more than he does us, and so he must take Spain's orders."

She staggered back against the wall. " It can't be – can't be true! He wouldn't be so cruel! "

He put his arms around her with a feeling that but for them she would fall. Ah, that out of his own misery he could find some barest shred of comfort for her!

" Where does he want us to go? " she shuddered out at last.

Even in his despair the pathetic irony of her question struck him. As if the least qualm about the future of his Jewish subjects would ever cross Manoel's mind!

He saw her turn a stricken face to the court; watched her eyes travel its sunny length; watched them come back to the workshop to linger, with tragic scrutiny, on the shelves, the bench, the table. He felt her suddenly quiver, felt her arms flung around him, and her cheek pressed to his.

" Abel, my poor Abel! "

He could only say her name, with a vague sense that somehow she was the comforter, he the comforted. They stood so, clinging to each other.

"We'll go together, Abel!"

"Together, Ruth."

"And Nejmi will go with us."

"Heaven be praised!"

"She's like balm to a hurt," Ruth sobbed, under her breath.

"A light in the dark – like her name!"

Ruth's arms tightened around Abel. "We must – must begin to plan – where to go," she got out in a voice that tried to be steady.

Instantly he understood what she meant. "For Nejmi's sake?"

She nodded. "After all she's gone through we can't let her think she's to be again a – wanderer."

"Wanderer!" The word seared itself into Abel's misery. He had thought he understood, when Abraham had tried to tell him of that terrible exodus from Spain. He knew now he had not. His gaze turned achingly to the massive walls of the court and the house. How impregnably they had seemed to shield him from all that was without, and now – "Wanderer!"

"No, Ruth, we won't let her be that," he said as calmly as he could. "I'll begin right away to plan."

"I wish we needn't tell her just yet, poor lamb!"

But, as it happened, at that moment, Nejmi came into the workshop, and clinging to her in a passion of gratefulness at her physical nearness, they poured out their misery to her.

Half-way through Abel's explanation she broke in:
"You must go because your God is different from your
King's?"

Almost he could have smiled at the innocent directness. "That's it, my child. That's the whole case in a
nutshell."

He saw the old fear creep into her eyes, and knew that
she was looking at their impending disaster in the light of
her own tragic exile.

"Ah, the trouble that it makes to call Him by different
names," she cried under her breath, "when, after all, he's
the same Allah!"

"We didn't want to tell you, my child," Ruth sobbed,
"until we knew where we were going."

"As if that made a difference!" She knelt between
them, fondled their hands. "We have each other, where-
ever we go!"

*   *   *

W HEN N ICOLO came, that evening, he found Abel sitting
on the bench under the grey old fig tree.

"I didn't know whether you'd care to see me so soon,
sir. If you'd rather be alone –"

Silently, Abel drew him down beside him.

"Isn't it chilly out here for you, sir?" Nicolo ventured. "Shall we go into the workshop?"

He felt Abel wince as if he had been struck.

"We'll stay here – if you don't mind?"

Nicolo glanced toward the workshop. It was unlighted.
There were lights in the other rooms. Had the great "lighthouse" lamp perhaps been forgotten? He shivered as his

gaze lingered on the dim outlines of the room that had been the glowing heart of Abel's house.

For a while neither spoke, and then Nicolo choked out, " I can't tell you the first word of my grief, sir. To stand by and not be able to lift a finger for you – "

" If it were my trouble alone! " Abel groaned. " But the thousands of us, that, tonight, are asking ourselves the same question: 'Where to go?' The business that we've built up here, our homes, all to be – " there was a sound of stifled agony as when a wound is probed – " to be as if they had not been! "

" I've been wondering, sir, if – if – I could help you find – a place – " He felt Abel's hand close convulsively on his, but no word was spoken.

" I've friends in Venice, you know, sir," Nicolo went on, " who'd do all they could if you wished to settle there. And Amsterdam – had you thought of it? They're progressive up there, I've heard, and they'd appreciate brains like yours. Some day," he broke out passionately, " Manoel will wake up to what he's lost! "

" If he would at least let us take our possessions with us! " Abel's gaze, as it travelled the length of the court, was a mute caress for each object that it touched. " But it will be as it was in Spain. We shall have to leave everything behind. Even our money – they will contrive to take that, too."

" That's something I wanted to speak of, sir. I was wondering if you'd care to invest your capital in my business. In that way no one could get hold of it, and it should grow with the business."

" My boy, I – I didn't look for anything like this! "

"Why, Master Abel, you're the heart of all this great future that is bound to come to Portugal. Why, in heaven's name, shouldn't you share in it?"

He started to mention Nejmi. But what was there to say? Should he ask if they would take her when they went? As if he didn't know without asking! The very thought was like a cold hand on his heart.

At last he got up, and gently asked if Abel would go in, for the night air was sharp.

No, Abel said, he would sit here a while longer. Chilly, was it? No matter. Almost it seemed as if he wished to be alone.

So Nicolo tiptoed away, shivering as he passed the silent workshop, and let himself out of the gate.

CHAPTER 12

The Lighted Workshop

I T was Abel's last day at his bank. The final meeting had been held, the investors refunded, and inevitable losses divided between the bank officials.

The bank was now, in Abel's own words, as if it had not

been. He had come to the building this morning only to take away his private papers, and now, with them in his hand, he sought, for the last time, the little side door which he had liked for its privacy.

As he opened it, someone on the threshold turned.

"Ferdinand – you?"

It was their first meeting since the pronouncement of the edict.

"I knew I'd find you here, sir. I came to give you a message from – from – " He bit his lips to hide their quivering, and Abel saw his shoulders heave.

"Come inside." Abel drew him within, and closed the door. "We can be alone here."

"It's a message from Master Abraham," the boy said in a voice thick, Abel knew, with suppressed weeping. "He's – he's gone."

"Gone?" Abel repeated. "Does Manoel know?"

"Manoel!" Ferdinand burst out. "I hate him! I never did like him, but now I'll never forgive him."

Abel put his arm around the heaving shoulders. "'Never' is a long word, lad."

"Not long enough for me! Look at what your people have done for Portugal, and now how does he repay you?" He broke off to draw his hand across his eyes. "I must give you Master Abraham's message," he said, with an effort. "He sailed, early this morning, in a packet bound for Tunis. There was no time to see you."

Abel received the news without surprise. "Did he take leave of the King?"

"Yes. Manoel assured him again he might stay on at the palace, but he wouldn't listen. Afterward I saw him for a minute and he whispered to me, 'See Abel as soon as possible, and tell him to go at the first chance. Manoel is sure to follow up this edict with forcing baptism on us.'"

"Baptism!" Abel cried, and his voice was full of horror. "That, too? Doesn't Manoel know what that means?" he groaned. Then, as Ferdinand stared, uncomprehendingly, at him, "You must go back to your duties, my boy," he said in a shaken voice, "and I – I must give Ruth that message at once."

All the way home the terrible word rang through his brain: Baptism! In letters of blood it seemed to play before his eyes, to mock and to threaten him.

As soon as he entered the court he called to Ruth.

She hurried out to him. "Oh, Abel – *what?*"

"Nejmi mustn't hear us," he warned her.

"Then come in here." She drew him into the workshop and closed the doors.

Sick at heart, he looked about it. The first time he had entered it, since Bartholomew had told him the worst. There, on the floor, were the shavings he had last made; the compass frame just as he had left it on the bench; the various tools on their shelves.

"Ruth," he said with an effort, "Abraham's gone," and he repeated his message.

Ruth's eyes blazed. "Why doesn't Manoel put us all to death, and have done? Do you remember – do you remember, Abel," she faltered, "what Abraham told us happened in Spain, when they tried to force baptism on our people? That parents killed their children and then themselves rather than be false to our faith? Oh, God above, must that happen here?"

Trembling, she sank on a seat. In silent misery Abel sat beside her, chafed her cold hands.

"If I could only shut it out, forget what he said!" she moaned. "Oh, those poor fathers! Those mothers drowning themselves and their babies!"

"Let Manoel try his baptism on us!" Abel said, vehemently. "Let him see what will happen if his priests come here!" He looked at her with sombre meaning.

For a minute she closed her eyes. When she opened them, they were brave and steady. "Yes, Abel, dear!"

From that day, ready at an instant's notice, there lay, in one of the workshop cupboards two little vials filled with a colourless liquid. Why they were never used, Abel, in the anguished days which followed, forgot to wonder or ask. And Diaz never told him of the exemption which Gama had begged from Manoel, and had received as a special favour.

"As long as we must go," Ruth said, heavily, "we'd better take Abraham's advice and go as soon as we can find transport."

"No!" Abel was firm. "Not until we know where we're bound. If it were only you and I, Ruth –"

"You're right," passionately she agreed. "For *her* sake, poor homeless lamb!"

Abel rose and began restlessly to pace back and forth. The necessity for decision forced itself on his misery like a blade in a mortal wound. He paused to look out of the windows. Could it be that he was to leave it all? The climbing roofs. The blue bowl of Tagus. The bustling harbour front. Oh God, it was too bitter!

Suddenly Ruth's arms were flung about him. "Abel –

Abel," she was stammering between her sobs, "we'll start over again! There's plenty of time – we're not old! "

"Of course we aren't," he managed to say. "Not for a long time yet, my dear."

"If I could only bear it all for you! " Her arms tightened about him. "Ah, Abel, there's no one like you in the whole world! "

"Well, my dear – " there was something like the old twinkle in his eyes – "if I'd thought there was another like you, I'd have been put to it to know which of you to marry! "

Nejmi's steps in the court made him say, quickly, "Go to her, Ruth. She mustn't suspect. And I'll begin right away to inquire about where to go. Rabbi Joseph may have something to suggest."

Left alone, he turned again to the windows and, standing there, gazing down on his Lisbon, he was seized by the impulse – not merely wish or desire, but consuming necessity – to go to the shipyards. Yes, even in face of engulfing tragedy, in spite of all, he must see those ships – the Expedition of the Spices! And without saying a word to Ruth or Nejmi he hurried out of the house and down the long stairway.

He was not half-way to the water-front, when someone stopped him with a ghastly rumour of a massacre somewhere outside Lisbon. A farmer, on his way to market, had brought the first report. Later, a Jewish lad, spent with hunger and crazed with terror, had staggered into town and gibbered out horrors that were past belief. And even as Abel sought here and there for further details, there arrived a small company of fugitives with a story that took Lisbon's breath: a band of Jews from outlying districts, on their way to embark according to Manoel's order, had been attacked by bandits who, on the strength of a report that the exiles had swallowed jewels and coin, had ripped them open by the hundreds.

In a very sickness of spirit Abel wandered blindly about. What streets he walked he would never know, and passers-by he saw as shadows moving in a sea of sunshine.

At last he became aware of noise, loud and insistent. A strong odour of hemp and resin stung his nostrils. Bewildered, he glanced about, and, with a stab of recognition, saw that he was at the dockyards. He recalled that, some time ago, he had meant to come here; in fact, this very morning, when he was standing at the workshop windows.

In spite of his leaden heart, his numb senses thrilled to the surge of life about him. Near by, carpenters planed huge timbers; over here, coopers were bending hoops; and there, billowed about with seas of canvas, tailors cut and sewed new sails. Caulkers' mallets beat a steady tattoo to the scream of saws; pulleys groaned, windlasses shrieked.

He caught his breath as his eyes rested on three tall caravels that reared against the sky: the ships that John had ordered for the finding of the Way! The ships that Diaz had designed! Well, at least, Bartholomew would have the satisfaction of seeing them put forth on the great adventure, and, undoubtedly, of seeing them return. But he, Abel Zakuto, where would he be when the Expedition came back? Ah, his compass that was to have guided it . . . his astrolabe! . . .

He walked on to watch a fleet of high prowed fishing boats toss the catch to waiting groups. The river bank swarmed with women and children washing and scaling fish, which others salted and piled. Farther along, he saw men skinning and quartering carcasses. Beyond were rows of barrels ready to receive the cured meat. " Gama's crews must eat and drink," Abel reflected, as a single-sailed wine carrier passed on her way to the warehouses.

How busy they all were – and how little they needed him! What was it to them that his tools were idle, the work-shop silent, the compass unfinished? Well, hadn't he told Diaz that Lisbon would go on just the same, even though half of it lay in its death agony? What cared the other half, going its triumphant way, drunk with the glory of this supreme adventure!

He stepped aside for a boy with a great bundle of flares. Abel watched him plant them at convenient intervals, and then set them afire. Could it be that work would go on after dark? Yes, here were fresh shifts to relieve the day workers.

In the jostle Abel felt a hand on his arm and heard his name spoken.

" Nicolo? "

" You, Master Abel, down here? Why, I was just going up to your house to tell you that I've stopped my own work – loaned my men to Diaz! " There was suppressed excitement in his tone.

" Loaned your men? "

" Haven't you heard, sir? The news came yesterday from England that Cabot is sailing in search of a north-west passage to India! "

Understandingly Abel assented. " So preparations must be rushed to prevent his getting too much of a start on – on Portugal! Is that it? " Almost he had said " on us " – for-getting that Portugal no longer counted him hers.

" And of course," Nicolo pursued, " it's no secret that

Columbus is moving heaven and earth to get off ahead of us. So, yesterday, as soon as we heard this latest news about Cabot, Master Diaz ordered night shifts. The least I could do was to loan him my men – but only on condition that Scander shouldn't be impressed into the Expedition. He's here, you know, at work."

A moment later, the tanned face peered out of the dusk. This was Scander's first meeting with Abel since the ban against the Jews. For a full minute the small, sunken eyes surveyed him in silence. Then the hairy fist grasped his hand.

"You're hard hit, sir! And I'm sorry – sorrier than I ever expected to be about anything." He hesitated, shifting from one foot to the other, then, "Odd, this business of religion," he broke out. "It's like a saw – works both ways. If you happen to touch it – " He clicked his tongue to indicate something swift and final. "It all but did for me once, and I haven't forgotten! "

From anyone else this frank handling of the subject would have rasped Abel, but, as it was, he felt a curious comfort in the simple directness.

"I don't wonder," he said, "that, after the Aden experience, you're firm on not going with Gama."

"Lisbon's good enough for me," Scander meditatively replied. " I'll stick here." He looked sharply at Abel, as if minded to add something. Evidently thinking better of it, he reiterated, " I'll stick here."

Long afterward Abel recalled the incident: that starting to speak, that change of mind, that stubborn " I'll stick here." But, at the time, it made no immediate impression on him, for both Nicolo's and Scander's voices, even the rush

and stir around him, seemed to come from very far away.
For between him and the roaring shipyards, between him
and, indeed, all else, rose up a host of mutilated corpses that
would never be avenged, that already were forgotten under
a pitiless sky.

"You did right," he said at last, to Nicolo, "to loan
your men."

He saw Scander go to join a knot of men at work in the
light of a flare, and mechanically he turned away with a
vague thought of home.

"I'll walk along with you, sir," he heard Nicolo say,
but was not again conscious of his presence until, on the
long flight of stairs, he felt a cloak thrown about him. "It's
raining so hard, sir!" Nicolo was apologetically explaining.

As the gate swung back, Abel halted, caught his breath.
Across the wet flags of the court, streamed light – light that
came from the workshop! He was dimly aware that Nicolo
walked by his side, and that together they entered the room.

Under the great "lighthouse" lamp, with something in
her hands, sat Nejmi, apparently too absorbed in it to notice
them. Abel took a step toward her. She looked up at him,
nodded absently to Nicolo.

"I've rubbed and rubbed," she said, anxiously, "but
I can't make it shine."

She laid aside a heavy cloth that Abel used for polishing and held out to him – the compass frame! Incredulously
he stared at it; at her who had shrunk from sight and mention of all that had to do with the sea, from all that had to
do with the Way and its finding!

"How do you polish it?" she was pleading. "If you'll
just show me–"

" Fetch me that bottle of oil, and that box, over there."

Abel spoke with an effort, and his hands were trembling. In spite of his fondness for her, he was conscious of bewilderment, even of annoyance. Why had she chosen this time to do this thing? Couldn't she see how spent he was? Hadn't she sensed his utter and heart-sick revolt from his instruments – she who was usually as sensitive to the moods of those about her as a flower petal to sun and wind?

But Nejmi, apparently engrossed in the business in hand, gave undivided attention to the oil and rotten stone that he was mixing.

*　　　*　　　*

ABEL LOOKED up at last, to find himself alone. How had Nicolo gone without his knowing it? Nejmi, most likely, had grown sleepy, and was in bed – Ruth, too.

His eyes returned to the frame in his hand. What a polish! Better even than he had expected; repaid him for that long process of selection from those many samples of wood. A beautiful colour, too, as of deep red roses dipped in wine. That paste he had mixed, he mused, was particularly effective. He took a pinch of it, rubbed it between thumb and forefinger, and smelled it. A good, clean smell it was, so wholesome, so real!

He rose and laid the instrument on its own precious shelf, and stood, looking down on it. Tomorrow he would try more paste, more rubbing. Tomorrow? Ah, God! For the moment he had forgotten! What had he to do with tomorrow or with any part of the future? Despairingly, his eyes sought the compass. That all that beauty of workmanship, of form and colour, should be wasted! . . . Wasted? He

felt himself trembling as something leaped in his breast.
Didn't Gama still need a compass? Wasn't the Way still to
be found? Well, then, why not *tomorrow?* And as many to-
morrows as would fulfill – yes, *his* part in the Way!

But after that? The old agony laid hold of him. Exile.
Hunger. Death.

Ah, for something to steady him, to keep that black
flood from again engulfing him! His glance fell on the paste,
the polishing cloth. He took them in his hands, grasped them
in a sort of desperate defense from himself. He would put
from him everything but the one thought that tomorrow he
would polish. Polish! And so, from hour to hour, not looking
ahead. For the present he mustn't reason about the future –
he wasn't clear-headed enough. He would hold himself only
to taking one step at a time, not thinking of the next.

He laid down the cloth and paste, and stepped into the
court for a breath of freshness. The rain had stopped, and
there was a broken sky. Great clouds raced before a clearing wind, and between their dark, fleeing masses Abel saw
the sweet radiance of stars.

CHAPTER 13

A Street Quarrel

NICOLO was sitting at a table in The Green Window, finishing the fish that Pedro had fried for his
breakfast.

"Hardly out of the water before it was sizzling in oil!"

announced the old man, and Nicolo made out that he was expected to praise its freshness.

"You take good care of me, Pedro," he said. "I'm lucky to be with you."

"Provisions, these days, aren't easy to get," Pedro plaintively remarked. "Meat and fish are highest I've ever known on account of so much being needed for the Expedition."

"Cheer up, Pedro! Gama'll soon be off, and when he gets home, there'll be such a rabble to sign up for the next trip to India, that The Green Window won't hold them, and you can charge anything for a meal; any price you like!"

Nicolo's banter was not so whole-hearted as it sounded. While he spoke of Gama's return he was heavily thinking 'Where will Nejmi be then?'

"That's what I hear," Pedro hopefully returned, "that prices are going up. There's a tailor friend of mine says he's even going to raise his figure before Gama sails."

"Good business!" commended Nicolo. Then, because Pedro's mention of a tailor stirred a half-formed thought, "Think your friend would make me a cloak for the big day?" he ventured.

It had occurred to him, some time ago, that he would like to have something new to wear on the day the Expedition sailed. To be sure, Nejmi wouldn't be among the spectators. He had heard Abel say they would watch the scene from the workshop. But, he reflected, afterward he could go up to Abel's. His fancy dallied with the notion: the new cloak with the sunlight in the court weaving patterns on it – and Nejmi near by. Even, he might drop a hint to her that she was its incentive! And at the same time he would make bold and tell her that his ship was to be named *The Golden Star!*

"He'd do it fast enough, if he had his regular help," Pedro replied, "but he's had to loan his men to make sails in the shipyards. You knew Captain Diaz was having two sets of sails for every ship? But I'll tell you where his tailor shop is; and say I sent you."

As Nicolo neared the address Pedro had mentioned, he became aware of some disturbance ahead. Loud voices rang out and, looking in their direction, he saw a knot of spectators already gathered, and others running to join them. He hurried forward, and came up in time to see, in the centre of the crowd, two sailors making unsteady passes at each other. One of them he knew, by his dress, was a Venetian; the other was unmistakably Portuguese, and they both were half tipsy.

"Funny, what you think you're going to do with those three or four little ships—caravels is it you call 'em?" the Venetian was drawling in bad Portuguese.

"You won't think they're so funny—nor so little—when you see your galleys coming home empty, one of these days," retorted the Portuguese. "Gama'll teach you a thing or two!".

"Oh, curse Gama!" shouted the Venetian as he reeled toward the other.

There was a growl from the bystanders, and several started for the Venetian.

"String him up and let him dangle!" cried someone.

Nicolo waited for no more. He dove through the crowd and stepped in front of the Venetian. "Better let me take you back to your ship," he sharply told him.

"Take me back to my ship, would you?" yelled the fellow. "Get out of my way before I take you where –"

Furiously he swung on Nicolo who, just in time swerved aside, while he, unable to stop himself, shot helplessly forward and struck the ground, face down.

"That's what you Venetians'll come to!" jeered the Portuguese sailor.

Nicolo stepped up to the grovelling figure, and jerked it upright. "Come along with me before you start trouble," he advised, in a low tone; then, to pacify the crowd, "He doesn't know what he's saying!" he laughed.

"I don't, don't I?" stammered the Venetian. He raised his fist, which Nicolo promptly caught and held.

Suddenly someone pushed toward them, and laid hands on the sailor. A tall, swarthy fellow, Nicolo noted, with bushy black hair.

"Been drinking again, eh?" he asked with a strong foreign accent; then, aside to Nicolo, "Shipmate of mine," he explained, as he walked the other man away.

The sailor looked back at Nicolo. "I'll settle with you, yet," he called, "you cursed Portygee!"

Nicolo burst out laughing. "As it happens, brother, I'm a Venetian!" Then, as the bystanders, including the tipsy Portuguese, had moved off, and there seemed no more chance of trouble, he continued on his way to the tailor's.

Some distance on, he was aware of someone falling in beside him: the tall, dark stranger!

"Lucky for me that you interfered," the man laughed, in his foreign accent. "If the crowd had got their hands on that mate of mine –"

"It might have been serious," Nicolo agreed.

"That chap," pursued the other, "is the handiest you ever saw on a deck. But he can't keep away from drink, and then there's no lengths to which his tongue won't go! "

"It was a poor time he chose, with the mood Lisbon is in just now! "

"Yes, the town's gone mad over Gama," the stranger admitted. "I stopped in here to see if I could pick up a cargo – being a small trader, myself – but a fellow has no chance at all at his own affairs, with everyone taken up with this Expedition."

"I'm in exactly that fix," said Nicolo. "I've a caravel half built, and there she'll stay till Captain Diaz gets through with my men! "

"You in the ship-building business? " The eyes under the bushy, black hair narrowed. "And didn't I hear you say you were a Venetian? "

Nicolo admitted this was so.

The man studied him with unconcealed curiosity. "Queer, you coming here, when you've about all the trade and ship-building in your own town. You must have heard some strong stories to make you shift to Lisbon."

"To my way of thinking," Nicolo replied, "what Captain Diaz did is strong enough to make anyone shift."

The other shrugged, and laughed. "Come, now! How can you tell that what he says is true? "

Immediately Nicolo was on the defensive. "If you knew Bartholomew Diaz as I do – "

"Oh, you know him, do you? " The note of eagerness made Nicolo wonder.

"Come in and have a drink, won't you? " added the stranger, as, at that moment, they were passing a tavern.

Nicolo suddenly remembered the tailor, but it was a hot morning, and he was thirsty! He followed the man into the tavern, and while they drank their wine, they talked about Portugal's slave trade.

" They say," said the seaman, " there's a fortune in it."

" Nothing like what there'll be in spice, after Gama gets things going in the East! " Nicolo confidently returned. With the relaxation and glow that the wine spread through him, he felt aggressively optimistic about Portugal's future.

" I hear that your friend Diaz is outfitting this Expedition. I suppose he's providing for a long cruise? "

" You'd think so, if you could see what he has ready for those ships! He has everybody working day and night, from packing provisions to casting cannon and caulking hulls. And he's bought up all kinds of merchandise to send, too: cloth and silks and jewellery and so on."

" Oh, reckoning on trading it? "

" Yes, and to give as presents to the native kings. There's nothing Diaz hasn't thought of! "

" You've been abroad, have you? " Again that note of eagerness!

Yes, Nicolo acknowledged, he had.

" Squat-built things, those boats, aren't they? " commented the other. " That square rig, and top-heavy castles, too! "

" How else could castles be," Nicolo defended, " but big and substantial, with the fighting that's to be done from them? "

" Expect fighting, do they? " The black brows were raised a trifle.

" Well, they're going prepared! "

The stranger's eyes appeared to explore the depths of his mug. "I suppose Gama figures on using gun powder?" he casually offered.

"If he has to! There's a trained squad for the powder pots and cannon," boasted Nicolo, secretly pleased to exploit his friends. "And besides that," he rambled on, "there are enough javelins and crossbows and pikes and—"

He checked himself with a curious and unaccountable feeling that the eyes under the lowered lids were only pretending to look into the mug, and that they were really taking stealthy account of what he was saying. Were they, too, a trifle derisive? It rushed over him that the questions might have been bait to make him talk. He was uneasily conscious that, proud of the Expedition, and eager to defend his own position, he had been only too willing to tell—to a stranger, at that—all that he knew. As well as he could, he picked up his broken sentence, and ended, a little lamely, "There's nothing that Diaz forgets or overlooks!"

The man's eyes, as he raised them to meet Nicolo's, were indifferent. "No doubt," he said, casually, "no doubt at all." He turned as a snatch of talk floated in from the street. "Ah," he said, pleasantly, turning back again, "I see the news has begun to get around." Then, as Nicolo looked mystified, "About the Jews, you know," he explained.

"What do you mean?"

"Why, the Pope's taken a hand, and made Manoel give them twenty years before they have to quit the country."

Nicolo's heart leaped to his throat. "Twenty years! Who told you?"

"Well, the proclamation hasn't yet been read," was the evasive answer, "but it's going to be!"

∽∽ *A Street Quarrel* ∽∽

In a tumult of hope and fear, Nicolo made some excuse, and went out. He must go right up to Abel's to find what he knew of this matter. How, he suddenly wondered, had this stranger got the information before it was made public? Yet, as he struck across to the hillside, he forgot everything but that he was keeping buoyant step to a measure his heart was beating: *Nejmi – Nejmi!*

The moment he opened the gate, and saw her and Ruth in the court, he knew, from their faces, that they had learned the news. He ran to them, stammering he hardly knew what, and seized Ruth's hands.

"I've just heard!" he choked out. He looked full at Nejmi. "Nothing's ever made me so happy!"

Between smiling and crying, Ruth was saying, while she fondled his hand, "You're a good boy, Nicolo! Yes, twenty years is a long time, a long blessed time."

Nicolo glanced about. "Master Abel . . . where is he?"

"Come!" Nejmi whispered happily, and tiptoed toward the workshop, while he followed, with a delicious sense of new intimacy. At the threshold she stepped aside, finger on lips, and gave him an ecstatic little push, so that he might look within.

Sunlight flooded the room; files and pincers strewed the bench; the floor was a litter of fresh shavings; and, in the heart of the happy riot, bent over the unfinished astrolabe, sat Abel. Rapt and absorbed, blind and deaf to all but his enchanted plaything – Abel, the Boy! Yet, not wholly the Boy, as Nicolo recalled him on that first visit to the hill-top house, for these last months had taken an irrevocable toll of his eager spirit.

Nicolo turned to glance behind him. Ruth was crying

softly. Strictly speaking, his own eyes weren't dry! But in Nejmi's was a light like sunshine at the bottom of a deep, deep pool.

Her hand touched his arm to draw him back, and they tiptoed noiselessly away, behind Ruth, who was whispering, over her shoulder, that he must see the pear preserve she was making for Gama.

He was made to look into the kettle of ruby syrup and translucent slices of fruit, and then to sample a spoonful dipped out especially for him.

While he lingered, Nicolo wondered how he could manoeuvre a moment alone with Nejmi. At last, over Ruth's head, he caught the dark eyes – and held them. In an ecstasy, he heard her say she would go with him to the gate!

As they passed the workshop, they glanced through the doorway at Abel and Nicolo whispered, "If it hadn't been for you, that night, with the compass frame –"

She seized his arm. "Do you think he guessed? Ah, Nicolo," she rushed on, "it broke my heart to see those idle instruments that used to be so busy . . . darkness, instead of light and voices! It was as if someone –" she caught her breath, sharply – "someone that we love had died!"

"Nejmi – Nejmi!" he cried. "You're thinking of your – of what happened there in Aden! Ah, Nejmi!" . . . How could he keep from pouring out his heart?

"Why, Nicolo, I didn't mean to distress you with my troubles." Now she was the calmer of the two. "I don't often let myself think about all that. I mean to keep it locked up in my heart, only, sometimes, it bursts the lock!"

"Tell me, when those times come, Nejmi!" He drew

close to her. "When you feel the lock bursting, promise
you'll tell me."

"If I tell anyone, Nicolo!"

"Nejmi!" This, he decided, was the moment to speak
of his caravel's name. "Would you mind if – if I called my
ship *The Golden Star?*"

She looked at him with shy, startled eyes that turned,
even as he watched them, tender and radiant.

"The best of luck, Nicolo," she said, very low, "to *The
Golden Star!*"

Somehow he got out of the court, somehow reached the
foot of the long flight. It was his instinct to keep by himself,
jealous of letting any thought outside the incident with
Nejmi invade its precious secrecy. Over and again he lived
every detail of it: the word, the gesture with which it had
begun, had progressed, had ended.

Down the hill he wandered, past the Cathedral. In a
vague sort of way he noticed how softly the evening light
touched the massive walls. He looked back at the grim old
Castle, aflame with the sunset's fire! A sudden loneliness
swept over him. Oh, that Nejmi were here to enjoy with him
this beauty! He began to wonder what she would say to him
the next time. And so, dreaming and hoping, he ran into
Ferdinand as dusk was falling.

"You've heard about the reprieve?" the boy hailed
him. "Gama sent me up to Master Abel's with the first news
of it. Oh, Nicolo, his face, when I told him!"

"I know! I saw him at work on the astrolabe, but he
didn't see me – wasn't even conscious of anything but of
what he was doing."

"Speaking of that astrolabe, the date for the

Expedition's sailing has just been set! " Then, to Nicolo's demand for details, " Yes," Ferdinand declared, " Master Diaz says everything is ready, and Gama's just called the last conference with his captains and pilots. I saw them all coming out from it, and they looked solemn, I can tell you! " He was silent a moment. " Lord, but I wish I were going! "

" I suppose everything at the palace is upside down with excitement! "

" Oh, yes. No one can talk of anything but the Expedition. Even Manoel's wedding comes second to that! "

" How does Gama take it all? "

Ferdinand's face softened. " I used to think, Nicolo, that he was overbearing. I don't think so any longer. He stands as straight as ever, holds his head thrown back just the same, but – I don't know just how to say it – somehow there's a new look in his face: proud and humble at the same time! And you know, he says if anything should prevent his finding the Way, that he's not coming back! "

" I like him for that. But he'll find it – barring death! "

Ferdinand's eyes danced. " He used to play the gallant with the women," he ran on, " but now, when they hang around him, and gush over him, he sort of backs off, says he's something to attend to, and vanishes! I told him the only trouble he'd have in picking a wife was to know which one to pick! "

" Just about like your impudence! "

Ferdinand assumed an injured air. " That's what he said! And then, into the bargain, one of the old cats, who'd give her eye teeth to marry him, overheard me and reached out to slap me – only I dodged. And me going on eighteen! "

"Women have a way of slapping truths they don't like!" laughed Nicolo.

The boy's eyes sobered. "All except Nejmi," he quali-fied, in a tone that made Nicolo glance at him with a sudden pang. Was it possible that Ferdinand, too, had set his heart on her?

But already he was rattling on: "By the way, I heard something about you, today."

"About me?" Nicolo's voice was incredulous.

"Yes. Manoel was talking about a street row that someone had reported, and then he turned around to the Venetian ambassador, and began to twit him with a Vene-tian's making all the trouble."

"What did the ambassador say to that?" chuckled Nicolo.

"Why, that was the curious part of it. 'Yes, sir,' says he as cool as you please, 'but, also, *another* Venetian put a stop to it!' and he mentioned you. He seemed to know all about the row. He spoke of your business, too – threw out something about Venetians knowing how to build ships!"

Who could it be, Nicolo puzzled, when he had left Ferdinand, that had told the Venetian ambassador of his part in the brawl and the other particulars about him? Carefully he reviewed the incident. To be sure, there was that seaman with the thick accent, who'd asked him about his ship-build-ing, but certainly a fellow of that class wouldn't be on fa-miliar terms with anyone at Manoel's court. Wait, though! Hadn't he, according to his own account, given evidence that he knew of the Jewish reprieve, before it was made public? Where else could he have got that first information except from the palace?

Well, granting that it was he who had mentioned him to the ambassador, what harm? Still, Nicolo reflected, it was just as well not to be too free with a stranger, and uneasily he recalled the eyes that had seemed to watch him through their dropped lids while he talked of the Expedition.

And by San Marco! It was because of drinking with that chap that he'd forgotten about Pedro's tailor friend, and the cloak that was to have been, ostensibly, for Gama's honour – but really for Nejmi. . . . Ah, Ferdinand's eyes, his softened tone, when he had spoken of her!

CHAPTER 14

Vasco da Gama

LATE on the night before he was to sail, Gama slipped
away from insistent visitors and climbed the hill to
Abel. He found him and Diaz in the court.

"I've been telling Abel," said Diaz, "of my orders to

leave the Expedition at the Verde Islands and proceed in my own caravel to Mina."

"You don't know when you'll be back?" Abel asked.

"No. But I know the spot that will see me first when that time comes." Diaz' eyes clung to the square of light from the workshop. Abruptly he turned toward the gate. "Well, Abel! . . ."

"I'll go a step with you, Bartholomew."

Gama saw the two figures linger at the head of the stairs. Then one of them disappeared. When Abel returned, alone, the desolation in his voice didn't escape Gama.

"Bartholomew gone, you gone – what will the workshop do without you? Nevertheless –" he laughed forlornly –"let's go in there, Vasco!"

"Master Abel," Gama said, when they had sat down at the big table, "I want to tell you something that no one knows; no one, that is, except Diaz and my captains. From the Verde Islands I'm going to put straight out to sea, fetch a wide compass to the southeast, and then head about toward the Cape."

"So! You aren't going to follow the coast, as Diaz did?"

Gama smiled. "That's all everyone thinks I have to do: repeat Diaz! But that's not the reason for my own plan, just to do something different. The reason is that by going well out and then making for the Cape, I avoid foul weather off the Guinea coast. You see, Master Abel, I've been studying our navigation charts and talking with my pilots. You knew, by the way, that I'd been lucky enough to get hold of Diaz' old pilot, d'Alemquer?"

"Good! What better could you ask than one of Bartholomew's veterans?"

"I wish I could have got Scander, too; knowing the Indian coasts as he does, he'd have been invaluable to me. Strange, how stubborn he is about sticking to Lisbon."

"Well, after that Aden experience, can you blame him? But I'm going to keep him busy here, helping me on maps. Between us we should be able to get out something that will be really useful."

Absently, Gama assented. Suddenly, he leaned forward. "Master Abel, there's something I want you to know: once I've set sail to find the Way, no mortal shall turn me back; but if I fail to find it and the world beyond, I shall not return."

"I should expect that of you, Vasco," Abel gently replied. "Just that."

"I want you to know it from my own lips in case — in case of the unforeseen."

"I, too, have something to tell you, Vasco." From a cupboard Abel took the completed astrolabe and compass, and placed them on the table. "That's the first metal astrolabe this side of the Orient," he said, a little proudly. "And this compass is the best I can make — though my next will be better! But if —" his voice sank to a whisper — "if it ever helps you a fraction as much as it did me . . . Vasco, it steered my soul out of hell!"

Silently Gama took up the instrument, turned it this way and that, ran his finger tips along the clean, true lines and the satiny surfaces.

"Master Abel," he said, very low, "if ever, on the long ways ahead of me, my courage slips, I shall look at this compass until I stand firm!"

Next morning it was very early, when Vasco da Gama

waked; much too early for anyone to be about. He was glad, so that he might meet, alone and quiet, this sovereign day. There had been so much to think of, to work out; details, questions, decisions, people in endless procession always waiting for him, always besieging him.

An arrow of flame shot across his bed. He sat up, to see the sun coming in at the window. His Day! Would that his father and mother were here! Ah, well, who knew but from some far, golden window a kind God would let them look forth? The thought filled him with a quick humility, for, after all, it was only a freakish accident that this day's choice was himself. Diaz should have been the man. Instead, Diaz had sweated under the gruelling of the past months, so that another should reap full honours.

How unflinchingly the old veteran had stood by, handled the practical end of the preparations with a resource that experience had made superlative. How patiently he had hunted up his own men of the famous Cape Expedition – those of them that were still living. How rigorously he had weeded out the new enlistments, until he had assembled a crew to his liking. And who but Bartholomew Diaz would have insisted that, in addition to his own craft, every man of them must learn how to handle carpenters' tools, do his turn at the forge, and caulk a hull!

The sun was now blazing full into the room, a midsummer sun that climbed strongly, since it must do a long day's work. Gama flung back the bed covers, and stood on the floor. As the morning air struck his warm body, a boyish tingling ran through him: to go – now! Now, while the day and he were keen and young, to slip away from the final ceremonies, the crowds and streets and noise and heat, and run with the tide. But there! Already someone at the door.

Time to dress for Mass, for the procession. For convention's sake he must wear this gorgeous velvet cloak, but a sailor's coat and breeches were more fit! This one and that one at his elbow, while he snatched a mouthful of breakfast. . . . "If you see a good buy, when you get out there, Gama, don't forget me! " Messages from so and so to save a moment for a last, private word. Lord! As if every moment weren't already full to bursting!

Now the Cathedral. Every flagstone of the floor crowded. Every niche jammed. Armour and head dresses and perfume and spurs and velvet. Paulo, Nicolau Coelho and himself, in the place of honour, next to a curtain behind which sat Manoel. He must listen to the service – the Bishop of Lisbon, himself, was officiating – but somehow it was impossible to fix one's thoughts on anything, in this air thick with flaring tapers, and one's eyes dizzy with so much gold and scarlet. . . . How white Paulo looked in the shifting lights! He wasn't over strong, and if anything should happen to him, this favourite brother . . .

The Litany had begun! He must pay attention, so he wouldn't be responding out of turn.

Hear my prayer, O Lord . . .

How the sails would gleam, as the crews swayed on the halyards! It wouldn't take long to get under way in this breeze.

Incline our hearts, O God . . .

That meant not only Christians but the heathen in the strange, glamorous lands where he was going. He'd see to it that their hearts inclined! He'd make Christians of them willy-nilly. That first, of course, and then – spice!

Let us pray . . .

Profound stillness among the kneeling uniforms and the taffeta trains. The Bishop had put aside his prayer-book, and was giving the final blessing.

Hold thy servants in the hollow of Thy hand . . .

The hollow of Thy hand? Three tiny ships between a vastness of tumbling waves and skies that stretched into eternity!

Be thou unto them an help when they go forward . . .

Right! The only time one deserved help was when one was going forward.

An haven in shipwreck . . .

Shipwreck? Trust Bartholomew to see that each timber was sound, each keel as true as his own true heart!

Guide them, O God, to their desired haven . . .

Ah, yes, O God, Thou – and dear Abel's compass! Even now it and the astrolabe waited aboard the flagship – sent out, first thing after breakfast, by Ferdinand. All the ships were supplied with hour-glasses, and sounding plummets, and compasses, but Abel's compass and astrolabe would be shrined in his own cabin – with his crucifix above them.

A great rustling and stir, everybody standing. Was it all over? Manoel's voice behind the curtain, wishing them all the best of luck. Diaz should have been there, getting those good wishes! Why in the world had Manoel chosen him and not Diaz?

Outdoors. A hot blue sky. Bells ringing and trumpets blaring. An endless procession, and at its head himself, on horseback. Faces lined along flag-hung streets and squares, peering over balconies, and from roofs. Well, it was a moving sight, and a solemn. Yes, solemn. For all this wild outburst was the people's way of saying, "Gama, we're for you. God bless you, Gama! "

Someone hailing him? Young Conti, waving his cap like mad! And what was that he was shouting? "Captain-Major! Captain-Major! " By heaven, the first time he'd been called that in public – gave one an odd feeling! Fine spirit that lad had, and a long head; not afraid to take a chance, as you could see by his leaving Venice for Lisbon. And there beside him, glum as a thunder cloud – Scander! Don't believe in going after the spice trade, eh? Every hatchful would be paid for in blood was what he'd said. Oh well, old croaker, just you wait till Portugal brings in the Oriental wealth. Then you'll change your tune! Still, it was strange how those words stuck in one's memory: spice . . . blood!

Now, going around this corner, one could look back along the line. There was Manoel, bristling with courtiers. There came Paulo and Coelho. Then the ships' officers and pilots and priests. Next, two and two, the ships' crews, stepping out brisk and fit, as if for a day's outing. For some of them, poor devils, it would be a jaunt into eternity! And there, clanking along in their chains, were the six jail-birds he'd begged of Manoel. They'd save risking the trained men for dangerous errands and if the natives got them – why, they were sentenced to hang, anyhow! How Manoel had laughed when he'd asked for them – said it was the most original scheme he'd ever heard.

The palace! . . . Hard not to show one's impatience to be off. Hard to go through with the feasting and the dancing, when all you could think of was those caravels straining at their anchors. Particularly hard to look pleasant with everyone pressing about you, to pour out compliments about your

'heroism.' And the women, with their prattle and their gush!
. . . Ah, Manoel beckoning! Come along Paulo, Coelho, and
all of you officers. Kneel, and kiss your King's hand, and
say your farewells.

Now, only to mount and ride to the harbour. And look!
. . . Who but Ferdinand holding the horse ready! Good to
have this last glimpse of the lad. How he stood out from the
other pages! Young colt that he was, with those big eyes that
burned their way right into your heart, and his impudence,
and his everlasting kicking at the harness of convention!
But, by heaven, he'd do something, one of these days,
that would make folks sit up. Eyes like that didn't often
happen.

Again those cheering throngs. God grant he should fulfill their hopes. Ah, at last the harbour – bursting at you like
a garden of wind-sown, wind-blown flowers! Flags . . . flags,
crimson and gold and scarlet and blue. Craft jammed in together thicker than crows in a wheat field. Lord! Where had
they all come from? And all in honour of those three caravels
that rode so soberly opposite the great sea-wall! The *San
Gabriel*, the *San Rafael*, the *Berrio*. The ships that King
John had named. The ships that Bartholomew Diaz had built.

After all the long readying, how simple to dismount, to
row out a little way, to stand on the deck of the *San Gabriel*.
His own vessel! At this poop would hang the huge official
lantern of the flagship. . . . Hear the people cheer! Manoel
himself had never got anything like this.

Now Paulo was on the *San Rafael*, and Coelho on the
Berrio. Lucky they were to have Diaz with them as far as the
Verde Islands. Nunez was just boarding the store ship. He
wasn't reaping as much applause as the other captains, be-

cause the store ship was to go only part way, but it took character to do those commonplace things.

There went the sails, fair and full as a gull's breast, each with its great, red Cross. And look! There, at the crow's nest – like heart's blood, splashed against Lisbon's sky – the scarlet flag of the Captain-Major!

By heaven, that salute! Almost forgotten it, thinking about the flag. Now let them have it: once . . . twice . . . and again! And once . . . twice . . . and again, the cannon on the quay are answering.

Now the hawsers are coming in. D'Alemquer is bringing the *San Gabriel* about. He'd have to beat to windward all the way down river with this wind rising. Might make the bar impassable, so they'd have to anchor at Belem. Everybody waving, cheering, laughing, crying . . . forms and faces on shore beginning to blur . . . fluttering handkerchiefs, distant good-byes.

One look back, before a turn in the river should shut off Lisbon. Ah, blue hills and climbing houses! Up yonder, in one of those houses, Abel was standing at the windows. He had said they would see it all from the workshop; that they didn't like to bring Nejmi down town. Ruth would be on one side of him; on the other, Nejmi, with her shining eyes. Star of the Way, old Abraham had called her. Well, however that should turn out, it was her evidence that had started Manoel up, evidence that had come, you might say, from the very lips of Covilham. And presently they would know, one way or the other. The main thing was to keep straight ahead – and overboard with any who talked of turning back, if it took every man jack of the crew. So God on his great white throne be witness!

Spice and the Devil's Cave

There went the last of Lisbon, sliced off clean by that turn in the river – Lisbon a-sparkle in the westering sun like a jewelled crest! The streets would be quieting down now, people talking it all over at home, some women crying – the ones he'd seen kissing his men on the quay. Everyone who could would be planning to come down to Belem for the final departure, but that couldn't be till this wind had died down; another day or two, likely.

But however long they were delayed, one thing was certain: their last night ashore would be passed in the rough little chapel of Belem which the Great Navigator had built, where men of the sea might pray for favourable winds and seas. Ah, he had known, this strange and solitary Henry, that the more alone a man was in his supreme moment, the more clearly would he hear what God whispered in his ear. . . . A strange thing, Life, giving the praise only to the consummation. For instance, he, Gama, getting all the credit for something that had started before he was born: a stupendous vision of the Great Navigator which had become the precious trust of his intrepid disciples. Diaz, daring the sea, and Covilham the land, had all but given that vision a body, had all but achieved what Henry had dreamed. Then had come Nejmi . . . that extraordinary night . . . her breath-taking story told in the language of a child. And now, the Expedition, and himself its Captain-Major!

*　　　*　　　*

M o r n i n g. Aboard the ships at Belem. Everything ready, after these three days of waiting for the wind to moderate. But it had been time put to good use. The crews had been reviewed, their names listed, payrolls made out of wages due on their return. And through it all Manoel had remained at Belem. A fine thing, that, for the men.

Manoel had spent the last night's vigil with them, too, when they had knelt the still hours through, under the flickering altar candles, each seeking according to his own need. For himself, Gama, there was but one prayer. There never had been but that one – from the hour that Manoel had said, "I want you to go, Vasco" – just man-courage to go forward in spite of entreaties to turn back, in spite of mutiny itself. . . .

Manoel! Manoel, stepping from the royal barge aboard the *San Gabriel;* walking with him between lines of men drawn up at attention; giving them all his God-speed; addressing him as the Captain-Major. (Hard to think of himself by that title!) A last whisper: "Vasco, you'll do this thing, I know you will! " Worth all the titlès in the world, Manoel's lips at your ear, like that. Put the heart into you, that " I know you will! " So, from ship to ship, reviewing the crews, giving each captain his royal blessing.

Now they were breaking out the Royal Standard at the *San Gabriel's* foremast. Please God it should carry the dominion of Portugal to the uttermost ends of the earth!

At last, in midstream. Crowds lining the shore, sobbing, praying. Hark! The priests chanting: *Kyrie eleison.* And the people responding: *Christie eleison.* The priests again: *Be with us that we may come to our home again in peace, in health, and gladness.* . . . Well, God, in his mercy, grant that the home-coming would be that. But, whatever might happen, the will to go forward!

Running, now, under full sail. Everything set, men at their posts, sails bellying in the wind. Astern, the other ships pounding a white wake to the *San Gabriel's* lead. On the poop of the *San Rafael,* a steadfast figure – Paulo. There was a heart that would never fail one, never ask to put back! Coelho and Nunez, too, fine captains as one could wish. D'Alemquer at the helm might almost be playing with it, so easily it swings in his deft brown hands.

A white swirl ahead. The bar! Feel the ship responding to d'Alemquer as he luffs her a little to meet the swell . . . as he eases her on. How confidently she leads the way! How confidently the other vessels follow! . . . Past shoals, through treacherous cross currents, and so, out into mid-channel. . . .

Over, at last! Over the bar. . . . Lisbon behind. . . . O God of battle and of sea, before Thee do I swear never to turn back one span of the way!

CHAPTER 15

Rumours

S CANDER, bent over the table, meditated a long minute
before he took a ruler, and carefully laid it on the unfinished map. Nicolo covertly watched the faces – Abel's,
Ruth's, Nejmi's – waiting for his instructions as for a judge's

sentence. That rapt attention was, of course, to be expected from Abel, but from Ruth! . . . A different Ruth from the one whose chief concern in the workshop used to be the "clutter" on floor and table. Had it been those days of death and threatened exile that had so changed her? Changed her into this person who brought her work to sit beside Abel – to brood over him with tender eyes when he wasn't looking? And Nejmi who once had shunned the mention of maps . . . Her head was as close to the drawing as Abel's!

"There! " Scander finished his measuring, and with the ruler beat a gentle tattoo on the table edge. "That's as near right as I can reckon. Safe to ink it in now."

Abel's waiting quill was promptly dipped into ink, and then applied to a pencilled outline. Nejmi's eyes travelled with the quill point; Ruth put down her sewing, and watched until it came to rest.

Abel straightened up, and surveyed his work with satisfaction. "How Bartholomew would like to watch this map grow! " he mused aloud.

"What are you making now, sir? " Nicolo drew up closer.

"The Spice Islands," Scander replied, as Abel was already engrossed in the next outline. "Near as I can remember them, that is."

"We're going to draw little trees on them to show that the spices grow there," Nejmi added.

"Not only that, but we'll write the names of the important products where Scander says they're shipped. It will be of the greatest help to merchants." Abel spoke without raising his eyes from his work, in the absent, jerky tone of one trying to keep his mind on two things at once.

"Like this. See! " Ruth dropped her sewing and indicated a port. " That'll be marked ' Slaves and Ivory '! " she importantly announced.

" No, not them from there, ma'am," Scander corrected with an amused smile. " From *here!* " He pointed to the East African coast: " Mombassa and Melinde."

" It's a long way to the Spice Islands," Nicolo observed, as he watched Abel's quill, " much longer than we'd thought."

" But," Scander broke in, " see how cheap you're going to get your spices, bringing 'em all the way by water. Why, I've seen cargoes re-shipped and re-caravaned as many as five times between Aden and the Mediterranean, and a fat toll piled on to the price every shift! " As he glanced at the map, an idea seemed suddenly to strike him. He dropped the ruler and sat back, staring before him. " I never thought before what the route 'round the Devil's Cave would do to the Red Sea! "

" I shouldn't wonder," Abel mildly suggested, " if the Soldan of Egypt had something to say on the subject."

Scander's eyes were faintly amused. " Well, seeing as he depends on those tolls for a living! . . . I can't picture it," he went on reminiscently. " That sea all a-boil with craft bursting their seams with stuff from everywhere – dead as a pond! "

Involuntarily Nicolo thought of Venice – of the Mediterranean. They, too!

Nejmi's voice broke in on him. She had straightened up from watching Abel, and in her eyes was the horror that came even now when she was reminded of the past. " Will Aden be ' dead,' too, Scander? "

He nodded, his eyes soft, as always, when he looked at

her. "I expect, child, we'd hardly know it in a few years. As far as I can see," he meditated aloud, "the whole world's going to be made over! "

"And all," Abel threw over his shoulder, "all, for a fragile thing of wood and canvas that is daring the unknown! "

"It's the same to me who gets the blasted spices," Scander observed.

"What? " protested Nicolo. "You wouldn't care, for instance, if Gama failed, and some other country stepped in on the spice trade ahead of Portugal? "

Scander took time to spit. "No, I wouldn't care, knowing it's as sure as I sit here that whoever gets the spice is going to settle for it in blood. But Master Gama's failing – that's something else. I'd give a year of my life to see him walk in here, this minute, and tell us he'd found everything as we " – he jerked his head toward Nejmi – " as we said 'twas! "

"You will see him! " she declared, with that look in her eyes as of sunlight in a deep, deep pool. "Some day you'll watch him sail up the river! "

Ferdinand's head suddenly appeared in the doorway. "Watch whom? "

"Where did you come from, so early? " Ruth asked him, as he stepped into the room and nodded to everyone.

"Oh, the King thought it was too warm to drive out, so I'm off duty for a while." He stood for a minute near the open door, and mopped his forehead.

"Summer's here, full force," he declared. He turned to Nejmi. "Who was that you were saying would 'sail up the river'? "

She was bending over the map, and hardly looked up to answer him: "Master Gama."

"I thought so! Do you know," he went on half talking to himself, "as I came up here I was thinking about the day he went away. My, but it seems a long time! People have begun to talk, too, about it's being too long – going on two years."

"Come see how this map's gone ahead since you were here," Abel broke in with apparent irrelevance. But when he had pointed out the freshly inked outlines, he quietly observed, "He could hardly have taken less than a long time to go as far as that, could he?"

"Still, sir, there's no denying it's being whispered around that Gama said he shouldn't return, if he didn't find the way to India."

"Yes," Nicolo agreed, "a man was complaining to me, today, that business hadn't come up to people's expectations, when Gama first went away. This chap had bought up land for warehouses, but now he didn't know whether or not to build."

Abel laid down his quill, and sat back in his chair, and in his face was a look of bitter reminiscence. "They've forgotten the time they were climbing over each other to get information about the Expedition, so they could make something out of it! I remember someone's coming to my office about that very matter of new warehouses."

He broke off, and there was a conscious silence in the room, for this was one of Abel's rare references to the office and the business he had given up in those black and terrible days of Manoel's decree against his Jewish subjects.

"That's just it!" Ferdinand contemptuously burst out.

"All that they thought of was the trade Portugal was going to get from Gama's finding the Way, instead of the glory
of just *finding* it!"

"I suppose," Nicolo shot back, with some heat—for
somehow, he felt that Ferdinand was covertly thrusting at
him—"that you'd be satisfied to give Portugal the glory, and
Spain the trade."

"You're both right," laughed Abel. "Ferdinand hates
to see adventure made into business—and Nicolo asks what
good is it unless it is?"

"Well, what is there to exploration," Nicolo insisted,
"if it's not put to use? You heard what Scander said about
the Red Sea when the Cape route gets started. Those who
don't follow the current are left in the backwash. If Venice
doesn't take care," he added, "that's what she'll come to."

Ferdinand looked up, as if to reply, when Scander play-
fully nudged him. "The trouble with you, youngster, is that
all you can think of is to go to sea and find something!"

"And just as soon as I'm through my tour of duty,"
Ferdinand retorted, "you'll see me go!" His eyes returned
to Nicolo. "Speaking of Venice," he said, "Manoel and
your ambassador are having a good deal to say to each other
these days. It seems that Venice wants to know if we're going
to keep a rigid monopoly on the Oriental trade—just in
case Gama finds the passage to India!"

"What?" Nicolo exclaimed. "I thought Venice scouted
the idea of the Cape route!"

"Then some of them must have changed their minds.
And that's not all, either," Ferdinand chuckled. "I even
heard that if we don't let Venice keep her monopolies in the
East, she'll get Egypt to make trouble for us!"

A minute of dumbfounded silence followed this amazing announcement. "It may be just gossip," Ferdinand added.

"Gossip or truth," Abel said at last, "it's astounding. Does Manoel appear to be disturbed?"

"Well, he isn't in as high spirits as when Gama went away, especially since people have begun shaking their heads over Gama's long absence. What with these rumours from Venice, and England's having sent Cabot on two voyages, and Columbus back from his third voyage – and yet never a word from Gama . . ."

"Bah!" snorted Scander. "What'd Cabot have to show for his two trips? A snare or two, and some fish-net needles that a civilized Arab'd laugh at. If 'twas any part of the Orient that he struck, 'twas the part next to nowhere! Anyway, John Cabot's dead, this half year; out of the way for good. And Columbus . . . a few pearls! Why, talk about pearls, I'll lay you those things he's showing around Granada would look like pebbles 'side of what I've seen in the bazaars."

"I suppose," Ruth ventured, "that the Queen's dying so soon after they were married has something to do with Manoel's low spirits."

Ferdinand grinned. "Not so you'd notice it! Already he has his eye on her sister." His face changed, and he thoughtfully observed, "But there's no doubt that he misses talking to Gama and Master Diaz; and I've even heard him say –" he stole a look at Abel – "that he wishes Master Abraham were here to consult the stars about what's happening to Gama."

"Humph!" A dull red spread over Abel's face, and it

was several moments before he said, "It's precisely my opinion of Manoel that he'd be willing to use poor old Abraham after he'd done him all the harm he could."

"Is he – poor? " Nejmi asked, and Nicolo saw that her eyes were very tender.

"Well, you know he could take nothing with him," Abel reminded her, "not even money. But he's happy enough, I dare say, there in Tunis, and at least he's doing what he likes best: writing the history and genealogies of our people."

Ferdinand cleared his throat, and fidgeted in his chair, his eyes watching Abel. "Would you," he at last blurted out, "would you, sir, come to Manoel, suppose he asked you? "

Nicolo saw Ruth drop her sewing with an exclamation, and Nejmi glance wonderingly from Ferdinand to Abel. Even Scander was stirred to sit up with new interest.

"I? " Abel's brows were scornfully raised. "I go to Manoel? " Suddenly, he gave Ferdinand a shrewd look. "What made you ask? "

Ferdinand laughed a little sheepishly. "Fact is, sir, I've heard Manoel hint that he meant to get you to read the stars for Gama's fate! "

"H'm! " was all that Abel had to offer to this confession, and then, as if indifferent to the incident, he asked Scander a question which brought their heads close together over the table.

Ferdinand moved up to watch them, and Ruth went on with her sewing. Nejmi had left her place by Abel and, with her back to the room, was leaning out of a window.

From his seat, near the door, Nicolo studied her. Soft,

dark braids against the pale gold of her dress. . . . Where did Ruth find those clinging, foreign-looking stuffs that she made into Nejmi's dresses? Invariably of some shade of gold, and unmistakably chosen for the delicate, ivory face. By the droop of her head he knew the look in her eyes: the shadow of sadness that hinted the reality – the remnant of the old fear.

He was debating joining her, there by the windows, when he saw her slip noiselessly into the next room and, presently, appear in the court. Apparently, no one but himself had noticed her go. He watched her as she wandered from flower-bed to flower-bed, gathered a spray of this or that, fastened a straggling runner, stripped off a faded bloom.

It was characteristic of her, he reflected, that she never stayed long, even in their intimate group. Spoken to, she would answer smilingly, but, as it were, from afar. Sometimes she volunteered a comment, but, again, from afar. The same delicate aloofness, the same exquisite remoteness, symbolic of her name. Was it intentional, this elusiveness, or instinctive, inherited? Hadn't Scander once said something about the reserve of Arab girls? Now and again, Nicolo recalled, she had let him come near, but the next time she was sure to offset the seeming intimacy. If he should go to her now, moving about in the flowery fragrance . . .

Someone brushed past him into the court – Ferdinand! . . . Now he was sitting beside Nejmi under the old fig tree. He, too, had seen her leave the room, but had acted while he, Nicolo, had deliberated! He felt his cheeks burn in fury at himself, at Ferdinand. He suddenly realized that he was staring at them, and turned his head. He mustn't appear to watch them, but from where he sat in the doorway, he could plainly hear them.

Abel's and Scander's talk resolved itself into monotone, occasionally broken by Ruth's higher key. He became conscious that Abel was raising his voice, as if he were repeating something.

" What's that, sir? " Nicolo hastily asked.

" Why, I was calling Venice pretty high-handed, demanding to know what Manoel proposed to do about the Indian trade. What do you think? "

" Oh, she's had her way in trade so long that she's a good deal like a spoiled child. I fancy it won't take Gama long to give her an answer. But that other business that Ferdinand mentioned, of threatening to get Egypt's help against Portugal – "

Abel nodded. " Ugly."

" Well," Ruth comfortably contributed, " I expect those that live in palaces relish a bit of gossip the same as common folks. Probably that's all it is: gossip."

" I don't know, ma'am," Scander objected. " 'Twouldn't be so out of the way for Egypt to send forces down the Red Sea, and waylay our fleets off India. And in that case – " he paused to rub his chin between thumb and finger – " you'd find I was right about the price I've always told you you'd pay for spice! "

" I hadn't thought of Egypt's attacking us from that end," Abel ruminated, " but I can see it's feasible; far fetched, though. I should hardly worry. By the way, Nicolo, do these things that people are hinting about Gama's long absence affect your business? "

Nicolo pulled himself together and replied, "Not a bit, sir."

He had just overheard Ferdinand's eager young voice – "Oh, Nejmi, why couldn't I have gone with him?" Speaking of Gama, he had thought, and had been listening for more, when Abel had broken in.

"Rodriguez was saying, a day or so ago," Nicolo went on, "that *The Golden Star* never lacks for full hatches. But he agrees with me: no more new ships till we're sure of the Devil's Cave!"

"I won't be sorry when that time comes," yawned Scander. "These maps are well enough " – with an apologetic glance at Abel – "but give me oakum and a mallet that I can bang all day!" He stripped a tattooed arm and vigorously flexed it.

Abel rolled up the map, and carefully fitted it into a brass tube. "Arthur Rodriguez," he said, as he stood it on a shelf of others like it, "always had the name of being dependable. How do you find he wears, Nicolo?"

"Better all the time, sir! In the year we've been partners his judgment has always proved sound. So far, we've kept busy with colonial trade, but of course I'm hoping to spread out into spice. My funds, with the help of your investment, will more than finance building any extra ships we need."

It was characteristic of Abel, Nicolo reflected, that he never referred to the capital he had entrusted to him when he had closed out his banking interests. Characteristic, too, that he had no comment whenever Nicolo reported its increase. Money never had meant much to Abel Zakuto. And as for active business, he, like those of his race here, was done with it. But at least, Nicolo thankfully reflected, Abel would never now leave Lisbon, rooted as he was, in this beloved house, with Ruth and Nejmi.

Her voice! . . . The impulse to turn his head almost conquered him. But he must keep his eyes away from the court – listen, with the appearance of not listening.

"Why do you want to go, Ferdinand?" she was saying. "To bring back gold . . . spice?"

For a moment there was silence. Then, a low, rapid outburst: "I hate that, Nejmi! I know trade must be, but it just isn't in me. To seek the unknown, for its sake only, seems so clean and sweet!"

Something clutched at Nicolo's heart. This talk against trade, his chosen calling! Did she, too, "hate" it?

Ferdinand's voice, low, passionate: "Can you keep a secret, Nejmi? Can you? . . . Some day I'm going to find where Sunset takes Dawn in his arms, and Day is born of their flaming kiss! I'm going to find where East and West meet . . . where there is no East and no West! Do you understand, Nejmi?"

In spite of himself, Nicolo turned his head. Ferdinand's eyes had the look of inward fire as on that first day, at The Green Window – glowing, smouldering. Ah, under this talk – this strange talk – of East and West, he was pouring out his heart to her! Yet, curiously, he seemed not to see her, but something beyond her: something hidden from physical sight, like a distant, beckoning vision – a radiant, solemn vision. And Nejmi was leaning toward him with the strangest smile of – of frightened happiness!

He started guiltily – Ruth was speaking, looking up from her work. Had she seen him watching those two outside? But she was only saying that the brass map-containers would soon need polishing.

Nicolo caught at the cue to cover his silence, and asked Abel where he got them.

"Scander attends to that," Abel replied. "He knows someone in the locksmith business."

Scander laughed, a little sheepishly. "Seems odd that one who's followed the sea all his days can settle down to land jobs!"

"Don't you think you'll ever change your mind," Nicolo pressed him, "and go as pilot to one of our fleets?"

"Not me!" The tanned face seemed to settle into its wrinkles. "I'm like a dog that's come back to his old kennel, and I reckon – " he chuckled, as if amused with the figure, – "I reckon I'll play watch dog the rest of my days!"

For a moment Nicolo fancied that Scander's gaze sought the court. Did he mean "play watch dog" to Nejmi? Yet why should she need to be guarded, surrounded as she was by the adoration of them all?

His own gaze followed Scander's. Ferdinand, he perceived, had gone, and Nejmi was kneeling by a bed of thyme, loosening the earth. On the impulse he got up, and went into the court. No more dallying, no more inward debate.

"I sometimes think," he said, going straight up to her, "that you'd rather not talk to me – alone."

Silent, startled, she looked at him. "What would you like to talk about?"

He could have ground his teeth at her adroit but complete parry. "That isn't my point, and – " plunging boldly – "you know it!" . . . How would she meet that?

But she only loosened more earth and heaped it around the roots, and at last it came over Nicolo that she was not going to answer him, that she was making a fool of him – or had he made one of himself? He angrily cast about for a pretext to argue with her.

" Is it that – that money I paid for the sugar – debt, you called it – that makes you keep at a distance? "

She raised her eyes to his. "It did make me feel uncomfortable, at first," she admitted, "but not any longer. Besides – " she flushed brilliantly – " I'm going to pay back that debt! "

"Don't! " he managed to say. " Don't talk that way, Nejmi! "

She continued to look at him, then bent again to her work. "You want me to pay you! " she breathed, hardly above a whisper.

He started back as at a blow – the more cruel that, for a fleeting instant, he could have sworn that laughter had lurked in her eyes.

In a daze he heard Scander at his elbow: " Going along, now, sir? I'll walk with you to the turn of the street below."

Mechanically, Nicolo murmured good-bye to Abel and Ruth standing together in the workshop door, and then he and Scander started down the long stairway. Through the chaos of his brain he became aware of Scander's voice insistently dwelling on a word, a familiar word: *Venice.*

" A bad business," he was saying, " that Ferdinand was telling us about Venice."

A vague recollection stirred Nicolo's memory. What was it Ferdinand had said? In a flash it came to him:

Venice . . . the Oriental trade . . . and that gossip about Egypt.

Ah, but those other things that Ferdinand had said: "Where Sunset takes Dawn in his arms . . . their flaming kiss . . ."

There was no forgetting those things!

CHAPTER 16

Abel Visits the Palace

In his long, black cloak and his conical, narrow-brimmed hat, Abel stood in a corner of the small room that Manoel used for informal audiences. He had expected to see Ferdinand, but Ferdinand was nowhere about, and another page had shown him where to wait until the King should be ready to see him.

He had been a little startled to find himself at once in Manoel's presence, though Manoel hadn't appeared to pay any heed when he entered. In fact, all that did seem to concern Manoel was keeping cool, and getting rid, as fast as he could, of the courtiers and pages who came and went around him. Half-dressed in a thin, silk lounging robe, he sat by an open window and spasmodically fanned himself with his handkerchief, for these days it was hot even by mid-morning.

Abel watched with amusement the dextrous way he managed to greet each visitor and, almost in the same breath, to wave him on. No one was encouraged to linger. Once, a good-looking young fellow in uniform, perhaps one of the aides, hurried in and whispered something. Abel saw Manoel frown, and, for a minute or two, one hand nervously clenched and unclenched. Then, he suddenly glanced up and, as it seemed to Abel, directly at him – or had he only imagined it? Manoel then turned to the young man, merely nodded, and went on fanning himself, while his visitors continued to file past.

Abel wondered when his own turn would come. As a matter of fact, his standing here so patiently, indeed his being here at all, struck him as grimly humorous, for when Ferdinand had hinted at Manoel's sending for him, he'd virtually said he wouldn't go. Then, as he had pondered the matter, something decided him to go – something that had troubled him for a long time: why did his people delay their going, postpone the exodus that finally they must face? How could they be roused from the apathy into which they'd sunk to see that anything was better than staying on, dishonoured and outcasts, where once they'd been free citizens? For Nejmi, and Nejmi only, he and Ruth had stayed, but now . . . Suppose, Abel had meditated, suppose, all unconsciously, Manoel could be manoeuvred into some measure that would so rouse the Jewish spirit, that . . . Yes! if he were summoned to the palace, he'd go!

He studied the figure by the window. It was hardly material to be " manoeuvred " into anything! Under the thin robe the lean, sinewy body was easily visible. Well, there was nothing in the way of physical toughening it hadn't gone through, and if the man within were as hard and unyielding as the man without . . . Almost ludicrous, the lanky arms were, in those flowing, feminine sleeves; the lanky arms whose fingers, it was Manoel's boast, could more than touch his knees when he stood upright – and that people said were a sign of his grasping nature! His face was as young as his less than thirty years, if one judged by the texture of the smooth, dark skin and the carefully parted hair and the crisp, short beard. But the expression in the odd, greenish eyes was that of a man far older. A man who was used to winning his game, and expected no opposition while he won it. One who expected to move his pawns without interference.

The procession of visitors was now dwindling. Abel saw the greenish eyes fix on a page, and a hardly perceptible lift of the brows. At once the boy came and whispered, " The King will see you now."

Deliberately Manoel turned from the last lingerers, who seemed to understand their dismissal, and forthwith left the room.

∾∾ *Abel Visits the Palace* ∾∾

" Close the door after you," he said to the page. " When I wish you, I'll rap."

He surveyed Abel attentively, then he motioned toward a chair. " Make yourself comfortable, Master Zakuto," he graciously told him. " I'm right, am I? " he added. " You're Abel Zakuto, kinsman of Abraham? "

Without changing his position, Abel nodded. " I've stood since I came in," he said, pointedly. " I'll remain standing. Yes, I'm Abel Zakuto."

For a moment this answer seemed to disconcert Manoel, then, " Well – please yourself! " he laughed.

He turned toward the open window, and absently gazed into the gardens beyond, and again Abel observed that nervous clenching and unclenching of one hand, while the other, holding the handkerchief, lay idle. A bumble bee flew in and buzzed about Manoel's head, but he took no notice of it.

" I sent for you, Master Zakuto," he said, facing back to the room, " because I understand that you, like your kinsman, Master Abraham, are skilled in the science of the stars."

He paused, as if for Abel to reply, but as Abel appeared to have no such intention, Manoel went on, while he rapidly fanned himself.

" You know, of course, that the people are beginning to doubt Senhor Gama's return. It's bad for the country, such a state of mind."

This time his eyes openly sought a response, but still Abel continued impassive.

" The worst of it is," – Manoel confidentially lowered his voice – " they're openly mentioning in certain foreign countries our fears for Gama."

∾∾ 183 ∾∾

"Aha!" thought Abel, recalling Ferdinand's talk of the other day, "I wonder if that means Venice."

"Now," Manoel said, "if we could give out a statement that the stars are favourable to his return – as they were to his going. . . . You see why I sent for you, Master Zakuto!"

The stars indeed! Inwardly Abel chuckled, as a certain night in the workshop, with Nejmi surrounded by an awe-struck group, flashed across his memory.

Aloud, he said, "My only business with the stars, Your Highness, is to learn from them a little navigation."

There was an impatient gesture, and the handkerchief dropped to the King's lap. "Surely you understand them as well as Master Abraham did?"

"Beyond a few matters of celestial degrees and computations, no."

Manoel thoughtfully regarded Abel, then, once more, his eyes sought the open window, and Abel saw that same perplexed frown as when the good-looking young aide had whispered a message. The room was very still, but the jessamine vine at the casement swayed in the warm breeze. A restless hand clenched and unclenched.

"Master Zakuto, I spoke of the rumour, in certain quarters, that we've given up Senhor Gama."

The King, Abel perceived, was choosing his words so as not to disclose too much.

"Unless we can give that rumour the lie, it may cause us trouble. In fact – " bringing a fist down on the chair arm – " it *is* causing us serious trouble. We must stop it. Suppose, Master Zakuto," his tone almost entreated, "I should make it worth your while to say Gama would return?"

Abel's face flashed. "As you made it 'worth while' for Abraham?" For a breathless instant he paused, almost expecting to be struck down for his temerity. But having gone this far, let him go all the way: "As you made it 'worth while' for the race who've built the prosperity of Portugal?"

Manoel's eyes dropped. "That measure was – was most unfortunate – most regrettable," he unexpectedly conceded, "but sometimes the State demands the sacrifice of the individual. If, for the good of the country, you could see your way clear . . ."

Abel studied, with a little less hostility, the tense figure opposite him. Did Manoel really feel sorrow at what he'd done, really "regret" it? Certainly his patience this morning had been past belief – no sovereign had ever borne as much from a belligerent subject! And after all, he was the sovereign. Ah, but the bleeding hearts and the broken lives that he had been willing to pay for his Spanish wife – and Abel hardened his heart.

"Why should 'the good of the country' concern me, now, Your Majesty?" he coldly asked. Dear Portugal, forgive him that!

The greenish eyes glinted unpleasantly. "If that's your feeling, I'd best clear the country of all you Jews – " he snapped his fingers – "like that!"

Inwardly Abel smiled. He was doing well! But he must do better, prick deeper. He feigned indifference. "That's within your power," he quietly replied. " But, Your Majesty, you'll find that Portugal will need her Jews more than they will ever need her!"

"By Saint Vincent!" Manoel choked out from deep down in his throat, and Abel could see that the fingers gripping the chair were twitching. Unconsciously he braced himself, for the fury in those green eyes brought to mind something that struck and clawed.

Suddenly, the fury faded, the fingers relaxed. Again Manoel lolled carelessly in his chair, and again began his lazy fanning.

"Then, perhaps, Master Zakuto," he said, maliciously, "I'll keep that valuable race of yours with me – forbid any of you to go! " He reached out and rapped on the door, and as the page outside opened it, "Show this person out," he said, without again glancing toward Abel.

His mind considerably bewildered, Abel walked through one corridor, and into another. Uniformed figures hurried past, but he was too busy with his thoughts to notice them. Where was this thing that he had started going to end? And why had Manoel let him go free? It was the first time, Abel was willing to wager, that young man had listened to such plain talk, and on the whole he'd not done so badly with his insulted dignity. But if he could know that, for once, he'd danced the puppet while a hand other than his pulled the strings! Now, if only he would carry out his threat and tell his Jewish subjects not to do what they had the right to do! . . . But even as Abel exulted within himself, he groaned: what had he, Abel Zakuto, brought on his people?

Ahead of him he saw the exit, and a sudden hankering seized him for the streets beyond it, the narrow twisting streets, the clatter of donkey hoofs, the cries of the vendors, the smell of fruit and vegetables in the hot sun.

From a side-entrance, two young men cut across his path, and sauntered along in front of him. One of them Abel recognized as the chap who had brought the message that made Manoel frown and clench his fingers in that nervous gesture.

"We've never stayed in town so late as we have this season," the other was complaining.

"Another day or so will see us in Cintra," rejoined the one whom Abel had recognized, and he looked as if he knew. "It's this Venetian business that's kept us broiling down here."

Could he mean the Venetian matter Ferdinand was telling of the other day? A murmur of voices followed, and scattered phrases floated unmeaningly back: "final audience this afternoon . . . their ambassador . . ."

He quickened his pace, intending to pass the two, when an impatient outburst from one of them made him draw back: "The insolence of those Venetians – wanting to know our terms in the Orient!"

Abel pricked up his ears. Still on the same subject? He took a stride nearer.

"I fancy Manoel will make short work, this afternoon, of telling them how he stands!" he heard the young aide exclaim.

The disjointed phrases that had drifted back to him now began to fit together: "final audience . . . their ambassador . . ." So that was what Manoel had on his hands, this afternoon! No wonder he'd looked disturbed. And was that why – could it possibly be why – he had swallowed his pride, had endured such plain speech? Was that why he had hoped to get assurance of Gama's return, so he could use it in his diplomatic game?

The other laughed, then quickly sobered. "The more credit to him, too, for down in his heart, like the rest of us, he's given Gama up – though he still keeps a brave front! "

Still chatting, the two turned off toward the gardens, and Abel went on to the exit and through to the street, pondering what he had just heard. If only these doubters could once hear Nejmi say, " You'll watch him sail up the river," once see the shining faith in her eyes! But Venice! Incredible how Venice had changed her skeptical front while Gama was gone!

He stopped in the shadow of a doorway, and threw back his cloak to feel the breeze. Then, with a pang, he realized that across the street was his old place of business. His gaze lingered on the familiar walls. At that door he used to go in. Around on that side was his own private room. He smiled as he recollected how impatient he used to be to get home early to the workshop. His eyes wandered on. That next building was where the Abrabanels had carried on the largest export business in Lisbon. What wouldn't they have done with the Oriental trade that Gama would surely start! Ah well, what Lisbon had lost in them, Antwerp had gained. And in that building yonder, his old friend, Samuel, had straightened out many a legal snarl. The best lawyer in town they had called him. Antwerp had got him, too. Down the street a way, was the old house of Abeldano and Gerondi, brokers and money lenders for generations. Now they were somewhere in the Levant, and doing well. On the other hand, the many and many who'd perished trying to find new homes, who'd died from poverty or persecution! Think of old Abraham, barely holding together soul and body till he should finish the chronicles of his people.

Abel drew his cloak around him and strolled on. He

found himself noting familiar aspects with a sharpened vision, as if to record them for future ingatherings of memory. Would he remember this high glory of summer noon? Ah, dear sky of Lisbon, would any other be as blue?

A little building that was mostly a huge window set in a bright green casement, caught his eye. He hadn't seen it for months, but he remembered it instantly: The Green Window, the little inn where Nicolo lodged. Perhaps Nicolo was there now. Abel halted in the shade of the doorway, and looked in.

By a fire that flared smokily into its great conical chimney, a little old man sat on a stool and stirred a steaming pot. Now and then he would look up and nod to a visitor leaning his elbows on a near-by table, and Abel could hear a desultory conversation. The old fellow he knew, from Nicolo's description, must be Pedro. All that he could see of the other was the back of a figure of more than usual height, in seaman's breeches and short coat, and a sailor's peaked cap snugly set on thick black hair. The man was speaking in tolerable Portuguese, but with a strong guttural accent. Nicolo, however, wasn't here, so Abel concluded he might as well go on.

A little reluctantly, he was leaving the cool doorway, when he heard his own name. He looked back, thinking one of the men inside had spoken to him. No, neither had stirred nor seen him. But now! – That voice with the foreign accent:

" Zakuto's the one who makes maps and such? "

How in the world did the fellow come to know about his doings with " maps and such " ? Abel moved back into the shadow and saw Pedro nod assent.

" Would he be there now – at this Zakuto's? " he heard the seaman inquire.

Pedro seemed to be uncertain, but, in a moment, he replied, " You'd more likely find him around the shipyards. He was going to look at some lumber this morning."

Ah – Nicolo! That was whom they were talking about. Lumber, eh? Perhaps the lad was going to change his mind and build another ship – and Abel walked on, reminded by a whiff from Pedro's pot that his own dinner would be ready for him. He remembered Ruth's saying something about a bean potage. Those savoury beans cooked overnight in the big old wall oven, with Ruth's inimitable flavouring of onions and thyme! Then, sometime when they could be alone, he and she, together. . . .

That time came only after Nejmi had gone to bed. On pretext of enjoying the full moon, Abel made Ruth sit with him in the court, and, presently, he spoke of his visit to the palace. She had heard Manoel's order delivered by a court messenger, but Abel had purposely not told her where he was going when he started out that morning.

" Why, Abel," she gasped, " was that where you were all that time? What happened? " she breathlessly demanded.

He laid his hand over hers before he answered her. " The King is going to forbid us – all of our people – to leave Lisbon. *Forbid* us, Ruth! "

He saw the startled look, heard her quick, indrawn breath. For a long time she was very still, not even responding to his caressing hand.

Suddenly he felt her tremble against him. " There's – there's plenty of work in the world for us, yet," she whispered. " Whenever you say, Abel! "

This was her way of telling him she understood the hard thing he was trying to say to her! In a rush of tenderness he put his arms about her.

For a moment she gave up to her grief. " Oh, Abel, must our people always be wanderers? "

What could he say to comfort her? For a woman's roots went deeper than a man's into the things of every day – the keeping of a house, the tending of a garden, the hundred intimacies that made the dear stability of home.

"We can't take any of our things, can we? " she asked him pitifully.

It was pouring salt into her wounds, but he must answer her. " Nothing but the clothes we wear, and what we might conceal in them, for after the King gives the order we must go secretly."

Nejmi, they agreed, mustn't know until the time came, and then, somehow, they would find a way to tell her.

" You see, Ruth," Abel faltered, " at first it was for her sake we stayed, but now – now, we couldn't stay, could we? "

"Oh, my dear, someone else is going to take care of Nejmi! " Ruth's eyes were wet, but her lips smiled at him.

"Which one," Abel whispered after a while, " do you think it will be? The way Ferdinand looks at her – "

"The way Nicolo *doesn't* look at her! " Ruth softly laughed. " Why, Abel, if you could have seen how hard that poor boy tried to keep his eyes off her, the other afternoon, when she and Ferdinand were in the court! "

" I suppose," Abel said, with the old, whimsical twinkle in his eyes, " that Nejmi herself may have a choice in the matter! "

" Something happened, that afternoon," Ruth pursued

with conviction. " Nejmi's been different ever since. It seems
as if she had shut herself away from everything – like one
of those lilies, when its petals close. And if you've noticed,
Abel, Nicolo hasn't been here since! "

No, he hadn't noticed, but Ruth's mention of his name
recalled the conversation in The Green Window, and made
Abel wonder if that tall chap had finally found Nicolo.

CHAPTER 17

The Venetian Ambassador

NICOLO came in late to The Green Window and, without a glance at the occupants of the benches, or even his usual word with Pedro, he absently dropped into a vacant place. It had been a long day, rather longer than he had

meant it to be, and he was too tired to take any notice of
what was going on around him.

He had started out by inspecting a shipment of lumber
from up-river that had been offered him cheap. The offer
tempted him, because he figured that, though he couldn't
use it now, later he might sell it at a good profit. For, he
argued, the time was coming – with Gama's return – when
everybody would go into Oriental trade. Then lumber for
caravels and warehouses would be in demand. He got an
option on the cargo, and afterward he had made a business of
sounding his acquaintances on future prospects.

"Keep your money," they all told him. "Better not
count on too good times."

As Nicolo well knew, times were dull, and growing
duller, as Gama's absence had stretched into a year, then
two years.

"Of course, if one were sure," his friends qualified, "of
Gama's coming back, or even of there being a sea passage to
India . . . "

Well, he thought to himself, as he listened, they didn't
know what he knew about that! And the end of the day
found him decided to close with the lumber dealer.

Still, as he sat staring past the faces at Pedro's scrubbed
tables, and unheeding of the talking and the drinking around
him, he knew that the prevailing doubt about Gama had
affected his spirits. Not that he had misgivings about
the existence of the passage around the Devil's Cave –
how could he have? But so many accidents could happen at sea! So easily the great, grey ocean could swallow
those fragile ships, and who would ever be the wiser?
Then, too, hadn't Gama repeatedly said that if he didn't

find the information for which he had gone, he should not return?

Nicolo was roused from his reverie by someone at his elbow, and discovered Pedro putting a steaming dish in front of him.

" A man was in, today, asking for you," whispered the old inn-keeper. He disappeared, and in a moment returned with a mug of red wine. " Said he'd stop in again for you tomorrow," he threw back, as he went off.

Nicolo nodded, and began to eat the hot food. He was hungrier than he'd thought. When he'd finished he began to sip his wine, meditating, as he sipped, on the morning's talk. Gradually, over the top of his mug, a face across the table disengaged itself from the others, and became focused into his absent gaze; heavy features, flushed with drinking, but, somehow, familiar.

Nicolo put his mug down, and carefully scrutinized the face. He saw the blood-shot eyes stare back at him with a sort of stupid recognition. Yes! Now he had it: that street row, two years ago, between the Venetian sailor and the Portuguese – and this was the Venetian.

" What have you been doing," Nicolo bantered, " since I heard you cursing Gama? "

The fellow continued to stare, then he began to mutter, thickly: " Gama . . . Gama . . . I've seen him! "

Nicolo laughed and glanced around, to see if anyone else had heard the idiocy. No, everybody was busy laughing and talking and drinking.

" You're a real wit! " he said, pleasantly. " Did the Senhor send us a message by you? "

" I've seen him since you have! " The thick voice rose

in an angry oath. The bloodshot eyes narrowed, and for a moment the inert body half-reared itself in a threatening attitude. " But you'll not see him again! "

There was a lull in the general talk, and two or three turned to look at the unsteady figure that was now slumping to the bench. Nicolo got up and went back to where Pedro was scouring ladles. The sailor was even more befuddled than he'd thought. He'd had enough of him.

" What did that man want who was inquiring for me? " he asked Pedro.

" Wanted to know where he could find you. I told him you were looking at lumber, somewhere down by the waterfront." After a moment, Pedro added, " He seemed to know you often went to Abel Zakuto's."

Nicolo received this information with a yawn. He was tired; he'd go to bed. Half-way to his room he heard hurried steps, and turned to look. A tall man in a seaman's jacket and peaked cap was standing in the entrance, and scowlingly scanning faces. Instantly Nicolo recalled him – the very man who'd helped handle this same sailor in the street row.

The next minute he saw the man swoop down on the half-conscious figure and savagely shake it; then, half-lifting, half-shoving it before him, he guided it to the door. As he passed Pedro, he paused and tossed him a coin.

" Has he – has he been talking? " Nicolo heard him inquire, as he jerked his head toward the sailor. " Sure he didn't say – anything? " he uneasily insisted, although Pedro, pausing in his work, told him he was too busy to listen to his customers' chatter.

Nicolo wandered to the door and watched them go down the narrow alley and turn a corner. Yes, he remembered the

tall chap perfectly, bushy black hair, guttural accent, and all. He was having all he could do now to handle his charge! Almost identical with the scene of two years ago. Odd that an able fellow would keep an ill-natured sot that long. Nicolo wondered, idly, why he had been so particular to know if the other had talked. As if anyone listened to drunken ravings! That gibber, for instance, about Gama!

But the tall one – trader he'd called himself – there was something uncomfortable connected with him. Nicolo recalled those eager inquiries about the Expedition, and his own feeling that he'd been too free with his answers. No, that wasn't it. It was Ferdinand's afterward telling him that the street quarrel had been reported at the palace, and that the Venetian ambassador had seemed to know all about him. Then there had been his own suspicion that the foreign-looking trader had posted the ambassador. There was something else, too. Hadn't the fellow spoken as if he knew of the Jewish reprieve before its public announcement? That had been extraordinary; it was what had made him suspect that the man had some direct communication with the palace.

The Jewish reprieve! Every moment of that day was graven on his memory: Abel in the workshop . . . Ruth making preserves for Gama . . . Nejmi and he alone, together, when they had come into a new intimacy. But now that was over. That scene in the court between her and Ferdinand, and then what she had said about her " debt " . . .

He stepped outside and began to walk to try to dull the ache at his heart. If only he could forget her last words – he could have borne anything but that. " I'm going to pay back my debt. . . . You want me to pay you! " How could she have dealt him that blow, she, who must know how he felt about her?

Well, he was not going to see her till he had himself in hand. As for Ferdinand, if she wanted him, and he, her . . . He meant to avoid Ferdinand for a while. That wouldn't be difficult, for the King's household was going up in a day or so to the summer palace.

There was a moon, and Nicolo continued to walk. His weariness seemed to have vanished. Pedro's hot supper was having its effect. Deliberately he put Nejmi out of his mind. He'd pin himself down to business.

That lumber, now! If only Rodriguez were here to consult, instead of at sea, somewhere between the Madeiras and Cape Verde! On impulse he decided to have another look at the lumber. It wasn't late, and the moon was bright. He ran back and called to Pedro that presently he'd return – not to lock him out.

The streets were deserted, but through tavern doors drifted talking and laughter. Down by the docks, he passed a knot of sailors. Once he heard a gang-plank dropped. He went on to the end of a dock where the lumber was piled. Beyond, there was a strip of sandy beach on which tiny waves lapped softly.

He walked slowly around the lumber, inspected it from end to end. Excellent stuff, sound as a nut. And its pungent odour was like a tonic. Standing there in the shadow, his ear caught the dip of oars, and he made out a row-boat coming in. As it neared, he saw two figures in it, one at the oars, the other in the stern, and both wore wide-brimmed hats. He watched idly as the keel grated on the sand. The figure in the stern jumped out, a man in a long cloak, whose face was hidden by his hat. The other remained in his seat, his face, too, in shadow.

The one who had landed stood, for a moment, with his hand on the bow. " Good-bye and good luck," he said, in a low tone.

Nicolo started. The man was speaking Italian.

" You'll be off, I suppose," he added, " as soon as you've got those – those things, so I shan't see you again."

He bent forward and gave the boat a shove. It glided off, and he turned and walked along the beach and toward the quay. In the shadow of the lumber and hardly a half dozen paces away from Nicolo, he halted, pulled up the collar of his cloak around his face, and then strode briskly on.

Nicolo stared after him. What on earth did this mean? For the face, a moment ago so close to him, was that of the Venetian ambassador! He watched the retreating figure disappear in the shadows, and then, recollecting the other cloaked figure, he turned around to see what had become of the row-boat. But it had blended into the harbour shipping.

In a whirl of puzzled thoughts Nicolo left the lumber pile and walked slowly back to The Green Window. He lay awake trying to account for the ambassador's strange excursion: an ambassador at the water-front at midnight, without a single attendant – and so evidently guarding against recognition!

Very early in the morning he was waked by a knocking on his door, and before he could swing his legs out of bed, he was surprised to see Ferdinand enter. With the memory of that scene with Nejmi still rankling, Nicolo's greeting was a little forced, especially as Ferdinand himself seemed conscious and ill at ease.

" I had to see you before we went up to Cintra," he burst out, sitting down on the edge of the bed, " and we're leaving today or, at latest, tomorrow."

Unconsciously Nicolo braced himself. The boy was going to speak of Nejmi!

" Nicolo " – Ferdinand leaned closer, and lowered his tone – " something's going on at the palace. I had to tell you! " He eyed Nicolo anxiously. " Probably you'll think it's my imagination, but I'm sure something's going on," he repeated.

" I'll get my things on," Nicolo told him as he began to dress, " while you talk." In his surprise at this unexpected turn he forgot his constraint.

" Well, here it is. Yesterday, toward evening, the Venetian ambassador – "

Nicolo almost dropped the long hose he was buttoning, but instantly smothered his exclamation in a pretence of coughing. Better keep last night's incident to himself.

" The Venetian ambassador," Ferdinand was saying, " came up to me and was very pleasant. He'd never noticed me before, but we talked for some time, and, after a while, he asked if I didn't go to an Abel Zakuto's, kinsman of the astrologer, Abraham, whom he used to see around the palace.

" He told me he'd heard Master Abraham say his cousin specialized in collecting maps of the Orient. Then I said he made them, too; that he had first-hand information about the Orient – meaning, you know, Scander. At that he burst out quick – ' Could you manage to have a friend of mine see Zakuto's maps? ' The next minute he'd calmed down and sort of apologized for getting excited. His friend, it seemed, was collecting maps, and if I'd take him to Master Abel's . . . I

told him of course I would, only I was going away for the
summer, and then, without thinking, I said I knew someone
who would." He looked quizzically at Nicolo, and they both
laughed.

"Meaning me?" Nicolo thrust his arms into his waist-
coat and quickly fastened his doublet over it.

Ferdinand nodded, but now his face was very grave.

"If it had ended there, I wouldn't have given it another
thought, but, Nicolo, I'd no sooner said that, than the ambassador fairly snatched at it – could he depend on me to
get his friend to Zakuto? 'I'll pay you well,' says he. That
was what gave me a queer feeling: that talk of paying. And
so eager too! I must have shown my surprise, for he laughed
and said, off-hand, 'Who is the person that'll take my friend
to Zakuto's?'

"I mentioned your name, of course, and then the next
queer thing happened. The strangest look came over his face,
and he half muttered to himself, 'Oh – *he!*' Then he said,
'Young Conti? Stays at The Green Window, doesn't he?'
You see, he knew all about you!"

"That's the second time he has appeared to know all
about me," exclaimed Nicolo. "Remember the first?"

"No," said Ferdinand.

Nicolo recalled to him how, just before Gama's departure, his own name had been mentioned by the ambassador in connection with a street quarrel that had come to the
King's notice.

As he talked, he buckled his cloak and sat down beside
Ferdinand. "I wonder why he's so particular about keeping
his eye on me."

"Nicolo!" Ferdinand grasped his arm. "That's what

kept me awake all night: his being so anxious to pay me if I'd get you to take his friend to see Master Abel's maps."

" Did you say any more about my taking his friend to Zakuto's? "

" Yes. I told him his man would find you here, where you lived, though I had an uncomfortable feeling about it all the time."

" When did you say you had this talk? " asked Nicolo.

" Late yesterday afternoon."

Then, meditated Nicolo, the " friend " couldn't have been the one who knew he went to Abel Zakuto's, because, according to Pedro, he had come in about noon.

" After I went to bed," Ferdinand continued, " I got to turning it all over. I didn't like the looks of it. And then, all at once, it popped into my head that early in the afternoon the ambassador had got his final answer about what we meant to do in the Orient, provided Gama found a sea passage. The gossip around the palace was that Manoel had been pretty short with him. Don't you see, Nicolo, the ambassador must have come to me right afterward! "

Nicolo's mind was in a chaos. Should he tell what he'd seen last night?

" I couldn't get it out of my mind," Ferdinand was saying, " that the two things, put together, looked – well – odd. And that's what kept me awake all night, that I'd got you mixed up in it. I wish to heaven I'd kept my mouth closed about your taking the ambassador's friend to Master Abel's."

For a moment Nicolo made no reply. Ferdinand sleepless and anxious about him, while he had been thinking resentfully of the boy, even avoiding him!

" Don't give it a thought, old fellow," he said heartily,

gripping Ferdinand's hand. " I'll look out for that ' friend ' !
You won't see him, by any chance? "

" Oh, I thought I told you! Yes, I did see him. Later,
in the evening, the ambassador took me into the garden and
introduced me to him and spoke of you."

A sudden intuition leaped to Nicolo's mind. " What'd
he look like? So I'll know him."

" He was tall," Ferdinand began, " dark, talked with
a foreign, throaty accent – "

" Wait a minute! " Nicolo clapped on his cap, seized
the surprised boy by the arm, and hurried him to Pedro.
" Tell Pedro what this person looks like who's to call for me,
so he'll know him."

" That's the one was here yesterday," Pedro exclaimed,
before Ferdinand was fairly started. " Him with the foreign
way of talking. Come to think of it," he said to Nicolo, " you
saw the man yourself, Master Conti. Remember when that
fellow came in here last night and carried that drunken
chap off? "

Nicolo gasped. " Was he the same one who'd asked for
me at noon? "

Pedro nodded. " I didn't think you'd want to talk with
him along with that mate of his, and then you went out and I
forgot to mention it. But he said he'd be in again today. Yes,
he was the one who knew about you being a friend of Zakuto,
and about Zakuto's making maps and such."

Ferdinand and Nicolo exchanged glances.

" There! " Ferdinand murmured. " You hear? Maps!
I wish I needn't go," he said regretfully, " so we could follow
up this thing, but it's good-bye now for the summer. If any
trouble should come of this – and I can help – "

Nicolo grasped both his hands. "Nothing's going to happen, or if anything does, at least my eyes are open! " On the whole, he decided, he wouldn't tell about seeing the ambassador at the docks.

As he stood at the door and saw Ferdinand hurrying away, he recalled their first meeting. Here their friendship had begun. Here, on this very threshold, and with this same warm little stir at his heart, he had watched the boy going back to his palace duty. The same luminous eyes that seemed always to be visioning some mystic world . . . the same open, boyish heart! Nothing, Nicolo vowed to himself, should ever again come between them.

But the Venetian ambassador! His inquiries about Abel's maps. His being out last night in that boat. Most of all, his connection with that foreign trader, that tall seaman. Could that other man in the boat have been he? "You'll be off as soon as you've got those things," Nicolo uneasily recalled. "Those things." Was he a fool to read a hidden meaning into those words?

If only he could talk the matter over with Abel. But that meant seeing Nejmi. Then – Scander! Yes, he'd go to him with this. He was busy, Nicolo knew, getting together stevedores to unload for Rodriguez, who was shortly due in port.

Scander was hurrying away from his lodgings when Nicolo overtook him. He was reluctant to be delayed because, as he said, good workers weren't too plenty, and one must be early at the docks to get them first. So Nicolo fell into step with him, and presently was pouring out his story and Ferdinand's suspicions.

Scander, however, refused to get excited. " Everybody's

interested in maps nowadays," he said, " making 'em or collecting 'em. As for your seeing anything in what the ambassador told the other fellow – rubbish! Why ' those things ' might 'a' meant anything, from salt fish to new sails! Ferdinand's imagination got started – and so did yours."

" Yes, but Scander, the ambassador pulling up his cloak to hide his face! And if the man who was rowing him was the same one that Ferdinand and Pedro and I all saw – "

" You saw him? You didn't mention that before. So you saw him, did you? "

" For just a minute, when he came into Pedro's to claim a drunken mate – and Lord, but his mate *was* drunk! " Nicolo grimaced at the recollection. " He'd lost every sense he ever had. Sat across from me at a table, and raved like a madman. And of all people in the world he chose Gama to rave about! Swore that he'd seen him since we had, but that we wouldn't see him again. Kept on saying it, too – in such dead earnest. It was really funny! "

A strange sound from Scander made Nicolo stare at him. Scander's mouth was gaping, and he was breathing hard. His face was very red, and the burnt gimlet holes glittered.

" ' *Seen him – since we had* ' " he was repeating. " By St. Vincent, he could have! "

Nicolo continued to stare. " What are you talking about? Are you drunk, too? " he half laughed.

" By St. Vincent! " Scander repeated, not seeming to hear him. " That's deep, that is! "

" What? " Nicolo impatiently demanded.

Scander regarded him pityingly. " If I wasn't working for you," he brought out at last, " I'd call you the thickest numbskull I'd ever met face to face. You pick up things that don't amount to that – " he snapped his fingers – " like those maps you kept harping on, and then you pass over the core of the whole thing. Certainly that drunk chap could 'a' seen Gama! "

"How could he? " Nicolo protested with some heat. " Not unless he'd followed him! And Portugal has too many forts and trading stations between here and Guinea to let a strange craft slip past."

Scander heaved a sigh. " Think you could put two and two together, if I was to tell you how? " he asked mildly. " How'd I get out of Indian waters, me and Nejmi? Don't you remember? "

He waited, while over Nicolo's astounded face crept slow understanding.

"Nothing could be easier," Scander continued. " Cut across by caravan and boat from the Mediterranean to Aden, and then down the coast a ways – and after that, all they had to do was to wait and see. If Gama got through at all, they was sure to see him." He meditated a moment, then struck his palms together. " That's what happened! "

"Put it in plain language, Scander! " Nicolo's voice had a new respect.

"Somebody was sharp enough to figure that all out," Scander meditated aloud. " Somebody must have been right here in Lisbon spying on the Expedition, and when Gama started out, the spies headed 'round the other way to meet him – through the Mediterranean and the Red Sea into Indian waters. They figured, of course, that if he didn't come it was proof that there wasn't a through passage to India."

"By San Marco! " Nicolo stopped short and seized Scander's shoulder. " I'll wager my head that one of the spies is the same chap who's been asking Pedro about me. He and that sailor that babbles were both here, just two years ago now! He asked me all sorts of questions about the Expedition. I'll lay you anything he was here to spy on it! "

Instead of replying, Scander regarded Nicolo with an odd expression. "According to that," he offered quietly, "wouldn't he be the same man that Ferdinand says is the Venetian ambassador's friend? "

"Great heaven! " Nicolo could only stare, aghast at the terrible implication. Was that why Venice no longer scoffed at the Way of the Spices? Was that why she had so persistently demanded to know Manoel's policy about Oriental trade?

"Deep, I call it," chuckled Scander. "Let us do all the work of finding the passage to India while they sit still and watch us! "

"See here! " protested Nicolo. "We're going pretty far on the drunken babble of a low fellow who couldn't walk straight. I'm not going to make up my mind about anything, until I've seen his running mate, the tall one. He told Pedro he'd be in again for me today."

At first Scander made no reply. "Tell you what," he declared, "the one that talks is the one to get hold of – but we must get him alone." He appeared to consider with himself. "Come along," he suggested, "and we'll look for him in the taverns and down at the water-front. Tell me when you see him, and then you leave him to me. Sailors have their ways – you leave him to me."

To this Nicolo promptly agreed. "But first," said he, "we'll stop in at Pedro's and leave word for the tall fellow in case he calls for me."

CHAPTER 18

The Will of Allah

Good!'' Scander exclaimed, as they looked into one tavern after another. "He's not there. Sober and alone is the only way he'll be any use to us."

At the harbour front they instantly saw that something

was afoot. The very air was alive with excitement. Across the rails of vessels, deck hands leaned and talked, and on the quay a crowd was gathered.

Scander and Nicolo pushed up to its edge, and heard two men in the midst rapidly exchanging experiences which they were evidently willing to share with the bystanders.

"First I saw of the vermin was three days out of Funchal. I was keeping fair close to the Moroccan coast to where I could cut straight across to St. Vincent when out shot two brigantines – "

"Ha!" Scander exclaimed to Nicolo. "Pirates!"

"That's my story to a word, Captain," cried the other of the two men, "only that I was bound from the Canaries. Half-way up Morocco I should say 'twas, too. I must have been just a day behind you. Goat hides and cheeses was my cargo. What was yours?"

"Honey, wine and Madeira beechwood. They never touched the lumber, but, saints above – the honey and the wine!"

"Good heavens, Scander!" whispered Nicolo. "This raid may have caught *The Golden Star*. Rodriguez expected to be down by the Madeiras and the Canaries at this very time!"

Scander, joining in the laughter of the bystanders, was evidently too engrossed to heed Nicolo. "Just listen to that!" he delightedly exhorted.

"They let my goat hides alone," the captain from the Canaries was saying, "but blast them if they didn't set to and fill their bellies with the cheeses, and then play ball with the rest of them till my deck was like a slime pit and stunk like a hog pen!"

Again the crowd laughed, and Scander's feet began to jig in a sailor's shuffle.

" Lord! " he whispered to Nicolo. " This talk makes me homesick for the feel of a deck."

" Yes, but Rodriguez – "

" Well – " Scander was frankly impatient – " what can we do about him? "

The words died on his lips, and Nicolo saw his gaze suddenly fix on one of the two captains.

" They started in by asking if I had any pepper," the man was saying. " *Pepper!* Now can you imagine that? "

" So they did me! " cried the other. " And ' cloves, too,' says they, in their heathenish jabber."

" ' Must think I'm Gama,' I told 'em," rejoined the first speaker. His face suddenly sobered. " By the way," he threw out to the crowd, " any news of Gama? "

A slight movement near them caught Nicolo's eye. The drunken sailor! Only now he was quite sober, to judge from his alert, eager face.

" There's our man," he murmured in Scander's ear.

They watched him as he edged nearer the speakers, evidently intent on not losing a word.

" I'll take care of him," Scander whispered back, " while you keep the other one busy when he calls for you. And don't leave The Green Window," he added, as Nicolo moved away, " without telling Pedro."

Hour by hour, Nicolo, from the rear of The Green Window, kept his eye on the front entrance. Pedro's regular customers came and went. Groups of sailors drank and bragged. More than once Nicolo's ears caught from them an echo of the story of that morning, only by now the two brig-

antines of pirates had swelled to a fleet, and the decks of the
attacked vessels ran with blood instead of cheese. Mid-afternoon came, and still the bushy-haired, foreign-spoken
stranger failed to appear.

"Are you sure he said he'd come in today? " Nicolo
asked Pedro, and invariably the reply was " That was what
he told me."

What would Scander have to report? Nicolo wondered.
Restlessly he reviewed the train of incidents of the last night
and day, from the maudlin words dropped by the drunken
sailor, to his own startling discovery of the Venetian ambassador, and Ferdinand's confidences of the morning. Was it
all a chain of intrigue or his own imaginings? He'd wait before he made up his mind. . . . By heaven, that lumber deal
he'd meant to close this morning! He'd go now to the dealer,
he hastily decided, and started to tell Pedro he would be back
before sundown, when he saw Scander and the sailor enter
the inn together.

He watched them sit down at a table while Pedro
brought them hot dishes and red wine. Even from the rear
of the room, Nicolo could see, under Scander's usual manner,
signs of excitement. He barely touched his food and only
sipped his wine. Presently he left the sailor heartily gulping
down his meal, and spoke to Pedro who nodded in Nicolo's
direction. Unhurriedly, Scander strolled over to him, but,
instantly, he dropped his leisurely manner.

"He said the same thing over that he told you, last
night – said it while he was sober, too! " he exploded, under
his breath.

Nicolo stared at him. Incredible! "How'd you get it
out of him? " he finally asked.

" I'll tell you," said Scander, " but we must be quick. We can't lose sight of him, so if he starts to go out . . . "

He sat down beside Nicolo where he could watch his charge.

" I began by trying to hire him to help unload when Rodriguez comes in – "

" If there's anything to unload after those pirates are done! " growled Nicolo.

" I asked him what he was doing here," Scander continued, " and he said he and another chap were fishing; had a small craft anchored out a-ways. ' When are you going out? ' I asked him. ' Depends,' he says. That was all I could get out of him: ' Depends.' "

Nicolo recalled that the ambassador had said to the man in the boat, " You'll be off as soon as you've got those things." It was clear enough that " those things," whatever they were, were what the departure " depended " on.

" The chap's name, by the way, is Marco," Scander was saying. " Wait," he broke off, " while I tell Pedro to keep him supplied so he won't go."

" Well," he continued, when he returned, " I told him I'd pay him extra high wages to help unload when our ship got in, and he finally agreed to hire with us provided he wasn't gone by that time. I noticed he kept talking about the captains who'd been raided, down Morocco way – seemed quite worked up and excited. So I asked him if he knew that coast. No, he didn't; but he'd wager his last coin there was nothing 'round the Mediterranean he didn't know! I let him talk, and then I let slip indifferent-like, that I'd sailed the Red Sea. So had he! I dropped a name or two – Aden, Melinde, Mombassa. He knew them – 'd seen them! "

" How in the world," Nicolo broke in admiringly, " did you know how to get him started? "

" Why a sailor'd rather brag about the places he's been than eat. It'd be a pity if I didn't know their ways by now. Well, after that you couldn't have pried him loose from me. All he wanted was to talk about the places he'd been – and I gave him plenty of rope! But all the time, I was saying to myself, ' Slow, now, Scander, easy – don't ground on a reef! ' Finally, when he was going top speed, I said, ' That's nothing to what happened when I was with Captain Diaz! ' "

" What? You didn't say you'd been with Diaz? "

" Well, in my own mind I have," grinned Scander brazenly. " Plenty of times! Anyway he swallowed the bait. ' And that's nothing,' he comes back, ' to the time I saw Gama coming down all loaded up – ' But right there he bit his words off as if they was twine, and I vow the sweat started on his face, so scared he was at what he'd let out."

" It doesn't seem possible," Nicolo ejaculated, half fearfully. " Gama! "

" I could feel his eyes on me," Scander went on, " watching to see if I'd noticed. The only way to do was to play the simpleton, and I said, cool and laughing, ' Ever hear the singing sharks around Goa? ' "

" ' Singing sharks! ' " laughed Nicolo. " More of your inventions? "

" Oh, it's one of the yarns they always tell land-lubbers. Well, I saw right away by his questions that he'd never set eye on Goa, nor on Calicut nor Cochin. I tried him on all those Indian ports, and I found out what I wanted to – that he'd never been near those coasts to the north'ard. Every once in a while he'd get harping on the pirates they were telling about this morning, and finally I twitted him with being afraid he'd be chased by them. I saw him give me a queer look out of the corner of his eye, and he changed the subject – but not back to Gama! Wouldn't say another word about Gama."

" But what's it all about? " Nicolo queried. " Suppose he did see Gama . . . suppose he's let Venice know it . . . "

" That's what I can't figure. What I'm working on is what this Marco fellow let slip: ' The time I saw Gama coming down all loaded up.' ' *Coming down,*' " Scander repeated.

" Well, what of that? " Nicolo's face was completely puzzled.

" I've turned it inside out and hind part foremost, and here's what I make of it: this Marco must have been somewhere off the coast south of Aden when he saw Gama's sails. That's sure, because he knew all about Melinde and Mombassa, but nothing about the Indian coasts. Remember I tried him on them?

" Now," Scander carefully continued, " if a vessel sailing north was to pass you, and another sailing south, which one would you say was *going up?* "

" The one sailing north, of course."

Scander's eyes glittered, and he ran his tongue around his lips. " Then the one sailing south . . . "

" Would be coming down," Nicolo glibly completed. Then – he was staring at Scander. He seemed to have lost sight of the room. " He meant that Gama was ' coming down ' *from India?* . . . ' Coming down ' – on his way home? " he whispered unsteadily.

" Now you got it! " But in spite of his bantering air,

Scander's hands shook. "So, of course," he went on, "if they saw him down Melinde way or off Mombassa, which isn't so far from the Devil's Cave, and the Devil's Cave not but six months' run to Lisbon – "

"Great heaven! Gama might – might almost be here! " gasped Nicolo. His head was bursting. Manoel must be told. All Portugal must know that Gama wasn't lost as they'd feared, but alive, coming home! But Venice – the Venetian ambassador! Suppose Marco and his mate were their spies. Could he tell Manoel without exposing them? And yet . . .

"Scander," he choked out, "we must take this to the King."

"Can't," Scander briefly stated. "He's gone. They were all leaving the palace two hours ago. Besides, we aren't sure enough yet of anything to talk. First thing you know, you'll get into trouble."

"Then I'm going to Master Abel! This is getting too thick for me."

"Wait till I get that chap out of here – he mustn't see you," Scander whispered, stepping ahead. "He's finished eating – getting ready to go. And he's not going out of my sight till I see where he stows away for the night." He glanced back at Nicolo. "Did the tall chap call? No? Then all the more reason to keep an eye on Marco. Neither'll leave Lisbon without the other."

"I don't blame him for being uneasy about Marco's talking! " said Nicolo. "Come back here tonight," he whispered, as Scander was going, "so you can hear what Master Abel has to say about this."

All the way up the hill he was tortured with the self-questioning that had started with Scander's tremendous news. Gama probably on the way home! But how, in common decency and honour, could he keep that from Manoel? Yet, if Venice were involved in a plot, had instigated it, even paid a price for it, then, what? Could he bring himself to expose Venice? Still, hadn't he cast his fortunes with Portugal? Again, if this thing should ever come to light, how could he hold up his head in Lisbon – Lisbon, where he'd built so carefully, so solidly, for his future?

He tried to put from him the thought of meeting Nejmi. He hadn't wanted to see her; in fact, he had deliberately planned not to see her, and he half hoped she wouldn't appear.

But the first person he saw, when he stepped inside the court, was Nejmi, sitting on the threshold of the workshop; Nejmi in palest, filmy yellow, her head against the door frame. Did he imagine it, or were the dark eyes wistful, even sad? And then, as they perceived him, did they change – quicken?

He steeled himself to speak casually, and then to pass by her into the workshop where Abel looked up from a map to exclaim, " Well, young man, it's been too long since you were here! "

" It's good to see you again, Nicolo," said Ruth, bustling in from the next room. She scrutinized him a moment, then, " Sit down here by the windows," she told him kindly. " You look warm – throw back your cloak."

" I mustn't stay," he murmured.

" Not stay! Of course you'll stay. I'm going to keep you for supper. There's a brace of young pigeons in the pot that'll tempt you, if – if nothing else will! "

Nicolo felt his ears tingle. Was there just the ghost of a

knowing twinkle in Ruth's round, bright eyes as she added that last clause?

"I'd like nothing better than to stay," he declared, "but I've agreed to meet Scander as soon – as soon as I've told you something, Master Abel, that's beyond my solving."

At the troubled voice, Abel looked up quickly. "Come over here, boy, by me." He pushed away his work, and turned his attention to Nicolo. "What is it?"

Nicolo made no answer at once. Again, everything was a whirl. Where should he begin? How weave together the tangled happenings of the past day and night? He seized on the one name, the one fact, that stood out from the confusion:

"Master Abel, Gama has been seen in Indian waters!"

He heard a sharp intake of breath as Abel started up. "Gama – Gama has been seen?" he gasped.

Nejmi came in from the threshold, and sat down at the table. She said nothing, but Nicolo saw the golden light that always came to her eyes when she was stirred.

"How do you know?" Ruth asked in an awe-struck whisper. "Who told you?"

"Was he alive?" Abel was demanding, his face close to Nicolo's. "Is Gama – alive?"

"When he was seen – yes."

Then, as well as he could, Nicolo told of seeing the Venetian ambassador the night before, of Marco's drunken outburst, and the boasts into which Scander had later trapped him.

"Think of it! Seeing Gama!" Abel murmured rapturously. "Why it's like looking into the future and knowing what's going to happen, before it does happen. The Way of the Spices is a certainty! "

" But suppose, sir," Nicolo said carefully, " Venice had got that information before we did – say some months ago . . . "

Abel's expression became intent. " I see! " he said. " I see now. You mean Venice's recent demand to know Portugal's intentions in the Orient? "

" How else could you account for such a demand? You see, sir, this Marco and his mate were here when the Expedition was outfitting. I fell into talk with the mate, and I'm sure now, from the questions he asked, that he was here to spy." Nicolo suddenly recalled that he had not mentioned Ferdinand's account of the ambassador's eagerness for his " friend " to see Abel's maps, for the effect of Scander's passing the maps over as unimportant had been to blur the incident in his own mind. " The fellow even went to The Green Window to get me to take him to you."

" When was that? " Abel shot back.

" Yesterday, about noon, according to Pedro."

" Then I saw him! I was passing, and stopped a moment to look in. I heard my name and something or other about maps. I heard Pedro speak of you, too. Said you were looking at some lumber. So that's the man who was here two years ago, and asked you about the fleet? "

" The same. Ferdinand was sure – and at first I agreed with him – that the ambassador's wanting this ' friend ' to see your maps, was suspicious because he was altogether too eager about it, and too willing to pay."

A slight movement from Nejmi made Nicolo turn his head. He noticed, then, that Ruth was watching her. Elbows

on table, and chin dropped on her clasped hands, she was following his account so intently that he had the impression of
breathlessness. He waited a moment – did she wish to say
something? Then, as she continued silently to gaze at him,
he went on:

"But Scander declares there is nothing to that – says
everybody's interested in maps just now."

Abel assented. "Likely as not the ambassador and this
friend of his are collecting them, just as I've collected them.
No, I hardly think there's anything in that."

"But there is! Ferdinand is right." In the pause that
followed Abel's words, Nejmi's low voice had the effect of a
stone thrown into a still pool.

"Of course they want our maps," she added, almost as
if she were talking to herself.

In utter and frank amazement Abel and Nicolo stared
at her. But Ruth, in her matter of fact way, asked, "Who is
it, child, that want the maps?"

At first Nejmi made no reply, but continued to regard
Nicolo with that peculiar intensity – only, now, was it sorrowful? "How can you help but see?" she asked almost in-
audibly.

And then he knew what she meant! Sharp across his
memory struck his own first misgivings when Ferdinand had
told him of the ambassador's eager curiosity about Abel's
maps. Scander – and Abel, too – had too quickly brushed
aside this item as insignificant, and afterward Marco's startling disclosures had taken his own attention from it. But
now, as clear as day, the ambassador's parting word to the
oarsman came back to him: "You'll be off as soon as you've
got those things." *As soon as you've got those maps,* Nicolo

silently translated – just as he had first suspected, until Scander had laughed at him. And of course it was easy enough now to complete Marco's repeated "Depends," when asked by Scander when he would leave Lisbon. "Depends on when we get the maps" was what he really meant.

"You mean – Venice wants Master Abel's maps," he said, as steadily as he could.

"Don't you remember that day," she asked him, "when Ferdinand first told us about the Venetians wanting to know what Portugal meant to do in the Orient, and you all wondered why they'd changed their minds – because at first they'd said there couldn't be a sea passage to India?"

Silently he assented. Remember that day, indeed! Would he ever forget its smallest detail? Though, to tell the truth, Ferdinand's talk was less clear in his memory than the scene he had later watched from the workshop door. He saw her eyes suddenly drop, and the colour steal over her delicate face. Had she guessed his thoughts?

"If the Venetians knew Gama had been seen, then they knew there was a passage," she was saying very low, and as if, it struck Nicolo, she were struggling with some pent-up emotion. "And so they – Venice – want the maps to show how to reach the Orient ahead of Portugal."

"Of course!" cried Abel. "To steal a march on Portugal before Gama can get home to tell what he's found, and before Portugal can claim it! How did we miss it, Nicolo? Certainly, Ferdinand was right when he suspected something behind the ambassador's inquiries. You see," he said, musing aloud, "Venice must make a desperate stand to keep her trade supremacy."

There was a sound of despair from Nicolo. "Then how

can I, a Venetian, hold up my head here if this thing ever comes to light? My business – the friends I've made – " He got up hastily to hide his emotion.

Abel pressed him down again in his chair. " My dear boy, has there ever been a time when there wasn't war over trade? "

" Portugal would do the same thing in Venice's place," Ruth impartially stated. " You mustn't take this so to heart, Nicolo! It's none of your doing."

" Assuredly, Portugal would do the same thing," Abel repeated. " Besides, your record here is too good to have this thing count against you, even if it should come to light."

" Do you think, if Manoel should hear of it, that he wouldn't let it ' count against ' me? " Nicolo asked bitterly. " And Gama – what would he say? I tell you the ground is cut from under me. I'll have nothing. I'll be discredited – dishonoured."

He saw Nejmi slip out of the room and felt, miserably, that it was the way she wished to slip out of his life. He became aware of Abel's voice . . . something about " an odd angle."

" A very odd angle to this business," he was saying. " Now, what if I should take a notion to revenge myself on Manoel, and give my maps up to Venice? "

" Abel! " gasped Ruth.

" Well, after all, I'm human! Would it more than even his account with our people? "

In the dead silence that fell on the workshop, Nicolo, dumbfounded, could only study Abel's face. Shrewd, keen, sagacious; jaw thrust ever so little forward; eyes narrowed. The face now of Banker Zakuto! Banker Zakuto, who held,

at last, the odds that would square, in part, at least, the long
account of his people.

Suddenly the old whimsical laughter twitched the corners of his mouth. " Don't be afraid, Nicolo! Ruth, did you
really think I would? " The boyish eyes were twinkling –
perhaps, too, were a bit wet. " Did you think I'd do any harm
to the child that Bartholomew and I have tended and watched
years before Manoel was born – the Way of the Spices? "

" Abel," Ruth said, with a catch in her voice, " there
was never another like you, my dear! "

" That's what was going through my mind," Nicolo
quietly seconded her.

" Nonsense! " declared Abel, vigorously clearing his
throat. " Now, about that chap who is after my maps – "

" I haven't yet seen him, sir, but I'm sure to. He might,
though, come to you first."

" I'll attend to him whenever he comes! " declared Abel.

" Then," Nicolo said, sombrely, as he started toward
the door, " I'd better go and tell Scander what Nejmi – what
you think about the maps."

" Keep us in touch with every step," Abel charged him.
" Especially anything you hear of Gama."

It was later than he'd thought, Nicolo saw, as he crossed
the court. The stars were out, and the moon just showed
over the high wall. He was reaching for the gate, when, from
behind the vine trellis, and directly in front of him, stepped –
Nejmi. Too startled to speak, even to think coherently, it
went through his mind that all the golden sweetness of the
night was gathered up into her.

" Nicolo," she breathed hardly above a whisper, " you
said – I heard you say – you had nothing."

Puzzled, he could only look at her. "Yes, I said that," he finally got out.

"Then, Nicolo, if you have nothing, now – now is the time I should pay my debt to you."

He steeled himself not to wince at this mention of that old hurt. And yet this look in her eyes, this tremulous tenderness of her lips, what was it? Was it pity? Though the pounding of his heart and the surge in his ears turned everything dizzy, he saw how pale she was.

Suddenly she moved nearer him. Then –

"Nicolo, I love you!"

Spellbound, he stared at her. He couldn't have heard aright. Was he stark mad – or was she? "You mean Ferdinand!" he said, and his voice sounded strange in his ears.

"I knew that was what you thought," she cried, with a little sobbing catch in her voice. "Ah, no, Nicolo – *you!* I – I have nothing to pay you with except – except love."

It was that "nothing to pay you" which broke, at last, the numbness in his brain, at his heart. "Nothing!" Yet not always "nothing." In fancy he saw her father's house, the great warehouses of Scander's description, the wealth and luxury that once were hers. And then, across that vision, flashed another: an empty barrel . . . a tender body, forlorn, destitute! He swept her up in his arms, murmuring he would never know what.

At last he held her back a little. Just enough to look full at her. Moonlight, Nicolo decided at that moment – moonlight that sifted through blossoming shade – was for the sole purpose of tracing patterns of delight on Nejmi's arms and on Nejmi's upturned face – patterns as uncapturable as the beauty of that face.

"But, Nejmi, that afternoon when Ferdinand talked to you about the 'flaming kiss' of East and West, he meant his feeling for you. I watched when you weren't looking!"

"I know," she laughed softly, "because I watched you when *you* weren't looking! No, Ferdinand didn't mean his feeling for me, and what you heard him say only showed his real heart."

But Nicolo wanted reassurance. "What is his real heart?"

"The love of adventure, of finding –" she hesitated, feeling for a word – "of finding a new Beyond! That will always be his great love, Nicolo; always it will be first with him. Can't you see it in that beautiful, flaming look that comes to his eyes when he talks about the time that he can go?"

"I was so sure, so desperately, wretchedly sure you loved him, Nejmi! There was such happiness in your face – only, somehow it was such frightened happiness."

"'Frightened,' yes," she said, very low, "for I'd seen *your* face at the workshop door! And I was afraid to believe what I saw in it, because –" her voice sank to a breath – "because I so wanted it to be true! I was afraid of myself, lest I couldn't keep from you . . ." She hid her face on his shoulder. "Oh, Nicolo, how shall I say it?"

He drew her closer. "Keep what from me, dear?"

"You remember that time, with the bird, when you told me not to be afraid? Ah, Nicolo, I loved you then – and ever since! That was what I tried to keep from you until I dared to tell you I'd pay my debt with love!"

"And how cruel I thought you were to say I wanted

you to pay me! " He was suddenly grave. " Why did you choose tonight to tell me? "

She turned a radiant face to him. " When I heard you say you would have no friends, nothing, I knew that it was time to pay my debt, and I came out here to – to find courage to do it! "

" But, Nejmi, if what we suspect of Venice should be known here in Lisbon, it would count against me. Do you want me, with a blot on my name? "

" What is against you is against me, too, Nicolo. What difference does anything but our love make to us? "

What difference, indeed? His arms tightened about her with a rapturous wonder at what she had said. Yet for her dear sake this plot should be set straight! Aloud he said tenderly, " Why have you kept me so at a distance – hardly ever let me talk alone with you? "

She made no answer until again he urged her: " Why, dear? "

" You know, Nicolo," she said at last, " that Master Abel and Mother Ruth would have gone away long ago but for me; so, how could I think of anything apart from them? "

" It won't be ' apart,' " he promised. " I'll share you – they shan't be left alone."

" And then, too," she said, looking away from him, " I couldn't wholly forget how I'd been brought up – how my people – my mother's people – believe a girl should be brought up."

He remembered how Scander had spoken of the seclusion of Arab women of her rank.

" And now – " she covered her face with her hands – " see what I've done! Among my own people I'd be in disgrace. But you were so unhappy when I said it was Venice that wanted the maps ... Ah, Nicolo, I had to pay my debt! "

" Losing everything was nothing to losing you," he told her ardently. " Yet how could I come to you with even a shadow of suspicion against me? Nejmi," he asked, suddenly curious, " what made you think of Venice? "

" I don't know. It flashed across me like a streak of light in the dark. And we Arabs say, when something comes to you like that, it's sent by Allah."

Silently he pondered what she had told him. What would Scander say now about the maps?

" I sometimes think, Nicolo," she went on, " that though my father was a European, my heart is all Arab! "

He assented, though not quite understanding her.

" Do you remember how long it was that I hated all mention of the Way or of anything connected with it? At first I forced myself, because I loved Master Abel so, to touch his maps, his instruments. Do you remember the night I was polishing the compass? "

Ah, didn't he!

" Now I know that from the beginning it was the will of Allah that my life should be linked with the Way. Else why – " she threw out her hands in a gesture that he recognized belonged only to the Orient – " else why all that horror – my father and mother – and afterward the sea and those men? And at last Master Abel and the workshop? "

" You mean," he said, with a sudden flash of understanding, " it was all part of the finding of the Way? "

" It was all part of Allah's will that the Way should be found! " she gently corrected. " Don't you see, Nicolo, how small all my trouble, even my whole life, seems, when you think of it as part of the great will of Allah? And so, from hating the Way, and then trying to like it for dear Master Abel's sake, I've come to think of it as something of which I'm part. And now, Nicolo, I feel as Master Abel does, as Master Diaz does: I'd do anything for the Way! "

"And I love it," he tenderly told her, "for its bringing us to each other. From the very first time I saw the fear in your dear eyes I've wanted to make you forget all that horror and fright. And that's what I'm going to do, from now on and forever! "

"Forever!" she repeated, with a strange look. "Did you ever think, Nicolo, how long that word is? That it reaches back as far as it reaches forward? "

"You mean," he said, softly, "that – that our love, too, is the will of Allah? "

She took his hands and covered her eyes with them. "From the beginning – forever! "

CHAPTER 19

The King's Marmosets

" A SCORE of marmosets . . . ordered special for the
King . . . and not a one of 'em saved – "

The words drifted out from a knot of passing sailors to
Nicolo hurrying toward The Green Window. Absently he

wondered why " not a one of 'em " had been saved. The next moment he was obliged to give way for another group. Where had they all come from – and all at once? Sailors in peaked caps everywhere you looked. Before tavern doors, at corners, swaggering by twos and threes along the street. Never before had he seen the town so full of them; and at so late an hour, too, though for all he cared or knew about time it might have been blazing noon as well as a radiant summer night.

All that really mattered now about time was whether or not it separated him from Nejmi! And all that mattered in the whole world was her happiness. Nothing must stand in the way of that, not even a shadow of suspicion against him – though she had said that would make no difference. His good name, doubly precious now, must be without reproach. Yet, how to steer an honourable course? How be loyal to the country of his adoption without dishonouring the country of his birth?

To his surprise he found The Green Window jammed with noisy sailors, whose calls for drinks Pedro was trying to fill, looking like a brown gnome as he scurried from one to another.

Concealed at his old post in the rear of the room, he waylaid the old man on one of those trips. " I've seen nothing but sailors," he declared, " all the way down here."

" Of course," returned Pedro. " With 'em all coming in to port and none shipping out, what'd you expect? "

" None shipping out? Why not? "

" Haven't you heard about the pirates? "

Vaguely Nicolo recalled hearing something or other about pirates, that morning on the docks, with Scander.

" By the way, has Scander been back here? " he inquired.

" Here now. Wanted to know when you came in. I'll go tell him you've come."

Pedro bustled off, and in a moment Scander appeared, yawning.

" That Marco'll keep me up all night," he complained. " He won't budge from anyone that he can get to talk about this pirate business, and I won't leave him till I see where he berths. I suppose you've heard the latest about the pirates? "

" No, and I don't want to, until I've told you something! "

" What Master Abel says? "

" No – what Nejmi says! That talk about maps between the ambassador and Ferdinand, that you said meant nothing, is the gist of the whole plot! " He forthwith described Nejmi's instant and unhesitating conviction.

" That child," said Scander, very quiet and humble, " is right! "

" But you as much as told me I was a fool," Nicolo reminded him," when I thought we should follow up the map item."

" I know," Scander admitted, " but where you just thought, Nejmi *knew!* It's just as she said, when a thing flashes at you out of the dark, you may be certain it's the truth."

He glanced at Marco, talking and drinking. " So that's why," he mused, " he's waiting around for the tall chap to get hold of the maps."

" Of course," Nicolo agreed. " I'm looking for that chap

any time, now, to come here to ask me to take him to Master
Abel's."

" Had you ever thought he might go there by himself? "

" Yes, and I mentioned it, too. Master Abel seemed sure
he could manage him."

Scander pursed his lips. "Hm! If he wants those
maps bad, it's not going to be child's play to prevent him
getting 'em."

" You mean," Nicolo said, " that one of us should stay
by Master Abel, in case – "

He was interrupted by a burst of voices. A group of
sailors trooped in, all talking at once.

" And the little beasts a-squealing and a-chattering like
demons, and a-clambering up the rigging " – a burly fellow
was bawling.

" Yes," shouted another, " and I a-yelling that they was
the King's marmosets and whoever laid hand to 'em – "

" The King's marmosets! " Nicolo exclaimed. " That's
the second time tonight I've heard about them."

" Yes," said Scander. " A ship bound back here from
the Verde Islands with a cargo of gold and a score or so of
marmosets, was boarded off Morocco."

" Another one? " Nicolo broke in with an alarmed face.
" Besides the two we heard about this morning? If Rodriguez – "

" Don't you remember, when you first came in, me
speaking of the latest pirate attack, and Marco being all
taken up with the talk about it? " Scander wheeled around
and hurriedly glanced about the room. " I must keep my
eye on him," he murmured. " Look – there he is! "

Absorbed, intent, and as near as he could squeeze to the

man who had come in with the marmoset story, sat Marco. "What were you carrying besides marmosets?" they heard him ask.

"Raw gold, mostly, and as rich as I ever saw," the man ruefully replied. "I'd have made a gift of it to the swine if they'd let those marmosets alone. Why, those marmosets – ordered special for King Manoel, they was – would've brought me in a snug bit."

"Lose the gold, too?" they heard Marco inquire.

"Every grain of it! And then they turned everything inside out looking for – *spice!* Did you ever hear the like of that?" he demanded from his audience. "*Spice!*"

At that word there was a sudden lull. Those who could, edged nearer him, and others craned their necks or stood up on benches to see him.

"I asked 'em how was I to get hold of spice – which doesn't come except from India – and all they did was to go on searching. Even started to break in the bulkheads!"

"Yes," put in another voice, "and they swore we were helping Gama get his cargo to Lisbon secret-like!"

Scander nudged Nicolo – "Look at Marco!"

Eyes glittering, lips caught hard between teeth, Marco, transfixed, sat staring at the last speaker.

Nicolo watched him a moment, and lightning-like came conviction: "He knows something about this pirate raid!"

"I was only waiting for you to say it!" agreed Scander. "By the saints –" as Marco suddenly rose – "he's going! I'll have to follow him."

"Here then, quick!" Nicolo jumped to fling open the back door, and as Marco, shouldering through the crowd, disappeared through the front, Scander dove out of the rear.

∽∽∽ The King's Marmosets ∽∽∽

Pedro, in high feather, stopped to whisper to Nicolo that never had his money bag been so heavy. If only the pirates would keep Lisbon bottled up a while longer, he'd presently be rich enough to retire.

Yes, thought Nicolo, but what if, at this moment, Rodriguez was fleeing with empty holds before those robbers?

He went back to his seat where, hidden in shadow, he could watch and listen. What did it all mean, this sudden onslaught of pirates, and their absurd demand for spice?

There again! A fresh batch of arrivals and loud cries for a retelling of the tale of the King's marmosets! Of the search for cloves – nutmegs!

" Must have thought you was Gama, back from India! " someone sputtered thickly, and was rewarded for his pleasantry by a shout of drunken laughter from his cronies.

But back in the shadows, Nicolo neither heeded nor joined in that laughter. In a daze he was whispering to himself the jest just stammered by that maudlin voice: " Must have thought you was Gama back from India." Almost to a word, he now recalled, what that captain had said, this morning, on the dock: " Must think I'm Gama."

Suddenly a memory of a flushed face flashed before him, an angry voice that yelled, " I've seen Gama. You won't see him again! " And staring at that fancied face, Nicolo was seized with an overpowering impulse to shout with laughter at himself, at this roomful of blind fools. Here he was, puzzling, twisting, straining after the truth, and there, staring him out of countenance, was the truth! If it had been less plain, less evident, he'd have seen it more easily. The pirates were lying in wait for Gama! Primed, of course, by those who had spied on him: Marco and his companion, perhaps others.

But that final word of Marco's "You won't see him
again!" He had dismissed it as nonsense, but now – He became aware that his heart was pounding, that a cold terror
had burst out on him. He knew now it was for more than to
waylay and to plunder Gama that the pirates were waiting.
. . . "You won't see him again!"

"Gama must be saved. Must be saved!" he heard himself saying, and realized that he was beating his knee with his
fist. Fool that he was not to have seen this thing sooner, for
now there was no time to spare. Hadn't Scander said only
six months from the Devil's Cave to Lisbon? And if Marco
had seen Gama somewhere near there, and Marco were *here,*
then Gama must be near. He started up. He must see Scander. Then he remembered: Scander was somewhere, following Marco. Besides, what if Marco's mate were to appear
here to ask about Abel's maps?

Maps! He'd forgotten about them in this terrifying discovery. What was he to do, which clue follow first? Gama
or the maps? What was the part of Marco and his companion? Were they in league with Venice to steal the maps?
In league with the pirates to destroy Gama? His heart seemed
to stop as a new possibility leaped to his mind: *was Venice
in league with the pirates?*

In a torture of uncertainty he felt himself tossed
in a swirl of angry currents, yet always he clung to one
thought: Gama must be saved! Gama and the Way must be
saved for Portugal. The Way, for which dreams had been
dreamed, for which hazard incredible had been risked
and the sacrifice supreme had been made, mustn't now be
lost!

He crossed his arms on the back of his chair and dropped

his head on them. He must think this thing through. His own loss, loss of friends, of business, seemed now really nothing compared to the loss that threatened Portugal. He had told Nejmi he loved the Way for its bringing them together. Now he knew that he loved it for itself.

He raised his head and studied the roistering room. Seamen of every age and degree still jostled for standing space, and drank and caroused. If, somehow, they and their vessels now bottled up in Lisbon harbour could be got to go out as one fleet, to be stationed at points, some of which Gama was bound to pass – at Cape Verde, the Canaries, the Madeiras, even as far north as St. Vincent's – they would soon have those Moroccan thieves on the run, and Gama would be saved. But what could he tell them to make them go? They wouldn't listen to him, to a land-lubber. Yet they might to Scander – if he'd only come!

He'd wait here for him, Nicolo decided, and not go to bed, for it must be nearer morning than midnight. He put his head down again on his arms, and in spite of the uproar that filled the inn he felt himself dozing off. Once he started at his own voice: "Gama must be saved!" Had he been dreaming – talking in his sleep?

Almost immediately, it seemed to him, someone was gently shaking him. He opened his eyes. Scander was bending over him and smiling. Through the huge window streamed the eastern sun. The little inn was empty and quiet except for Pedro sweeping the floor, and for the voices of people passing the open door. What were they all talking about so earnestly?

"Sat up all night, did you, lad?"

Nicolo scanned the tanned face. There was a curious

glint in the burnt gimlet holes. " Scander, you've heard some news! "

" So've you! " Scander shot back. " Let's have it."

" Gama must be saved " – the words he last remembered saying before he had waked. " We must save him, Scander! "

" How'd you come to see that? " Scander asked, with the odd glint still in his eyes.

" The wonder is that I didn't see it sooner! It flashed on me while they were telling how the pirates kept searching for spice and dropping remarks about Gama. What else could those raids mean, one after the other, in the very place where Gama was sure to pass, but that the pirates were expecting him? And that spice talk! Who but Gama could have spice? What's the matter with our Portuguese crews that they didn't suspect what was up? "

" Likely would have, if they hadn't got used to thinking Gama was dead. The only reason the pirates don't think the same is because " – Scander paused significantly – " because they've been told different."

Nicolo nodded. " Of course. By Marco and the other one. There was something else that came to me last night, what Marco told me that first time: *' But you won't see him again.'* "

" Just so," said Scander. " Seemed as if you took the words out of my mouth when, first thing, you says to me, ' Gama must be saved.' "

Nicolo gave him a keen glance. " Then something you found out since I last saw you put that into your head. The minute I looked at you I saw something had happened to you."

" Yes," said Scander. " This morning, just after I came ashore."

" Ashore? Where'd you been? "

" I stayed up all night, same as you," grinned Scander. " You remember I dodged out after Marco? Well, I followed him right down to the water-front. I could see by the way he stepped along he was worked up, just as he was when he was listening to that fellow whose ship was boarded. Now what was there about that talk, I kept asking myself, to excite him? " He paused as Pedro, smiling and complacent, came toward them. " Don't let him suspect anything's up," he warned in an undertone.

" Well, Pedro," laughed Nicolo. " I can see you made a good thing of last night."

Pedro reiterated his hope that not a ship would leave Lisbon harbour for a long while yet.

" Did you have a good rest, Master Conti? " he anxiously inquired. " I tried to wake you so you could go to bed, but you were like the dead! Why," turning to Scander, " he slept through all that noise the town crier made – and he beating his drum in the square just yonder! And afterward, every-one that passed the door was talking about it, but Master Conti never so much as lifted an eyelid! "

Nicolo recalled the footsteps and voices when he had first waked. " What was it all about? " he inquired indif-ferently.

" There's to be a proclamation read to the Jews today," Scander replied.

Instantly Nicolo's indifference vanished. That would af-fect Master Abel, and if him, then Nejmi. " An edict? " he asked in a startled voice. " What about? "

Scander laughed. "I heard that 'twas to forbid the Jews to leave the country."

"Forbid them to go?" Nicolo exclaimed. "Why, it's only two years ago that the King was ordering them to go!" He was immensely relieved. Now there would never be any more question of Abel's and Ruth's going nor of Nejmi's parting with them.

"Yes," put in Pedro, "I heard people saying the King left town a-purpose, so he wouldn't be here to hear folks laugh at him for changing his word so quick! Reckon he's found out the Jews are his best citizens – doesn't want to lose 'em. Anyway," he ended, as he moved away, "every man, woman and child of them, so the crier said, must come to hear the proclamation one hour before sundown today."

"I'm glad it's no worse," Scander declared. "I couldn't bear to see Master Abel suffer any more."

"It will be a blow to his pride," Nicolo mused – "to the pride of all the Jews, in fact. But for myself, I'm glad they're to stay."

"So am I," Scander warmly agreed. "As Pedro says, they're our best citizens. Now, let's see," he said, drawing closer to Nicolo and lowering his voice, "where was I when Pedro broke in? Oh yes – I was telling about following Marco and noticing he was all worked up. Well, when he got down to the quay, he made straight for a boat that was tied up there, and before I could borrow or lay hand to one, he'd jumped in, and rowed off."

"You found him again, I'll warrant!"

Scander acknowledged the compliment with a grin. "It wasn't too hard! You see I was sure he wouldn't leave Lisbon at that time of night, and if he did, his ship would be the only one going out and I'd have no trouble sighting her. So I rowed around, and after a while something shiny in the moonlight caught my eye. 'Twas a pair of *wet* oars in a rowboat astern of a small craft."

"He'd forgotten to take his oars in!" exclaimed Nicolo.

"Just what I figured. Excited and forgot 'em. I hung around near by and early in the morning I sighted him, sure enough, clambering down from his vessel into the boat."

"You didn't see the other chap?"

"Not a sign of him. Afterward I found out he was in town all night. Well, I trailed along behind Marco and watched him go ashore. He appeared to be concerned about something, talking first to one, and then to another. Finally I lounged alongside of him and made as if I was going to pass him, when he catches up to me and says, distressed and nervous, 'No one'll take us out over the bar. They're all afraid of pirates outside. I've offered three times the regular fee, too!' "

"Then they're planning to go right away!" exclaimed Nicolo.

"I looked at him close," Scander continued, "and I saw he was in a regular panic lest he couldn't get off. Thinks I, 'You're counting on your mate's getting Master Abel's maps and then both of you making a dash for it.' If somehow I could take him unexpected, and surprise the truth out of him! So I says, cool and offhand, 'If you can't get a pilot, it'll kind of delay your going to Venice.'

" 'Venice!' he grunts. 'We aren't going to Venice!' Then, like lightning –" Scander drew close to Nicolo and his voice was barely a whisper – "*I knew where he was going!*"

With one impulse each gripped the other. " To join the pirates against Gama," Nicolo's lips formed.

" Odd," said Scander, " how it came so quick to you and me both. I swear I was shaking so, I was afraid he'd see, but I managed to say I'd had a bit of pilot service, and I'd take him out, over Belem bar, when he and his mate was ready."

" We can't wait for them! We've got to reach Gama without delay. The pirates aren't going to stop at lifting his cargoes, you know! "

" I know," Scander nodded. " They're going to do their cursed best to make true what's being gossiped around about him! "

" That he's dead! Of course. I tell you we haven't a day to lose. You said yourself it was only six months from the Cape to Lisbon. If we could get some of these ship masters, who are cooped up here, to form a fleet and start right out for some point that Gama's bound to pass – "

" Well, you couldn't," said Scander shortly, " so you'd better stop planning anything like that."

" You mean," Nicolo retorted, " they'd be afraid to take the risk for Gama, who's risked his life over and again! "

" It's not that, either – not exactly. Don't any of 'em half believe he's alive, and 'twould take more than you and me to convince 'em."

Nicolo brought his fist down on his knee. " Then, by heaven, you and I must do what we can to save Gama! "

Scander gave him a searching look. " How far'll you go with that? "

"*All the way.*" Nejmi's " I'd do anything for the Way," flashed through his mind. " Remember," he said, looking Scander in the eye, "that I've a ship due any day."

" But what good is it to you, when you aren't even sure where Rodriguez has her? "

Nicolo didn't answer at once. " Let's talk that over while we have something to eat."

He got up, stretched vigorously. They both went over to Pedro who was doing something over a brazier of glowing coals.

"About time you were hungry! " the old man told them, and he held up two skewers with little cubes of broiled mutton. He made them sit down, and brought plates and bread.

'" Scander," Nicolo presently said, as he tore off a morsel of bread and soaked it in meat juice, " you'll have to take care of the map end of this business – you and Master Abel – because I'm going to start for Cascaes [1] as soon as you can hire a boat and take me down there."

Scander stopped eating to stare. " What you going to do at Cascaes? "

" I'm going," Nicolo answered deliberately, " to wait there for Rodriguez. He'll stop for a pilot. If he hasn't run afoul of these pirates he's sure to be along in a day or two at latest, and we won't waste an hour putting right about for Cape Verde or for wherever he thinks Gama is likely to pass."

" What? " cried the astonished Scander. " You aren't going to have him first bring the cargo to Lisbon? "

[1] Cascaes. Fifteen miles west of Lisbon, where ships bound for Lisbon take on pilots.

"No. We'll leave the cargo at Cascaes – if there is a cargo!"

"Why, man, you'll lose your profits that way! To unload at Cascaes, and then to re-ship to Lisbon'll cost – "

"I told you I was going *all the way*," Nicolo impatiently broke in.

For a moment Scander was silent, and his keen eyes softened. "I'd ask for the job of pilot to you and Rodriguez," he said gruffly, "if 'twasn't for having to keep an eye on Marco. But we can't risk either of those fellows giving us the slip. As to that," he confidently added, "they won't leave Lisbon without me knowing it, for they can't get anyone else to take 'em over the bar."

"How would it be to go down to Cascaes right away, so you could be back here, all ready for them?"

"Right!" agreed Scander, briskly pushing back from the table. "We'll hire a skiff, and be off at once. I suppose," he grinned, as they left The Green Window and turned down the little alley, "you can make out with a sail, if I take the helm and tell you what to do?"

"Yes – or even the other way around!" Nicolo grinned back. Suddenly he sobered. "I shan't wait more than two days for Rodriguez."

"I was wondering what you had in mind in case he didn't come," Scander admitted, "but I didn't like to ask."

"Get another ship. Some of those Cascaes seamen might like nothing better than to show their heels to a pack of pirates.

"I only wish you were going," Nicolo added, guessing Scander's thoughts. "But what with the maps, and Marco and the other fellow to be looked after . . ."

" I've settled one thing," chuckled Scander, " which is that Lisbon quay is the limit of those chaps' travels, till every bit of this pirate business has blown over. They're mixed up, somehow, with that, and they don't mean any good to Gama – so here they stay, where they can't hurt him! "

" Then you'll have to have some help ready, when they find out you aren't going to take them down river."

" Let them try and start something! All I'd have to do would be to tell about Marco's seeing Gama. The crowd would take care of him! "

" I wish I could be with you and at Cascaes at the same time," Nicolo said anxiously. " If those fellows should make some move for the maps – "

" I'd already thought of that," Scander assured him, " and I'd about decided to go up to Master Abel's every little while so's to be on hand in case of trouble. Besides," he added, " even if they did get his maps, they'd find themselves in a blind alley – with me at the open end! By the way, what shall I say if Master Abel asks where you are? You can't tell, of course, how long you'll be gone."

For a moment Nicolo was too startled and confused to reply. His plan to try and warn Gama had shaped itself so quickly – taken him, as it were, by surprise – that he had hardly thought beyond Cascaes. But, as Scander had hinted, who knew how long he might be gone? For the first time, the hazard, the actual danger of what he meant to do, confronted him. What if he never came back? Yes, he must see Nejmi! He must tell her, as he held her close, where he was going, and why. But wouldn't that delay the start for Cascaes, and hinder Scander's return to Lisbon?

Irresolute and perplexed, he wavered. Then he

remembered that he hadn't told Pedro he was going away. He'd run back to The Green Window.

"Scander," he said, "I forgot to speak to Pedro. I'll meet you presently at the dock."

At the door of The Green Window he hesitated. He was so near now to Nejmi. Just up the hillside, and the flight of stairs! Who could tell what might happen after Cascaes?

"Look here, Master Conti!" Pedro was hurrying toward him, carefully holding something between his palms. "That tall fellow was just in – him that wanted to see you about maps or something."

"How long ago?" cried Nicolo.

"Just after you'd gone out. But this time he didn't mention you. Said he wanted a word with Master Zakuto, and asked me to point him out when the proclamation's read to the Jews this afternoon. And see –" he held up a gold coin – "what he gave me to do that!"

Nicolo glanced at the coin in the brown fingers. Marco's mate was at work! Instantly his mind was made up. "Pedro," he said abruptly, "I'll be gone for a while. Don't expect me back just yet."

He stepped into the alley and hurried toward the docks. As fast as they could, Scander and he must be on their way to Cascaes. There might soon be need of Scander back in Lisbon.

It came to him strangely that his decision had been made – but not by himself! Was it by a self that he had never known until now? "I'd do anything for the Way!" Nejmi had said. Was that why, longing to go to her, he had not gone, because he, too, would do "anything for the Way"?

CHAPTER 20

The Workshop Lamp

F ROM the top of the stairway Nejmi watched Ruth and Abel descend, and waved to them when they turned back to look at her. How closely they clung to each other, the broad-shouldered figure in its conical hat and black cloak, and the stout, short figure in the long cloak and hood! Though they both stood very straight, neither leaning on the other, that close clinging made Nejmi think, somehow, of two lonely children comforting each other. But they should never be lonely, she said to herself with a rush of tenderness, as she watched them disappear around a corner. Nicolo and she would so surround them with warmth and love, so try to atone for all the suffering Manoel had brought on them, that there would never be room for loneliness. This edict that they had gone now to hear proclaimed was another humiliation, but, she reflected, not actual cruelty.

Everything should welcome them when they got back. Supper would be ready and the house lighted. It would be dark by then, for the reading of the edict would hardly be over at sundown, and Master Abel had said that afterward they might stop a moment to see Rabbi Joseph, who was too old and infirm to leave his house. She would even leave the gate ajar, Nejmi thought to herself, as she stepped back into the court, so that they could see the light from the workshop lamp as soon as they reached the head of the stairs.

But before it was too dark, she must do what she had decided to do when she had heard Nicolo say, "What if the Venetian ambassador's friend should come here! " Master Abel had seemed not to heed, but it had come to her like a command that the maps must be hidden. It was better that she should hide them, so that if they were demanded of him he wouldn't know where they were.

She crossed the court to the workshop. At the threshold she paused and surveyed the room. Shelves . . . cupboards . . . table drawer. No chance for concealment. Under the carpenter's work-bench? She stooped down to look. Plenty of room of course, but anyone would be sure to search there. Again she scrutinized the room, from floor to ceiling, absently noting that the draught between door and windows was gently stirring the great lamp above the table. Her eyes came back to the swaying lamp, fixed on it. The very thing! No one would ever dream of looking there.

She ran to the row of brass containers, slipped the maps from them, and made several tight rolls. Then, standing on the table, she opened Abel's "lighthouse." Carefully she fitted the rolls inside. Now, just to latch its door – But what was that sound? The gate swinging on its hinges? Perhaps Nicolo! Surely not Master Abel and Mother Ruth so soon. She jumped down, and ran to look.

A tall figure in seaman's coat was pausing, motionless, in the act of stepping into the court. The man might have been a statue, but for eyes that seemed live fires and for quivering nostrils and twitching lips. The air grew dark, whirled with a million shining specks. Her body seemed not to be there on the threshold of the workshop, seemed not to be a body at all but only a sensation of deathly faintness, of hideous, endless sinking. A mad thing leaped and tore at her breast. Was it the heart in the body that had been hers? If she could only move – speak. A curious fancy possessed her that she was a bird unable to stir before the evil glitter of narrowed eyes in a weaving head; that she was a creature of the wild, beyond motion in the shadow of a hovering hawk.

Something in her suddenly snapped, and she was conscious of struggling, like one in a nightmare, against death-like numbness. She felt something cold at her throat, and looking down, she saw that her hands were gripped there. Her gaze went back to the figure at the gate. Slowly, almost as if he were feeling his way, the man was coming toward her.

Ah Nicolo! Scander! Dear Master Abel! Where are you? She didn't deserve this – not after the anguish of Aden . . . of the slave market . . . of the *Sultana.*

Now he was standing before her, breathing hard through dilated nostrils, as she remembered he breathed when he was stirred or angry. She hadn't forgotten the black, bushy hair that showed under his peaked cap. The old terror flooded over her. Her knees were shaking. With a supreme effort she locked her fingers together. So, O Allah, hold her sinking spirit from this fear that was worse than death.

" You haven't forgotten me I see! "

The Arabic that she hadn't heard for so long, the awful familiarity of the guttural tones!

" Say my name! " he ordered.

Her tongue rasped her parched mouth, but no sound came. The only effort she could seem to make was to grip her hands still more tightly.

He took a step nearer her. " Say it! Say my name! "

" Abdul! " at last she choked out.

His eyes narrowed in the way she remembered so well. Would she ever forget their expression when he and Slaiman had debated whether or not to make a present of her to this or to that Bey?

" Ah," he swore softly, " you haven't forgotten! " Then, " How'd you get here? " he demanded, peering into her face.

So, just so, had he peered at her through the bars of the cage he had ordered built for her! But she must summon now, as she had summoned then, the will not to flinch, lest he should guess her sick revulsion and wreak worse vengeance on her.

"How'd you get here? " he repeated. "No matter – " as she cast about for an answer – "I'm in a hurry." Then, "Where does Zakuto keep his maps? " he snapped out.

In puzzled dismay she stared at him. How should he know or care about Master Abel's maps? Then . . . great Allah above! Could it be – could it possibly be that Abdul and the Venetian ambassador's "friend" were one? Had he found out that Abel and Ruth were to be away? Involuntarily her eyes sought the lamp. She hadn't fastened its door! The next moment, in a panic lest his eyes had followed hers, she again fixed her gaze on him.

"You know where those maps are – I can tell by your looks! "

Ah, he had seen her expression change!

"Come! Hand them over. Zakuto'll be coming back."

She saw him scan the sky and noticed that the sun had left the court. The proclamation must be at an end. If she could play for time, perhaps some kind chance, or the tiny, inner voice that sometimes warns humans, might make them come directly home instead of stopping at Rabbi Joseph's.

"I know what you're thinking! " he flashed at her. "But if you figure you can keep me dangling till they get back – " He took a step nearer and seized her wrist. "Get those maps – and get them now! "

His touch on her flesh roused her. The blood that had seemed to freeze within her was suddenly thundering in her ears. She threw back her head and faced him.

"Oh yes, you'll get them. Look here! " His free hand

slid something from his belt. His knife was gleaming at her throat.

How easily, she recalled, it had sunk into Slaiman's back! She braced herself against memory. This time her face shouldn't betray her.

"Will killing me," she coolly asked him, "give you the maps?"

"Then I'll kill you anyhow!" he raged. "Kill you for the sport of it." His grip on her wrist tightened into agony. "I swear I'll wait here for Zakuto, and if he refuses me, I'll kill him, too."

"It will be the same with him," she calmly assured him, "as with me. Kill us – but you won't get the maps." But within herself she was wildly praying, 'O Allah, keep them from coming home – delay them!'

She saw him stare past her into the workshop, followed his glance as it roved along the shelves – the bench – the table.

The next moment he flung her aside. "That's where he makes them," he muttered, as he burst past her.

She stole a terrified glance at the great lamp still gently stirring in the breeze. Its door was ajar! If it should open wider, and he should happen to look up at it – Oh, how could she get him away?

Panic stricken, she watched him dart from shelf to shelf, tear open cupboards, snatch at the table drawer, peer under the bench, tip up the empty brass tubes. Her heart stood still – his eyes were fixed on the lamp! No, he was staring at the windows! In her relief she felt suddenly weak.

But immediately she heard a frightful oath. The sun was setting, and Abdul was still unsuccessful. O Allah,

send him away before he should see that unfastened lamp
door. Before Master Abel and Mother Ruth should come
home! For Abdul, she knew too well, would do to them exactly as he had told her he would do. She tried to close her
memory on a vision of Slaiman sinking on the deck of the
Sultana, with Abdul's knife deep in his back. Oh, not that!
Not that in this beloved court. And Nicolo! Good, kind Allah,
what if he should happen in? Neither he nor Abel carried
what Abdul carried in his belt – and Abdul would do what
he had said he would do.

" I'll give you one more chance! " He stood stock still
in the midst of the disorder he had made, and even at that
distance she could see his quivering nostrils. He sprang toward her, thrust his face into hers. " You'll make it all the
worse for yourself, girl, if you don't give them up, for I'm
going to take you, maps or no maps! You hear me? "

Instantly she caught at the change from his first con-
fident order: " Get those maps. Hand them over." Now it
was " Maps *or no maps."* From certainty he had come to
compromise, to admission of possible failure. Another step,
and he might give up his search. She had only to offer herself and he would take that step – and Master Abel and the
maps would be safe! But she must be quick, for it was fast
darkening, and they would be back. And Abdul would keep
his word.

O Nicolo! O love and life, to put you forever away!
It was too much, too much to ask of human flesh, of human
spirit. She would delay, risk some incredible chance to step
between her and this black abyss. Something would happen,
something must happen, to save her and Nicolo for each
other.

But yet, what if after all, Abdul should find the maps, and the Way should be lost to Portugal? A sudden memory flamed within her of last night, when she had said to Nicolo that she would do anything for the Way. Her hands clutched at each other for support. Oh, Allah, of the boundless wisdom of thy will, strength to do what of her own will she could not!

She knew that her tongue moved, and her lips. But that voice – could it be hers?

"If I come with you, will you go away, now – at once?" said that unreal voice. Where was it that she was going with him? No matter! The maps would be safe.

He ripped out a savage oath. "You'd play with me, would you?" He jerked the blade of his knife up against her bare neck.

If it would only bury itself there, as it had in Slaiman's back! "I'm ready. I'll go with you," she calmly told him.

He stepped back, and the hand with the knife dropped to his side. "Aren't you afraid of dying?" he asked, with grim curiosity. "I remember we had to build that cage to keep you out of the sea." He came closer, so close that she could see the puzzled scowl of his black brows. "What are those maps to you that you won't give them up?"

A wild hope sprang in her heart. Was there in his curiosity just a bare hint of mercy? But instantly, as if he had forgotten what he had asked, she saw him glance at the dimming light, and saw his face set.

"Killing her isn't going to give me the maps!" she heard him soliloquize as if he defied an unseen accuser. He slipped the knife into his belt, turned impatiently on her.

"We must make the bar in a hurry. Put on something – quick."

It was like a blow that struck the breath from her; a black void that closed irrevocably over her. She knew now that, though she thought she had given up hope, she had not given it up till this moment! But he had said "the bar." Thank Allah for that! For just beyond the bar was the ocean – but this time her face mustn't let him guess her thoughts.

"Quick!" he repeated. "Something that'll cover you up."

Of course. The pale gold of her dress would at once mark her on the streets. She remembered an old cloak of Ruth's, and with a strange, bodiless feeling she went into the house, took the cloak from a chest, and went back with it to Abdul. He watched her while she fastened the hood.

"Lower over your face!" he ordered.

He seized her arm and hurried her through the gate. She heard it close behind them. The last link, as it had been the first, between her and blessed refuge. She fought down the anguish that welled up at the image of bewilderment, when Abel and Ruth should open it and see no light streaming out to welcome them. Would the empty tubes and the wild disorder of the workshop tell them what had happened? Inside the dear "lighthouse" would they find and understand her hidden message? And Nicolo – when they should tell him . . . Ah, let her not think of Nicolo now. Let her remember only that the maps were safe!

At the foot of the stairs, Abdul told her to pull the hood down still further. "Keep close to me," he whispered, "and if you make any sign for help . . ."

Silently she assented. The escape that she would make needed no help but the ocean. She would be so docile that he would forget to watch her, and as soon as he put to sea . . . Would there be a crew, she wondered in sudden terror – a crew like the *Sultana's?* No matter! She would feign obedience. This time she would need no cage. And somehow she would find a way to slip past them all. Allah wouldn't deny her that.

She could see that Abdul was making toward the harbour, by a round-about route to avoid, of course, the streets which would be full of people going home from hearing the proclamation. They would never know, Master Abel and Mother Ruth, how near she had passed! But who had told Abdul that they would be gone? The Venetian ambassador? Wouldn't he have heard this new edict talked of at the palace, and known that all Jews must be present to hear it read?

A cold fear seized her: it wasn't impossible that she should pass Nicolo or Scander. They were often at the waterfront. It wouldn't be in human flesh not to cry out to them. Yet if she did so forget her agreement, Abdul's knife would remind her!

In her anguish she hardly noticed that they had come to the docks. The docks that she had never seen since that night she had stolen away from the *Venezia!* Now, as then, they were silent and deserted. The gleam of tossing water caught her eye, and for the first time she was conscious of a strong breeze and that wind clouds swept across a bright moon.

As Abdul and she walked rapidly on, she saw a man move out of shadow, and slowly approach them. At that

first glance, her heart leaped. The short breeches and bare
legs were like Scander's! But the next moment showed her
an unfamiliar face below the peaked cap.

Abdul halted. " Marco! "

Marco? Marco, whom Nicolo had mentioned? Wasn't
it he who had let drop the stupendous news of Gama?

At Abdul's voice the man came closer. Nejmi could see
his amazement as he glanced inquiringly from her to Abdul,
but all he gave vent to was a breathless inquiry: " Have you
got them? "

" That's my business! " she heard Abdul retort. " Boat
and pilot all ready? "

" Curse him, I can't find him! " Marco stammered, and
Nejmi saw him step back as if to avoid an expected blow.
" I've been scouring the town for him, too, but – "

" What! He isn't here? "

At the contortion of Abdul's features Nejmi felt herself trembling even more than at the stream of oaths he was
choking out.

" Hell take you! " he raged. " I – I've depended on you
for that part of the job, while I – "

" Well, I did it, didn't I ? " The surly tone, Nejmi de-
tected, was only a blind for the fear that looked out of the
heavy face. " Found the only pilot in town who'd take us,
didn't I? " he continued. " If you'd told me sooner that you'd
changed your mind about leaving tomorrow morning, I
likely'd have found him."

" Stop your drivel, you fool," cried Abdul under his
breath. " Get someone else! " He glanced up and down at
the anchored craft as if he somehow expected help from
them.

"It can't be done, I tell you," declared the other. "There's not a soul'll do it. Don't I know? "

" Then by – we'll make it alone! " Abdul seized Nejmi's arm. " Where's the boat? "

She steadied herself against the shuddering terror that came over her at his touch. But she must do nothing to make him watch her. After all, it was not so far to the silent deeps that would grant her safe haven.

" Boat's over there." Marco jerked a thumb toward the end of the dock. He surveyed the harbour. "We've got the wind against us," he said sullenly. " That craft of ours won't stand everything! "

He stole a glance at Nejmi, and at once she guessed that he was speculating whether, in case of danger, her presence would lessen his own chances.

" Curse you," Abdul cut him short, " untie that boat! " He tightened his grasp on Nejmi, and they went forward, breasting the wind, while Marco ran ahead.

They were up with him almost as he drew the painter from its ring, warped the boat alongside. Without a word, Abdul lifted Nejmi and swung her into the rocking tender. Instantly he was behind her, pressing her down into the stern, while Marco leaped in and seized the oars.

" Everything ready out yonder? " asked Abdul, as the boat shot forward, and Nejmi saw him jerk his head sidewise.

" Except hoisting anchor," replied Marco.

Oh, where were they taking her? To another *Sultana?* She caught her breath as a wave broke over the side and dashed her with its spray.

" If it's this bad here," Marco said, half aloud, " what'll it be down river? We'd best wait for the wind to go down."

Abdul turned on him with a volley of oaths. " You'd wait and risk Gama's slipping through our fingers? Why, they might be sighting him now – devil take him! "

Gama! Her heart seemed to stop and then to batter furiously at her breast. Were her ears playing tricks? Could she have mistaken that name? Suddenly she remembered. Was this the treachery that Nicolo had suspected behind Marco's having seen Gama in Indian waters? And she, with her mind on the maps, had paid no attention! " *You'd wait and risk Gama's slipping through our fingers.*" She knew now where Abdul was taking her. He was on his pirate way to waylay Gama! Something flamed through her: perhaps she would see Gama! Then – she could warn him! Somehow she would find a way. With a strange feeling she looked down at the surging water whose refuge, only a moment before, she had meant to seek. Not that – yet!

She hardly knew that the boat had stopped. Mechanically she let Abdul lift her over the side of another vessel. She saw Marco set the row-boat adrift, and then hoist anchor. Together the men set the sails.

" Take the helm! " said Abdul. " I'll tend the sheets."

Marco hesitated, then walked reluctantly aft. " I don't claim to be an expert in these waters," he grumbled, " I won't promise to go beyond Belem without a pilot, either."

" Take my orders and stop your talk, you lubber! " roared Abdul, and Nejmi saw his face flame and one hand clutch at his belt. She dropped her eyes, sick at the thought that, only for the need of him at the helm, Abdul's knife would even now be sunk in Marco's neck.

Slowly the bow swung around, and the ship began to

move. Nejmi watched Abdul work the sheets as they tacked down the rough, moonlit river.

Stealthily she turned her head, that no one should see her backward look at the dark blur that was Lisbon. She locked her hands against her breast as if to crush down the agony that was bursting it. Ah, Nicolo – Nicolo!

Yet, O Allah, let her remember only that the maps were safe. That somewhere, beyond, in need of help was Gama!

CHAPTER 21

Arthur Rodriguez

A T dusk Nicolo and Scander were pacing Cascaes beach.
High prowed little fishing boats, dragged up on the
sand after discharging their catch, scattered the shore. Beyond, where the beach swept oceanward, the old Moorish

lighthouse pointed sombrely upward, and right and left glittered a choppy sea under a bright moon.

They had made slow work of beating down river against a slight breeze and a tide now near high, and, as he expected the wind to freshen, Scander was lingering to keep Nicolo company.

" At latest, I'll make Lisbon before midnight. Those fellows won't be leaving before then," he said confidently.

Voices made them look back. Behind them two men strolled toward an outspread fish net and sat down near it, hands clasped around their knees. Presently, a third joined them. Sitting there, peering out over their hunched knees, they looked to Nicolo like three wary old hawks, sweeping the landscape for prey.

" Pilots waiting for a call, I'll wager you," said Scander. " I'd like to know," he mused aloud, " what that tall fellow said to Master Zakuto when Pedro pointed him out."

" What makes me uneasy," said Nicolo, " is that he bribed Pedro to do that. Why didn't he ask me to take him to Zakuto, as he told Pedro he meant to? "

" I've wondered about that, too," Scander admitted. " He never did call at The Green Window for you, did he? There's one thing, though: whatever passed between him and Master Abel happened after the proclamation was read, about sundown, and nothing much can happen between sundown and sunrise, when I'll be back. Those fellows can't get very far without me."

He raised his head and snuffed the wind. " Breeze is freshening," he observed, " but it'll be with me going up river."

Nicolo looked anxiously at the water. "It won't be so easy for you, alone."

"There's not a tiller made ever got the best of me, nor a sail either! It's you, Master Conti," Scander said, gravely, "who's taking the real risk."

"It's nothing to the risk Gama's taken every day since he left us," rejoined Nicolo. "Nor to the one he's taking at this very moment – all unaware, too, poor chap! You know, Scander," he declared, "I've about concluded, if Rodriguez comes, not to discharge cargo, but to put to sea at once. Why, what if this minute Gama were steering straight into that nest of robbers!"

They had faced back and were retracing their steps. The three men sitting on the sand looked up, as they approached, and again Nicolo thought of hawks. Those gaunt, tight-skinned faces, that peculiar listening expression that comes from long intimacy with the sea – Yes, these men, or their like, would do for his errand, if Rodriguez couldn't go with him.

"When is the tide high?" Scander asked, as he and Nicolo halted.

"Just turned." One of the three pointed to a barely visible lag in the incoming water. "Are you going out?"

"Yes," said Scander, "to Lisbon. Pilots, are you," he inquired, "all of you?"

They nodded. "Want a lift over the bar?" one of them asked.

"I reckon I can manage. I made it down."

"If you're looking for work," Nicolo struck in, "I've pressing business down Cape Verde way."

"Going after the pirates, eh?" chuckled one.

There was a quick sound – " Look there! " One of the three was pointing seaward.

Scander and Nicolo wheeled around. Out on the rough, moonlit water a vessel was heading toward Cascaes beach.

" Do you suppose it could be Rodriguez? " cried Nicolo to Scander.

" Rodriguez? " one of the pilots took him up. " Know him? I've often taken him in. Whoever it is, see the sail he's carrying – in this wind, too. Must be in a hurry."

" That's putting it mild! " exclaimed Scander. " See that! . . . And they not yet hove to! "

Smashing along, with no sign of slackening, and as yet too far out to anchor, the pilot signal light had nevertheless been run up between the masts.

" That's surely *The Golden Star!* " Nicolo declared, as the vessel suddenly came up into the wind.

One of the pilots jumped up. " I'll take her on," and he started down the beach.

" Let's go," cried Nicolo. He seized the surprised Scander by the sleeve, and they both ran after the pilot. " Mind if we go along? " Nicolo called. " If it's Rodriguez I've business with him – he's my partner," and as the man hesitated, " Take our skiff," he offered. " She's already afloat."

" Fair enough," the pilot returned. " It'll save launching mine."

In a moment they had shoved the skiff into deeper water, and leaped aboard.

" Yes, that's *The Golden Star,*" exclaimed Scander as they drew nearer the caravel. " I can tell by the way she rides."

He had hardly got the words out when they heard the rattle of an anchor.

" What? " cried the pilot. " Signal for pilot service and then anchor out here? What's the meaning of that? "

As the skiff came alongside there was a loud hail from the caravel.

" That's Rodriguez! " Nicolo and Scander exclaimed together, and Nicolo made ready to clamber aboard first, for he must lose not a moment in telling his plan.

Several forms appeared at the rail, and among them, by the light of a lantern, Nicolo caught a glimpse of Rodriguez' face.

" Stand by for a line," shouted the pilot above the wind.

" Rodriguez! I'm coming aboard! " Nicolo peered up at him, expecting to see the usual, broad smile. ' He'll be surprised to see me here,' he thought.

But the face that he saw by the flickering light was possessed by something deeper than either laughter or wonder. What had happened? Nicolo wondered. Could it be pirates?

And then Rodriguez, leaning far out, was speaking, entirely ignoring the pilot, too – and asking such a curious question: " Master Conti, is the King at Lisbon, or at Cintra? "

" The King! " Nicolo blankly repeated. " The King – " Almost he'd added, " What the devil! " but managed to stammer, " He went to Cintra yesterday."

" D'you get me out here to gossip? " bellowed the pilot. " Want me to take your vessel on to Lisbon or not? I'll give you two seconds to make up your mind."

"My vessel stays where she is," Rodriguez snapped back, "but you're to set me in at Cascaes!"

"Wait, Rodriguez! I'm coming aboard," Nicolo shouted, hardly believing his ears at his astonishing order. "I've got to see you."

But already the man's legs were over the rail – he was sliding down the side of *The Golden Star*.

"What's the matter with him?" muttered Scander. "Never saw him before like this."

A minute later, Rodriguez' feet were feeling for the skiff, and, as he dropped into the stern, he ordered the pilot to cast off.

"No, wait!" Nicolo sharply interrupted, "I've something to tell you that'll make you change your mind about going to Cascaes. We must put to sea immediately!"

"Sorry, Master Conti," Rodriguez struck in, "but I mustn't lose a moment in getting to Cintra. I've news for the King that – that *won't wait*. Tell your pilot to cast off – do, sir!"

Nicolo looked closely at him. The man was plainly under great strain and in deadly earnest. But what news for the King could possibly count now, when every moment was telling either for – or against – Gama? Besides, the pilot was grumbling at the delay.

"Listen, Rodriguez!" He bent forward and whispered in rapid succession, "Gama's on his way home! There's a pirate fleet somewhere off the Moroccan Coast waiting to destroy him. We must warn him, you and I. We must put right about as fast as we can – lose no chance to intercept him."

As Nicolo spoke, he saw an extraordinary expression

spread over the other's face. " Holy Mother! " he heard him
murmur, and then, to his amazement, Rodriguez raised an
arm and sang out to the pilot: " Cast off! "

"What d'you mean ' cast off ' ? " cried Nicolo angrily,
" after what I've just – "

" Master Conti – " Rodriguez thrust his face close to
Nicolo's – " cross yourself, and swear that you'll ask me no
questions, and that you'll tell no word of this." Then, as
Nicolo, in utter bewilderment, touched forehead and breast,
he felt the other's lips at his ear: " Set your heart at rest –
Gama's safe! "

It was at this particular moment that Nicolo, staring
dumbfounded at Rodriguez, heard the pilot bawl out some
order, and saw Scander scramble forward.

" I'll manage alone," he called as he passed. " You
and Rodriguez'd better have your talk out."

The two dropped into the stern, while Nicolo, bursting with the tremendous news, tried to keep from shouting
it aloud.

So it was Rodriguez who spoke first. " How did you
get wind of this pirate plot against Gama? "

Briefly Nicolo described what he had learned during
the last three days. " By putting together what this fellow
Marco has let drop, and the talk from the ships that have
been attacked, Scander and I are certain that there's a pirate
fleet waiting to make a clean sweep of Gama."

Rodriguez shook his head gravely. " A terrible blow it'd
have been to Portugal. Terrible. Everything would have
been lost – Gama's work would have gone for nothing. It
was just mere chance that those scoundrels didn't get
me."

" I was eaten up with worry lest they would, and we'd lose cargo and all! "

" I'd have run square into them if I'd gone where I was headed, the Algarve[1] and Cape Verde. What saved me was this: four days ago, I was putting out from Terceira[2] loaded with sugar, when I heard this – this news. So I changed my course for Lisbon, and ever since I've been going at full speed, day and night, with all the canvas I could carry."

" Only four days between here and Terceira? " exclaimed Nicolo. " Why, Rodriguez, you've made a record! But you must yet get to Cintra. How will you – "

" Oh, that's just a matter of borrowing a horse from a man that I know here. I can make Cintra by midnight." He was silent a moment, then, a little shyly, he added, " I'd like to tell the King what you were going to do for Gama! "

" Don't, Rodriguez. Things of this sort sometimes take odd twists – turn 'round and slap one in the face! No, not a word."

" As you say, Master Conti," Rodriguez unwillingly conceded. " But I'll tell you this: I'd have been proud to take *The Golden Star* out with you, if there'd been need for her – and, as it is, I'm proud to be sailing her for you, sir! I'll be back by sunrise to take her in."

Nicolo glanced at the fast nearing shore. In these last few moments should he reveal the rest of the plot – about the maps? Yet, why expose the Venetian ambassador and Venice? No, Scander and he would attend to that. And Scander – didn't he deserve to be taken into the great secret?

[1] Most southern province of Portugal.
[2] One of the Azores Islands.

" Rodriguez," he whispered, " tell Scander what you've told me! He's done more than I have in ferreting out this plot. You can trust his tongue! "

" Right! " the man came back heartily. " But it must be quick – we're here now! " He moved forward just as the keel grated, and leaped on the wet sands. Hardly a pace behind him was Nicolo, with the astonished Scander in his wake.

" Rodriguez has something to tell you," Nicolo said to him. " Keep her where she is! " he called, as he passed the pilot. " We're leaving in her, directly."

They started across the beach, while Rodriguez, without slackening speed, made Scander swear secrecy. Then, " Gama is safe," he solemnly announced. And while Scander stared, open mouthed, " I've sworn to myself," he rapidly continued, " that none shall know the whole of this matter before the King knows. That was why I anchored so far out, and would let no one aboard. Lest my crew should be tempted to talk! "

He broke into a run, and only swung up an arm as sign that he'd heard Nicolo's " Good-bye and good luck! "

" I knew, first thing I saw him, that something'd happened," Scander exclaimed. "Lord, but it's wonderful! Where d'you suppose Gama is? "

" Wherever he is, he doesn't need me! " Inwardly Nicolo hoped that he wasn't too openly happy over the fact that he was returning to Lisbon.

" I'm not sorry we're going to finish this job together! " Scander confided, as they walked back to the skiff.

Nicolo paid the pilot, and they put off, this time with Scander attending to the sails, and Nicolo at the helm.

"We're in luck to have the wind with us," Nicolo remarked, "even if this ebb tide is against us."

"And we're in luck to have this moon as bright as day and not to have to go around through the South Channel, with all those cross currents dragging a body over to the shoals."

"If currents were our only worry!" returned Nicolo. "I don't feel too easy, I can tell you, about the maps."

"Oh, those chaps won't leave without me. And as soon as it's daylight we'll find out from Master Abel what's happened."

"As soon as it's daylight!" Nicolo reflected happily. . . . Morning in the court! Cool fragrance of dew-wet bloom. Early sunlight tiptoeing across slumbrous shade, touching a filmy dress, soft, bare arms, sweet, shy eyes.

"Shall we change places?" Scander sang out as they neared the narrows of the North Channel. "I cut my teeth on the Cachopos, you know!"

"Stay where you are, and call the course!" Nicolo returned. "You can see Cascaes light. This wind should take us through, square as a die."

For the remainder of the narrows, Nicolo, at the tiller, steered by Scander's quiet directions.

"Not much room to spare, is there?" Scander chuckled, as at last they passed Lage Point and came inside the bar.

"But at that, I'll chance this side every time against the hellish rip in the South Channel," rejoined Nicolo. "Still, if it hadn't been for the moon so bright, you and I might be on the North Cachopo now!"

"Better ease her off a little," Scander called, letting out the sail. "The wind'll be square behind us past Belem."

"She's rough over there, off South Cachopo," Nicolo remarked.

"Yes. The breakers sound plain even here," said Scander as he made a half turn in the main sheet.

For some time they were silent. The skiff forged ahead under tight canvas. They should make Belem in less than half an hour, Nicolo ·calculated. Then Lisbon, and after that –

A gleam of white off the Belem shore caught his eye.

An outbound boat!

"Odd, that is," he heard Scander comment. "Carrying that much sail, in such a wind!"

Yes, thought Nicolo, it was odd; a considerably larger craft, too, than their skiff – but of course she wouldn't try the bar on this tide against an inshore breeze. As he watched, the craft came up into the wind and lay over toward the south shore, and somehow, then, he got the impression that she was feeling her way out to sea.

"She'll cross us," he heard Scander say in a low tone.

"Yes, we'll go astern," rejoined Nicolo. He suddenly felt a shift in the sail. "What's that for?" He wheeled around to see Scander motionless, eyes riveted on the approaching vessel. The next minute Scander let out more sail.

"Do you want to hail them?" exclaimed Nicolo.

Scander nodded. "Bring her nearer," he said, in the same low tone.

A little puzzled, Nicolo obeyed, and eased the helm. The two vessels, he saw, must now pass very close. The sound of the oncoming prow grew audible. What could Scander possibly want of her – leaning far over the port side like that, straining his eyes on her?

He heard a startled exclamation – " They've given us the slip! " Before his wits could seize Scander's meaning, the vessels were passing, two faces glaring down at them from her stern – Marco and Marco's running mate!

But who was behind Marco, staring out at them as the stern flashed by? A face – a woman's face! Was he stark mad? It couldn't be! Yet – it *was!* That face like carved ivory – Oh, merciful heaven, *it was Nejmi's!*

For a stunned moment Nicolo stared at Scander. He saw the sailor pale under his tan.

" Come about! " he yelled to him like a man frenzied. " We must follow them! "

But already Scander was furiously hauling in the sheet. " Too slow! " he shouted back. " We've got to gybe. We've got to risk it. . . . That's Abdul – the captain of the *Sultana!* "

CHAPTER 22

The Bar

A T Scander's cry Nicolo's blood seemed to freeze. The
foreign captain who wished to see Abel's maps . . .
the Venetian ambassador's friend . . . the captain of the
Sultana – one and the same! And this man now had Nejmi!

271

How had he found her? What had happened? Why, why, had he taken Scander to Cascaes at the very time Scander would inevitably have come face to face with Abdul and saved Nejmi? In his torture every thought of the maps left him. In that ship ahead was Nejmi . . . Nejmi! And with every second the distance between them was widening!

Suddenly and violently he came to himself. That distance mustn't widen! By every power on earth and above, no! What was that Scander had yelled? That they must gybe, must risk it? Risk! What was risk when the dearest that life held was being snatched away under your very eyes? He put all his skill into the manoeuvre as Scander, with unbelievable strength, hauled in the sheet. He realized that the next moment would need all their effort to prevent disaster. He must keep the skiff in line as the sail swung over – he knew the shock would be terrific.

A moment the little craft shuddered, and the beating of the sails was like gun shots. Instinctively he managed the helm, fastening his whole strength to it, as Scander braced himself for the shock. It seemed an age until the sail snapped over to the full length of the shortened sheets. Then, with unexpected smoothness, the boat stood away on her new course, following the bright wake of Abdul's speeding craft.

Seconds passed before either spoke. In a frenzy of hope and horror, Nicolo watched the vessel dancing in front. With such start, was it humanly possible to overhaul her? But they must – they would overhaul her! No one but Scander and he could possibly save Nejmi now. Perhaps she had seen him. Perhaps she could see him coming now!

But Abdul, Nicolo recalled, had seen Scander, and

would do his cursed best to escape. By what monstrous trick of fate had he found Nejmi? Oh, how, how had it happened? The cruelty, the irony of it, after her flight from him – after Abel's careful shielding of her! His heart contracted as he recalled his vow that he would never let fear come again to her dear eyes. There must have been violence, for Abel and Ruth would never have given her up. Oh, that he had only left Scander in Lisbon!

Nearer and nearer came the sound of the breakers on the bar. Nicolo saw that Scander eased the sheet a fraction.

" Whew! " cried Scander, as a wild expanse of boiling surf broke before them. " See the rollers the wind and this ebb tide have kicked up in the South Channel! They're breaking clean over the bar! "

At times the little boat sank in the huge troughs, and then Abdul's vessel was out of sight. The uproar increased. Nicolo saw Scander's lips form words that he could not hear. But there was no thought of their own safety now, for ahead, speeding toward destruction, was Nejmi.

" If he goes any closer to the shoal," yelled Scander above the boom of the surf, " he's lost – the shore current will catch him."

" Our chance," shouted Nicolo, " is to gain on him when he comes about – if he can make the turn! "

It was now a matter of seconds. Both boats were in the raging seas of the South Channel. Nicolo could already feel the drag of the inshore currents of the strong ebb. Abdul's vessel, a half league away, changed her course. The flash of the moonlight on the moving sails was plain. For a moment she seemed to stand still, and lay over almost on her beam ends, as, close hauled, she headed northward across the tossing rollers. But in that brief moment the skiff cut down the lead.

Slowly the larger vessel righted, but again seemed to stand motionless. For a few instants she held her course. Then, heavily, the bow swung toward the oncoming skiff.

"She's lost her helm," yelled Scander, and the two saw the sails lay over again, almost flat against the water.

"We'll be in the same fix," cried Nicolo, bearing his full weight down on the tiller. "The current has got them!"

The skiff struggled, but, almost to their amazement, answered perfectly, and in a moment they were tearing away on the starboard tack, passing almost within hailing distance.

But horror! Abdul's vessel was plainly sweeping helplessly into the breakers, head swung completely around, sails furiously slatting.

"She'll go aground in another minute," cried Scander, "and everyone'll be washed overboard."

Aground in this pounding surf! Inwardly Nicolo groaned. Could anything survive that? He dashed the spray from his eyes. "Hard down!" he shouted. "It's our only chance to save her. We'll have to risk it and stand over there!" What was risk now, with Nejmi rushing toward possible death?

Again the skiff came up, hesitated, and swung over on the southwest course, bearing, now, directly toward the fury of the breakers – a desperate hazard, but, as Nicolo had said, the only one.

They saw the ship ahead list, stagger, pitch helplessly forward, and then, as she lay over on her side in the bright moonlight, a man's figure wildly scrambled forward. The next moment she struck. Their skiff passed like a shot.

" He's cut the halyard," shouted Scander.

The big sail crumpled. A huge roller broke completely over the stranded hull. Another followed, and with a crash the foremast, unable longer to withstand the strain of the big foresail, went into the water.

" If she'd been three lengths farther west," said Scander, " she'd have floated. There's deeper water here."

But Nicolo, eyes strained on the other ship, hardly heeded him. Clinging to the stern rail were two figures! Suddenly the tiller was torn from his hands by Scander's full strength, and at the same time he was violently thrust into the cockpit as the skiff came up again into the wind and tacked away northward. Nicolo's eyes never left the stranded vessel. Now he could plainly see two clinging figures.

"What you doing? " he cried.

" Got to keep afloat, haven't we? So when this millrace of tide slackens we can come up on Abdul's vessel from deeper water." Without turning, Scander spit out the words sideways.

"Idiot! " Nicolo exploded. "We must get to them at once! That craft can't live an hour."

Scander shook his head. "She's in soft sand. She won't break up in weeks."

Nicolo barely heard the answer above the noise of rollers.

" But Scander," he yelled back, "look at that! " He pointed to the seas that now swept Abdul's boat continuously. "Nobody can live on her in that surf."

"Not unless they're lashed! " called Scander.

"We must get nearer at once! " Nicolo shouted angrily.

But Scander stood his ground. " I figure if anyone goes overboard this tide will take 'em out," he said shortly. " That's where we've got to be – outside; and as close as we dare."

Instantly Nicolo saw the force of that reasoning. Another short tack brought them astern of the stranded boat, and perilously near the first line of breakers.

" It's still deep here, though the surf's worse," cried Scander above the breakers. " It's soft bottom, and a fathom or more under us."

Nicolo suddenly realized how well Scander knew his ground; how he had indeed " cut his teeth on the Cachopos! "

Scarcely an hour had passed since they had sighted Abdul. He glanced at the moon. If they could only hold their little boat for another hour!

Scander turned and pointed to the sail. For a second the canvas had spilled the wind! "Wind's going down," he shouted.

Incredible as it seemed, Nicolo sensed the truth, for when they again came about, it was easier. With amazing strength and skill Scander had managed to shorten sail, and, braced against the windward rail, was easing and tightening the sheet to meet the combers. Then again, and still again, they manoeuvred to hold their position.

In agony of suspense Nicolo watched the waves wash over the wrecked vessel. Would the tide never turn so they could approach her? Still, her condition was growing no worse. As Scander had said, she lay fast in soft sand.

A crash of surf made him shudder. Another wall of foam

swept over the grounded ship. Could anyone live through that?

At times, when the skiff's position was favourable, he could dimly distinguish figures clinging to the rail. Ah, what if Nejmi were not one of them! He braced himself against an overwhelming fear. He fixed his mind on the helm, realized that at last they were actually approaching the wreck.

Suddenly a faint call seemed to mingle with the wind and sea. A man's voice! Nicolo strained his ears.

"A line! Stand – by – for – a line! " Scander began to let down the sail as Nicolo eased the skiff still nearer.

And then it came, whistling through the air – a rope flung with unmistakable skill. But to Nicolo's horror the line fell short. Conflicting thoughts raced through his mind. Would those scoundrels save themselves – leave her alone out there?

Hark! That call again! Between the crash of the breakers came detached words: "Stand in closer – as close as you dare! You must take off a woman! "

A woman – a woman! Thank God, a woman! In ecstasy of relief Nicolo almost dropped the helm, but quickly recovered. Scander lowered the sail, and together they worked the tossing little boat through the now lessening rollers toward the wreck.

" That's not Abdul's voice," he heard Scander exclaim. He finished stowing the sail.

Again came the whistling line. This time Nicolo caught the wet coils and took a turn through the forward chuck. Violently as the skiff still tossed, they had now worked her close under the stern of the wreck.

"That talk about taking off a woman may be to put us off guard," Scander said briefly. "Better let me stand forward—you haven't a knife!"

"What! Abdul would . . . when we're saving him?"

"Humph! He'd slit our throats and then get away in our boat!"

They were now as near as they could be to the stranded vessel. Plainly two figures only were at the stern rail. Suddenly, to Nicolo's incredulous joy, he heard Nejmi's voice—"Nicolo!"

"Nejmi!" he called back, all but choking over the dear word.

Scander took position in the tossing bow. The still strong ebb stood off their boat, with the fastened line taut.

"Send the girl first!" cried Nicolo.

Words unintelligible to him floated back, but there was an astounded cry from Scander:

"There's only Marco and Nejmi! Abdul's gone—washed overboard!"

"Thank heaven!" cried Nicolo on first impulse.

"Best thing that could have happened," agreed Scander. "There it comes," he shouted as a second line whirled aboard. He caught it, bracing himself with feet wide apart. "I'll haul in. You stand ready to take her."

In spite of being soaked to the skin, Nicolo, as he fixed his eyes on the far end of the line, felt moisture break out on him. If at this last moment Marco should play them some treacherous trick . . . if the line should break . . . But at last, a slender figure swung off from the wreck. He saw that Scander was breathing hard, as length after length of line disappeared through his deft hands. Now she was half across.

Now he could plainly see the delicate face, the wet, clinging clothes.

And, now, reaching, stretching out for her, he had drawn her, with tremendous effort, to the rail. For a moment she clung, dazed and breathless. In another moment he had raised her, drenched and limp, into his arms.

" Nicolo! " she gasped. Then her eyes closed. " Gama! " she murmured faintly. " They're plotting to kill him! "

Something blinded Nicolo, took him by the throat. Herself at death's very door, yet thinking of Gama – of the Way!

" Nejmi, darling! " He caught her to him, trying to think what he should tell without breaking his promise to Rodriguez. " Gama doesn't need us, dear," he whispered. " They can't hurt him now! I mustn't tell you any more yet – I've promised."

She leaned back from him, staring at him with startled eyes. " Nicolo! Where were you going? " she asked him breathlessly.

" I was coming back from Cascaes. I'd just heard there what I've told you."

An instant he felt her arms go around him. Then Scander was saying, gently, " My child, I must take off this line."

She looked up at him, and for the first time seemed to realize his presence. " Scander! Dear Scander – " Wildly weeping she dropped her head on his shoulder. " You've always saved me! "

His rough hands soothed her. " I'd give ten years of my life not to have had this happen to you, my child! "

" It's my fault! I took him off to Cascaes," cried Nicolo. " Did you know us when we passed, Nejmi? "

"Yes! And I was so afraid Abdul would – know! " she panted. " I was sure you'd come. And I watched you following all the way – " She broke off with a sound of anguish. "Master Abel, Mother Ruth! What are they thinking? Oh, Scander, hurry, hurry back to them." She seized his hands, her face convulsed. " We must get back to them! "

"Are they alive – safe? " Nicolo and Scander cried in the same breath.

"Abdul never saw them," she said, reading their thoughts. "When he came to the house I – I – " She closed her eyes, shuddering uncontrollably.

" Spread your coat out for her, Scander," cried Nicolo as he untied the line about Nejmi's waist. "And hand me mine – under the seat there. She mustn't talk any more now. We know Master Abel and Mistress Ruth are safe."

"Heaven be praised for that! " Scander fervently exclaimed. He snatched the coats they had flung off, laid one in the cockpit, and tossed the other to Nicolo, who stripped off Nejmi's wet cloak, and wrapped his coat around her.

As they lifted her into the cockpit, she opened her eyes. "Abdul didn't find the maps," she whispered. " They're safe! "

" Maps! " cried the two men in the same breath.

" They'd gone clean out of my mind! " Nicolo declared.

" So *that's* how that blackguard found her! " Scander said between his teeth. " I've a mind to leave that scoundrel of a Marco out there for his part of it! " he wrathfully burst out.

"Why, Scander – " Nejmi's hand reached out for his sleeve – " it was Marco who saved me! If he hadn't lashed me to the rail, I'd have – have gone – the way Abdul did.

Do save him, Scander," she shuddered. " You – you don't
know how dreadful it is out there! "

Scander's only reply was an uncompromising
" Humph! " but he nevertheless hurled the line, and presently they saw a bulky figure drop over the stern of the
foundered ship.

Both Scander and Nicolo took a hand with the line,
for Marco's weight was a different matter from Nejmi's.

" Wind's going down fast," observed Nicolo, as they
hauled. " See the difference in the waves just since Nejmi
crossed. We won't have any trouble getting home." Home!
Blessed thought! Nejmi, Abel, Ruth – safe. Sunshine flood-
ing court and workshop. He could have put his arms around
all Lisbon!

" Good enough for you if we'd left you out there,"
Scander greeted the bedraggled Marco. " Helping that partner of yours to steal this poor child! "

" But he didn't! Abdul came alone! " cried Nejmi.

" I swear I never laid eyes on her till I saw her with
Abdul at the dock," Marco declared.

" That makes it a little better," Nicolo told him shortly.
" We'll settle with you later. Sit down now and dry your
precious self in what's left of this breeze," he directed the
abject sailor, who blankly took off his coat.

With a stroke of his knife Scander cut the line. For
one moment Nicolo stopped to draw his coat still closer
around Nejmi, and to feel her hand in his. Then he had
grasped the helm, while Scander was once more raising the
sail. Within minutes – though it seemed hours – they had
picked up headway against the remnant of tide, and were
making slowly toward the lights of Belem.

"What happened to Abdul?" Nicolo inquired, when steering had become a matter of merely guiding the helm.

"Last I saw of him," replied Marco, "he was cutting down the fores'l. A breaker took us broadside, and when it cleared, he was gone!"

Nejmi raised her head a moment above her coverings. "And if Marco hadn't lashed me to the rail," she added, "I'd have gone with the next breaker." Wearily she lay back, and when Nicolo looked at her again, he saw she was fast asleep.

"What made you try the South Channel in ebb tide and an inshore wind?" Nicolo inquired after a while.

"It wasn't my doing," Marco sullenly replied. "I looked everywhere for Scander to take us out, and when I couldn't find him, Abdul swore we'd make it alone."

Scander shrugged. "What could you expect? All he knew was the Mediterranean, that never saw a tide! Still," he mused, "it's hard to believe. Abdul, who laughed at Allah and the devil, and stuck his knife into anybody that crossed him, carried off like the greenest lubber! Kind of spoiled your plans, didn't it?" he asked pointedly.

Marco's eyes shifted, and he fidgeted in his seat.

"Yes!" Nicolo put in sarcastically. "You were expecting to accomplish quite a stroke with Gama, weren't you?"

Marco's heavy face puckered up like an aggrieved baby's. "How'd you know so much?" he whimpered. "I don't care, though, if you do know," he quickly added. "It's all up now."

"What made Abdul change his mind so sudden about leaving?" Scander demanded.

"He heard that Zakuto was to be at the proclamation

about sundown. He figured he could steal the maps while the old chap was away from home, and get off before he came back."

"So that was his hellish game!" Nicolo exclaimed, as he suddenly recalled the coin Pedro had held up to him. "He made a cat's paw out of old Pedro, you see, Scander, to point out Master Abel, so as to be sure no one was at home."

Scander's palms came together in sudden enlightenment. "*That's* how he found Nejmi alone!" He glanced at the sleeping figure. "We mustn't speak so loud!"

"But he never got the maps," Marco said, in a low tone. "I knew the minute I saw him at the dock that something'd gone wrong."

Involuntarily Nicolo's eyes sought Nejmi. That slender loveliness to pit herself, alone and defenceless, against the very cause of all her fear – fear worse to her than death! What if they had missed seeing her on the river? What if she were lying now where Abdul lay? A kind heaven be praised that the sea had forever settled with Abdul!

He looked up to find Scander watching him, and, as if he had guessed Nicolo's thoughts, "She'll never again need to be afraid," he said, half smiling. His face hardened. "If only Master Abel and Mistress Ruth knew she was safe! I hate to think of them when they found her gone."

"We'll be with them soon," Nicolo told him. "The tide has turned – doing its best for us this time!"

"Wind's doing us a good turn, too! I'm more'n half dry. So are you."

Presently they had sighted Belem, had come abreast of it, had passed. They were on the home stretch!

Marco, head sunk on breast, stared moodily at his feet.

Scander's burnt gimlet holes were fastened on the horizon except when they stole a glance at the sleeping figure in the cockpit.

Nicolo, coming about, noticed that the stars were dim in the eastern sky. The sun was on his way. A new day; a new world! For today would bring news of Gama – news of the Way, and of the world beyond the great Cape!

Somewhere outside on the tumbling seas, the steadfast spirit that had vowed never to turn back was coming home! With the Arab world against them, with the Western world on jealous watch, even ready to stab, Gama and his little fleet were coming home. He glanced at the delicate ivory face nestled against his coat – and something smarted in his eyes. But they would never know that, for their sake, a girl had laid down her all. A girl in whose blood met both East and West!

CHAPTER 23
Nejmi's Dowry

IT was pale dawn when the skiff slipped into Lisbon harbour crowded with what might have passed for ghost ships, for any sign of activity they showed.

"'Twon't take 'em long to come to life," Scander chuckled, "when they know what we know!"

Nicolo was silent a moment before answering and then nodded. " Some time today, Rodriguez said." His face suddenly lighted. " Scander! Ferdinand knows all about it by now! "

" I expect those big eyes of his haven't had a wink of sleep since Rodriguez told his news! Wouldn't wonder if Manoel came back to Lisbon pretty quick, would you? "

Absently Nicolo nodded, his eyes on the nearing docks. " We'll tie up by the old ladder," he said. " That'll be easiest – for her."

" What you going to do with me? " Marco uneasily demanded, as he put on his coat.

" I'll tend to you later," Scander told him. " But till then, just stick to me. Walk when I walk, stop when I stop. Understand? " And for all his casual tone, there was a glint in the burnt gimlet holes that was unmistakable.

As easily as he could Nicolo brought the skiff alongside of the ladder. " Make her fast," he ordered Marco, as Scander seized the piling.

As the skiff bumped, Nejmi sat up, staring about her. Nicolo dropped the helm and leaned over her. She looked up at him with radiant eyes. Suddenly, she sobered.

" Nicolo! We must hurry as fast as we can! " She sprang up, while Nicolo handed Scander his coat, and then wrapped his own about her.

" All ashore! " called Scander, and the next minute he was half-way up the ladder, with Marco at his heels. Next came Nejmi with Nicolo close behind, while Scander, leaning over, warned her to hold firm to the slippery rungs.

As Nicolo stepped on the dock, Scander turned to him.

"You two'd best go up to Master Zakuto's alone. I'll be up after a while." He returned to Marco. "We've some business to settle," he told him shortly. "Come along, and mind what I said: don't lose sight of me, see?"

The two walked off, and Nicolo, alone at last with Nejmi, caught her to him.

"Ah, Nejmi, when I thought I might lose you . . ."

"Nicolo – Nicolo! When I looked back at Lisbon, and thought I should never again see you . . ." Breathlessly she poured out to him the story of Abdul's capturing her.

"It seemed the only way to save the maps and Master Abel and Mother Ruth – to go with him. But I meant, when we got out to sea . . ."

"Nejmi, if you had gone, my whole world would have gone, too!"

"It was only the thought of helping Gama that kept me steady," she whispered. "And then, when I saw you – ah, Nicolo, I knew that you'd come to me. Even on that terrible bar, I was sure of it!"

"Nothing shall ever keep you from me," he told her. "Nothing and no one in all the world!"

Her head sank on his breast, and he saw how pale she was, and exhausted. She was shivering, too. He drew his coat more closely around her, and they started on.

"But you'll be cold," she protested.

"No, the wind dried me off. Feel!" and he rubbed her hand across his sleeve.

Arm in arm through the silent, twisting streets they went, and up the hill. Once they stopped to gaze down at the harbour and river, calm enough now, like an angry child that has cried itself to sleep.

"And look – behind you! " Nicolo said. He turned her
around to see, above them, the workshop windows rosy in
the first sunlight. He heard her catch her breath, felt her
press forward.

"Ah, Nicolo, quick! They're waiting up there."

He tried to hold her back, to save her strength for the
stairway. A short lane, another corner – and the long flight
lay before them. He felt Nejmi clutch his arm – glanced up.
Slowly climbing the stairs, shoulders sagging, and head bent,
was a beloved figure in conical hat and long, black cloak!

Together they started after him, when, all at once, he
turned and looked back. An instant Nicolo saw a face seared
with grief and weariness unutterable. The next, something
flashed over it, as if a light had suddenly appeared in the
dark – and Abel was coming toward them, his arms held out.
With a little wordless sound Nejmi rushed into them, while
Abel, head bent over hers, stroked her quivering shoulders.

It was characteristic of them that at first neither spoke,
and that when Abel at last did speak it was about the thing
then most essential. "My child, you must have dry clothes
and food."

The same kindly, even tone of every day, Nicolo said
to himself – only that you could see his hands shaking.

"Come. Ruth is waiting for us." Abel motioned to Nicolo, and they started slowly up the stairs with Nejmi between them.

Once she tried to speak. Nicolo caught the word
"maps." "Wait a little, child," Abel said. "There's plenty
of time."

"She's been on the river all night," Nicolo told him in
a low aside, motioning toward the harbour.

Understandingly Abel nodded. " I was sure of that from the first."

As they paused at the head of the flight, " Open the gate carefully, Nicolo," he whispered. " Ruth may have dropped off to sleep. She's been waiting all night."

Softly Nicolo swung back the gate and stepped into the court. It was as if Morning, herself, gazed out at him from cool, deep shade and lilting sunlight and dewy, half-shut petals. Sweeter even than he had visioned it, out there on the tossing water. Sweeter by far!

A murmur behind him caught his ear. He turned, saw Nejmi and Abel looking at something behind him, followed their gaze. On the seat, under the old fig tree, just as she had flung herself, he saw Ruth, asleep. Every line of the drooping figure told of the night's cruel vigil.

" I'm going to her," he heard Nejmi breathe, and saw her steal across the court, while Abel and he followed.

For a moment she paused, tenderly gazing down on the worn face, and in that moment Ruth woke. There was a gasp, a look of incredulous joy. Then Nejmi had dropped beside her, fondling, caressing, begging her not to cry, while Ruth sobbed wildly that Abel and she should never have left her alone – oh, why had they?

" Everything is safe now," Nejmi comforted her. " Everything is safe and right, dear Mother Ruth! "

" But where did you go, my child? " Ruth managed at last to get out. " Oh, when we called you, and you didn't answer . . ."

" Ruth," Abel struck in, " Nejmi is wet and cold and faint! Can't you give her some warm food? Let the rest wait."

Ruth sprang up. "My blessed child!" she cried remorsefully. "You must be hungry, too, my poor Abel – and you, Nicolo. I'll bring you both something hot. But first, Nejmi!"

She hurried her inside, and Abel sank down on the seat.

"I've walked the water-front all night," he said, apologetically, as he made room for Nicolo, "for the minute we found the maps – "

"In the workshop lamp!" Nicolo broke in. "Nejmi told me."

"I was instantly sure that seafaring fellow had been here – the one I'd heard asking Pedro about me – and had wreaked his vengeance on our poor child for not giving up the maps. I didn't dare tell Ruth all I feared – "

"If you'd only known the truth of the matter, sir! That man was Abdul!"

"Abdul?" Abel appeared to search his memory, then, suddenly, he leaped to his feet. "That pirate captain? How did he know she was here?"

"He didn't!" Nicolo told him, and then repeated Nejmi's story.

"The monster!" cried Abel. "The black – "

"Don't waste your breath on him, sir! He's gone where he'll never again make trouble. He was swept into the South Channel rollers from the boat in which he had Nejmi and his man Marco. It was only Marco's lashing her to the rail that saved her until Scander and I could take her off."

"Pedro told me you'd gone somewhere," Abel exclaimed, "when I ran down there first thing to find you. How did you get wind of Abdul's carrying off Nejmi?"

"We didn't! It was pure accident that we met them on our way back from Cascaes."

"Cascaes! What took you down there?"

For a second Nicolo hesitated. If he said "To warn Gama of danger," Abel would, naturally enough, ask, "Then why did you come back?"

"We'd heard rumours of pirates," he said casually, "and I was afraid Rodriguez might have run afoul of them. So we slipped down to Cascaes to find out what we could – you know they always get the first news there – and on our way back Scander recognized Abdul in the moonlight, and then we both saw Nejmi, and we – "

He broke off as Ruth appeared with two steaming bowls. "There's the chicken broth I made yesterday," she told them, "and there's plenty more." She waited while they ate. "Abel," she said in a low, horrified voice, "has Nicolo told you that it was – was *Abdul* who took her away?"

He put his arm about her. "But you know that he'll never come back?"

"Yes," she shuddered. She stooped swiftly, and kissed Nicolo on the forehead. "Nejmi's told me how you and Scander saved her."

Abel looked up with the old twinkle in his eyes. "You deserve her now, my boy, if you never did before!" Then as Nicolo blushed and tried to stammer something, Abel gripped his arm. "I always wanted a son," he said. "Haven't you, Ruth?"

"Neither Nejmi nor I would be here," Nicolo said gravely, "if it hadn't been for Scander. You should have seen him work! Besides, if Marco hadn't lashed her – "

A flash of colour in the workroom caught his eye: Nejmi

in one of those dresses like a primrose sky! Nejmi, bending over the great table; lifting, one by one, long rolls from it and slipping them in turn inside brass tubes.

" I forgot to put the maps away after we'd taken them out of the 'lighthouse,'" whispered Abel.

" Abel! " There was a catch in Ruth's voice. " Abel, it seems as if, from first to last, that child's life has been bound up with the Way! "

A click of the gate startled them, and brought Nejmi to the workshop door, as Scander stepped into the court. She ran to him, and they crossed the court together. Nicolo sprang up to meet them, and, as they all came toward Ruth and Abel, " Scander," Abel said warmly, " there's so much to say to you that I can't say anything! " He reached out and pulled him down on the seat.

" It's not in words to say what's in our hearts for you," Ruth seconded him. " We never can tell it to you."

" Anyone'd have done as much," Scander protested. " It was Master Conti who put the heart into me, when I thought we were done."

" You were all that kept my heart up more than once! " Nicolo retorted. " And but for your knowing that South Channel, I'd have come to grief."

Nejmi's eyes rested affectionately on Scander. " It seems as if you'd always been ready when I was in danger! "

" That's why I've stuck to Lisbon," he exclaimed. " I've never forgotten that Abdul got off alive when the *Sultana* went down."

" What! " cried Nicolo, " You suspected all the time he'd come here? "

Scander shrugged. " Well, I always kept this on me."

His fingers caressed the knife handle in his belt. "And
I always saw to it that it was sharp! And then, after
all, I wasn't here when he did come! " He looked closely at
Nejmi. " How are you, child? No worse for that terrible
soaking? "

" And you, Scander? " She touched his sleeve with her
delicate hands. " Have you had something to eat? " she inquired anxiously.

" I'll get him some broth! " cried Ruth.

" Thank you, ma'am, I've eaten," Scander protested.
" Besides, I've more on my mind than vittles." He paused
and surveyed them all. " I've something to tell you," he announced. " I got everything out of that Marco before I was
done with him! "

" Where is he? " Nejmi and Nicolo exclaimed together,
and, " The fellow who babbled about Gama? " Abel asked.

" He saved me! " Nejmi said in a gentle aside.

" He's where he won't get into mischief for one while,"
replied Scander. " I found him a berth on a packet that's
bound for Southampton in a day or so, and from there he
can pick up a galleon for Venice. But first, I bought him a
good breakfast, and then I got him to tell me everything.
Whew! " he cried. " What we'd pieced together from his
babble was bad enough, but not half of the whole scheme.
Why, it seems it began in Venice over two years ago! What's
more, the Venetian ambassador had his eye on you, Master
Conti, even then! "

" So, after all, Venice was involved! " Abel exclaimed.

" Started it, so Marco says. If I had a map now –"
Scander's eyes questioned Abel's – " I could make it all as
plain as day to you."

"Yes," Ruth chimed in, as by common consent they all made for the workshop. "It's getting warm out here, too."

They settled themselves around the table, Nejmi between Abel and Scander, and Ruth and Nicolo opposite them.

"In a nutshell, here's what's been going on." Scander spread a map out, and thoughtfully inspected it.

"According to Marco, there was some merchants in Venice who thought there might be something in a sea route to India. Somehow they got hold of this Abdul, who, it turns out, was half Venetian and half Moor. They bargained with him to spy on Gama, and he picked Marco up to go along with him."

"There!" Nicolo struck in. "Didn't I tell you I suspected that was what brought them here when the Expedition was outfitting – to find out all they could?"

"You mean that Abdul was here *then?*" cried Nejmi.

"Don't you remember my telling Master Abel about seeing Marco and another stranger at that time, and having one of them ask me about Gama's preparations? That was Abdul!"

"Come to think of it," Abel exclaimed, "I must have seen him myself! The man I heard asking Pedro about my maps, you know, Nicolo."

"Seems as though everybody'd seen him," Scander observed, "except the two people most concerned: me and Nejmi! I can't figure how I missed him the first time he was here."

"You were working on night shift for Captain Diaz," Nicolo reminded him. "Don't you remember?"

"So I was. And this time, when the reports about the

pirates started, it seems he got instructions from the Venetian ambassador to keep out of sight."

"Then he was mixed up with that pirate business," said Nicolo, "just as we thought!"

"He was on his way to harm Gama," Nejmi confirmed him. "I heard him say so to Marco."

Scander nodded. "That was the chief scheme. You see, as soon as Gama left Lisbon, Abdul and Marco put out for Egypt, and then followed the mainland south. Along the way they picked up news of him from the natives, and found he'd sailed for India. Well, they waited around for months, and finally, off Mombassa –" the stubbed forefinger that had traced south stopped at a spot labeled "Ivory" – "they had the luck to sight Gama's fleet coming back from India. Marco told a wild story about one of the ships being burned at Mombassa. I can hardly believe it, but he stuck to it."

"That's not impossible," said Abel. "The vessel might have been unseaworthy and beyond repair."

"Well, as soon as they saw the other two ships sail on, back comes Abdul and Marco to Venice and tells their employers what they'd seen."

"So Venice really knew there was a Way of the Spices before we did!" cried Ruth.

"Or before anyone else, ma'am. She had cause to worry about what King Manoel meant to do in the Orient!"

"And we wondering why she'd so suddenly changed front!" mused Abel.

"Well, then Venice went to work in earnest," Scander continued. "She put out her claws in every direction. First, the government started this question of what was we going to do about trade in case Gama found a sea route. Meanwhile, this group of merchants I was telling about, was working hand in hand with the government, but secret-like, too. They paid Abdul a big fee to get together a pirate fleet to patrol the waters off Morocco and St. Vincent's, where they figured Gama would pass. Abdul was to keep in touch with the Venetian ambassador and pass the signal to the pirates according as Manoel's answer to Venice was favourable or unfavourable. Favourable, and they was to let Gama alone. Unfavourable, and they was to split the cargo amongst 'em and sink the fleet clean, so's no one'd be left to tell whether or not they'd found the Way."

Abel's head dropped to his hands. "The cargo was nothing," they heard him groan, "but to lose the Way for Portugal! . . ."

"After going so far," Ruth murmured, "then to die almost as they're home! "

"I knew Abdul meant harm to Gama," Nejmi said, "by what he told Marco."

"But Nicolo! . . . Scander! " Abel was looking at them with horrified eyes, and they saw that great drops stood on his forehead. "The pirates don't know that Abdul is dead, and they're still waiting for Gama! "

"Set your heart at rest, sir! " Nicolo broke in, unconsciously using Rodriguez' words. A glance shot between him and Scander: what to say without betraying Rodriguez? "I've learned, within a few hours," he went on, carefully choosing his words, "that the pirates will do no harm to Gama." Then, as Ruth stared, and Abel started up with a flood of incoherent questions, he quickly added, "I can't tell you more now, sir. I've promised! "

For a moment Abel's eyes bored into him. Slowly a
look came into them as of happiness incredulous of itself. As
if afraid of asking forbidden questions, he abruptly turned
to Scander.

" It seems unbelievable that the Venetian government
would make allies of pirates! "

" Well, of course it was done under cover, with the
government shutting its eyes. You see, sir, Venice could depend on them for a thorough job, for the pirates themselves
was in a bad fix: how was they to make any kind of a living
off the Mediterranean, if the Indian trade got started 'round
by the big Cape? Same fix as Venice. But – " Scander paused,
impressively – " this pirate plot wasn't half of what was
really going on, so Marco told me. Look here! " He bent
over the map and planted a stubby finger. " See this bit
of land between the Mediterranean and the Red Sea?
Now, suppose Venice was to open a passage through
there . . ." He waited, while Abel and Nicolo looked
incredulously from the map to him, and then at each
other.

" Impossible! " Nicolo burst out at last.

But Abel's face was rapt. " It's the thought of a master
mind! " he declared. He hung, fascinated, over the map.
" Why Venice would have the Orient in her arms! "

" Most as smart as finding the Way, I call it! " Scander
admiringly conceded. " Well, that's Venice's scheme, so
Marco told me, to cut that passage and to build forts at
each end and at the main seaports of the Orient. They even
sent an agent to get the Soldan of Egypt to help them put
the plan through."

" That's why the ambassador needed Master Abel's

maps," Nicolo exclaimed. " *You* guessed that! " he smiled across to Nejmi.

Scander grinned broadly. " That was the job the ambassador meant for you, Master Conti: to take these maps to Venice, so they could see where to build forts! Then he found out you were a friend of Master Abel's and couldn't be bribed."

" But Abdul kept telling Pedro that he was going to get me to bring him up here to see the maps! "

" That was a blind. He knew all the time that he himself was to steal them when Master Abel was hearing the King's proclamation read. The ambassador had given him advance information."

Disapprovingly Ruth shook her head. " And yet they say ambassadors are to keep nations from having trouble with each other! " she murmured.

" Poor old Pedro would be out of his mind if he knew the part he'd played in this affair," smiled Nicolo, and he told of Abdul's gold coin.

" It's odd," chuckled Scander, " that in the end 'twas the maps that did for Abdul. If he hadn't waited for the proclamation, Marco wouldn't have been idling round town, tippling and babbling, and we'd never have suspicioned what was hatching under our very noses! "

" How on earth," Abel exploded, " came that loose-tongued Marco to be chosen for such a mission? "

" Just what I asked him! " rejoined Scander. " 'No more wits than a puppy ' says I. ' Abdul had to have someone,' he blubbers, ' and no one else would stick with him – he'd such a name for knifing.' Which, of course, was true enough! "

"I wonder," Nicolo mused, "whether the ambassador will have anything to say about all this."

Abel's eyebrows lifted. "You'll never have any trouble in that quarter. If you told what you knew, he would have to take a quick leave of absence!"

"He nor anyone else will ever hear a breath of it from me," Nicolo declared. He looked around at the others. "Let's bury this thing here – not tell even Ferdinand or Gama."

"That's the only way," Abel agreed. "Nothing but harm could come of its being known." His face suddenly lighted and he bent again to the map. "I can't get that passage out of my mind," he declared. "It's so intelligent! Yet once it's been pointed out, you see it's the thing to do. Look how beautifully it works out!" He made Ruth and Nejmi watch, while he drew a quick line from the Mediterranean, down the Red Sea, to the far ports and coasts of Scander's description. "Some day," he declared, "that passage will go through, and everybody will be talking about it, just as, now, everybody is talking about the Way!"

"But won't it," Ruth asked doubtfully, "take the trade away from Portugal?"

He gave her an amused look. "By that time perhaps Portugal will have had her turn long enough! Besides, my dear – "

A rush of footsteps across the court cut him short, and before anyone could turn, Ferdinand burst in – Ferdinand in riding clothes, and hot and dusty. Instantly a glance flashed between Nicolo and Scander – At last!

For all his haste, there was an expression in Ferdinand's flushed face that at once struck Nicolo. As always, when he was stirred, the great eyes were on fire, but now there was in them a certain awe that was almost reverence.

Deaf to Ruth's astonished " I thought you were in Cintra! " and Nejmi's quiet " Why, Ferdinand! " and Abel's " Well, young man, how is this? " he brushed past them all, and walked straight to Abel.

" Sir," he said – and Nicolo saw that his face was working – " Gama has returned! "

There was dead silence, as if the world had stopped for this tremendous moment. Abel – his face working, too – was panting, " Where – where is he? "

" I'll tell you everything I know, sir," said Ferdinand, " but it must be quick, for I've promised to be back at the palace as soon as I've given you the news."

He dropped on the table edge, and flicked the dust from his breeches. " I heard it almost as soon as the King did! " he jubilantly announced. " It happened I'd just brought him a cool drink, when someone came in to say there was a man with an important message that he refused to deliver except to the King himself. Well, it was midnight, and an odd time for anything of that sort, but, finally, they showed the chap in, and who d'you suppose it was? " Quite the old Ferdinand, he glanced around the table, enjoying the suspense of his audience. " Rodriguez! Arthur Rodriguez! Your man, you know, Nicolo."

" What? " cried Nicolo, avoiding Scander's eyes, and trying to look surprised. " You don't mean it! " he added, aware that from under her lashes Nejmi was stealing a glance at him, and that a peculiar expression had come to Abel's face.

" He was in his rough sea clothes," Ferdinand con-

tinued, " but the minute I saw him, I knew something was afoot. He knelt down before Manoel and whispered to him for a few moments, and then, all of a sudden, the King looked up, and called right out, ' Gama has returned! ' "
Ferdinand drew a long breath, and swallowed hard. " I –
I felt queer, I can tell you. Shaky inside and out! "
" No wonder," said Ruth. " I'd have cried! "
" There was a great to-do, of course," Ferdinand ran on. " Everybody crowded around and talked at once. Then Manoel made them all listen, while Rodriguez told his story.
" He said that four days before, he was sailing away from Terceira to Portugal, and met a ship that appeared to be having hard work to navigate. He hailed her, and someone aboard called out that she was the *San Gabriel* from India where she'd been in command of Vasco da Gama! You could have heard a pin drop when he came out with that. Everyone went wild, and I saw Manoel pretend to smooth his hair – but actually he was wiping his eyes! Well, Rodriguez had sailed day and night, landed at Cascaes, and ridden at top speed to Cintra, so as to be first with the news! "
" Then Gama will soon be here," cried Abel. " Perhaps today! "
In the same breath, Scander demanded, " Where's the other two ships, the *Berrio* and the *San Raphael?* "
Ferdinand's face fell. " Wait a minute," he told Scander. " It's not all good news. Paulo da Gama has just died at Terceira. So Vasco – "
" Paulo dead? " Nicolo broke in. Almost he had said: " Rodriguez didn't tell us that! "
" Poor Paulo! " Ruth murmured, but Nejmi said, softly, " Poor Vasco! "

"Yes, 'poor Vasco,'" Abel repeated. "He loved Paulo so."

"When we rode down from Cintra this morning, expecting to find Gama already here, we didn't know about Paulo," Ferdinand went on. "Rodriguez didn't, either. All he'd stopped to hear was just the word that Gama was back. But at the palace we found messages from the *San Gabriel* and the *Berrio*. They've –" he caught his breath – "they've both come in! They're anchored off Belem."

"Hurrah!" shouted Scander. "The *Berrio* down river, you say? I caulked the old girl's seams! I'm going down to see her! But how about the *San Raphael?*"

"Stop your noise," laughed Ferdinand, "and let me finish! Didn't I say I was in a hurry?" He turned to Abel. "Do you know, sir, I took my courage in my hands and begged permission of Manoel himself to bring you the news!"

The corners of Abel's mouth twitched, but all he said was, "At worst he could only have refused you! Go on, lad."

"Well, here's the message the *San Gabriel* sent to the palace. In the first place, the *San Raphael's* gone!"

From the corner of his eye Nicolo caught a covert glance from Scander, while Ferdinand was hurriedly explaining:

"She was in bad shape and had lost most of her crew, so they burned her. Later on, the other two ships got separated in a storm, and the *Berrio* came on here alone. Paulo grew so much worse that Vasco put in at the Verde Islands, and sent the *San Gabriel* on, while he took Paulo in a small vessel to Terceira. Some ship has just now brought in news of his death at the monastery there, and that Vasco will stay on to mourn for him! "

For a while no one spoke, till Scander said, "Now I suppose everybody's saying they knew all the time Gama would come back! "

"Oh, falling over each other to see who can shout it oftenest and loudest – especially when the King's near to hear them! " rejoined Ferdinand. "And Manoel's as bad as any of them, too! "

"I fancy he'd even take a good, stout oath that he'd never harboured any doubts on the subject," Abel mildly suggested.

Ferdinand jubilantly swung his cap around. "He's already planning another expedition, sir. And I'm going on it if I have to play stowaway! " He bent toward Abel, and lowered his voice. "That's the first thing I'm going to ask Gama," he confided. "To take me the next time."

He uncrossed his knees, and stood up, stretching and yawning. "I didn't even go to bed last night," he exclaimed, "thinking about the new expedition! " He began to move toward the door. "I won't be able to get off for a while, on account of all that's going on, but I'll send word as soon as Gama says when he's coming."

At the door he hurriedly turned. "Nicolo! I forgot to tell you what Rodriguez got for being first with the news: the King has made him a gentleman of the household and his sons, pages! And by the way," he threw over his shoulder, "nothing come of – of what I told you in your room? "

"Nothing," Nicolo carelessly answered. But as soon as the gate had closed after the boy, he gave a sigh of relief.

" It's not so easy to pretend surprise when all the time you know what's coming! "

" Marco was right after all, about their burning the ship, wasn't he? " Nejmi exclaimed. She looked shyly at Nicolo. " It was Rodriguez, wasn't it, who told you – "

" Yes – about Gama! " Abel struck in with an amused look at Nicolo. " I guessed it the minute Ferdinand spoke his name – while you were trying so hard to look innocent! "

" There's one thing I'll wager you don't know about Master Conti's going to Cascaes," Scander volunteered, and before Nicolo could stop him, he was telling the real reason for the trip, and the plan to send *The Golden Star* in search of Gama.

" I wish everybody could know that! " Abel's tone was quiet, but the look in his eyes – and in the eyes next to him – brought the blood to Nicolo's face.

" Rodriguez said about the same thing, sir," he stammered, " but I made him promise not to mention it." He turned to Scander. " I suppose he's made his last trip on *The Golden Star*. We'll have to find someone to take his place."

" I'll wager you he'll miss the smell of pitch, and the feel of a sheet in his palm! " Scander pensively observed.

" I wonder how his wife'll like being a lady," murmured Ruth.

" We'll have to find someone to take Rodriguez' place," Nicolo repeated. " And I know a good man, too! " He looked hard at Scander. " How about it? "

For a moment the burnt gimlet holes stared back. Then, over the brown face, crept a deep red.

" I mean it," laughed Nicolo, as he reached over and slapped Scander on the back.

◇◇◇ *Nejmi's Dowry* ◇◇◇

" Oh, I'm so glad! " cried Nejmi. " Scander should have our – " she caught herself up on the telltale word – " our very best. Yours and mine, Nicolo! " she ended, flushed and radiant.

Scander beamed as he looked round the table. " There's nothing on earth I'd exchange for the captain's job on *The Golden Star!* I wouldn't have taken it a minute sooner, though," he added. " But now that I know Abdul'll never come – "

He broke off, fumbling at his belt, and brought out a dingy leather bag wound around with a thong. " Here's something else, besides my knife, that I've kept on me," he said, without raising his eyes. " You remember I once told you how – how I got hold of the price my old captain took for Nejmi, in the market at Aden? "

" Scander! . . . That? " As if she doubted her eyes, Nejmi reached out and timidly touched what lay between the brown hands.

Silently Scander passed the bag to Abel who weighted it for a moment, gave a surprised whistle, and then handed it across the table.

" Good Lord, man! " Nicolo exclaimed, when Ruth and he had had their turn, and the dingy packet was again in Scander's hands. " You told me you starved when you first landed in Lisbon, and with all that coin in your belt . . ."

" Think I'd touch *that* for vittles and drink? " Scander scornfully demanded. His eyes softened as they fell on Nejmi. " I always figured that sometime she'd be needing a dowry, and I reckon – " he laid the bag in her lap – " I reckon that time is right now! "

CHAPTER 24

Dom Vasco da Gama

A GLITTERING day of summer, with Lisbon's hills cut sharp into deep blue sky. A breeze-crinkled harbour of crowded craft and fluttering pennants.

Everywhere, throngs. They jammed the steep streets

and streamed out on water-front and river shore; fought for foothold on the quay edge; clung to pile heads.

Gusts of cheering, of shouting, of laughter; breathless intervals of waiting, watching; then, pent-up hearts bursting forth again. A town gone mad with joy. That was Lisbon on the day that Gama came home!

On the edge of the quay overhung by the House of Mines, stood Abel Zakuto. Not an inch, in any direction, could he have turned, for the mass of humans behind him. But, at least, no one was in front of him! This was precisely why he had come down here at sunrise – to make undisputed claim to this particular spot with its stout pile to hold to. Nothing must be between him and Gama's ships! There was no doubt that Gama would anchor off this quay, in line with the House of Mines; for he wouldn't have forgotten, even in this long absence, that the King always sat in the balcony to see any action in the harbour. Of course, too, that was where Manoel would first receive Gama.

Any moment now he could be expected. Already there was a rumour that he had left Belem. A long time it had seemed to Abel since Ferdinand had burst in with the first news – these weeks, while the *San Gabriel* and the *Berrio* waited down river for Gama to mourn, first at Terceira, where he had buried Paulo, and then at Belem. Of course, Abel reflected, he might have gone down and visited the ships. Scores had; so had Scander – and had returned with excited accounts of foreign pilots that Gama had brought back. But not that for him! He would see those caravels come in as they had gone out – led by their Captain-Major!

Oh, for Bartholomew – that together they might have stood here! And for Covilham, no less. Hail to your valiant soul, Pedro de Covilham! Of all the workshop group that young rascal, Ferdinand, would be the first to take Gama's hand! It would probably be days before Gama could come to the familiar old meeting place, besieged as he would be by visitors and fêtes and one thing and another. Hard, too, this noise and to-do for him, still wrapped in his grief for Paulo.

A stir on the balcony caught Abel's eye: Manoel arriving, with his suite, and decked out in his royal best. Well, it was an occasion worth the finest ermine ever trapped! Now he'd sat down, as excited as a boy! You could tell it by the way he rested those long arms of his on the railing and leaned far over them to gaze where everybody else was gazing – at that bend Gama must now soon round.

Abel tightened his hold and looked back over the sea of heads. Somewhere, at an overhanging window, safe above the jostle and press, Nicolo had found standing space for Ruth and Nejmi. That child, Nejmi! What would they all say if they knew her part, first and last, in this tremendous affair?

A sound like low thunder! Cannon! A tense moment, as if all Lisbon held its breath. And then, from every throat in that vast throng, a wild clamour: " Gama! Gama! " Another instant, and cannon from harbour and from shore were booming their answer to that distant salute.

Again the thunder, much closer. Then, slowly, almost wearily it struck Abel, two caravels, the royal colours at their mastheads, glided into sight.

If Lisbon had shown its joy before, it was nothing to what it did now. It was a city abandoned to joy, gone literally mad with it. From crowds and from cannon went up a roar that shook the air and turned one deaf and dizzy. Almost Abel wondered whether he could keep his footing.

∽∽ *Dom Vasco da Gama* ∽∽

On came the caravels, over the crisp little waves. Wholly lost to all else, Abel watched them draw nearer and nearer. That was the *San Gabriel* ahead, with the tattered scarlet pennant of the Captain-Major at her crow's nest. Gama must be aboard her! And close behind, the *Berrio*. Welcome home to you, Nicolau Coelho! Even at this distance one could see the battered hulls, and the gaping seams. Men were at the pumps! In a sort of ecstasy Abel's eyes noted the stained sails, the weathered spars, the faded rigging – and mentally saluted them. Ah, dear and gallant scars of war-worn conquerors! He knew tears were streaming down his cheeks, and he didn't care.

Now the *San Gabriel* was coming about. He could see sailors laughing and gesticulating, and waving from the rail. There were the officers, standing together on the main deck. Was it his fancy that their faces seemed lifted in a sort of homesick rapture to Lisbon's crowded, climbing roofs? And see – those dark faces standing out sharp from the others! The foreign pilots Scander had told about! Gaudy as parrots in their red and yellow rig and as eager as boys.

Ah, that figure on the poop, apart from all the rest! In black, from the small, round cap to the close fitting tunic and cloak. Pale, grief-stricken, yet with an air of quiet resignation that sent a moment's hush over the throng. The Captain-Major! Now they were at it again, splitting the very sky: " Gama! Gama! " And now Gama himself was moving forward, bowing gravely.

A woman's sob behind him caught Abel's ear: " He'd give it all up, if he could have back his brother! " He looked over his shoulder – a young woman, eyes swollen with long weeping, a baby in her arms. One of those whose man had stood his last watch. A sad number of his mates were with him, too, according to the accounts Scander had brought back from his visit to the *Berrio.*

The rattle of metal brought Abel's head around: the *San Gabriel's* anchor – and now the *Berrio's!* And there went a royal boat, manned with the King's own sailors, drawing alongside the *San Gabriel.* He would wait only to see it bring Gama ashore. After that he would go home, to think over from first to last this great day; to relive each detail, that to the end of his life never a jot of it should fade from his memory. For this day would change the face of the world!

He forgot the boom of cannon and the cheering as he watched Gama descend into the boat; stand, as he gravely acknowledged the oarsmen's salute, and then seat himself, a sombre figure among splendid uniforms. The boat shot forward and, for a few moments, his face came into plain sight. Worn, and lined with grief it was, and years older, Abel noted with a pang. Yet, it had a serenity that had not been there when he had gone away, the serenity of a spirit, Abel said to himself, that has tried itself and kept the faith of its own making.

The boat swerved toward the landing, and Gama was hidden from view. Immediately there was a mad surge to follow him. At last, Abel was free to move – to go home. In the rest of the day's celebrations he was not interested. He had seen what he had come to see: Bartholomew's ships, and Gama!

It was slow work through the crowded streets, but finally he was climbing the stairs, then entering the court. He glanced about. No one back yet.

He went into the workshop, walked eagerly to the win-

dows. There they were! Somewhat hidden by the other shipping, but distinguishable by the Royal Standard. Brave,
beautiful things, those shabby, leaking ships! Themselves
outworn, the thing they had done would never die. And from
that doing still greater would come, just as their accomplish-
ment had had its roots in those first venturings of the Great
Navigator's frail barks. Ah, straight back to him, must
Portugal trace this great day! Other expeditions would follow – Portugal would have her rivals! But in the end it was
more than Portugal or any nation. It was Man uncovering
the face of his world – searching out Truth. Oh, he was glad
that he had a part, small though it was, in those ships down
there! His compass. His astrolabe!

He turned, and exultantly surveyed the shelves, the
tools, the bench. He had hardly touched them since Gama
had been gone – he'd been so busy with the maps – but he'd
done some long thinking about ways to improve his instruments. And now, with the message those shabby, gallant ships
had brought him . . .

From shelf to shelf he went, taking up this instrument
and that. Oh, but he was hungry for the twirl of a bit, the
rasp of a saw! He critically examined a compass, the counter-
part of the one he had given Gama. He could better that!
There must be a transparent top to the box. The compass
card should be at the bottom of the box, below the needle,
instead of the present awkward arrangement. At a glance,
then, a man could get his bearing. And that astrolabe he'd
made for Gama – the first metal one in Europe! There must
be more like it. No excuse for wooden ones with Abel Zakuto
able to make better!

He returned to the windows to gaze, not at Gama's

ships now, but at the town itself; at the crowded houses that climbed from blue harbour to blue sky. Ah, let him look well – that he might remember well!

Voices made him turn. They were all back again; Scander, too. Abel studied them as they came toward him: thoughtful – almost reverent. Even Scander seemed subdued.

"Abel, you passed right below us," Ruth was saying, as they entered the workshop. "We called and called, but you never so much as looked up! "

" I didn't hear you, my dear. I was thinking."

Nejmi ran to him and caught his hand, and he saw that the golden light was in her eyes.

" You were thinking about the ships! " she whispered. " Oh, Master Abel, when I saw them sail into the harbour, it was as if Allah said to me, ' See, now! Wasn't it worth all the pain and trouble? ' "

" I couldn't help but think," Nicolo said quietly, " how hard it was that Master Diaz couldn't be here today, and Covilham – and Paulo da Gama! "

" Poor Vasco," Ruth murmured. "He looked so sad in that black suit."

" Different enough from that gay velvet cloak he wore when he went away," exclaimed Scander. " Why the man's aged ten years! "

" It was pitiful, the way he tried to smile when the people cheered him," said Nicolo. " We caught a glimpse of him when he was walking up to the House of Mines between a count and a bishop – at least so people said they were! We didn't see Manoel receive him. Too many heads got in our way! "

" I saw everything," Scander chuckled, " from the mast

of a little craft. I bribed the captain to let me aboard! Lord! When Master Gama knelt down front of the King, and kissed his hand, I couldn't help thinking 'twould be more fit if the King had knelt and kissed *his* hand! "

"What do you think, Master Abel! " Nejmi broke in. "Scander talked with the foreign pilots that Master Gama brought."

" I saw them," Abel declared. " Black as ebony, aren't they? "

" The king of Melinde sent them," Scander explained, "to find out about our side of the Devil's Cave. You should 'a' seen their jaws drop when I sang out to 'em in their own language! 'Most made me homesick for old times."

" Gama never got as far as the Spice Islands, so these pilots told Scander," Nicolo said. " But they say he's brought back plenty of spice."

" Calicut and Cananor is as far as he went. That's where, so they tell me, he had to drive some pretty sharp bargains for his spice." Scander's face suddenly changed, as he appeared to recall something. " Master Conti," he exclaimed, "I forgot to tell you that Rodriguez left a message for you at Pedro's. Said he'd been delayed by the King and wanted to know if you cared if he didn't bring *The Golden Star* in till tomorrow. Said for you to leave word at Pedro's."

" Let him take his time," Nicolo cried warmly. " Go and tell Pedro so, Scander, and if you should happen to see Rodriguez, introduce him to our next captain! And wish him the best of luck."

He went into the court to call out the last word as the wiry form disappeared through the gate, and presently Nejmi followed him.

From the workshop Abel could see them strolling, arm in arm, about the court. He glanced at Ruth, and saw her tender eyes on them. How should he tell her what was in his mind – what he had been thinking before she came in? By common consent they had never mentioned their talk that moonlight night, after Abel's visit to Manoel, but her forlorn cry still rang in his ears: " Must our people always be wanderers? " It was too cruel to remind her on this day of triumph.

Unexpectedly she said, motioning toward the court, " They need each other, Abel. More than we need her! "

A little puzzled, he studied her. What did she mean? " More than we need her."

" Abel, dear . . ." Her voice faltered but her eyes were calm and sweet. " Nejmi doesn't need us. Not any longer! "

He looked at her with sudden understanding. He knew now what she was trying to say but all that he could get out was a choked, " Bless your brave heart, Ruth! " They drew close to each other and he whispered, " Just to see Gama – talk once with him. Then, when those two children out there decide to go to the priest . . ."

" I'm ready when you are, Abel."

He braced himself against the desolation that surged over him. " Tomorrow I'll go down to the docks and find what vessels are sailing," he said, with his hand tightening on hers. " Then I'll tell Rabbi Joseph what we've decided. You know he's helped so many of us to get away. Brave old soul! If he weren't bed-ridden he'd have been the first to go."

" You're sure we can't take any of our things, Abel? " she asked him wistfully.

He tried not to see the caress of her eyes as they lingered

on this and that familiar object. " Dear," he answered,
" they're watching the ports, strictly. At best it won't be easy
to get by."

" But once you said small things that we could hide in
our clothes. And a few cuttings from the plants we love
best . . . and some bulbs of your yellow lilies . . ."

He nodded, not trusting his voice.

" We'll take a little of our own earth, too, so the new
garden will have something of Lisbon! "

" Home will be wherever you are! " he told her.

She drew a long breath. " Then – then as soon as you've
seen Master Gama."

Silently he put his arms around her. " And when Nejmi
and Nicolo – "

Nicolo's voice from the doorway broke in on them.
" We've been talking about the house I'm going to build," he
jubilantly announced. " Nejmi says it must be just like this
one! "

For a minute Abel's eyes and Ruth's exchanged glances,
and then Abel was saying, " You children don't need to wait
for a house! Live in this one till you get yours built."

Flushed and radiant the two came in from the court,
and Nejmi slipped down beside Ruth. " Would you like that,
Mother Ruth? " she asked a little tremulously.

Ruth bent over and kissed her, and Abel said, " The
sooner the better, child! What do you say, Nicolo? "

" As soon as Nejmi says! " Nicolo happily declared.

" Then be off with you, you two! " Abel pretended to
wave them violently into the court. " Talk it over! "

For a while he and Ruth were silent, conscious of the
low hum of voices outside.

"I suppose," he said at last, "that to them we seem old." He laughed a little, softly. "Ruth, do you feel old?"

"It's like climbing a mountain, Abel. To those watching at the foot, it seems as if we'd reached the top, while to us the top is always beyond!"

* * *

THAT NIGHT Abel sat late in the workshop. It was too soon yet to expect Gama, but he was sure to come the first chance he got, and Abel wished to be ready and waiting for him and for those precious hours together. Ah, so precious, for they would be the last – though Gama mustn't suspect that.

The next night, too, he sat late, long after Ruth and Nejmi had gone to bed. Gama would hardly come even yet, Abel mused, taken up as he must be with celebrations and receptions and services of thanksgiving in the cathedral. Still, he left the gate unbarred, and when, past midnight, he heard it click, he was more glad than surprised. He reached the workshop door just as Gama entered it.

"I knew you'd come!"

"I knew you'd be waiting!"

Grasping hands, they stood silently surveying each other. Yes, Gama had aged. Lines in his face, grey at the temples. But, withal, that look of inward fulfillment!

"It's good to be here, Master Abel!"

Into Abel's fancy crept the vision of a child saying "I'm glad to get home!"

Gama's eyes wandered about the room. "This place," he said at last, "is nearer perfect content than anything I know. It lacks only –" he looked gravely at Abel – "only Master Diaz."

" Ah, Vasco, you've said what I've thought every evening since he went away. And when I was watching you come
into the harbour – "

" I was thinking the same thought that you were," Gama
broke in. " That he'd built those ships. That he'd paved the
way for me! "

" But no one in all that crowd would have been prouder
of you than he," Abel declared, "unless it was I! " His eyes
rested affectionately on Gama. "It was good of you to get
up here so soon."

" I thought I never would," Gama admitted. " Such a
procession of ceremonies and visitors and questions, even
after I was in bed trying to snatch a bit of rest! Just as it
was when I went away, only a thousand times worse. You
know Master Abel "– he stopped to laugh – " they're all like
a pack of children for the first time listening to a fairy story.
And the King is the youngest of them all! Wants to
know how the Orientals look and dress, and even what
they eat. He's having a huge time with those Melinde pilots I brought back! And how do you think he greeted me
when he sent for me this morning? ' Good morning, *Dom
Gama* ' ! "

" So! " cried Abel. "*Dom!* That's splendid, Vasco –
though how could Manoel have done less? Why, man, you've
more than earned every letter in the word! "

" It's the first title in our family," Gama said a little
shyly. " But – " his face suddenly clouded – " I'd have foregone everything, title and glory and applause, if – if Paulo
and I could have come home together! "

" I felt for you," Abel said simply. " It was cruel hard
for you, all this joy-making, when your own heart was

bleeding. But, thank God, Vasco, Paulo lived to help his country's dearest dream come true."

"How often he spoke of that, all the time he was so ill! 'Vasco,' he'd say, when he'd see me grieving and anxious, "what's a man's life compared with those white pillars we've put up for Portugal?'"

"He'd been ailing long, then?" Abel asked gently.

"Oh, for months. I had him on board the *San Gabriel* where I myself could care for him. His own ship, the *San Raphael*, we'd burned because she was beyond repair, and sickness had taken so many of the crew that there weren't enough left to run her. The store ship had gone to pieces long before that. We saved the figure head of the *San Raphael* – it's aboard the *San Gabriel* now. The men did their best to make speed, but at last I saw Paulo couldn't live to reach Lisbon. I couldn't bear to let him die at sea, so I put the *San Gabriel* in at the Verde Islands, and took him in a faster boat over to the monastery at Terceira. The *Berrio* hadn't caught up – Coelho had been delayed by storms. I buried Paulo there – at St. Francis'. The brothers were more than kind."

For a while Gama was silent. Abel mused on what he had just heard. So it was doubtless this bearing toward the Azores, instead of making direct toward St. Vincent's and Lisbon, that had thwarted Venice and the pirates!

"I didn't mean to talk about my trouble," Gama said at last. "I really came to tell you some of the things I've stored up for you these two years – only I don't know where to begin!"

"Begin with the pillars, Vasco!"

Gama's grave face suddenly relaxed. "What'll you say," he asked, "when you hear that Mistress Ruth's preserved pears impressed one native king almost as much as the white pillar we put up on his domains! King of Melinde he is."

" Melinde, eh? " Abel recalled inking in the word Melinde on one of the maps; a spice and ivory port. " That will tickle Ruth's pride! " he chuckled. " Is he the chap who sent the pilots back with you? "

" Yes, as pledge of good will, as well as to take him information about our part of the world. But about the pears. I had a few served up to his majesty in a covered silver dish – with napkins, too! He vowed he'd never eaten anything daintier. Couldn't do enough for us – loaded us up with rice and mutton and all sorts of fruit. That was the first time we stopped there; and the second, on our way back, he gave me magnificent presents for Manoel, silks and ivory and jewels. But," Gama paused impressively, " the best thing he did was to write Manoel a friendly letter – on *gold leaf,* if you'll believe it! "

" That means a trading post there for Portugal! " exclaimed Abel.

" Yes. He's ready to meet us half-way. When we told him we wanted spice, he gave me nutmegs and pepper for Manoel."

The old, whimsical smile twitched at Abel's mouth. " When you started out, you were going to get spice, and make Christians of the foreign folk. You certainly got the spice! How did the other notion work out? "

Gama laughed a little sheepishly. " To tell the truth, when we got to Calicut, I was taken off my feet by that civilization out there! I'd had the idea that I was superior because I was fair-skinned and a Christian, but when I saw what they had – "

"They seemed to have done pretty well on their own brand of religion, did they, Vasco?" laughed Abel.

"The gardens and fountains of the King's palace, a little way out of Calicut, and his tapestries, and bronze furniture, made our palace here seem tame! And talk about carved ivory! There were whole panels of it. As for the jewels the King wore – well, I hadn't really seen rubies and diamonds and pearls till I saw his! The presents I'd brought him from Manoel looked pretty puny by comparison, I can tell you! Oil, sugar, honey; a few hats or so."

Abel burst out laughing. "Did you have hard work to save Manoel's dignity?"

"Well – " Gama shrugged significantly – " I confess I had to cudgel my wits considerably! But on the whole, the King – Zamorin they call him – treated us very well. In fact, I don't know how I'd managed if he hadn't taken my part against the merchants in Calicut. They refused to trade with me, told the Zamorin I was a spy, even tried to capture me. You see the Arabs have their grip on all that Eastern trade, and they don't propose to yield a finger's hold."

"But surely this King of Calicut isn't an Arab?"

"No, a native of India, but the Arab traders in his kingdom have to do as he says. Finally, the Zamorin brought pressure on them, and they agreed to trade with us. But the tricks they tried! For instance, the natives cover their ginger with a little clay, to hold the flavour. What did those rascals do but plaster on three times as much again to the ginger they brought us, and then try to sell it to us for the solid stuff! They tried to pass off poor cinnamon on us, too, and half rotten nutmegs."

"Persevering devils!" Abel commented. "How did you get around them?"

"Oh, I shut my eyes to a good deal. I thought I'd gain in the long run if the thing went off smoothly. And I did! I got –" Gama's face lighted up – "what I wanted: all the spice I could load, cloves and nutmegs, cinnamon and pepper and camphor. We put up a pillar, too! And best of all, the Zamorin wrote a letter to Manoel, practically agreeing to trade with us!"

"I should say, Vasco, that you're as expert a diplomat as you are trader – or sailor!"

"That letter, by the way," Gama continued, "was written on a palm leaf! So, with the gold leaf one from the King of Melinde, I had two letters for Manoel. Then I got a third – gold leaf, too – from the King of Cananor – that was the last port we made before we turned 'round for home. I'd have liked to go further, but the ships wouldn't have stood it. Besides, so many of the men had died – fully two thirds of them, poor fellows."

"Well, Vasco," Abel spoke out impulsively, "you've done a splendid thing. Done it magnificently! You've given Portugal the Way of the Spices."

"Ah, but now to *keep* it for Portugal! You know, sir, the Orient isn't going to let us into its trade without a struggle. The Arabs are against us, and they're the traders. As to that, our own European neighbours will probably have something to say to our spice cargoes!"

"Scander always said we'd pay for our spice in blood. Remember?"

"I'm afraid he's right. By the way, I saw Scander, when the King was receiving me down at the House of Mines. I happened to look around, and there was the good old leather face grinning at me from the shrouds of a vessel! Yes," Gama continued, "for every warehouse we put up in the Orient, we must have a garrison. Manoel is already talking about a huge campaign that includes everything from fighting, to building forts and factories. He says he's going to recall Captain Diaz from Mina to outfit another expedition, and he hinted he might send him along with it."

Bartholomew coming back! For a second Abel's eyes lighted. Then he remembered. By the time a ship could sail from Mina to Lisbon . . . He put down something that rose in his breast, and said quietly, " If the King is planning another expedition, there's evidently no doubt about the profits of this one! "

Gama smiled. " You can judge of that for yourself, sir, when I tell you that the freight of the spice on the *San Gabriel* and the *Berrio* is as sixty to one, compared with the cost of the voyage! "

Gama's figures drew an amazed whistle from Abel. " There's other merchandise, too, I suppose? "

" Bales of it! Silks and brocades and cottons and gold thread stuff, besides porcelains and gold and silver trinkets. In short – " Gama's eyes twinkled – " the things Venice's galleons used to bring us! "

Inwardly Abel smiled. Venice indeed! Aloud, he asked how Gama himself had come out.

" Manoel has been more than generous. Gave me exemption from duty on all the spice I wish to import! " Gama suddenly fell silent, evidently meditating something. " How do you think young Conti would like to distribute my spice to our colonies? " he presently asked. " I always had a fancy for his pluck in leaving Venice on what was then a pure venture. I want to see him prosper."

"Capital!" cried Abel. "The spice trade was always his object. You know he saw the need of building ships for carrying Oriental merchandise when Portugal was only thinking about laying hands on it. By the way, did you know that it was his man, Arthur Rodriguez, who brought the first news of your arrival? And now that Manoel's rewarded Rodriguez, Scander is going to captain *The Golden Star*." Abel paused to laugh softly. "This idea of yours, Vasco, will please Nicolo hugely. In fact, it's quite by way of being a wedding present! For Nejmi and he –"

"Oh, so?" beamed Gama. "I saw that coming the night those two met – couldn't keep their eyes off each other! That strange, wonderful night!" he mused aloud. "Sailing past Sofala and the Devil's Cave, I often thought of that child as she stood before us – so frightened, so lovely!" Impulsively he leaned toward Abel, "I'm going to pick out a piece of embroidered silk for her, and send it over by Ferdinand!"

A curious look came into Abel's eyes. "Could you manage it, say, tomorrow? I myself want to see Ferdinand then, if he can get off. Tell him to come about – about mid-afternoon.

Gama, rummaging in his pockets, nodded. He finally produced a sealed tin.

"That," he said, "is for Mistress Ruth: nutmegs to flavour her syrups and mutton stews! When you give it to her, tell her I saved her pear preserves – barring the few I gave the King of Melinde – until provisions ran low. Then, when I opened them, I was seized with panic lest I'd let them go too long and they were spoiled."

"You don't know Ruth!" laughed Abel. "She boiled that fruit in its own weight of sugar, so it *would* keep."

"Well," continued Gama, "she'll never know in what stead it stood me. It was the end of a hard day, and the crew was on edge. There'd been one mutiny, and I could feel another brewing. I suddenly thought of that preserve. I got it out of my box, and had it handed around at supper. Why –" Gama's eyes were smiling – "after that, the men would have done anything for me! All evening I could hear them talking and laughing, as good-natured as boys."

"You say you had one mutiny?" Abel asked. "Was it serious?"

"It would have been, if we hadn't caught it in time. It was the old story: homesick, discouraged men who wanted to turn back. But – well . . ."

"Ah!" cried Abel warmly, "I can guess what you said to that! I've not forgotten what you told me about 'turning back' – here, in this very room."

Gama's fist came down on his knee. "I'd have scuttled every ship first! All I actually did do was to put the ring leaders in irons. I brought them back in irons, too, for the King to pass judgment on them. Then, to show the crew who was who, I threw overboard the navigation instruments. All except your compass. No one knew about it. I kept it always in my cabin."

Abel leaned eagerly toward Gama. "It proved exact, Vasco?"

Gama now was leaning toward Abel. "You told me it had steered your soul out of hell. Do you recall, sir?"

Silently Abel assented. Ah, didn't he!

"I used to think of that," the other continued, "when

things looked dark, and failure seemed surer than success. And in my sorest need, when I could see Paulo slipping away from me, and I myself seemed adrift, then, Master Abel, your compass did more than steer my ship exactly. I came to need it to steer myself by! "

"Ah, Vasco! " Abel's voice was hardly a whisper. "Who of us doesn't need something by which to steer himself? "

CHAPTER 25

A Letter

OUT of a side chapel of the great Sé Patriarchal, Nejmì
and Nicolo stepped into the late afternoon sunshine.
Behind them came Abel and Ruth, and then Scander and
Ferdinand.

∞∞ *A Letter* ∞∞

Ruth had been first to kiss Nejmi when the old priest had given his final blessing, and Abel first to call her " Mistress Conti." Rapturously Nicolo watched her as, a little shy, but smiling, she stood with them all around her wishing her joy. Her dress was one of every day. She had refused to have anything new. But it was one of those golden, clinging things that Ruth had made for her, that put one in mind of soft sunset skies. Banded across her forehead, and braided into her hair, were the pearls Nicolo had given her. More than ever, he told himself, she looked her name: a star, radiant and tender.

" I always knew this would happen some day," sighed Scander. The burnt gimlet holes rested lovingly on Nejmi. " But now that 't *has* happened, I don't deny it makes me feel odd in the pit of the stomach! "

"And me! " declared Ferdinand. He turned to Ruth. " Aunt Ruth, did anyone cry at your wedding? "

She laughed tremulously. " They say it's good luck to have some tears at a wedding! "

" I can't ask anything better for you children than that you'll be as happy as Ruth and I have been," Abel quickly added.

Nicolo's arm went suddenly around Nejmi. " If I make her half as happy as she's made me – "

An exclamation from Ferdinand stopped him. " Look! I'd almost forgotten." From under his coat he produced a package wrapped in bright cotton cloth, and handed it to Nejmi. " From Gama – I mean *Dom* Gama! He said not to open it till you get home."

" There's another present waiting for you there," said Abel, " from Ruth and me. Go along, you two, and find it! "

∞∞ 327 ∞∞

"Yes, go and find it," Ruth repeated. "We – we've an errand. Those bulbs and things for someone who's going to start a garden."

All morning, Nicolo recalled, she and Abel had been busy at something or other in the court. He'd been too blissful to notice what!

"I'll walk a ways with you, sir," Scander proposed to Abel, and so would he, too, said Ferdinand.

As they turned away Ruth ran back to Nejmi. "I must kiss you once more, child – you look so lovely! " Her eyes were misty, Nicolo noticed, but she was smiling. Then she was again with Abel, her arm through his.

"You'll come home soon, Mother Ruth, Master Abel? " Nejmi called after them.

As if they had not heard her question, they smiled back at her, and then hurried on.

Afterward Nicolo remembered that they had made no reply. Always would he remember Abel's face in that short moment. The eager eyes were those of Abel the Boy! But neither to Abel the Boy nor to Abel the Banker belonged that look of shining peace, of sweet majesty. A seldom used word stirred Nicolo's memory – Abel the *Seer!*

The next moment, putting Nejmi's cloak around her, he forgot everything but her. "Let's go home, darling! " he whispered, only half believing that this wasn't all a dream.

She slipped her hand into his, and they started off.

"I'm so glad 'home' is that dear house, aren't you? " she asked him.

"But you'll love, just as much, the one I'll build, won't you? "

As they reached the top of the long flight she said in

a low tone, "I love these stairs! They've always meant warmth and light and safety after the dark and the cold."

He flung open the gate. "I love them because they've always meant *you* at the end! "

Together they stood looking about them. All so familiar, yet so rapturously unfamiliar! Into the western windows, and out into the shadowed court, flooded the sunset's gold.

"Let's open Master Gama's present in the workshop." Nejmi nodded toward the doorway.

"You must say *Dom* Gama now," Nicolo laughingly reminded her.

"Then, afterward, we'll look for our present from Master Abel and Mistress Ruth! Where do you suppose it is? " she said, as they entered the workshop.

Almost as she spoke, a folded paper on the table caught their eyes.

Nicolo bent over it. "It's addressed to us both."

"It's about the present! " exclaimed Nejmi. "See if it isn't." Hastily she laid Gama's package aside, and looked over Nicolo's shoulder.

He opened the paper and ran his eye over the first lines. "Why – why what does this mean? Listen! "

He began to read:

"THE WORKSHOP,
The morning of Nejmi's wedding day.

"You two children are in the workshop, and you're wondering where the present is that we told you to find. You've already found it! Yes, when you opened the gate

and looked within: the court, the house – your present from
Ruth and me. (No need, Nicolo, to build another home!) "

A quick cry stopped him. "Ah, Nicolo – Nicolo! "
Nejmi's hands were suddenly gripping his.

He stared at her in startled alarm. She was trembling,
and very pale; and in her eyes was a look of tenderness and
grief that wrung his heart.

" I – I know now what the letter means," she said, very
low. " Read on, Nicolo."

So, with his arm around her, her face against his,
Nicolo " read on ":

" We thought you might guess, when we were cutting
those slips this morning, and taking up those bulbs! They
are for our new garden – child of the one we planted together. So shall we take with us a little of the homeland.
(Ruth says she can coax yellow lilies to grow anywhere.)

" How could we tell you before? No, this was the better
way: for you not to know till we are gone. But through Rabbi
Joseph you will hear of us in our new home – when it is safe
for us to send him word. Go and see him sometimes. Perhaps he'll whisper to you how, one late afternoon, Ruth and
Abel Zakuto went in at his front door. How, a little later, a
middle-aged carpenter, carrying his tools, walked out of the
back door. How, still later, a woman with a basket of vegetables on her head, also walked out of that back door. (They
were not to be seen together, you'll understand.) That is all
that Rabbi Joseph actually saw! But, for yourselves, imagine, now, the middle-aged carpenter and the vegetable
woman on a trading vessel speeding down river – into the
sunset!

" Nicolo, your business will grow with Lisbon's great,

new traffic. You may want more capital. Use mine freely. I meant it that way when I deposited funds with you, my boy. What I need of it you may send me through Rabbi Joseph.

"There will be another workshop! (Ruth says that even if, at first, we have to live in two rooms, one of those rooms shall be a workshop.) Other Ways are waiting for their Covilham, for their Diaz, for their Gama! The rims of new worlds already peer above the western horizon. Columbus has shown us them. So, there must be better compasses, better astrolabes. One of these days Ferdinand will be starting off to discover something. He knows who will make his navigation instruments for him! Bartholomew, too. Who can tell but he'll be needing a compass for the next expedition to India? (When he comes home to build the new fleet, show him and Vasco the maps Scander helped me to make.)

"Our undying love, Ruth's and mine, to you both: to you, Nicolo; to you, Nejmi – Star of the Way!

ABEL ZAKUTO."

A CATALOG OF SELECTED
DOVER BOOKS
IN ALL FIELDS OF INTEREST

A CATALOG OF SELECTED DOVER BOOKS IN ALL FIELDS OF INTEREST

100 BEST-LOVED POEMS, Edited by Philip Smith. "The Passionate Shepherd to His Love," "Shall I compare thee to a summer's day?" "Death, be not proud," "The Raven," "The Road Not Taken," plus works by Blake, Wordsworth, Byron, Shelley, Keats, many others. 96pp. 5$\frac{3}{16}$ x 8¼. 0-486-28553-7

100 SMALL HOUSES OF THE THIRTIES, Brown-Blodgett Company. Exterior photographs and floor plans for 100 charming structures. Illustrations of models accompanied by descriptions of interiors, color schemes, closet space, and other amenities. 200 illustrations. 112pp. 8⅜ x 11. 0-486-44131-8

1000 TURN-OF-THE-CENTURY HOUSES: With Illustrations and Floor Plans, Herbert C. Chivers. Reproduced from a rare edition, this showcase of homes ranges from cottages and bungalows to sprawling mansions. Each house is meticulously illustrated and accompanied by complete floor plans. 256pp. 9⅜ x 12¼. 0-486-45596-3

101 GREAT AMERICAN POEMS, Edited by The American Poetry & Literacy Project. Rich treasury of verse from the 19th and 20th centuries includes works by Edgar Allan Poe, Robert Frost, Walt Whitman, Langston Hughes, Emily Dickinson, T. S. Eliot, other notables. 96pp. 5$\frac{3}{16}$ x 8¼. 0-486-40158-8

101 GREAT SAMURAI PRINTS, Utagawa Kuniyoshi. Kuniyoshi was a master of the warrior woodblock print — and these 18th-century illustrations represent the pinnacle of his craft. Full-color portraits of renowned Japanese samurais pulse with movement, passion, and remarkably fine detail. 112pp. 8⅜ x 11. 0-486-46523-3

ABC OF BALLET, Janet Grosser. Clearly worded, abundantly illustrated little guide defines basic ballet-related terms: arabesque, battement, pas de chat, relevé, sissonne, many others. Pronunciation guide included. Excellent primer. 48pp. 4$\frac{3}{16}$ x 5¾. 0-486-40871-X

ACCESSORIES OF DRESS: An Illustrated Encyclopedia, Katherine Lester and Bess Viola Oerke. Illustrations of hats, veils, wigs, cravats, shawls, shoes, gloves, and other accessories enhance an engaging commentary that reveals the humor and charm of the many-sided story of accessorized apparel. 644 figures and 59 plates. 608pp. 6 ⅛ x 9¼. 0-486-43378-1

ADVENTURES OF HUCKLEBERRY FINN, Mark Twain. Join Huck and Jim as their boyhood adventures along the Mississippi River lead them into a world of excitement, danger, and self-discovery. Humorous narrative, lyrical descriptions of the Mississippi valley, and memorable characters. 224pp. 5$\frac{3}{16}$ x 8¼. 0-486-28061-6

ALICE STARMORE'S BOOK OF FAIR ISLE KNITTING, Alice Starmore. A noted designer from the region of Scotland's Fair Isle explores the history and techniques of this distinctive, stranded-color knitting style and provides copious illustrated instructions for 14 original knitwear designs. 208pp. 8⅜ x 10⅞. 0-486-47218-3

Browse over 9,000 books at www.doverpublications.com

CATALOG OF DOVER BOOKS

ALICE'S ADVENTURES IN WONDERLAND, Lewis Carroll. Beloved classic about a
little girl lost in a topsy-turvy land and her encounters with the White Rabbit, March
Hare, Mad Hatter, Cheshire Cat, and other delightfully improbable characters. 42
illustrations by Sir John Tenniel. 96pp. 5³⁄₁₆ x 8¼.   0-486-27543-4

AMERICA'S LIGHTHOUSES: An Illustrated History, Francis Ross Holland.
Profusely illustrated fact-filled survey of American lighthouses since 1716. Over 200
stations — East, Gulf, and West coasts, Great Lakes, Hawaii, Alaska, Puerto Rico, the
Virgin Islands, and the Mississippi and St. Lawrence Rivers. 240pp. 8 x 10¾.
                                                                        0-486-25576-X

AN ENCYCLOPEDIA OF THE VIOLIN, Alberto Bachmann. Translated by Frederick
H. Martens. Introduction by Eugene Ysaye. First published in 1925, this renowned
reference remains unsurpassed as a source of essential information, from construction and evolution to repertoire and technique. Includes a glossary and 73 illustrations. 496pp. 6½ x 9¼.   0-486-46618-3

ANIMALS: 1,419 Copyright-Free Illustrations of Mammals, Birds, Fish, Insects, etc.,
Selected by Jim Harter. Selected for its visual impact and ease of use, this outstanding
collection of wood engravings presents over 1,000 species of animals in extremely
lifelike poses. Includes mammals, birds, reptiles, amphibians, fish, insects, and
other invertebrates. 284pp. 9 x 12.   0-486-23766-4

THE ANNALS, Tacitus. Translated by Alfred John Church and William Jackson
Brodribb. This vital chronicle of Imperial Rome, written by the era's great historian,
spans A.D. 14-68 and paints incisive psychological portraits of major figures, from
Tiberius to Nero. 416pp. 5³⁄₁₆ x 8¼.   0-486-45236-0

ANTIGONE, Sophocles. Filled with passionate speeches and sensitive probing
of moral and philosophical issues, this powerful and often-performed Greek
drama reveals the grim fate that befalls the children of Oedipus. Footnotes. 64pp.
5³⁄₁₆ x 8 ¼.   0-486-27804-2

ART DECO DECORATIVE PATTERNS IN FULL COLOR, Christian Stoll. Reprinted
from a rare 1910 portfolio, 160 sensuous and exotic images depict a breathtaking
array of florals, geometrics, and abstracts — all elegant in their stark simplicity.
64pp. 8⅜ x 11.   0-486-44862-2

THE ARTHUR RACKHAM TREASURY: 86 Full-Color Illustrations, Arthur Rackham.
Selected and Edited by Jeff A. Menges. A stunning treasury of 86 full-page plates span
the famed English artist's career, from *Rip Van Winkle* (1905) to masterworks such as
Undine, A Midsummer Night's Dream, and *Wind in the Willows* (1939). 96pp. 8⅜ x 11.
                                                                        0-486-44685-9

THE AUTHENTIC GILBERT & SULLIVAN SONGBOOK, W. S. Gilbert and A. S.
Sullivan. The most comprehensive collection available, this songbook includes
selections from every one of Gilbert and Sullivan's light operas. Ninety-two numbers
are presented uncut and unedited, and in their original keys. 410pp. 9 x 12.
                                                                        0-486-23482-7

THE AWAKENING, Kate Chopin. First published in 1899, this controversial novel
of a New Orleans wife's search for love outside a stifling marriage shocked readers.
Today, it remains a first-rate narrative with superb characterization. New introduc-
tory Note. 128pp. 5³⁄₁₆ x 8¼.   0-486-27786-0

BASIC DRAWING, Louis Priscilla. Beginning with perspective, this commonsense
manual progresses to the figure in movement, light and shade, anatomy, drapery,
composition, trees and landscape, and outdoor sketching. Black-and-white illustrations throughout. 128pp. 8⅜ x 11.   0-486-45815-6

Browse over 9,000 books at www.doverpublications.com

CATALOG OF DOVER BOOKS

THE BATTLES THAT CHANGED HISTORY, Fletcher Pratt. Historian profiles 16 crucial conflicts, ancient to modern, that changed the course of Western civilization. Gripping accounts of battles led by Alexander the Great, Joan of Arc, Ulysses S. Grant, other commanders. 27 maps. 352pp. 5⅜ x 8½. 0-486-41129-X

BEETHOVEN'S LETTERS, Ludwig van Beethoven. Edited by Dr. A. C. Kalischer. Features 457 letters to fellow musicians, friends, greats, patrons, and literary men. Reveals musical thoughts, quirks of personality, insights, and daily events. Includes 15 plates. 410pp. 5⅜ x 8½. 0-486-22769-3

BERNICE BOBS HER HAIR AND OTHER STORIES, F. Scott Fitzgerald. This brilliant anthology includes 6 of Fitzgerald's most popular stories: "The Diamond as Big as the Ritz," the title tale, "The Offshore Pirate," "The Ice Palace," "The Jelly Bean," and "May Day." 176pp. 5⅜ x 8½. 0-486-47049-0

BESLER'S BOOK OF FLOWERS AND PLANTS: 73 Full-Color Plates from Hortus Eystettensis, 1613, Basilius Besler. Here is a selection of magnificent plates from the *Hortus Eystettensis,* which vividly illustrated and identified the plants, flowers, and trees that thrived in the legendary German garden at Eichstätt. 80pp. 8⅜ x 11. 0-486-46005-3

THE BOOK OF KELLS, Edited by Blanche Cirker. Painstakingly reproduced from a rare facsimile edition, this volume contains full-page decorations, portraits, illustrations, plus a sampling of textual leaves with exquisite calligraphy and ornamentation. 32 full-color illustrations. 32pp. 9⅜ x 12¼. 0-486-24345-1

THE BOOK OF THE CROSSBOW: With an Additional Section on Catapults and Other Siege Engines, Ralph Payne-Gallwey. Fascinating study traces history and use of crossbow as military and sporting weapon, from Middle Ages to modern times. Also covers related weapons: balistas, catapults, Turkish bows, more. Over 240 illustrations. 400pp. 7¼ x 10⅛. 0-486-28720-3

THE BUNGALOW BOOK: Floor Plans and Photos of 112 Houses, 1910, Henry L. Wilson. Here are 112 of the most popular and economic blueprints of the early 20th century — plus an illustration or photograph of each completed house. A wonderful time capsule that still offers a wealth of valuable insights. 160pp. 8⅜ x 11. 0-486-45104-6

THE CALL OF THE WILD, Jack London. A classic novel of adventure, drawn from London's own experiences as a Klondike adventurer, relating the story of a heroic dog caught in the brutal life of the Alaska Gold Rush. Note. 64pp. 5³⁄₁₆ x 8¼. 0-486-26472-6

CANDIDE, Voltaire. Edited by Francois-Marie Arouet. One of the world's great satires since its first publication in 1759. Witty, caustic skewering of romance, science, philosophy, religion, government — nearly all human ideals and institutions. 112pp. 5³⁄₁₆ x 8¼. 0-486-26689-3

CELEBRATED IN THEIR TIME: Photographic Portraits from the George Grantham Bain Collection, Edited by Amy Pastan. With an Introduction by Michael Carlebach. Remarkable portrait gallery features 112 rare images of Albert Einstein, Charlie Chaplin, the Wright Brothers, Henry Ford, and other luminaries from the worlds of politics, art, entertainment, and industry. 128pp. 8⅜ x 11. 0-486-46754-6

CHARIOTS FOR APOLLO: The NASA History of Manned Lunar Spacecraft to 1969, Courtney G. Brooks, James M. Grimwood, and Loyd S. Swenson, Jr. This illustrated history by a trio of experts is the definitive reference on the Apollo spacecraft and lunar modules. It traces the vehicles' design, development, and operation in space. More than 100 photographs and illustrations. 576pp. 6¾ x 9¼. 0-486-46756-2

Browse over 9,000 books at www.doverpublications.com

CATALOG OF DOVER BOOKS

A CHRISTMAS CAROL, Charles Dickens. This engrossing tale relates Ebenezer Scrooge's ghostly journeys through Christmases past, present, and future and his ultimate transformation from a harsh and grasping old miser to a charitable and compassionate human being. 80pp. 5³⁄₁₆ x 8¼.   0-486-26865-9

COMMON SENSE, Thomas Paine. First published in January of 1776, this highly influential landmark document clearly and persuasively argued for American separation from Great Britain and paved the way for the Declaration of Independence. 64pp. 5³⁄₁₆ x 8¼.   0-486-29602-4

THE COMPLETE SHORT STORIES OF OSCAR WILDE, Oscar Wilde. Complete texts of "The Happy Prince and Other Tales," "A House of Pomegranates," "Lord Arthur Savile's Crime and Other Stories," "Poems in Prose," and "The Portrait of Mr. W. H." 208pp. 5³⁄₁₆ x 8¼.   0-486-45216-6

COMPLETE SONNETS, William Shakespeare. Over 150 exquisite poems deal with love, friendship, the tyranny of time, beauty's evanescence, death, and other themes in language of remarkable power, precision, and beauty. Glossary of archaic terms. 80pp. 5³⁄₁₆ x 8¼.   0-486-26686-9

THE COUNT OF MONTE CRISTO: Abridged Edition, Alexandre Dumas. Falsely accused of treason, Edmond Dantès is imprisoned in the bleak Chateau d'If. After a hair-raising escape, he launches an elaborate plot to extract a bitter revenge against those who betrayed him. 448pp. 5³⁄₁₆ x 8¼.   0-486-45643-9

CRAFTSMAN BUNGALOWS: Designs from the Pacific Northwest, Yoho & Merritt. This reprint of a rare catalog, showcasing the charming simplicity and cozy style of Craftsman bungalows, is filled with photos of completed homes, plus floor plans and estimated costs. An indispensable resource for architects, historians, and illustrators. 112pp. 10 x 7.   0-486-46875-5

CRAFTSMAN BUNGALOWS: 59 Homes from "The Craftsman," Edited by Gustav Stickley. Best and most attractive designs from Arts and Crafts Movement publication — 1903–1916 — includes sketches, photographs of homes, floor plans, descriptive text. 128pp. 8¼ x 11.   0-486-25829-7

CRIME AND PUNISHMENT, Fyodor Dostoyevsky. Translated by Constance Garnett. Supreme masterpiece tells the story of Raskolnikov, a student tormented by his own thoughts after he murders an old woman. Overwhelmed by guilt and terror, he confesses and goes to prison. 480pp. 5³⁄₁₆ x 8¼.   0-486-41587-2

THE DECLARATION OF INDEPENDENCE AND OTHER GREAT DOCUMENTS OF AMERICAN HISTORY: 1775-1865, Edited by John Grafton. Thirteen compelling and influential documents: Henry's "Give Me Liberty or Give Me Death," Declaration of Independence, The Constitution, Washington's First Inaugural Address, The Monroe Doctrine, The Emancipation Proclamation, Gettysburg Address, more. 64pp. 5³⁄₁₆ x 8¼.   0-486-41124-9

THE DESERT AND THE SOWN: Travels in Palestine and Syria, Gertrude Bell. "The female Lawrence of Arabia," Gertrude Bell wrote captivating, perceptive accounts of her travels in the Middle East. This intriguing narrative, accompanied by 160 photos, traces her 1905 sojourn in Lebanon, Syria, and Palestine. 368pp. 5⅜ x 8½.
0-486-46876-3

A DOLL'S HOUSE, Henrik Ibsen. Ibsen's best-known play displays his genius for realistic prose drama. An expression of women's rights, the play climaxes when the central character, Nora, rejects a smothering marriage and life in "a doll's house." 80pp. 5³⁄₁₆ x 8¼.   0-486-27062-9

DOOMED SHIPS: Great Ocean Liner Disasters, William H. Miller, Jr. Nearly 200 photographs, many from private collections, highlight tales of some of the vessels whose pleasure cruises ended in catastrophe: the *Morro Castle, Normandie, Andrea Doria, Europa,* and many others. 128pp. 8⅞ x 11¼. 0-486-45366-9

THE DORÉ BIBLE ILLUSTRATIONS, Gustave Doré. Detailed plates from the Bible: the Creation scenes, Adam and Eve, horrifying visions of the Flood, the battle sequences with their monumental crowds, depictions of the life of Jesus, 241 plates in all. 241pp. 9 x 12. 0-486-23004-X

DRAWING DRAPERY FROM HEAD TO TOE, Cliff Young. Expert guidance on how to draw shirts, pants, skirts, gloves, hats, and coats on the human figure, including folds in relation to the body, pull and crush, action folds, creases, more. Over 200 drawings. 48pp. 8¼ x 11. 0-486-45591-2

DUBLINERS, James Joyce. A fine and accessible introduction to the work of one of the 20th century's most influential writers, this collection features 15 tales, including a masterpiece of the short-story genre, "The Dead." 160pp. 5³⁄₁₆ x 8¼. 0-486-26870-5

EASY-TO-MAKE POP-UPS, Joan Irvine. Illustrated by Barbara Reid. Dozens of wonderful ideas for three-dimensional paper fun — from holiday greeting cards with moving parts to a pop-up menagerie. Easy-to-follow, illustrated instructions for more than 30 projects. 299 black-and-white illustrations. 96pp. 8⅜ x 11. 0-486-44622-0

EASY-TO-MAKE STORYBOOK DOLLS: A "Novel" Approach to Cloth Dollmaking, Sherralyn St. Clair. Favorite fictional characters come alive in this unique beginner's dollmaking guide. Includes patterns for Pollyanna, Dorothy from *The Wonderful Wizard of Oz,* Mary of *The Secret Garden,* plus easy-to-follow instructions, 263 black-and-white illustrations, and an 8-page color insert. 112pp. 8¼ x 11. 0-486-47360-0

EINSTEIN'S ESSAYS IN SCIENCE, Albert Einstein. Speeches and essays in accessible, everyday language profile influential physicists such as Niels Bohr and Isaac Newton. They also explore areas of physics to which the author made major contributions. 128pp. 5 x 8. 0-486-47011-3

EL DORADO: Further Adventures of the Scarlet Pimpernel, Baroness Orczy. A popular sequel to *The Scarlet Pimpernel,* this suspenseful story recounts the Pimpernel's attempts to rescue the Dauphin from imprisonment during the French Revolution. An irresistible blend of intrigue, period detail, and vibrant characterizations. 352pp. 5³⁄₁₆ x 8¼. 0-486-44026-5

ELEGANT SMALL HOMES OF THE TWENTIES: 99 Designs from a Competition, Chicago Tribune. Nearly 100 designs for five- and six-room houses feature New England and Southern colonials, Normandy cottages, stately Italianate dwellings, and other fascinating snapshots of American domestic architecture of the 1920s. 112pp. 9 x 12. 0-486-46910-7

THE ELEMENTS OF STYLE: The Original Edition, William Strunk, Jr. This is the book that generations of writers have relied upon for timeless advice on grammar, diction, syntax, and other essentials. In concise terms, it identifies the principal requirements of proper style and common errors. 64pp. 5⅜ x 8½. 0-486-44798-7

THE ELUSIVE PIMPERNEL, Baroness Orczy. Robespierre's revolutionaries find their wicked schemes thwarted by the heroic Pimpernel — Sir Percival Blakeney. In this thrilling sequel, Chauvelin devises a plot to eliminate the Pimpernel and his wife. 272pp. 5³⁄₁₆ x 8¼. 0-486-45464-9

AN ENCYCLOPEDIA OF BATTLES: Accounts of Over 1,560 Battles from 1479 B.C. to the Present, David Eggenberger. Essential details of every major battle in recorded history from the first battle of Megiddo in 1479 B.C. to Grenada in 1984. List of battle maps. 99 illustrations. 544pp. 6½ x 9¼. 0-486-24913-1

ENCYCLOPEDIA OF EMBROIDERY STITCHES, INCLUDING CREWEL, Marion Nichols. Precise explanations and instructions, clearly illustrated, on how to work chain, back, cross, knotted, woven stitches, and many more — 178 in all, including Cable Outline, Whipped Satin, and Eyelet Buttonhole. Over 1400 illustrations. 219pp. 8⅜ x 11¼. 0-486-22929-7

ENTER JEEVES: 15 Early Stories, P. G. Wodehouse. Splendid collection contains first 8 stories featuring Bertie Wooster, the deliciously dim aristocrat and Jeeves, his brainy, imperturbable manservant. Also, the complete Reggie Pepper (Bertie's prototype) series. 288pp. 5⅜ x 8½. 0-486-29717-9

ERIC SLOANE'S AMERICA: Paintings in Oil, Michael Wigley. With a Foreword by Mimi Sloane. Eric Sloane's evocative oils of America's landscape and material culture shimmer with immense historical and nostalgic appeal. This original hardcover collection gathers nearly a hundred of his finest paintings, with subjects ranging from New England to the American Southwest. 128pp. 10⅝ x 9. 0-486-46525-X

ETHAN FROME, Edith Wharton. Classic story of wasted lives, set against a bleak New England background. Superbly delineated characters in a hauntingly grim tale of thwarted love. Considered by many to be Wharton's masterpiece. 96pp. 5³⁄₁₆ x 8 ¼. 0-486-26690-7

THE EVERLASTING MAN, G. K. Chesterton. Chesterton's view of Christianity — as a blend of philosophy and mythology, satisfying intellect and spirit — applies to his brilliant book, which appeals to readers' heads as well as their hearts. 288pp. 5⅜ x 8½. 0-486-46036-3

THE FIELD AND FOREST HANDY BOOK, Daniel Beard. Written by a co-founder of the Boy Scouts, this appealing guide offers illustrated instructions for building kites, birdhouses, boats, igloos, and other fun projects, plus numerous helpful tips for campers. 448pp. 5³⁄₁₆ x 8¼. 0-486-46191-2

FINDING YOUR WAY WITHOUT MAP OR COMPASS, Harold Gatty. Useful, instructive manual shows would-be explorers, hikers, bikers, scouts, sailors, and survivalists how to find their way outdoors by observing animals, weather patterns, shifting sands, and other elements of nature. 288pp. 5⅜ x 8½. 0-486-40613-X

FIRST FRENCH READER: A Beginner's Dual-Language Book, Edited and Translated by Stanley Appelbaum. This anthology introduces 50 legendary writers — Voltaire, Balzac, Baudelaire, Proust, more — through passages from *The Red and the Black*, *Les Misérables*, *Madame Bovary*, and other classics. Original French text plus English translation on facing pages. 240pp. 5⅜ x 8½. 0-486-46178-5

FIRST GERMAN READER: A Beginner's Dual-Language Book, Edited by Harry Steinhauer. Specially chosen for their power to evoke German life and culture, these short, simple readings include poems, stories, essays, and anecdotes by Goethe, Hesse, Heine, Schiller, and others. 224pp. 5⅜ x 8½. 0-486-46179-3

FIRST SPANISH READER: A Beginner's Dual-Language Book, Angel Flores. Delightful stories, other material based on works of Don Juan Manuel, Luis Taboada, Ricardo Palma, other noted writers. Complete faithful English translations on facing pages. Exercises. 176pp. 5⅜ x 8½. 0-486-25810-6

Browse over 9,000 books at www.doverpublications.com

CATALOG OF DOVER BOOKS

FIVE ACRES AND INDEPENDENCE, Maurice G. Kains. Great back-to-the-land classic explains basics of self-sufficient farming. The one book to get. 95 illustrations. 397pp. 5⅜ x 8½. 0-486-20974-1

FLAGG'S SMALL HOUSES: Their Economic Design and Construction, 1922, Ernest Flagg. Although most famous for his skyscrapers, Flagg was also a proponent of the well-designed single-family dwelling. His classic treatise features innovations that save space, materials, and cost. 526 illustrations. 160pp. 9⅜ x 12¼. 0-486-45197-6

FLATLAND: A Romance of Many Dimensions, Edwin A. Abbott. Classic of science (and mathematical) fiction — charmingly illustrated by the author — describes the adventures of A. Square, a resident of Flatland, in Spaceland (three dimensions), Lineland (one dimension), and Pointland (no dimensions). 96pp. 5³⁄₁₆ x 8¼. 0-486-27263-X

FRANKENSTEIN, Mary Shelley. The story of Victor Frankenstein's monstrous creation and the havoc it caused has enthralled generations of readers and inspired countless writers of horror and suspense. With the author's own 1831 introduction. 176pp. 5³⁄₁₆ x 8¼. 0-486-28211-2

THE GARGOYLE BOOK: 572 Examples from Gothic Architecture, Lester Burbank Bridaham. Dispelling the conventional wisdom that French Gothic architectural flourishes were born of despair or gloom, Bridaham reveals the whimsical nature of these creations and the ingenious artisans who made them. 572 illustrations. 224pp. 8⅜ x 11. 0-486-44754-5

THE GIFT OF THE MAGI AND OTHER SHORT STORIES, O. Henry. Sixteen captivating stories by one of America's most popular storytellers. Included are such classics as "The Gift of the Magi," "The Last Leaf," and "The Ransom of Red Chief." Publisher's Note. 96pp. 5³⁄₁₆ x 8¼. 0-486-27061-0

THE GOETHE TREASURY: Selected Prose and Poetry, Johann Wolfgang von Goethe. Edited, Selected, and with an Introduction by Thomas Mann. In addition to his lyric poetry, Goethe wrote travel sketches, autobiographical studies, essays, letters, and proverbs in rhyme and prose. This collection presents outstanding examples from each genre. 368pp. 5⅜ x 8½. 0-486-44780-4

GREAT EXPECTATIONS, Charles Dickens. Orphaned Pip is apprenticed to the dirty work of the forge but dreams of becoming a gentleman — and one day finds himself in possession of "great expectations." Dickens' finest novel. 400pp. 5³⁄₁₆ x 8¼. 0-486-41586-4

GREAT WRITERS ON THE ART OF FICTION: From Mark Twain to Joyce Carol Oates, Edited by James Daley. An indispensable source of advice and inspiration, this anthology features essays by Henry James, Kate Chopin, Willa Cather, Sinclair Lewis, Jack London, Raymond Chandler, Raymond Carver, Eudora Welty, and Kurt Vonnegut, Jr. 192pp. 5⅜ x 8½. 0-486-45128-3

HAMLET, William Shakespeare. The quintessential Shakespearean tragedy, whose highly charged confrontations and anguished soliloquies probe depths of human feeling rarely sounded in any art. Reprinted from an authoritative British edition complete with illuminating footnotes. 128pp. 5³⁄₁₆ x 8¼. 0-486-27278-8

THE HAUNTED HOUSE, Charles Dickens. A Yuletide gathering in an eerie country retreat provides the backdrop for Dickens and his friends — including Elizabeth Gaskell and Wilkie Collins — who take turns spinning supernatural yarns. 144pp. 5⅜ x 8½. 0-486-46309-5

Browse over 9,000 books at www.doverpublications.com